The Bookshop of Memories

Also by Elise Darcy

The Sunrise Coast Series

New Beginnings at the Harbour Inn
The Secret of the Summerhouse
The Cottage by the Sea
The Guest House at Shingle Cove
The Houseboat by the Quay
Return to Willow Tree Cottage
The Bookshop of Memories
The Beach House
A Summer to Remember

The Scottish Highlands Series

Winter in the Scottish Highlands
The Secrets of the Glen
Return to the Lake House
The Boathouse by the Loch
Summer in the Scottish Highlands
Coming Home to Aviemore

The Living Apart Together series

Living Apart Together
It Takes 2 to Tango
Dear John
Love on the Rooftop

Standalone books

Lola & The Man
A Mallorcan Affair
The Villa in Sicily
We'll Meet Again

The Bookshop of Memories

A Novel

ELISE DARCY

ISBN 978-1-913147-19-8

"Nothing is ever really lost to us as long as we remember it." – LM Montgomery

1

'You will come, won't you? I know it's a bit last minute, but I want to introduce him to my family. Well, the closest I've got to family right now, that is.' Thea lurched forward as the bus accelerated. She turned to Gracie expectantly.

'Of course I will.'

'You won't be too tired, will you, after work today?'

Gracie placed a tender hand on Thea's arm. 'Is that your way of saying I should retire?'

Thea looked at her wide-eyed. 'Oh, no – of course not. I didn't mean—'

Gracie burst out laughing as she grabbed the handle on the back of the seat in front of her to steady herself as the bus slowed down for the next stop. 'Now, child, after all these years working together, you should know me by now. Not a serious bone in my body.'

Thea ran her fingers through her long dark hair. 'You had me there,' she said.

'I certainly did, didn't I? Now, I'm the one who normally throws the parties. What is the occasion, really? I mean, I've seen your boyfriend already, in and out of the apartment. Are you two finally moving in together?'

Thea leaned forward and rang the bell for the next stop. Thea and Gracie loved taking the bus back to Pimlico from the British Museum. Although they chatted amiably on the journey, mostly they took the time to just enjoy the London vista from the top of the bus. Gracie often said she had a bus tour every day – the same bus tour enjoyed by the many visitors who flocked to the capital, except that she lived there and experienced the different seasons, each with its own appeal.

They both loved Christmas with the festive lights and the hustle and bustle as pedestrians scurried from one shop to another, seeking out special gifts for loved ones. Spring always came with its promise of warmer evenings, and the best part was that when they caught the bus after work, it was still light. Thea also loved summer and the tourist season; she liked people-watching as tourists stood capturing special moments of their time spent in London. Now, though, it was autumn, and she could see pedestrians struggling to keep their umbrellas up in the blustery weather as it started to rain.

Glancing out of the window as the bus passed the Dominion Theatre, Thea noticed the trickle of theatregoers already arriving for the evening show.

Gracie noticed too. She turned to Thea, who was also quietly taking in the familiar scene. 'Do you fancy a trip to the theatre one evening? We could make it a Friday and stop for a bite to eat and take the Tube home afterwards.'

Thea turned to Gracie and smiled. 'Yes, that would be a great idea. I haven't been to a show for quite a while. Miles isn't interested in going when he's in London. It's a shame, really, with so many shows to choose from.' Thea noticed that Gracie didn't comment, choosing to keep any thoughts about Thea's boyfriend to herself.

Gracie and Thea went back to people-watching as the bus crawled slowly along in the commuter traffic. As the bus skirted Trafalgar Square, Thea looked out of the window at the four imposing lion statues, which tourists loved to clamber over.

Gracie had once told her that if a person touched one of the lions in Trafalgar Square, they were destined to come back to London again. But Gracie had also said that she couldn't tell if this was true; even though she had taken her own daughter, Tanya, to see the lions and they had stroked their beautiful manes – which apparently were not identical – Gracie had never left London since her parents had arrived from Jamaica.

Although the bus always took a little longer than the Tube, Thea particularly enjoyed the views from the top of the bus as it skirted Green Park and the Wellington Arch, especially at this time of the year. The old-fashioned streetlamps adorning the pavements gave London a magical, Dickensian feel that she never tired of.

At their stop, Thea followed Gracie down the stairs of the double-decker. Even though Gracie found going up the stairs a struggle, they both preferred to sit on the top deck and see the sights. As they stepped off the bus and began to walk through Pimlico, Gracie remarked, 'You didn't answer my question, Thea.'

Thea got the housekeys out of her handbag. She sighed. 'No, we're not moving in together yet.'

'Oh, that is a shame. How long have you been stepping out?'

Thea smiled at that old-fashioned turn of phrase. *Stepping out.* It sounded so outdated – even coming from Gracie, who was in her mid-sixties. Perhaps it was a turn of phrase that Gracie had heard her older relations use back in Jamaica. She felt like asking, but imagined Gracie would just think she was trying to change the subject. 'We've been stepping out for nine months. I keep hoping he'll get a transfer back to the UK office.'

'How long has he been working out in Hong Kong?'

'Around five years, I think.'

Gracie shook her head. 'Long-distance relationships. It's not easy.'

Thea was beginning to wonder whether, contrary to what Gracie thought, it *was* easy. As Miles often said, when they were together they did all the fun things, like meals out and cosy nights in, and occasionally going to his hotel, but mostly meeting up at her flat. It was way more fun spending quality time together than having to do mundane things like shopping and household chores. She agreed with his sentiments – up to a point. She had been quite happy with the arrangement at first, when he'd promised he would reduce his stints abroad and get a 'regular' job in the office in London. But so far, that hadn't happened, and there wasn't even any hint that he was putting anything in place to change things.

Just lately, for some reason, it had started to play on her mind that it was beginning to feel less and less like a real relationship. Although at some level every couple would like it all to be romance and roses around the door, at some point real life always intruded. The mundane side of living with somebody and doing everyday things together – wasn't that part of what being in a relationship was all about?

Perhaps that was the reason she had made specific plans for that evening. She felt that finally introducing Miles to her friends would make her feel a bit more normal. She would have loved to invite her sister and brother-in-law over, but they no longer lived in London, and although she could have arranged it for another evening or a weekend, it had been a spur-of-the-moment thing. She knew Miles was flying in from Hong Kong that day. They hadn't seen each other for two weeks.

Thea and Gracie walked up the steps of the Georgian terraced townhouse, which was just a couple of streets away from the bus stop near Pimlico Tube station. Thea noticed Gracie fumbling in her handbag. 'It's all right, I've got the key,' she said. Each of them had a key to the front door of the house and a key for their own flat. Thea's flat was on the ground floor.

They walked into the hallway, Thea's comfortable flat shoes slipping on the smooth, old-fashioned decoratively tiled floor.

'I'm just going to nip upstairs and take my coat off,' Gracie said. When do you want me to pop down to yours?'

'You can come straight away. We could have a cuppa while we wait for the others to arrive.' It wouldn't exactly be a party like the ones that Gracie threw. Gracie knew so many people, and her parties were tremendous, with amazing music belting out from her old record player. 'It's a shame that Tanya can't make it,' said Gracie.

'I know.' Thea was disappointed too. Gracie's daughter Tanya was also Thea's best friend, and if she had been able to come, she would have brought her husband too. They were good fun, and it would have made for a more lively evening. But Tanya was a physiotherapist and was on a late shift at St. Barts.

Gracie was starting up the stairs as Thea opened the door to the flat. 'Are you sure it's okay?'

Thea looked up. 'Of course. I haven't got much to prepare food-wise.'

'No, I meant a pair of oldies like us coming to your party.'

'Oh, I wouldn't call it a party. Just a little get-together. I want you to meet Miles.'

'The question is,' said Gracie as she continued up the stairs, 'will he want to meet us?'

Thea stared after her, thinking, *Why wouldn't he want to meet my friends?*

2

'What is going on? Why are all these people here?'

Thea slipped off the oven gloves and turned to Miles, who had followed her into the kitchen. She had wondered why he'd said he was coming in with her to help. He'd never done that in all the time he'd been coming round to her flat.

'What do you mean?' Thea frowned. 'I told you as soon as you arrived that I'm throwing a little dinner party and invited my friends. I wanted you to meet them. And what do you mean, *all these people*? There's just Gracie and Edward.'

Miles looked confused. 'Your friends? They're so ... old. Where did you meet them?'

Thea heaved a sigh. She was pretty sure she'd told him about them before – several times, in fact. She was hoping that introducing them might mean he'd introduce her to some of his friends too. He hadn't so far. He didn't even bring them up often, let alone talk about them. And on the rare occasions he did mention them, it was only very briefly. She got the impression that even his personal relationships pretty much revolved around work, just as hers did.

'Haven't you got any your own age?'

She sidled up to him, and stroked his cheek. 'I've got you.'

He looked towards the kitchen door. 'Why didn't you tell me you'd be doing something like this?'

'I wanted it to be a surprise.'

'It's a surprise alright.'

Thea looked at his grim expression and took that comment as it was intended – an unsubtle dig that he wasn't impressed at all.

'But – why?'

Thea wished he'd keep his voice down. Fortunately, she'd put some music on in the lounge, which she hoped was drowning out his raised voice.

'I told you.'

He looked at her sceptically.

Thea breathed a sigh. 'Okay. We've been dating for a while now, and I wanted you to meet my parents.'

'They're your parents?'

'No, of course not. Do we look alike?'

'Well – no.'

Thea was getting annoyed. 'Then why did you ask such a dumb question?' She could feel like this was going to turn into a row.

'Look, I'm getting confused. You said that you wanted me to meet your parents. Is that guy your father?'

'No.'

'Then I don't get—'

'They are the closest thing I've got to you meeting my family right now. My mum is in Nepal at a yoga retreat. I told you that already.' Thea knew that he wouldn't be meeting her mum any time soon. Her mum was always travelling and was into learning something new on her travels. A few months ago it was cooking exotic dishes and visiting the souk in Marrakesh to seek out spices to take with her to the cookery classes she was attending as part of her trip. Now she was into yoga. It sounded, from the postcards she'd sent, as though she rather fancied learning the craft and becoming a yoga teacher.

Thea remembered reading that and thinking that her mum probably wouldn't get that far before she lost interest and moved on to something else. What Thea would have loved was for her mum to come home, but with her state pension, and the rent from the upstairs flat, it turned out cheaper for her to spend the autumn and winter abroad.

Thea had grown up in this house. Her mum had decided to convert the house into two flats and gift the ground-floor flat to Thea. Thea's older sister was married, and would eventually own the flat upstairs; their mum had placed it in a trust for her.

Thea felt so lucky to have her own place in London. She didn't imagine many young women in their early thirties were that fortunate. What she would do with it if and when she married, Thea hadn't decided. Why would she? Thea gave Miles a sideways glance. The topic of marriage and settling down permanently together had not, so far, come up. That was because of his work. But Thea wasn't exactly pressuring him to change their long-distance relationship.

'Don't touch that!' She caught him absently picking up one of her cookbooks.

He put it down on the kitchen counter.

Thea picked it up and slipped it back in its rightful place, where he'd found it. The cookbooks were on a shelf above the kitchen worktop, organised in alphabetical order. It wasn't just the cookbooks that she'd carefully arranged. Everything in her flat had its place. Thea liked her orderly flat and her orderly life. She wasn't quite sure how a guy would fit, living there properly. Miles only ever stayed a few days on a flying visit, and then left. Would she cope with the possibility of having to clear up after someone else, with more laundry and piles of ironing, and with someone else using her stuff and not putting things back just so?

She'd had a taste of what it might be like on one occasion when he'd stayed a few nights in one go. It wasn't like him; he normally came over for a night or two and then had to leave. Sometimes he had late work commitments, and the only time they got to spend together was a few hours over dinner. But she'd experienced what it was like to have somebody leaving dirty clothes on the floor. He had picked them up, but she was concerned about the fact that such things bothered her. How could she live with someone twenty-four-seven if she lifted off when a cookbook was out of place? She had realised that she only felt everything was under control when she could control her environment.

Thea stared at Miles. She didn't want to think about that right now. What she did want to think about was the reason she was cooking dinner. Despite her reservations about eventually moving in together, she wanted the evening to work. Miles wasn't helping.

'And your dad?'

'Pardon me?'

'You said they were like your substitute parents.'

'That's not quite what I said.' In all the time they'd been together, he'd never taken much of an interest in her background or her parents. Whenever she had brought up her past, his eyes had glazed over, and she had been pretty sure he wasn't listening.

She watched him shake his head in frustration. 'Whatever. But what about Edward?'

Thea smiled. 'Edward has been like a father to me since I was nine. He is a close friend of my mum's.'

'Close? How close?'

'Just a family friend. He's been happily married for forty years.'

Miles walked up to the kitchen door and opened it a crack. He turned around, and whispered, 'So, where's his wife?'

Thea didn't know what to say to that. She had invited Edward's wife too, but Edward had said that she had a prior engagement and couldn't come.

Thea checked the timer on the oven, then turned down the heat under the vegetables.

'You never speak of him, I notice.'

'Him – who?'

'Your father.'

Thea stared at him. 'There's nothing to talk about. He disappeared when I was nine, and we never heard from him again.'

'God, I'm so sorry.'

'Yeah, well – that's all in the past. It's been twenty-five years.'

Miles walked over and put an arm around her shoulders. 'You still miss him, don't you?'

'What makes you say that?'

He shrugged. 'I guess you're bound to.' He shuffled from one foot to the other. 'When you say *disappeared*, you mean like he took off and left you and your mum?'

'And my sister.' Thea paused, deep in thought. 'Not exactly. He owned a bookshop.' In the school holidays I used to spend time there, helping out. I would sit and watch him bookbinding.' She smiled at the memory.

'Bookbinding?'

Thea rolled her eyes.

'Oh, right.' He grinned. 'You mean attaching a load of sheets of paper together.'

She shook her head. 'You make it sound as though anyone can do it.'

He held up his hands. 'Hey, don't bite my head off.'

'Sorry. I suppose it just irritates me that people assume it's that easy. You know, not everyone can bind a book. it's quite a skill. You need to be taught by a skilled artisan, and even then you've either got the patience and the aptitude, or you haven't. Few have. I've heard there is quite a shortage. It's a dying art, which is a shame, but they can command really good money.'

'Maybe I should change jobs.'

Thea looked at him quizzically. 'That's a joke, right? I imagine your job is really well-paid, jetting off to Hong Kong.'

He frowned and shook his head, laughing. 'Of course it is.'

'If you admire it so much, why didn't you continue the tradition, learn from your dad and become one too?' He stopped abruptly. 'Shit, sorry. I just remembered you said you were nine when your father left.'

Thea folded her arms. The trouble with Miles was that he wasn't a good listener. It seemed that most things she said to him went in one ear and out the other; it was almost impossible to have a serious conversation with him, or any conversation that didn't revolve around their plans for the evening, where they would dine out, or what takeaway they would have. Sometimes she wanted to talk about other things, rather than always being in the moment. Miles was quite the opposite.

'Maybe I might have become one if he'd been around long enough to show me. But then even if he had, he was still away a lot.'

'How come?'

'He was often away for weeks at a time travelling to bookfairs and book conventions, finding or selling rare books – sometimes to private collectors. I used to hear my dad and Edward talking when I was little. They thought I wasn't paying attention, but I was.' Thea had felt at the time like she was spying, which now seemed silly; she had been just a young child. She still felt bad about it all these years later, though, for some bizarre reason she could never quite put her finger on.

'Edward? The guy out there?' Miles flicked his finger in the direction of the door.

'Yes. I told you he was a family friend. They went back years, Mum, Dad and Edward.'

'Okay.'

Thea said, 'So, the fact that he was gone for periods of time wasn't unusual. It's just that one time he never came back.'

'So, you never found out what happened to him?'

Thea shook her head.

'We tried to find him. Edward tried to help us, but with no luck.'

He put an arm around her shoulders. 'I'm so sorry, Thea.'

Thea stepped back and looked at him. 'You won't do that to me, ever, will you? Just disappear and never come back.'

He stared at her.

She frowned at him, thinking he was taking far too long to answer the question – when the door to the kitchen suddenly opened.

'Oh, I've found the two lovebirds,' said Gracie, grinning at Thea before casting a gaze over her shoulder at Edward, who was peering over her shoulder in the doorway. 'So you have!'

'Do you need any help?' Gracie asked. Her smile faltered when she caught the look on Thea's face.

Thea shook her head. 'No, I'm fine. I'll be dishing up the meal very soon.'

'Oh, wonderful,' said Edward. 'I'm feeling a bit peckish.'

Thea looked at Miles. 'Why don't you go and join Gracie and Edward in the lounge. I won't be long.'

'Are you sure you don't need my help? I could carry something out for you.'

'No, you'll just get in the way.' Thea surreptitiously gave him a look that said, *Go out there and be sociable, go on!*

With his back to Edward and Gracie, he looked at Thea wide-eyed as if to say, *Do I have to?*

'Come and join us, Miles,' said Edward.

'We won't bite,' Gracie said good-humouredly.

As he walked out of the kitchen door, Thea saw Edward put an arm around Miles's shoulders. 'Now, you must tell me all about yourself. But first, have we told you what a gifted archivist our young Thea is? We are so lucky to have her at the museum – aren't we, Gracie?'

Miles looked back at Thea as the door swung shut, the look on his face saying *Help me!*

Thea just grinned. Her smile faded when she thought about Edward's interest in Miles's life. Perhaps that was the reason Miles was hiding out in the kitchen. That was what it felt like. She was interested to find out whether Miles did speak to Edward and Gracie about his job, because he didn't ever say much about it to her. In fact, he didn't like talking about work at all. Thea was quite the reverse. She could talk about her job non-stop. Perhaps that was because she loved her job working as an archivist at the British

Museum Library and Archive. Working in one of the most famous museums and libraries in the world was such a privilege and a dream come true for Thea.

She smiled as she popped on the oven gloves. She opened the oven door and was about to lift out the hotpot when she stopped. She closed the over door, turned down the temperature dial and sat down at the kitchen table. Perhaps Miles would open up about himself, and his job, to Edward and Gracie. She would give the food a few more minutes.

When she finally walked out of the kitchen, wearing the oven gloves and carrying the large hotpot to the extendable table she'd set up in the centre of her living room, she felt like she could almost have cut the atmosphere with a knife. There was no friendly banter or any conversation at the dinner table. They were all sitting in stony silence.

Gracie broke the silence. 'That smells delicious.'

'That it does,' added Edward, picking up a paper napkin and tucking it into the top of his jumper.

Thea caught Gracie and Edward both look at Miles and then exchange a glance. She put the hotpot down on the table and looked crossly at Miles, who was making no effort whatsoever to make even polite conversation.

3

Edward left first. In the doorway, he put an arm around Thea's shoulders and gave her a squeeze. 'That meal was delicious, Thea. If you don't mind me saying, it reminded me of the family meals your mum used to cook years ago. She was a good cook too.'

'You think I'm a good cook?' Thea looked at him in surprise. Miles had never once complimented her on her cooking.

'Of course I do.'

'I wish Frances could have come.'

'Well, maybe next time.'

Thea had known Edward long enough to catch something in his voice. It suggested that his wife would not be coming next time. Thea wondered why.

He lowered his voice as Thea walked with him to the front door of the house. He stopped, glancing over her shoulder at the door to her flat. His eyes dropped to her. 'How long have we known each other?'

Thea smiled. 'Like, forever.'

'Yes, it feels like that doesn't it? Well, I don't want you to take offence when I say this, but ...'

'What is it?' Thea searched his face, taking in his dark brown eyes, craggy features and mop of grey hair.

'Are you sure he is right for you?'

'Miles?'

'Yes.'

Thea sighed. 'Look, I'm sorry he wasn't very talkative at the table. When he gets in from Hong Kong, we always spend the time together, just the two of us. I think I should have at least pre-warned him about my bright idea of holding an impromptu dinner party so that he could meet my best friends.' *Perhaps I should have asked him first*, she thought. Although she couldn't imagine he'd have said no to meeting her friends. She guessed it was the surprise element that hadn't gone down well. Perhaps that was why they got along so well; they were both creatures of habit. She didn't like surprises either.

'It's not that, Thea. I get that he probably finds it a bit awkward trying to find something to talk about, some common ground with us older folks.'

Thea hadn't thought about that either. She remembered that he'd asked her something about whether she had any younger friends. It made her wonder if he would have got on far better in the company of Gracie's daughter and her husband, if they'd been able to make it.

'Did he talk much about his job, his life?'

'No. He spent the time asking about mine. I did find it rather odd.'

'That he was interested in your job as an archivist?' *He's never appeared interested when I've talked about it*, she thought.

'No. Well, yes – maybe. It's a bit like saying you're an accountant. In my experience, people's eyes glaze over the moment the word *archivist* is out of your mouth.'

Thea grinned at him. She knew what he meant. Miles had actually yawned in her face when she'd first told him what she did. Thinking back on it now, although she'd laughed, she'd thought it really rude of him to do that.

He'd done it intentionally to stop her talking. They'd kissed instead, which had defused the situation, but Thea felt that she could have taken it as quite an insult. If you like someone, if you love them, don't you sit down and listen to them when they want to share details of their lives?

Thea asked, 'What else did you find odd, other than the fact that he appeared interested in your job?'

'I don't know. I'm probably speaking out of turn, and do tell me off if I've overstepped the mark, but ... well he just doesn't come across as someone who ...'

'Someone who ...?' Thea prompted.

Edward shook his head. 'You know what? It's a daft thought. I don't know what I'm talking about. In fact, I think it was that rather nice bottle of wine that I'm pretty sure I drank all to myself.'

Thea shook her head. 'Actually, I'm pretty sure you didn't.' She had seen the way Miles had been drinking one glass after another. It wasn't like him.

'Well, I do feel a little lightheaded in any case, so it's just as well I ordered a taxi to take me home rather than going on the Tube,' Edward said. He opened the door. Thea could see the black cab sitting at the kerb, its light off, showing it had a fare.

He bent down and gave her a kiss.

Thea said, 'Before you go, will you share that daft thought with me? About Miles?'

He shook his head. 'No, really – it's so silly. It's nothing. I don't even know why the thought entered my head.'

'But what was it?'

He stood there and sighed. 'Oh, all right. I just thought that he doesn't come across as some high-flying executive who jets off to Hong Kong.'

Thea stared at him.

'There. I told you it was a daft thought.' He shrugged. 'I mean, who am I to know? It's not like I've met any. I work in the basement of a museum, locked away in the archives, so it's not like I get to meet those types of high-flyers.' He frowned. 'Look, don't listen to me. It's the wine talking, and the overprotective father-figure who believes nobody is going to be good enough for my best friend's daughter.'

Thea laughed. She knew that was true. Ever since she'd had her first boyfriend in sixth form, Edward had been very critical of anyone she'd had a relationship with. Perhaps that had come through as Miles was talking to Edward; the scrutiny, the questioning that she hadn't been privy to when she was in the kitchen.

As Thea walked back to her apartment, Gracie appeared at the door. 'Well, I'm off now too.'

Thea nodded. 'Okay.' She glanced through the open doorway to her apartment, and lowered her voice. 'What did you think of Miles?' After what Edward had said, even though he'd persuaded her that he was talking a load of old tosh, she was interested to find out about Gracie's opinion.

Grace said, 'I don't like him.'

Thea frowned. This hadn't been how she expected the evening to go at all.

'Oh, Thea! I'm joking.'

'You are?' She looked at Gracie, grinning.

'Of course. Conversation was a bit awkward, but I bet that we weren't what he was expecting when you told him you wanted to introduce him to your friends.'

Thea smiled. 'That's true. I couldn't help thinking that the evening might have gone a little better if your daughter and her husband could have made it. Sorry, I shouldn't have said that.'

'Why not? Of course you want to be with people your own age.'

Thea gave Gracie a hug. 'I'm so lucky to have you as a friend, and a neighbour.'

Gracie drew back. 'And I, you. I feel so lucky to be renting the flat upstairs. I know my daughter has a spare room, but I wanted my own place. The trouble is until the divorce was finalised I couldn't sell the family home, then it was a case of starting to look for something else to buy, but where would I live in the meantime? It was serendipity that your mum decided on an extended stay at that yoga retreat.'

Thea nodded and smiled. It had coincided with Gracie looking for a rental. But the rental market was buoyant and so competitive that prices were rocketing in London. Although Gracie had the money from her share of the house, it would cost thousands to rent while she looked for somewhere permanent. Thea knew Gracie wasn't sure she would even buy in London. She was starting to think of the future, not long down the road, when she wasn't in work, and was wondering where she'd like to spend her retirement.

Gracie said, 'I still feel as though I'm not paying enough rent. I don't like charity.'

Thea rolled her eyes. 'We've had this conversation before. It isn't charity. My mum didn't want to rent her flat out, I told you that. She was worried she might get a bad tenant who stopped paying their rent; we've all heard about that sort of thing, where it then takes months to get them out. But of course renting it out to a friend avoids all that.'

'But it feels like a peppercorn rent.'

'I know. But she knows you are looking after her flat while she's not there, and she actually feels bad about taking any money from you. I knew you wouldn't move into her flat unless you were paying rent, and I persuaded her that the extra income would top up her teaching pension.'

Gracie nodded. 'I imagine the yoga retreat isn't cheap.'

'No, not at all. She's not exactly roughing it out there.' Thea had received an email from her mum asking her to come for a week's holiday at the retreat, but when Thea had checked out the cost of the hotel, she had realised that she couldn't afford to spend all that money on just one week's holiday. She imagined her mum wasn't paying a weekly rate, but had paid for a package which included the extended stay, and the yoga classes – that must have made it cheaper overall. Although she was desperate to see her mum, she had declined the invitation.

'Have you spoken with your mum lately?'

Thea shook her head. 'As you know, Mum's kind of off-grid. I mean, the hotel is all mod-cons, apart from where it is, up a mountain in Nepal with, like, a crap mobile phone signal, or none at all.' Thea grimaced. 'Although they have the internet, they don't encourage guests going online. In fact, by the sound of things, they discourage it. I suppose that's the point – getting away from the outside world and just immersing yourself in your surroundings – and yoga, of course – with no distractions. I guess that's why they call it a *retreat*.'

'Now, there's a thought when I retire. Perhaps I'll take up yoga.'

'You know that Mum will be the first to persuade you to go for it. Last time I heard from her, it sounded as though she'd decided to extend her stay and train to be a yoga teacher.'

'What a nice idea. You know, even when I retire, I can't imagine doing nothing. I'll have to have things to occupy me and keep me stimulated.'

Thea smiled. She imagined that was why Gracie and her mum were such good friends. They'd met through Edward when Gracie had started work as an archivist.

'She must have snuck online, because she did send me a lovely email with some photos. It looks as though she's having an amazing time.'

Thea had received similar emails. Thinking of her mum being thousands of miles away, Thea sighed. She didn't have a problem with it in itself; she just wished her mum wasn't staying somewhere so remote. 'The trouble is that if I just want to speak to my mum, I can't. I send emails, but she has to go to the nearest town for mobile reception, to get my voice messages. And because they discourage using the internet at the retreat, she isn't always online, and doesn't read my emails straightaway. If she wants to spend time sending lengthy catch-up emails, she has to visit a local internet café.'

Gracie nodded. 'I know.'

'Thea?'

They both turned to see Miles approaching the door. 'Oh – you're still out here?'

'Yes, I was just saying goodbye to Gracie.'

'Well, you're taking an age about it.'

Thea turned to Gracie and caught her eyeing Miles. She knew that look. It made her wonder if that comment Gracie had made about not liking him was in fact the truth, but she'd pretended she was joking to save Thea's feelings.

Gracie said, 'Well, have a nice evening.'

'What's left of it,' mumbled Miles.

Gracie raised her eyebrows at him before heading for the stairs.

Thea watched her walk up the stairs. She heaved a sigh and turned towards the door.

4

'What was that?' Thea asked, rounding on Miles as soon as she walked back into her apartment. He was sitting on the sofa, feet up on her coffee table.

'What was what?'

'Oh, my god! The whole time we were sitting up the table, you made no effort at all to engage with them.' She didn't even know what to say about how rude he'd been to Gracie when she'd said, *Have a nice evening.* 'Why did you say to Gracie, *what's left of it*? She was just being nice.'

Standing in front of him, arms folded, she watched him sit up and take his feet off the coffee table. He reached out, taking her hand. She had the impulse to pull away, but didn't. His expression changed, dark brown eyes looking up apologetically. 'Look, I was just surprised you were having people over, that's all. I'm used to having you all to myself. You can't hold that against me – can you?'

Thea sighed. He sounded sincere. 'It was a spur-of-the-moment thing, really. I should have let you know in advance.'

'Yes, you should have.'

'I think the evening would have gone better if Gracie's daughter had come.' Although on the other hand, Thea did wonder whether Tanya would have failed to warm to Miles too. The problem was that they didn't know him. He didn't normally behave like he had in front of Gracie and Edward.

'Come, let's sit together and watch a movie.'

Thea didn't sit down. 'Why don't we go out to a bar instead?' It was Friday evening, and she felt like going out.

'I'd prefer not to go out. I'm not all that interested in seeing a show. The time we get to spend together is precious. I'd much rather spend time with you here rather than sitting in a noisy bar where we have to shout at one another to be heard.'

They rarely ventured out, for that reason. Thea understood. How many times had he told her that he just wanted her to himself?

'All right. Do you have to work tomorrow?' Although it was the weekend, Miles had told her with the time difference that he often had to work at head office over the weekend. She hoped not. 'I was thinking we could have a day out in London. Would you like to see where I work? We could go to the British Museum and I could show you The British Library and Archives. It's not open to the public anymore, so it would be a rare privilege to see it.'

She stared at him eagerly, hoping he had the time off and would say yes. That was the problem with their long-distance relationship. Nothing was ever really planned. Even when he said he was in the country, his work intruded on their weekends together. Sometimes he flew in mid-week, and they were lucky to spend one evening together.

They'd been together months – if you could call it *together*. There was no sign of him leaving his high-flying jet-setting position to be with her. Obviously, the job came first. Perhaps it was just as well her friend hadn't been able to come that evening. In the past, she'd told Thea to move on. Thea had thought Tanya might change her mind when she met Miles, but after the disastrous dinner party, she was beginning to doubt it.

'Will there just be you and me there?'

'Oh, yes. Nobody works there at the weekend, and as I said, it's not open to the general public.' She expected him to say no, as he did with most suggestions she came up with which involved doing things in London.

He had been very different when they had gone away together on a long weekend to Brighton, and there were lots of things he had wanted to do – seeing the pier and the Royal Pavilion, taking a long walk along the promenade, eating out. In fact, they had been out all the time, only spending time in their hotel room to sleep. It had taken her aback. She wondered why it wasn't like that at home too, where they spent most of their time.

'Yes.'

Thea looked at him. 'Did you just say yes?'

He nodded.

'In the morning?'

'Why not?'

Thea sat down beside him and threw her arms around him. 'You're the best.'

'Yes, I know.' He reached towards the coffee table and picked up the remote. 'Now, what shall we watch?'

5

'So, this is it!' Thea opened the door, indicating the little office where she worked. She glanced over her shoulder at Miles. 'I'll show you the library next.'

'What is he doing here?' Miles whispered in her ear.

Thea turned from Miles. 'Oh, hi Edward. I didn't know you were working today.' Edward had his back to her, and was hastily doing up his old leather briefcase. He turned around. 'Oh, I'm not working today. I just came in to collect some paperwork I wanted to get done over the weekend.'

Thea walked into the room. 'Oh, okay.'

He smiled at Thea. 'Now, I'm the boss here, so I can do overtime. What's your excuse?' he said by way of friendly banter. His smile faded when Miles followed her into the room.

Thea's smile faded too. She hadn't expected anyone to be there. By rights, the public weren't really allowed access to this part of the museum unless it was a pre-arranged tour, which they often set up for schools.

'I wanted to show Miles where I worked – I hope that's okay? I thought it better at the weekend so that we weren't interrupting work.'

'Fine, fine.'

Thea noticed he didn't sound fine about it. 'You don't have to leave. I was literally just pointing out the office on the way to the library.'

'No, it's all right. It was only a flying visit. You can lock up afterwards?'

'Of course. I've got the key.' She gazed after him as he left the office, wondering why he'd locked the door from the inside. In all the years she'd been working there, since she had left university with her Master's degree in archives and record management, she'd never known anyone to lock themselves in.

She looked about her and thought how eerily quiet it was. Although she did work down there on her own on occasion, during the week there was always the sound of footsteps outside – colleagues popping in to use the photocopier or accessing the archives for research purposes, and the general hustle and bustle of staff. Of course, the museum itself was busy upstairs at the weekend, but not the parts that were generally closed to the public.

Miles touched her arm, making her jump. 'Are you all right, Thea?'

'Oh, yes, sorry. I was lost in thought.' She turned to Miles. He was peering around the office. He said, 'I thought it would be bigger, seeing as it's an archive.'

'Ah, this isn't where all the collections are stored.' They walked past a row of filing cabinets and rounded a corner. 'This is my cubicle.'

He walked over to her desk and looked at the artwork on the wall.

Thea smiled. She felt so fortunate to handle amazing collections of artwork and priceless books, and she felt privileged as an archivist that her job was to look after them for future generations.

'So, what is it exactly that you do as an archivist?'

'Well, I guess you could say there are three parts to my role. Here – let me show you what I enjoy the most.' Thea picked up a pair of white cotton gloves from the desk drawer and slipped them on as she walked out of her cubicle. In the centre of the room was a long table where there were some documents she was in the middle of archiving. 'So, this part of my job involves actually handling the collection.'

She pointed. 'Here we have a new document to add to the collection, so I have to carefully separate the document pages, take off any elastic bands, paper-clips, that sort of thing, ready to store in folders, or boxes – whatever is appropriate for the document or artefact in question. Then they have to be archived correctly to ensure they can easily be found.'

Thea carefully unfolded the map. After checking the document over, she decided where the most appropriate place was to file it. 'Now, if only my job was all about doing this.' Thea reluctantly took off her gloves and walked over to her cubicle. She sat down at her desk. Miles followed. 'So, now I have to do something we call *establishing intellectual control*.'

Miles said, 'What does that mean?'

Thea switched on the computer. She swivelled around in her seat to look at him. 'Basically, it's one thing taking physical care of the collections, but we also need to keep records of where we are storing or archiving these items too. We refer to our online databases as finding aids, so those boxes and files can be easily located and are referenced at the collection level and item level so researchers and the public know what we have. That's the second part of my job. The third part of my work really revolves around kind of supporting or championing what we have. I guess like spreading the word online through places like Wikipedia so researchers and the public are aware of our collections. Anyone can get in touch and view our archive.'

Thea caught Miles yawning.

She didn't take offence. 'Too much information?'

He nodded. 'Yeah. Sorry.'

Thea stood up. 'Shall we go and see the library?'

Miles yawned again. 'Can we save that for another time?'

Thea looked at him. 'It's a really impressive library.'

He apologised again. 'Can I be honest?'

'Of course.'

'I'm not that into books. You'd have to twist my arm to visit a bookshop, let alone a musty old library.'

'But it's not—'

'I really don't know how you do this all day. I thought my job was boring.'

'Your job – boring? What's boring about jetting off to the Hong Kong?'

'Oh, yes – right. I think when you've done it so many times, like I have, it just gets a bit, well ... old.' He looked at her a long moment. 'Do you mind if we get out of here?'

Thea was disappointed. She had been looking forward to showing him The British Library. 'All right. Just let me get my bag.' Thea walked over to her desk and picked up her bag. As she turned around to go, she noticed that one of the filing cabinets was slightly ajar. 'That's odd.'

'What is it?' Miles called from the door.

Thea pushed the cabinet door shut, realising that Edward must have opened it for some reason. She hoped he hadn't taken something home with him. He was her boss, and the chief archivist, and the one who had the most experience, decades of managing the museum archive, so it was his prerogative if he chose to work at the weekend. But taking material home, archived material, unless it was your own material you were working on, was strictly prohibited.

Thea walked over to the door, where Miles was waiting for her, took one more look around the room, and switched off the light before closing the door. She locked it and put the keys back in her bag. She turned to face him. 'What shall we do now?'

Miles looked at his watch.

Thea sighed. 'Don't tell me you've got to work this weekend?'

He reached out and tucked a dark wisp of hair behind her ear. 'I'm sorry to disappoint, but there's this big contract, and the law firm need my expertise.'

Thea wasn't surprised. How many weekends had started out like this? They would get to spend one night together, and then he would have to go the next day. 'It's just not fair.'

He nodded empathetically. 'I know, but then I suppose that's my fault for being such a hot-shot lawyer.'

She nudged his arm playfully. 'Yes, it is. Why can't you do a boring job like I do?'

He looked at her a long moment.

She knitted her brow. 'What?'

'Oh, nothing.' He glanced at his watch again. 'I got a text, so I'd better go.'

'All right.' Thea took his arm, and together they walked down the hall, up the stairs and along a corridor that led to an exit through a door into the main atrium of the museum. The door closed and automatically locked behind them.

They left via the side entrance into Montague Place. Miles stopped outside the entrance. 'Well, I'd better head off.'

'Isn't there time to have lunch together before you go?'

He glanced at his mobile phone and vigorously shook his head. 'I'm afraid not.'

Thea's face fell. She perked up when she had a thought. 'Will you have to work this evening? Perhaps we could meet up after work?'

'That's a thought. I'll try. I'll text you. Work might go on until really late, though. You know what it's like with the time difference.'

Thea didn't know personally, but she understood he was working with clients from different time zones all over the world. 'It's a shame, isn't it, with the modern technology like Teams and Zoom, that you have to live and work abroad. Why is that? Can't you ask for a job here?' She stared at him. She really hadn't meant to bring that up. A part of her was quite happy in her ordered, structured little life, with her own little flat. Sometimes, she wasn't sure she wanted to share it with anybody – not all the time.

She'd voiced that thought to Tanya once, who'd scoffed at the notion of a permanent long-distance relationship. 'If you were really, really in love with him,' she'd said, 'then you wouldn't be able to bear being apart for a minute, let alone weeks on end, and the thought of not seeing him at the end of the working day, of not living together, well ... that's just crazy in my mind.'

Thea stared at Miles, thinking about what Tanya had said. He still hadn't responded to her question.

He looked at his watch. 'Look, I've really got to run. I'll let you know if I can make it tonight, okay?'

'And if not? When will I see you again?' It wasn't something she normally asked. It was always very fluid, very as and when.

'I don't know.' He put an arm around her shoulders. 'Look, I'll make it up to you about this weekend, I promise.'

'I've got some leave coming up. When is yours? We could go away for like a whole week, rather than just a long weekend. I even thought of flying to Hong Kong to surprise you, but I don't know where you work.'

He shook his head vehemently. 'That would not be a good idea at all.'

'Why not? Of course I couldn't surprise you at your place of work, or the hotel, but I could phone you from the airport.'

Thea had been mulling this over. She'd even looked it up. It was only a five-hour flight from Hong Kong to Nepal. Would he accompany her to meet her mum? The look on his face said there was no point even asking. He looked appalled at the thought of her just turning up in Hong Kong, and that was before she had even had a chance to suggest meeting her mum.

His mobile phone rang. 'Look, I have to go. I'll phone you.'

Thea stood outside the museum, watching him answer his phone as he walked away. She heard him say, 'Yes, I know I said I'd be there, and I will. It's not my fault I had to pull an all-nighter.'

Thea hoped he wasn't going to get in trouble with work. He was obviously late for whatever meeting he had on a Saturday morning.

She turned on her heel and walked along Montague Place, wondering what she was going to do with the rest of her afternoon. *It's not my fault I had to pull an all-nighter.* She wondered what he had meant by that. *He wasn't at work last night – he was with me.*

Thea took a bus back to Pimlico and decided to spend the afternoon tidying up her flat. There was a mountain of washing-up in the sink from the dinner party the previous night. Miles had said he'd help her with the washing-up in the morning, but that hadn't happened. It never did. It was always left to her to do all the chores once he'd left. She didn't normally feel bothered. After all, as he always said, this was their quality time together. But today, the thought of all that washing-up wasn't exactly encouraging her to return to her flat. It didn't help that when she'd mentioned the state of the kitchen, he'd asked what she expected after a dinner party.

Thea stepped off the bus and returned home. She walked into her flat, looked at the state of it, and didn't know where to start. She glanced in at the kitchen, heaved a sigh, and walked down the hallway to her bedroom. She was going to start by making the bed and tidying her room. She would leave the kitchen until last.

Thea was kneeling down to tuck the sheet in under the mattress when she noticed something on the floor by Miles's side of the bed. 'Oh, no,' she exclaimed when she realised it was his wallet. It must have dropped out of his pocket when he had got dressed that morning. She walked into the lounge and found her mobile phone where she'd left it on the coffee table.

She'd already called his number when she realised he might be in a meeting by now. As expected, his phone when straight to voicemail. 'Oh, hi – it's me. Look, I've found your wallet. It was in the bedroom.' Thea didn't want to wait in all day for him to pop round and collect it; she had no idea how long he'd be at work. 'When you get this, let me know – we could meet up later.'

She smiled. Wouldn't this be the perfect excuse to get together again later that day or even that evening? She eyed the stack of washing-up through the open doorway to the kitchen and decided that she fancied a meal out that night. She put her mobile phone down and picked up the wallet, intending to put it in her bag so that she didn't forget it when they met up later. The wallet was open. She glanced at the cards inside and had a thought. What if his meetings went on until really late? Sometimes they'd have conversations on their mobiles at really odd times, very late at night or in the early hours. She imagined that when he was back in England, and he had work meetings with colleagues abroad, it would be the same story – unsocial hours. Thea decided she would prefer it if he didn't call round very late, or early on Sunday morning. It wasn't herself she was thinking about, but her upstairs neighbour, Gracie.

She looked through the wallet, trying not to feel as though she was prying. It was only a wallet, with bank cards, a driver's licence, and a little hotel card; just what she was looking for.

Thea took the card out. If she hadn't heard back from him by the time she'd got her apartment back to some semblance of normality – which for Thea would involve cleaning, hoovering, dusting, and making sure everything was in its place – then she thought she'd take the wallet to his hotel and text him. Perhaps he'd be there later, or the hotel staff could keep it in a safe and leave a note by his hotel key for him to collect it when he arrived after his meetings.

Thea set to work. It occurred to her, not for the first time, how she'd cope if she lived with someone twenty-four seven; someone who would disturb her daily routine and cleaning rituals. She didn't mind clearing up after herself, but what would it be like if she had to clear up after someone else all the time? She was thinking of Miles. He didn't exactly go out of his way to do anything on the domestic front.

She finished plumping the cushions on the sofa and went to fetch the hoover. *Am I a bit over the top when it comes to cleaning?* she thought. *But I like everything in order*, she said to herself. She'd seen a therapist once, after the breakdown of her last relationship. At first, she'd thought it hadn't been her fault that things had fallen apart when she and her partner had moved in together. Although the therapist had suggested they try couples' therapy, and had assured her that, to borrow a phrase, it invariably takes two to tango, it was too late for couples' therapy; they'd already split up permanently. But she had brought up Thea's mild OCD and discussed where it might have originated.

Thea put the dishcloth down and looked around the kitchen. It had taken her an hour to wash and dry the dishes and put them back in the kitchen cupboards. It wouldn't have taken her that long if she hadn't felt compelled to wipe every surface, clean the front of her kitchen cupboards, mop the tiled floor, and clean the sink until the stainless steel gleamed.

Normally, she felt satisfied when she'd finished going around her little apartment. Today, she just felt sad when she caught sight of the time by the clock in the kitchen. Three hours of her life wasted. Had it really taken that long?

6

Thea thought again about her past therapy sessions. She supposed that what had happened twenty-five years ago – her father's disappearance – had been bound to come up. The therapist had told her that the event was something outside her control, so it could well be bound up with her need for things to be orderly, and to feel in control. Thea hadn't liked the therapist reading too much into her past, so she'd left, deciding that there was nothing wrong with being a tidy person, even though she knew she was a little over the top. She looked around her sparkling kitchen and mumbled to herself, 'Okay – perhaps a lot over the top.'

She walked out of the kitchen, taking her mobile phone out of the back pocket of her jeans. It was now late in the afternoon and there had been no call or text from Miles; no acknowledgement whatsoever of her message.

Thea threw on her jacket, grabbed her bag and popped his wallet inside. She strode out of the door with the hotel card in her hand. It had the address on the back. She found Google Maps on her phone and discovered that the hotel was only a thirty-minute walk away. It probably wouldn't be any quicker on the bus in the traffic.

Thea set off through Pimlico. She loved this area of London. vasn't as posh as Belgravia next door, but Pimlico had its own le vibe, with its Regency architecture and its residential streets l out around garden squares that were a haven for wildlife.

As she closed the front door of the house, she thought of her m, who had inherited the property from her parents. Rather n sell it, she'd decided to keep it as an investment for Thea and sister. Little had she known that a few years later, she'd be ving in to live permanently as a single parent with her daughters. ea had only been nine at the time, her sister twelve. Perhaps her er sister had understood, but Thea remembered the scary feel- when she realised that something bad had happened; living on Suffolk Coast, in a rental cottage near the sea, was all she'd own. She had often spent time in her father's bookshop in the n, and her dad had always said that he was saving up his money ouy the cottage they were renting.

She remembered her favourite bedtime story – the one he had en told her about finding a very special lost book that would ke their fortune. That was why he had travelled a lot, leaving three of them to mind his shop when he was away, buying and ing books.

They hadn't had much in the way of material things – even cottage hadn't been theirs – but they had always had each other. it was what her father had often said. They had enjoyed spend- time together, with cosy evenings around the open fire playing rd games, or walks on the beach.

Everything had changed when he failed to return from a book he'd said he was attending in London. Worse still, when their n eventually reported him to the police as a missing person, e were no leads as to where he had gone. It was then that her mum found out he had not attended the book fair at all. Her mum had wanted them all to go with him in his campervan – the one he used to travel around the country. She had not long inherited her parents' house in London, and was in the throes of deciding what to do with it; whether to sell it and buy the cottage they were renting, or wait for her husband to buy the cottage – he was still insisting that he would find the money. In the meantime, her parents' house stood furnished but vacant.

She saw it as an adventure that they could all travel down to London to stay in the house while her husband visited the London Book Fair. Years later, Thea remembered the tremendous row between her parents when he'd refused to let them accompany him to London. Her parents never rowed, or fell out. They had always been very much in love – she remembered that. She had always been catching them kissing and holding hands, carrying on like two love-struck teenagers.

Her mother had been bereft when he had disappeared, and had been left wondering if the row had precipitated his disappearance. Of course, Thea had no notion of that when she was nine – just of the ramifications of the disappearance when she had to leave the cottage, and her school, and the little bookshop in which she'd adored spending time with her father, and move to London.

It was only later, when her older sister and her mum spoke a little of that painful time, that it came to light what her mother was afraid of; that she'd driven him away. 'Of course you didn't,' Thea had told her mum. 'He wouldn't have left you, or us.' But of course, no one could answer the next question: 'So, where is he? Why didn't he come back?' And for a very long time, Thea's mum had not stopped searching, looking, hoping that one day he'd come back. Thea had an idea that it was the reason her mum had kept the house – because then he would know where to find them if he ever reappeared.

Thea locked the front door and stood for a moment on the porch. London was the last place he'd been – or so her mum had thought. But the police had found no evidence of his old camper-van in London.

That was not to say he hadn't travelled to London, but there were hundreds, if not thousands of security cameras all around London, and her dad's campervan, which was painted yellow, wasn't exactly something you drove around in if you wanted to stay under the radar.

Thea had asked her mum once why they hadn't stayed in Suffolk. But of course she already knew the answer – her mum wanted to be in London, where she believed her husband had disappeared. Perhaps she thought she'd spot him one day, riding a Tube, or driving by in his campervan. Desperately in love with her husband, aching to have him back, it had seemed that she'd never give up looking.

At some point, as Thea got older, she had started to think that he was most likely dead. She knew her sister thought so too alt-hough Jenna had come up with another possibility; perhaps he'd had an affair and left them for someone else.

She wouldn't ever share that thought with her mum, though. It would probably destroy her.

Her mother threw herself into teaching, to support her girls, and the years passed. They grew up, and she converted the house for them before taking early retirement and leaving London.

For a long time, she had spent her time walking around Lon-don, attending book fairs with his photo, asking if anyone remem-bered him. That all stopped when she retired. Thea knew she'd spent long enough, years, waiting, hoping she'd find him. And now she'd finally moved on.

Thea had a feeling that in Nepal, with the yoga, her mum had finally found something that gave her a reason to look to the future. Leaving London had enabled her to stop searching. It was the happiest news for Thea that her mum wanted to be a yoga teacher. For the first time since her husband had vanished, she was finally facing the future alone.

Thea sighed. If things had been different, if her father hadn't disappeared, perhaps she wouldn't be living in this flat. Perhaps her mum would have sold the house earlier and bought that cottage, and her parents would be living there now, growing old together, just as Thea had imagined they would when she was a child. Her dad, rather than Edward, would have walked her sister, Jenna, down the aisle. And her mum wouldn't be on holiday in Nepal on her own, searching for something ever elusive, something missing from her life – her lost love.

Thea wiped a tear from her cheek. Although she hadn't told her mum and sister, sometimes she walked the London streets on the lookout for her father too. But it had been twenty-five years. He would be an old man now, in his seventies; would she even recognise him? She doubted it. But it didn't stop her looking, hoping, that one day he'd turn up, even though she knew in her heart he was most likely gone. After all, surely people didn't just disappear into thin air.

Thea's phoned beeped, reminding her that she was meant to be following Google Maps on foot to the hotel. She sighed and put her key away in her handbag, thinking of Miles and how it would be nice if they could meet up for a meal that evening. Thea wanted to ask him again if he might consider taking another position in his firm that meant he could spend more time in the UK – or preferably move back permanently. There was still no text, voicemail or phone call from him. She imagined there would be, though, as soon as he realised his wallet was missing.

Thea walked through Pimlico and along the Thames on her way to Hyde Park. She arrived at a rather nice-looking, imposing hotel near Lancaster Gate, overlooking the park. She walked through the swing doors into the large reception hall, which had wooden floors, comfortable wing-backed armchairs by the floor-to-ceiling windows, and a huge chandelier in the centre of the ceiling. It was all rather grand, and just the sort of place she expected Miles to stay in when he was in London; it certainly befitted his position as a top lawyer working in Hong Kong.

Miles said he much preferred to spend the evenings at her cosy flat rather than in his bland hotel room. She saw nothing bland about this hotel or the lovely room his company paid for. She had visited the hotel once before, ages ago. There had appeared to be no expense spared; he had a suite with amazing views of Hyde Park across the road. But she understood; he didn't want to spend any more time in the hotel than he had to. It just reminded him of work.

She got his wallet out of her bag as she approached reception. 'Hi. My boyfriend dropped his wallet. He is at work at the moment, and I don't want to disturb him. May I leave it with you? If there's somewhere safe you can store it, then you could give it to him with his hotel room key on his return.'

'Of course, madam. That won't be a problem. One moment while I check he is staying with us.'

'Well, of course he is.' Thea shook her head. *What a silly thing to say*, she thought.

The receptionist looked up and smiled. 'Of course, madam. May I have his name?'

Thea got out his wallet and showed him Miles's driver's licence. 'There, his name is Miles Bannon.'

'Very good, madam. Do you know his room number?'

Thea shook her head.

The receptionist glanced at the driver's licence, and then turned to his computer, typing on the keyboard. 'Hmm.'

Thea stared at him. 'Is there a problem?'

He handed the driver's licence back. 'I'm afraid he is not staying here.'

Thea frowned. Miles had mentioned this hotel, she was sure of it, and she'd found the card in his wallet.

'Are you sure? Can you double-check?'

'I have. He is not staying with us.'

Thea picked up the licence, feeling rather foolish. 'Sorry,' she mumbled.

The receptionist said, 'I did notice an address on the licence.'

Thea looked up. She'd been in the process of tucking it back in the wallet. She slipped it out and took a look.

'It's a London address,' the receptionist continued. 'I recognise the postcode. It's not that far from here.'

Thea stared at the address. Why hadn't she thought to look herself? Because he was meant to be at the hotel. There was an explanation; he likely had his own property in London that he rented out. He'd never mentioned this before, but then she'd never asked. Why was that? In fact, when she really thought about it, she knew very little about him, his background, where he was from, who his parents were – were they even still alive?

'Can you call me a taxi?'

'Yes, madam. Please, take a seat. I'll let you know when it arrives.'

Thea walked over to one of the armchairs by the Georgian window and sat down. She opened the wallet. This time, she didn't feel the least bit guilty about thumbing through. Miles was obviously staying at another hotel. She hadn't noticed any other cards of that nature in his wallet, but she thought it wouldn't hurt to have another look. However, aside from the normal bank cards, there was nothing else but some bank notes – all sterling. That surprised her a little. Wouldn't someone who lived abroad most of the time have some foreign currency in his wallet?

'Madam, your taxi is waiting outside.'

'Oh, okay. That was quick. Thank you.'

The receptionist gave her a little bow and returned to his desk.

Thea gathered up her bag and coat and stepped back through the swinging door. A black cab was waiting by the kerb. She read the address out to the taxi driver through his open window before she got inside. 'Do you take cards?'

'I prefer cash.'

Thea opened Miles's wallet and pulled out a twenty-pound note. She'd have to pay him back another time or go Dutch on their meal tonight – if he agreed to eating out, that was.

Twenty minutes later, after crawling along in the heavy traffic, they arrived at a modern apartment block in Soho. She was just reaching for the door handle, intending to get out of the taxi and see if Miles was there, when a taxi arrived and parked a couple of cars down. She saw Miles in the back of the taxi as it passed by. 'Oh, that was well timed!' she said, smiling as she handed the taxi driver the fare. She couldn't believe he'd turned up the same time. Thea looked in her bag for his wallet. Any minute now, he'd discover he hadn't got his wallet. In the back of her mind, though, she wondered why he hadn't mentioned this address.

The taxi driver turned in his seat. 'Who – the guy with the young woman and kids?'

Thea looked up. 'Pardon me?' Miles was standing on the pavement with two young children, helping a young woman with shopping bags out of the taxi.

She saw him patting down his jacket, obviously looking for his wallet. She had no clue who that woman was that he was sharing the taxi with. Thea was about to jump out of the taxi and surprise him, when she saw him lean over and kiss the young woman on the cheek. One of the young children tugged on his trouser leg. He bent down, picked the child up, ruffled his hair and handed him to the young woman, who had left the carrier bags on the pavement by his feet. She said something. He shook his head and smiled, pointing at the flats. Thea opened the taxi door and heard him say, 'No, it's all right. You go ahead. I won't be long. Must have left my wallet at the damn office. That will teach me to pull an all-nighter and be so exhausted. I don't know what I'm doing.'

Thea stepped out of the taxi, but she was too shocked to move any further.

He didn't notice her standing on the pavement. She watched him wait until the woman and children had entered the apartment building. Then he got out his phone. Thea's mobile rang. Over the sound of the engine of his taxi ticking over, he didn't hear her mobile ringing a few feet away. Thea slowly got out her phone and answered it.

'Hey, Thea. Look, I've lost my wallet. I'm thinking I may have left it at yours. I'm coming round.'

'No need,' Thea said, 'I'm right here.'

'What are you talking about?'

Thea stared at him. 'Turn around.'

He turned around and nearly dropped his phone in shock. He smiled nervously, casting a furtive glance in the direction of the apartment building. 'Thea, darling,' he said. 'What are you doing here?'

'I might ask you the same question.'

'Excuse me, mate,' the taxi driver interrupted, leaning across the passenger seat and talking to him through the open window. 'Are you paying for the fare – or what?'

Miles looked at Thea. 'I don't suppose you've got my wallet?'

Thea got it out of her handbag. 'I left you a message on your phone.'

'Did you? Sorry, I've been so busy at work, I didn't get a chance to—'

'Mate? You can carry on your conversation after you've paid me.'

'Oh, right, sorry.' He walked up to Thea. 'My wallet?'

She handed over his wallet. She didn't know how she was holding it together. She glanced at the flats. She didn't know why she was still standing there and why she hadn't just thrown the wallet at him and left.

He followed her gaze. 'That's my sister. I haven't got a permanent address here, obviously, so I use her address for correspondence. We meet up when I'm in London.'

Thea breathed a huge sigh. 'Oh, right.' The possibility had not occurred to her. Of course, that was plausible.

He looked at her. 'Oh, god. You thought …'

Thea felt really foolish. 'Well, of course. What else would I think?' She stared at him. 'Why didn't you tell me you had a sister?

Do you stay here sometimes, then?'

He shook his head vehemently.

'Mate, can I have that twenty?'

'Oh, yes – sorry.' He handed over the money. Then he looked at the taxi driver. 'Wait.'

'Do you need a taxi somewhere else?'

He nodded. 'You might as well take the taxi home, Thea.' He got out his wallet and looked at the driver. 'I'll give you her address.'

7

Thea looked at Miles. Something wasn't right. She looked at the flat. 'Are you visiting your sister, then? I'd like to meet her. You never talk about your family.'

He shook his head. 'No, not really. I just literally bumped into her, so we got a taxi back here together. I might pop in, but it wouldn't be a great time for you to visit, you know, with the kids under her feet.'

Thea stared at him. 'Why can't I just say hi?'

He looked at her. 'I just said why.' He glanced up at the flats. 'Look, why don't we go back to your place? You said you wanted to meet up later. Well, here we are. Let's go.' He opened the taxi door.

'Why don't we go to your hotel for a change?' she asked. She recalled her visit to the hotel first. She hadn't told him she'd been there.

'Pardon me?'

'You know, the hotel where you're staying. The hotel card is in your wallet.'

'You went through my wallet?'

'Well, you didn't respond to my voicemail.'

'I was in meetings all afternoon.'

Thea looked at him, wondering whether anything he'd said was true. There was one way to find out for sure. 'I saw the name of the hotel in your wallet. It's not far.'

His grin faltered. 'It's not a very nice room. Let's go to a nice coffee place instead.'

Thea nearly let it slip that she'd been there already. She couldn't imagine a hotel like that didn't have nice rooms.

Thea persisted. 'No, I'd like to see your hotel room.'

'Why? It's just a hotel room.'

She noticed he sounded irritated.

'I'd just like to see where you live when you're in London.'

'Look, I'd rather not. My room is a bit of a mess with dirty laundry. I'd be embarrassed to take you back there. I'll tell you what. I promise the next time we hook up, we'll stay in my hotel room. How about that?'

He was standing there with the taxi door open, motioning for her to get in. She caught him glancing at the flats and looked over at them too. If it had been a house, she would have run up to the front door and knocked, insisting she speak to the woman inside.

He turned to her. 'We could pass it in the taxi.' He turned to the driver. 'Will you pass by my hotel on our way?'

'Yeah – sure.'

Miles gave him the name of a different hotel.

Thea looked at him surprised. 'But the card in your wallet said—'

'Oh, I'm not staying at that hotel. The company has put me up in a different hotel. I think they're cutting costs. It's not as nice.'

'Really?' Thea's heart leapt. All the things that had been going through her mind – namely that everything coming out of his mouth was an outright lie – vanished the moment he explained that he was staying elsewhere. Thea smiled at him. She got in the taxi. He was about to follow when his phone rang. He closed the door to the taxi and then answered his phone, walking a few paces away from the car.

Thea frowned at him as she watched him turn his back. A moment later, he came back to the taxi. 'Sorry, that was work. Look, it turns out I haven't got the afternoon free. Why don't you go home. I'll call another taxi.'

Thea shook her head. 'It's all right. I don't mind sharing. Where is your office?' She'd never seen his office building before. He'd said he worked for a foreign bank. She imagined it was in The Square Mile in the heart of the city. She eyed him.

He smiled. 'All right. The taxi can drop you off first.'

'No, I'm sure your office is on the way.'

The taxi driver said, 'It would be quicker to swing by your office first, mate.'

Thea turned to him.

'Oh, all right.' He leaned forward in his seat, and gave the driver the address. He caught her surprised expression when he leaned back in his seat. 'What?'

'Oh, nothing.' Thea glanced out of the window, feeling stupid for doubting him. He had said he worked at that bank, and that was where they were headed.

'Do you want to do a detour and pass by the hotel?'

Thea shifted her gaze from the window. 'Huh?'

'You know, I said I could show you where—'

Thea smiled at him, and took his hand in hers. 'No, that's all right.'

'Okay then.' He returned her smile and squeezed her hand.

The taxi took longer than expected to get through the traffic, during which time Thea enjoyed making plans for when they would next meet up. She was disappointed to discover that Miles was flying out the next day. It had already been arranged. Something had come up as a result of the meeting, and he was being sent off to Dubai urgently.

'Dubai! Wow,' Thea exclaimed.

He nodded.

'I know you're busy the rest of the afternoon, but what about this evening? Let's meet up. Come round to mine. We could go out to a restaurant for a meal.' She saw his smile falter. 'Or we'll eat in. Get a takeaway.'

'I'm not sure, Thea. Depends what they've called me back in the office for.'

Thea sighed. 'You might have to work late again?'

'Quite possibly.'

'That's going to be disappointing.'

'Yeah, sorry.'

'Oh, don't apologise.'

He leaned towards her and kissed her cheek. 'I'll make it up to you, I promise, next time I'm in London.'

'You sound pretty sure you won't be able to make it this evening.'

He sighed heavily. 'Well, I know work. When they call me in, it means there's something pretty important that they need my expertise for.'

'What do you do, mate?' the taxi driver asked.

'I'm a lawyer.'

The taxi driver nodded as he pulled into a layby outside the bank.

Miles said, 'Well, this is me.' He squeezed her hand, and cupped her face in his hands to kiss her goodbye.

'I'm going to miss you,' said Thea, feeling the tears welling up.

'And I you.' He leaned over to open the car door.

'When you're next in town, I'd love to meet your sister.' Thea caught the taxi driver staring at her in the rearview mirror. He quickly looked away when he realised she'd seen him.

'Er, yeah, sure. I'll, um … arrange it.' Miles shuffled along the seat to get out. 'Well, I'd better dash.'

Thea smiled 'Bye.'

'Yes, see you.' And with that he shut the door and walked into the building.

'Where to? Is it the address in Pimlico?'

'Yes, please.' Thea stared at the entrance to the bank.

The taxi driver put his indicator light on and was about to move out into the traffic when Thea suddenly leaned forward and tapped him on the shoulder. 'Wait!'

The taxi driver slammed on the brake. He glanced over his shoulder. 'Yes?'

'I, er … I've forgotten to tell my boyfriend something. Will you wait while I pop into the bank?'

'Sure. The meter will still be running though.'

'That's fine. Thank you.' Thea stalled for a moment or two to see if Miles emerged from the building, but he didn't. She got out of the taxi. The multi-storey, ultra-modern building had huge floor-to-ceiling glass windows, so she could see inside the foyer even from the taxi. As she approached the revolving door, she saw a security guard sitting at a reception desk. There was nothing else in the reception foyer apart from the desk, a row of seating by the door, and two lifts past the security desk.

Thea was aware that this was nothing like a high street bank. You didn't just walk in off the street to take out cash or make a deposit. This was an office building, the head office of a foreign bank.

She went inside and wasn't surprised when the guard looked up, and said, 'May I help you?'

'Um, well, a guy, a … friend who works here just walked in, and I forgot to give him a message.'

'Okay. Can you text him?'

'Well, no.' Thea had to think on her feet. 'I think he has a meeting, so he must have switched off his phone.'

'All right. The security guard got out a piece of paper. 'What's his name?'

'Miles Bannon.'

The security guard looked up. 'Oh, yeah – I've just seen him.' He looked at the system. 'I can't see any meetings arranged for today.' Not sure why they'd hold a meeting at the weekend.'

'They work with clients all over the world,' said Thea.

'Okay, well that's as may be, but there aren't any meetings.'

'Did he say why he was here, then?'

The security guard eyed her. 'He was collecting some work from his desk to do this evening.'

'Oh, okay.'

'He's a nice fella – keeps himself to himself.'

Thea thought that sounded like him.

'But he says good morning to me every morning, unlike a lot of 'em.'

Thea furrowed her brow. It was probably just a figure of speech. Even so, she had to ask, 'What do you mean every morning?'

'Just like I said. Well, when I'm here on my shift. I do unsocial hours some of the time, like this weekend. No one else wanted these shifts, but then I get paid more, and still have time off during the week, so it works for me.'

Ah, that explained it. She wouldn't be surprised if they were like ships passing in the night. It probably felt like he said good morning to Miles every time he was here, because he did – on the rare occasions they were in the building at the same time.

'What was the message?'

'If you could write down, *Can't wait to see you when you're back in London.*'

'Is he going somewhere?'

'Yes, I believe Dubai.'

'Lucky fella. I'd love to go on holiday there.'

Thea shook her head. 'Oh, it's not a holiday; it's work. He's just come back from Hong Kong, then he's off there.'

'Oh! Really? When was he in Hong Kong?'

'He lives there, and works over there for this bank. He comes back here and there, mostly at weekends, touching base with head office.'

The security guard stopped writing and looked up. 'Look, are we talking about the same guy? The Miles I know works here nine to five, Monday to Friday, in the accounts department. I think he's some sort of support worker, you know – not exactly a high-flying lawyer.'

Thea felt like the ground was moving beneath her.

'Ma'am? Are you all right?'

Suddenly Thea could feel an arm around her waist as her legs gave way. 'I'm so sorry,' she said. 'I came over dizzy all of a sudden.'

'Here, come into the back office.' He guided her through a

door behind the desk and sat her down in a comfortable leather swivel chair. There was another person in the office who was monitoring some screens which were linked to CCTV inside and outside the building.

'Let me make you a cup of tea.'

'Oh, no – really. I haven't got time. I've got a taxi waiting.'

'A glass of water, then.'

'All right.'

He handed her a paper cup of ice-cold water from the water cooler beside the desk. She sipped the water, feeling her heart pounding in her chest. The security guard knelt down in front of her chair. 'Feeling better?'

Thea wouldn't exactly say she was feeling any better, even though the dizzy spell had passed, but she nodded all the same. 'Yes, thank you.'

'Good. Look, I think we are talking about two different people. I don't mean to sound condescending, but are you sure you've got the right building?'

'Of course I have. I saw him walk in!'

The security guard walked up to his colleague and leaned over, looking at the security cameras. He pointed. 'Is that him?'

Thea carefully stood up and walked over. There Miles was, on the little screen, sitting at his desk. 'Yes. Yes, that's him.'

He turned to his colleague. 'He's the guy who works in accounts – isn't he? He's not one of the lawyers on the top floor.'

The young woman swivelled around in her chair. Despite the bland grey security uniform, she was very pretty, with blonde hair. 'Yes,' she said. 'He jokes every time, saying that if he was ten years younger, he'd ask me out. Happens pretty much every morning. It's like an in-joke, because he's married.'

Thea let out a gasp.

'Well, I know it's against protocol, as you're not an employee here, but if I put you in our logbook as a visitor, and issue you a pass, I can take you up to his office, if you like.'

Thea hesitated, her heart pounding in her chest. *It can't be true – it just can't!* she thought.

There was only one way to find out – confront him. She looked the security guard in the eye and said, 'Give me that pass. Please.'

'Sure thing.' He walked over to filing cabinet, took out a log-book and sat down to fill in her details.

Thea stared at the security guard, still in two minds as to whether she should confront Miles right there in the building.

'Right – this is for you.' The security guard gave her a lanyard with a small plastic wallet hanging from it containing her pass. 'I'll take you to his office.'

Thea hesitated when she stepped back into the reception area. She wished she could just walk out of the building now, get in the taxi, go home and carry on in blissful ignorance until the next time they met up. But how could she after what she'd seen today?

She cast her gaze back into the security office at the young, blonde-haired woman. She'd said he was married. Thea was still having a tough time believing that was true.

'Are you sure you want to do this?'

Thea looked at the kindly young man. 'No, but I need to know if the person I … I…' She choked back tears, turning her face from the guard. She composed herself before turning back. 'Let's go.'

'All right.'

Together they walked to the lift and rode up to the next floor in silence. Thea thought about Miles flirting with that young woman, and what the other guard had said about the high-flying lawyers and executives, whose offices were on the top floor. 'So, you said the lawyers and executives work on the top floors – is that some hierarchal thing?'

'Oh, yes – that's why us security guards work on the lowest floor,' he joked. 'But yes, that is the case. Right, this is us. This is the admin staff's floor.' They got out at the next floor.

'Where is his office?' Thea asked, looking around the large, open-plan office with its rows and rows of little cubicles.

The security guard said, 'Oh, folks who work on this floor wouldn't have their own office.'

Thea shook her head. She had somehow expected him to say just that.

'I don't see him,' said Thea.

'No, you wouldn't if he's sitting down. I do know where his desk is. If he's not at his desk, he's probably gone to the restroom.'

The security guard weaved his way past lots of cubicles, each containing a desk, a chair, a computer, and paperwork. There were also personal photos and mementos pinned to the soft panel boards that separated one cubicle from the next. It wasn't unlike her own cubicle in the museum's offices, except that she didn't work in an open-plan environment like this.

The office was quiet, like the archives were most of the time, but she could just imagine what it was like there on a Monday morning with the room full of people. There would be phones ringing, people talking and keyboards clicking as people typed. The thought of it filled her with dread.

'So, this is him.'

As they rounded the desk, Thea saw that the cubicle was

empty. She picked up a gold name plate, embossed with Miles's name in black lettering.

'Oh, yeah – that's a bit of a running joke. Everyone else has their name written on a piece of paper and pinned to the outside of their cubicle. He has to be different; everyone says he's got ideas above his station.'

Lexi stared at the name plate; there was his job title. 'Oh, my god. He isn't a lawyer.'

'Yes, I think I mentioned that.'

Thea turned to him, wide-eyed, holding the fancy name plate. 'What does this mean?'

The security guard looked at the name plate and didn't quite get her meaning.

'He's a pen-pusher, like the rest of them.'

Thea wasn't asking what the job title meant. She was asking what all of it meant; the fact that Miles had lied to her about who he really was and what he really did, and worse still – Thea caught sight of the photos of the woman and two children that had alighted from the taxi when she'd arrived at the address on his licence – about the fact that he was married.

She slowly lowered herself into his office chair and stared at the photos.

'Are you all right?' the security guard asked again.

'I don't think so.' She looked up at him. 'Has he left, do you think?'

'One moment.' He pressed a button on the little radio device on his shoulder. 'Hey, has Miles Bannon left the building, do you know?'

'No, he hasn't. I saw him walk out of the door in the direction of the toilets.'

'Great – thanks.' The guard turned to Thea. 'He's still here.' He hesitated. 'Look, I've got to get back to the desk. Will you be okay?'

Thea stared at the photos. It felt like the dumbest question she'd ever heard. Of course she wasn't okay. Her boyfriend, her partner, the guy she had made grand plans with – if only in her head – wasn't who he'd said he was. She had hoped that they would move in together, get married. She had liked the idea of travelling, of living abroad, but she loved her job and had hoped he would stay and work in London. But that was what he'd been doing all along – living in a flat the next borough over. When she'd thought he was in Hong Kong, he'd been just a thirty-minute cab ride away the whole time.

She now understood why he never wanted to go out much. He was scared of being seen. It was no wonder she got phone calls and texts from him at odd hours; he could only contact her when his wife was out or asleep or when he was at work.

The odd hours that he apparently kept because he was in a different time zone were one big horrendous lie – as was this fantasy of his life as some hot-shot, jet-setting international lawyer. The only truthful thing he'd told her was that he worked in this bank.

She heard the lift door open and the security guard head back to his desk. She got out her phone and dialled Miles's number. From somewhere out in the corridor, she could hear the faint sound of a mobile phone ringing.

He answered. 'Hi, Thea. Did you get home all right?'

Thea swivelled around in his chair, holding a photo of him and his wife. She imagined that he was biding his time, hanging around in the office until he was sure she'd left in the taxi. Wasn't her phone call the perfect timing for him to leave and head back to his wife?

She looked towards the door at the end of the room. She presumed he'd have to walk back through the office to get to the lift and exit the building.

'Thea?'

She said, 'Not exactly.'

'Why what happened?'

Thea heard the sound of a door opening, and footsteps. 'I got waylaid.'

'Really? Why?'

'Something happened.'

'On the way home?'

Thea could hear his voice getting closer.

'You could say that.'

'Oh, dear. I could try and come over later. It would have to be quite late, though. Would you like that?'

'No, actually.'

'I think that's probably for the best.'

'You think so? Is that because you're jetting off tomorrow?' Thea stared at his desk, shaking her head. *How could I have been so stupid?* she thought.

'I'll call you as soon I touch down.'

'Another big contract abroad?'

'I'm afraid so.'

Thea could hear his footsteps approaching. 'There's a strange echo on the phone.'

Thea stood up. He was but a few cubicles away. She'd never seen him look so shocked as when he spotted her right there in the office. 'Thea! What on earth—?'

'Am I doing here?' Thea finished off his sentence. 'What do you think?'

'I have no idea. I thought you were going home. I'm in a meeting. I just came back to my desk to collect some paperwork.'

Thea's eyes went wide. 'Oh, my god. Is there no end to your lies? You're not in a meeting, and you are certainly not going to Dubai, or back to Hong Kong. I doubt you've even been there, let alone lived there.'

He bit his lower lip. 'Oh, Thea. I can explain—'

She held up the photo of him cheek to cheek with the woman Thea recognised from the taxi.

He'd almost reached his desk when he stopped and caught sight of the photo.

'Oh really? Explain this!' Thea threw the photo at him and ran for the lift. She stopped at the lift door, frantically pressing the button. She glanced over her shoulder and saw him bend down and pick up the photo. He looked at her. 'Oh, my god. Thea, please – wait. I love you. I … I shouldn't have lied. I ... I don't know why I said those things about myself when we first met. Well, I do. I didn't think I was good enough for you. And the lie became bigger, and I didn't know how to tell you the truth. It was stupid mistake. Let me make it up to you. I'll leave her, I will.'

She had known he would come up with excuses. He was a master liar. She didn't want to hear it. There was no excuse for the lies he'd told her, the way he'd strung her along all this time, along with the lies he'd told his wife. Her friends had been right: she should have dumped him ages ago. She ran into the lift when the doors opened, and kept pressing the button. Miles didn't move from his spot beside his cubicle. He had obviously realised that chasing after her was futile.

'Let me make it up to you. I'll call round tonight. We can go out for a meal ...'

'Are you insane?'

'I'll leave her. Things aren't going well between us. I'll disappear. We can disappear together.'

'Don't you dare!' she shouted at him as the lift doors closed, crying uncontrollably. 'Don't you dare disappear and leave your family.'

'Miss – are you all right? What happened?' said the security guard.

'I dumped him – that's what happened,' Thea said as she ran out of the building, thankful that at least the taxi was still waiting for her. She jumped in. 'Please, take me home.'

8

Thea slammed her front door shut and stood there looking at her spotless apartment. She felt numb. She jumped at the sound of her phone. There was a text, then a voicemail. She threw her handbag across the room without even bothering to get out her phone. It landed on the sideboard, knocking off the vase filled with fresh flowers, which shattered on the wooden floor.

'If you think I'm even going to look at your text, or listen to your voicemail—' Thea didn't finish her sentence. She collapsed in a heap on the floor, tears rolling down her face, letting out a silent scream.

She hadn't been lying there long when there was a soft knock on the door. 'Thea? Is everything all right in there?'

Thea sniffed and wiped her runny nose with the sleeve of her coat. 'Yes.'

'I heard a loud noise, like glass shattering. Are you okay?'

Thea slowly got up from the floor. She undid the lock and opened the door. She could tell by Gracie's expression that her friend was shocked at the state of her. Thea imagined what she looked like. Her normally sleek hair was all askew, some of it plastered to her tear-streaked face. She bet her mascara had run, and imagined her lipstick was a mess where she'd wiped her face with her coat sleeve.

'Oh my goodness, child – what happened?'

Thea stepped forward and almost fell into Gracie's arms, sobbing into her friend's shoulder. She wished her mum was there. A part of her felt stupid; a woman in her thirties crying like a baby. 'Sorry. I'm so sorry.'

Gracie held her shoulders. 'Now, don't you be saying sorry to me. What I want to know is, what has he done?'

Thea looked at her in surprise.

'It's got to be a man. And the only man I know in your life right now is Miles.'

Thea managed to nod her head, a sob escaping.

Gracie nodded. 'I thought so.' She put a reassuring arm around her shoulders and steered her back into the flat, closing the door behind her with her foot. Let's start with a nice, sweet cup of tea. How about it?'

Thea nodded her head. Gracie followed Thea into her flat and immediately spotted the glass vase shattered on the floor, the beautiful roses swimming in a puddle of water.

'Did he get you those flowers?'

Thea shook her head, realising what it must look like. 'No, they weren't from him. I bought them myself. I think he texted me, and left me a voice message, so I threw my bag with the phone inside. I didn't expect to smash my lovely vase.' She started to cry again.

Gracie rushed over. 'Now, now. Let me put the kettle on and you can tell me all about it. I'm sure when you've talked to someone about it, it's not going to seem half as bad as you think it is.'

Thea stared after her as Gracie walked into the kitchen,

thinking that she'd given anything for that to be true. Unfortunately, it was every bit as bad as it seemed.

❖

'That bastard!'

Thea sipped her tea, not surprised by Gracie's reaction when she told her what had happened that afternoon – although she'd never heard Gracie swear before. She heaved a sigh. The sweet tea had helped, but only to the extent that she was no longer lying on the floor, sobbing her heart out. That was not to say she wasn't still *feeling* like sobbing her heart out, though.

She sat down on the sofa and tucked her legs under her. 'Now I know why we never really talked about moving in together.' She didn't add that she hadn't been entirely sure that moving in with Miles was what she'd wanted anyway. Cohabiting hadn't exactly worked out with her last boyfriend. When he had moved in, her little flat had no longer felt like her own; no longer tidy and ordered, with everything in its place. So, she hadn't exactly pushed Miles on the subject of his work or his personal life.

Now she knew that if she had asked him, he would have had to refuse. 'I can't believe he had a young family all along. I'm the other woman. He said he loved me and that he'd leave her.'

Gracie interrupted her monologue. 'That's what they all say.' She patted Thea's hand. 'Listen to me, I'm the voice of experience.'

Thea remembered Gracie saying that she'd throw a party when she got the decree nisi through. She knew why that was; after nearly forty years of marriage, Gracie's husband had left her for a younger woman who worked in the same building.

'I don't want to be the other woman. And I don't want to break up a family.'

Gracie's eyes shifted to the sideboard. 'How about I get a broom and sweep that up?'

'No, that's my fault.'

Gracie patted her hand again, and smiled. 'I insist.'

Thea heaved a sigh. 'All right. There's a dustpan, brush and broom in the little cupboard in the kitchen.' She watched her good friend and neighbour disappear into the kitchen and come out with the dustpan and brush, the broom, and an old carrier bag and newspaper. Thea finished her tea while Gracie swept up.

'There – all done. I'd hate to think what might have happened if you'd actually aimed your bag at something.'

Thea turned around in her seat, frowning until she caught sight of Gracie's broad grin. At a time like this, she was still making jokes. Trust Gracie to make her smile.

'There, now – that's much better. I know it hurts right now, very much, but no man is worth putting your life on hold for, or worth not moving on from, I'll tell you that.'

'Tell that to my mum,' blurted Thea.

Gracie cocked her head to one side and regarded her a long moment. 'Your dad disappeared years ago, didn't he?'

Thea had always been aware that Gracie knew about her father's disappearance. But what Gracie didn't know was that Thea's mum and dad had been in love. When Thea was older, her mum had told her there had been no reason for him to leave – he had not been involved with anyone else, and neither had Thea's mum. Apparently, they had been the perfect little family: Thea, her sister, Jenna, and their mum and dad. It was a situation that was worlds away from the one she found herself in with Miles.

'Thea, I knew Miles wasn't right for you.'

Thea finished her tea and leaned forward to put it on the

coffee table. 'After dinner yesterday, when you said you didn't like him – you weren't really joking, were you?'

Gracie put a consoling hand on her arm. 'There was something about him I couldn't put my finger on.'

Thea sighed. 'Edward said something.'

'About Miles?'

Thea nodded. 'He said, *are you sure he is right for you*? He said something else too. That he didn't think Miles came across as some high-flying executive who jets off to places like Hong Kong. He said it was a daft thought, and to ignore it.' Thea's bottom lip quivered.

Gracie stood up and fetched Thea's handbag. She returned to the sofa, and handed it to her.

Thea threw her a questioning look.

'He is only going to keep texting and leaving you voice messages,' Gracie said. I think you should reply now – make sure he knows there's no coming back from this. You're ending it. It's over.'

Thea stared at her.

Gracie took her handbag, opened it, and found her phone. She handed it to her. 'Do it now. You don't want him texting and calling anymore.'

Thea nodded and took her phone. She hesitated.

Gracie said, 'You're still so very young, Thea. This might seem like the end of the world right now. Your trust has been betrayed, and you can't imagine trusting anyone again, let alone opening your heart to anyone. But there is someone else out there – someone you will meet who is right for you, who is your soulmate.'

She caught Thea's sceptical expression. 'Think of it this way; if this hadn't happened, it could have gone on for years.'

Thea shook her head. 'No, it wouldn't.' She was thinking of that young security guard who Miles had flirted with at work. She looked as though she was in her early twenties – almost ten years younger than Thea. When would he have got bored of her and start to look for someone younger? It seemed like he was already well on his way to doing so.

'Yes, you would have found out sooner or later when he refused to move in with you.' Gracie smiled. 'So, read those texts, listen to that voicemail, and send him packing!'

Thea smiled at Gracie. 'What would I do without you?' She leaned over and gave her friend a hug. She picked up her phone, took a deep breath and scrolled through her messages. 'Oh, it's not him – it's my sister.'

Gracie grinned. 'All the better.'

But it wasn't, not for Thea. Although she'd said to Gracie that she didn't want to be the other woman and break up a family, Miles had said he loved her and that things weren't going well with his wife. He had said he was going to leave her. Gracie had said that such men never left their wives, but her sister's husband had. He had left his first wife for her sister. Who was to say, despite what Gracie had said, that Miles wouldn't leave his wife for her, now she'd found out the truth?

She recalled what he'd said. That he'd spun an absurd lie because when they'd first met, he just hadn't thought he'd be good enough for her, so he'd come up with some stupid, insane lie about himself that had got way out of hand. Thea bit her lower lip. She realised that despite everything that Gracie had said, deep down there was a part of her that believed him.

Gracie said, 'Was it your sister who left you a voice message too?'

Thea nodded. She'd listened to the message; her sister had asked her to phone back straight away as she had something really important to discuss. Thea sighed. She expected Jenna needed her kids babysitting. She guessed a babysitter had let them down at the last minute. The twins weren't little anymore; they had started secondary school a month earlier and had just turned thirteen. She was just wondering whether they were old enough to spend one evening at home alone when Gracie said, 'Do you want me to stay with you tonight?'

'No, it's all right. I'm going to make myself a hot chocolate, curl up on the sofa and watch Bridget Jones. He never did like those movies. He thought Darcy was a loser.'

'Well, it's not Darcy who's the loser, is it?' Gracie's face broke out into a wide grin. 'Well, if you need anything, you let me know, all right? And if you need some time off work …'

'Oh, I'll be in work on Monday. I'm not going to sit around my flat and mope, feeling sorry for myself.'

'That's the spirit.' Gracie got up and walked to the door. 'Now, remember what I said – there's someone else out there for you. Just you wait and see.'

But how will I find him? thought Thea.

As if reading her mind, Gracie said, 'Serendipity will bring you together, I'm sure of it.'

9

'You're my agent – why can't you tell me why the work is drying up?' Callum walked over to the window, his mobile phone to his ear, and gazed at the view from his luxury penthouse apartment. It was a home he could no longer afford; he'd missed two months rental payments, and the bill reminders for the utilities were stacking up. He was only there because the electricity had been cut off at his mansion in Beverley Hills.

It was the same story there, except that it wasn't rent he'd missed paying; he had a mortgage on it. He'd put it up for sale the previous month, hoping a potential buyer could be found quickly. That was why he'd moved out and taken on this rental instead, hoping the house would sell quicker if he wasn't there. In hindsight, he should have just stayed in the house and not taken on more financial commitments with the rental. But he hadn't been able to abide the thought of staying in that mansion – which he knew he shouldn't have bought in the first place – while watching his Hollywood dream descend into a nightmare before his eyes. The worst part was that it was all of his own making.

He stared across the road to where he could see some young people roller-skating along the wide boulevard and others enjoying themselves on the white sandy Malibu beach. He sighed heavily and turned his back on the window. If only he had listened to his agent ten years earlier. Instead, here he was anxiously calling him, worried about work and money. It was the weekend, and he should have been relaxing on the Malibu beach and doing a bit of surfing – not desperately hoping some work would turn up.

'I heard about your last audition.'

'Who from?'

'How many times have I told you that Hollywood is a small place? Besides, I'm your agent. I set it up, don't you remember? So, of course I'm going to know about it.'

Callum groaned. 'Look, I messed up.'

'I'll say. How on earth did you think you could turn up drunk and not flunk it – big time? If you're not careful, you're going to get a reputation for being unreliable, and then you really will be screwed in terms of work.'

Callum thought it was already heading that way.

'Do you know what my advice is to you?'

Callum rolled his eyes. He didn't need advice. He needed a break. A job. Money.

'Take some time out – and for god's sake, you'd better get your shit together if you want to work in this town again.' His agent paused. 'Do you remember what I said to you when you got your first break?'

Callum bit his bottom lip and walked over to the sofa. He sat down. 'Yes, I do.'

'And did you follow my advice?'

Callum rubbed his forehead. He could feel a monster of a headache developing, on top of the dull ache he already had. He was still hungover from his drinking session in a bar the previous night. He didn't answer that question, although he was sure that at some point in the conversation his agent would get around to reminding him just what that advice was.

'I remember when you first started out fifteen years ago, fresh-faced, like all the others who have walked through my door, thinking you were going to be the next big thing in Hollywood. You started out, like all the others, when you got those bit-parts in terrible B-movies.'

'You got me those parts!' exclaimed Callum.

'Yes, I know.'

'I wanted movies.'

'Yes, but what you needed was work and money.'

So, what's changed? thought Callum, still rubbing his forehead.

'What piece of advice did I give you back then, when you landed the lead in that show?'

'Here we go,' thought Callum.

'An opportunity like that comes along once in a lifetime for the lucky few. Don't squander it. Save the money. Buy a property. I hope you set yourself up for life because in this business, one minute you are someone, the next you're a nobody.'

Callum decided he probably need a Tylenol to ease the headache. He got up from the sofa and walked into his bedroom to look in his bedside drawer. 'Hey, honey. What are you doing up already? Come back to bed.'

Callum frowned at the young woman.

'Who is that?' asked his agent. 'Is that your girlfriend?'

Callum stared at her. 'No, she dumped me when I moved out of Beverley Hills and put my house on the market.'

He winced. He hadn't meant to say that out loud. He could almost see his agent sitting at his desk, shaking his head in dismay.

'That's a shame. You two looked good together.'

And doesn't that comment hit the nail on the head, thought Callum. They looked good together. The golden couple of prime-time television. Their relationship had been built on appearances – and when she'd discovered he'd mismanaged his money, and they wouldn't be living in a Beverley Hills mansion, it was all downhill from there.

'So, who's the girl?'

Callum scratched his head, and looked at her. 'Sorry – what's your name?'

She frowned at him. 'I told you last night when we met in the bar.'

'Shit … sorry.'

She scrambled out of bed, taking the sheet with her, and stalked into the bathroom, slamming the door.

Callum held his thumping head. 'Oh, god.'

A few moments later, she flung open the door, fully clothed. It hadn't taken her long to slip on her little black dress, sans underwear, and slinky, high-heeled sandals. 'You're nothing like Fergus MacGregor,' she said.

Callum rolled his eyes. 'Well, of course I'm not. That's a character on a television show. I'm not really a Scottish laird.'

'Why have you suddenly slipped into character?'

'What are you talking about?'

'Your accent.'

'That is my accent. I am actually Scottish.'

She stared at him. 'So, what was with the American accent last night?'

'Really?' He frowned at her. 'I have no idea. I was drunk.'

'God, you really are pathetic. Anyway your American accent is terrible. I'm not surprised you can't get any more parts.'

'Pardon me?'

I heard you on the phone to your agent.'

'I'm still on the phone to him, so will you keep it down?'

'I will not.'

'Look, at least stay for breakfast.'

'I can't. I've got an audition.'

Callum dropped the phone from his ear. 'You've got an audition?'

'Yeah – for a part in a movie. I told you that last night too.'

Callum looked at her, wide-eyed.

'I thought you could give me some pointers, tips for my audition. Help me out to get the part.'

'Is that why you singled me out in the bar?' Callum had been minding his own business, which never really worked out if he went out. Even now, three months on from the end of the show he'd starred in, he was still recognised and called Fergus MacGregor.

When the show had first started airing nine years earlier, it had won awards. He had walked the red carpet with his co-stars at events and had attended conventions. He had loved the attention back then and hadn't mind being called by the name of his character. He had been earning incredible money and living the Hollywood dream; had been under the impression that it would never end. But end it did, and with the demise of the show – it had not been renewed for a tenth season – went all his earnings too.

Now he could see how much money he had wasted on people he barely knew – and in some cases didn't know at all, on buying his Beverley Hills home and throwing lavish parties, on buying expensive cars, and on buying his so-called friends cars and gifts and helping them out whenever they needed money. Now those friends were gone, along with the money, the lifestyle, and probably any chance of landing another high-profile, long-lasting role ever again.

Of course he'd remembered the advice his agent had given him almost ten years earlier when he'd landed a part in a show that had the makings of a winner and the chance of longevity that was unusual in Hollywood.

He'd taken his advice – well, some of it, at least – and had bought himself a property, but had stupidly thought that after nine seasons, the show would just go on. The writers not only had the tenth season all planned out, but the next five seasons after that. A whole story arc. But that meant absolutely nothing. The show's ratings dropped as it competed with new shows starring much younger casts, and it was cancelled before the final episodes of the last season had even aired.

Callum had been shocked, but his agent had been philosophical. *You've had quite a run*, he'd said. *Why don't you go back to Scotland and buy a castle for real?* he'd joked.

What with? Callum had thought of throwing back, but he had stopped himself. He had been too embarrassed to tell him that all the money was gone. He was back to square one, but not as the fresh-faced twenty-one-year-old he'd been when he'd started out.

Now, if someone called him Fergus MacGregor, it just got on his nerves. And if ever he was approached and asked whether he was the guy in *The Scottish Laird*, he always vehemently shook his head and said no. Always, that was, except for the previous night. He'd been sitting on his own in the bar, deserted by all his so-called friends, when a cute young woman had approached. For the first time in an age, he'd answered the usual question with, 'Aye, I am.'

She'd laughed when he'd spoken in his native Scottish accent. 'You really are, aren't you?' she'd responded. Although it had turned out she'd thought he was putting it on. He couldn't remember what had been going through his mind when he'd decided to use an American accent for the rest of the evening. He hadn't intended to take her back to his place and sleep with her. It wasn't the sort of thing he usually did. But he had been lonely, and too drunk to think rationally, and she'd reminded him of his long-term girlfriend, who had recently dumped him.

His ex-girlfriend's career was still on an upward trajectory. She hadn't left him because of his failure to land another role straight after the demise of the show, but they had been drifting apart anyway, and his loss of the mansion had not been what she was expecting. Rather than helping him out, she'd taken her stuff, and had just left. The golden Hollywood couple were no longer.

His best friend, who lived in England, had said it was good riddance, if that was the way she was going to treat him. It wasn't his fault the show had ended. Callum was inclined to agree, although it *was* his fault he'd lost the house – *and all his money.* He had a small amount of savings – enough for a one-way ticket to Scotland, and some extra cash to get by – but how long would it last?

'Cal – are you still there?'

Callum was still holding the phone to his ear, and heard his agent down the phone, as he followed the young woman out of the bedroom to the door of this apartment. 'Look, I'm sorry about what I said. Good luck with the audition – I wish you every success. I mean it.'

She turned around and eyed him. 'You know, I liked you better last night.'

'Gee – thanks.' He frowned. 'Why?'

'You were fun. You made me laugh.'

'I did?' He hadn't been in the frame of mind at all to have fun, or laugh – let alone make anybody else laugh. He hadn't been in that frame of mind for months. He guessed it had been the drink talking.

'But then you were drunk, weren't you?'

He cast his gaze down on the floor.

She surprised him by lifting his chin and placing a hand on his cheek. 'Don't despair, and don't give up. Something will turn up. If you really want it, you'll get it – you'll see.'

He stared at her as something odd occurred to him. 'What if that was the problem? What if he didn't want something to come up? Perhaps that was the problem – he was done with that life. But then it was all he'd ever known since he had gone to London at eighteen and signed on with an agency before unexpectedly landing a gig in Hollywood, and finally being cast in the TV series. Now, he was already the wrong side of thirty-five; in three years' time he'd be forty. And what did he have to show for his life?

The last nine years might have earned him a lot of money, and made him famous, but the lifestyle wasn't without its downsides. The hours were gruelling; the fifteen-hour days took their toll. The money was good, but he felt like he'd earned every single cent. Working in TV wasn't like doing a movie, where you could earn a packet and then rest on your laurels, waiting for the next one. Starring in television shows felt too much like hard work. And then there was the publicity – the conventions and the junkets. His agent was right: perhaps even though he'd been out of work for the last six months, fretting and worrying about where or when his next role would come up, he needed to take a break – a proper break. He needed to go home. But maybe what he was really afraid of was that if he did that, he wouldn't want to come back; perhaps he was well and truly burnt out. Or maybe it was the case that if he gave in, and went home, it would be admitting defeat.

'I agree with her, Cal.'

Callum had forgotten that he was still on the phone. 'You heard that too?' He looked at the young woman as she mouthed *goodbye*. As she left and closed the door behind her, he got the feeling he wouldn't see her around again. The next time he'd see her face would probably be on a screen, in a movie.

'Can I be brutally honest, Cal?'

Callum sighed. 'I wouldn't expect anything less.'

'You're a good-looking guy, Cal,' his agent continued. 'I'm not surprised you got the part in that show, but I'm wondering if your heart isn't in the game anymore.'

'What makes you say that?' As he wandered into the kitchen, he opened the fridge door and stared at a pot of healthy yoghurt. Perhaps he wanted more out of life than yoghurt in the morning and a jog along the beach, with young women recognising him and wanting to know him, thinking he was made of money.

'I don't know. You sound tired Cal. I think you should go home.'

'But what's there for me if I go home?'

'Your family. When was the last time you saw your parents?'

Callum didn't want to talk about them. They hadn't been proud when he had been successful, so what would they think when they found out the work had dried up, the money was gone, and he'd hit rock bottom? He sighed and kicked the fridge door shut with his foot.

He would never forget how they hadn't encouraged or

supported his choice to become an actor. Once he had become successful, it had seemed as though they liked it even less. His mother had insisted that he use a stage name, rather than his real name, which he'd thought was weird. But he had acquiesced to her wishes, changing his surname.

Although he hadn't got the movie roles he'd envisaged, he had achieved some success in a well-known sitcom, and a movie, even before his big break in the long-running drama. He had thought his parents would be happy and proud, but they had not been happy at all – to the point that it felt as though they could become estranged. But that wasn't all down to them. He hadn't been back to see them for five years, and he hadn't exactly made much effort to stay in touch in the intervening years.

'Go home and see your friends, then. I assume you still have some friends back home?'

'Yes, I have. Very close friends.'

'Well, there you go. Go stay with them for a bit. Recharge your batteries. I promise I'll keep in touch, and if something comes up ...'

Callum almost felt like telling him not to bother. He was pretty sure nothing would. In his heart, he doubted he would be back.

'Never say never,' his agent scolded him down the phone.

Callum smiled for the first time that morning. 'I swear you can read my mind sometimes.'

'Yeah, well, I've known you for ten years, and in this industry, that is a long time. Whatever happens, I'd like us to stay in touch – even though I might not be representing you for much longer.'

'What? Why not?'

'I'm retiring. Getting a bit long in the tooth for this game.'

Aren't we all, thought Callum, although his agent really *was* long in the tooth; he must have already been in his mid-fifties when he and Callum had started working together.

'I'd like to retire and finally write a film script. Did I tell you that's my dream – to see it made into a movie?'

Callum smiled. 'Many times.' He knew that his agent, the one good friend he could count on in Hollywood, had always aspired to be a scriptwriter, even now that he was nearly retired. 'How's it going? Have you got an idea for your script yet?'

'No, not yet. But when I do, I know it's going to be a corker, and I'm going to insist you are in the starring role.'

'Well, that's very kind of you,' Callum said, with genuine feeling. 'Do you mind getting a move on with that? I've got bills to pay and a house that is going to be repossessed.'

His agent guffawed down the phone. 'I see you haven't lost your British sense of humour.'

Callum laughed too. 'Of course not.'

'Well at least if I can't sell my script I know a very good bookbinder, so I can gift it to my friends.'

'Oh, I haven't done that in an age.' Callum had no idea why he'd put that down on his CV when he had approached agents. What it had to do with acting, he had no idea. He'd just put it down there under *Other skills*.

'Where did you learn to do that, anyhow? I've heard it's a bit of a dying skill.'

'My father.'

'I see. Well, you do realise you've got something to fall back on?'

'What – the lost art of bookbinding?'

'I wouldn't call it a lost art. I've read that skilled bookbinders are very much in demand. You, my friend, should think about that.

You could start over. Perhaps you could go into business with your father.'

Callum went quiet.

'Cal?'

'Just write that script will you?' This time Callum wasn't joking.

10

Callum touched down at Edinburgh Airport the following day. He'd been lucky; he'd got a standby ticket after waiting at the airport in the hope that someone would fail to turn up for their flight, leaving a spare seat.

The previous day, before setting off to the airport, he'd handed in the keys to the fully furnished apartment, packed his clothes in a holdall, and made a phone call to the realtor dealing with the sale of his house in Beverley Hills. There were still no potential buyers. The realtor had the keys. He'd told them his financial situation, and that if it was repossessed, they could hand in the keys to the bank.

Some of his personal possessions were in the house, but only furniture – nothing of particular value, sentimental or otherwise. His ex had already stripped the place of the pieces of artwork that had been on the walls, which he imagined had been the only things of real value besides the house. But as usual, he hadn't been thinking of money when she'd left; he had been in a state over her leaving him and hadn't cared what she took. In hindsight, that had been a mistake – that artwork could have paid his mortgage for a few more months. But now it was too late.

His agent had said he'd be in touch if anything came up. As he'd sat in the taxi on the way to Los Angeles International Airport, less than twenty miles away, he'd stared out of the window, thinking that while it had been nice of his agent to say that, they both knew it wasn't going to happen. And anyway, if an audition *did* turn up, he'd be thousands of miles away, so what was the point?

He stared glumly at his passport as he waited in line, shuffling along in the queue towards one of the desks to have his passport stamped. Behind him, he heard some teenage girls giggling. He felt someone tapping on his shoulder. He turned around to see a middle-aged man looking him up and down. 'Hey, man, aren't you that guy in the TV show, *The Scottish Laird*?'

Callum looked at the American man and pursed his lips. He was tired after the long-haul flight and could well do without the encounter. He was about to deny it when the man said, 'My girls would love your autograph.'

Callum looked at the two teenage girls. They looked away, embarrassed. He ran a hand through his spiky blonde hair and fixed his dark brown eyes on the American man. As much as he really hadn't envisaged that this would happen once he got home, he didn't want to be that git of a celebrity who was stand-offish. It was people like this, those who had watched the show religiously, who had kept him in a job – up until now. It wasn't their fault he'd screwed up, and made a mess of his life. 'Yes, that's me,' he said. He smiled at the two teenage girls.

'We adored that show. That's why we're here on holiday. We just had to come to Edinburgh. Say, are you a Scottish laird in real life?'

He didn't want to burst their bubble, but decided to tell the truth. 'Nah – I grew up on a council estate on the outskirts of

Edinburgh,' he said. His parents had bought their council house years earlier and had put their stamp on it. It was a nice area with neighbours that his family had known for years. His background was the complete opposite to that of the Scottish character he'd played in the TV series, who'd fled his tyrant of a father in Scotland to start a new life in America. Callum's own motivation for fleeing his background was far more mundane; he had just wanted to be somebody.

He looked down the queue of people, realising that the long, boring wait at passport control had just got a lot more interesting. There were whispers of, 'Is he famous? What did he star in? I recognise his face, but I can't place what I've seen him in.'

'God, he's even more good-looking in real life,' he heard someone else remark.

'Are you here to see your folks?' asked the American as Callum wrote a nice message for his girls, and signed it, *love Fergus MacGregor.*

Callum nodded. 'Yes. I haven't been back to Scotland in quite some time.'

'What a nice guy,' he heard them say. 'Remember when we asked for that autograph from ...'

Callum turned around and zoned out of their conversation. He saw other passengers in the queue staring at him. Those not in the know about the TV show were probably wondering who he was.

Fortunately, it wasn't long before he was handing over his passport to be checked. The young guy looked at his passport, looked at him, and handed it back. That was it. Callum sighed in relief when he wasn't asked for an autograph. 'Thanks.'

He walked into the vast arrivals hall, looked for the nearest exit, and headed outside to find a taxi into the city. He looked up at the grey overcast sky and shivered. He noticed that the other people weren't even wearing coats. He guessed it was a mild autumn, but the difference in the weather between Edinburgh and LA, especially the cold chill in the air, was a bit of a shock.

He paused to get out his mobile phone. So far, he hadn't even contacted his parents to let them know he was coming. They'd be in for a shock when he told them he was at the airport in Edinburgh. Perhaps they'd offer to come and pick him up from the airport. *Chance would be a fine thing*, he thought. At least his best mate would be pleased to hear from him.

Callum stared at his phone. He hadn't told Jack either that he was on his way home. Jack would want him to travel down to Suffolk and stay in one of the holiday cottages in the grounds of their working farm, if one was available. Luckily for him, he knew that they'd insist on him staying there for free if he were to visit. And he knew why. It was not just because they were best friends. It was more than that. Callum didn't really want to revisit the reasons, though. He'd done a good deed, and it had almost lost him his best friend.

On his last trip back, when the TV show still had good ratings, and there was no indication that it would be cancelled, and he still had money, Callum had discovered that Jack and his wife had got into financial difficulties. They had over-extended themselves by taking out loans and re-mortgaging – all because Jack had been pursuing grand ideas of how they could do more with the farm by converting the old barn into holiday accommodation.

They had been on the brink of losing the farm, which had been in his wife's family for generations. When Callum had found out, he had stepped in and paid everything off, including their loans and mortgages. He had also provided the rest of the money for converting the barn into three super holiday cottages. While he was at it, he'd paid for the old farmhouse they lived in to be renovated too.

He might not have spent the rest of his money wisely, but he knew he would never regret helping his best friend. Jack and his wife Beth hadn't wanted charity, but he'd said he had more money than he knew what to do with.

Although Beth had been over the moon at Callum's generosity, Jack had not. In hindsight, Callum should have seen it coming: Jack's reaction to the hot-shot, good-looking actor rolling in money arriving to save the day. Callum had dented his best mate's pride, making it appear that Jack could not provide for his family. The only thing that had saved their relationship after that was that Jack had insisted they became business partners; even though Callum had told him, in the nicest possible way, that he had no interest whatsoever in a farm. It wasn't even in Scotland.

He hadn't needed the few hundred pounds they'd deposited in his bank account each month as his share of the rental income from the holiday cottages. He'd put that money to one side in a separate savings account for their child. Now he felt terrible that it was nearly all gone. That small amount of money, which he'd privately scoffed at, had been his lifeline since the work dried up.

He breathed a heavy sigh as he stared at his phone. Jack didn't know the other reason Callum couldn't see Beth's family farm go to the wall. Callum and Beth had a history. Perhaps going to stay with them would not be a good idea. Besides, he'd have to check what he had left in his bank account. Getting a flight or the sleeper train down to London wouldn't be cheap, and then he'd have to buy another train ticket to where they lived in Suffolk.

On the other hand, he thought of his agent's advice that he should go home and recharge his batteries. He couldn't imagine doing that in Edinburgh; he wouldn't want to hang around his childhood home. The small three-bedroomed semi he had grown up in would seem so claustrophobic, and moving back in with his parents was just unthinkable.

Callum realised he'd made a huge mistake. He should never have listened to his agent; there was nothing for him there. In fact, he found it hard to believe he'd grown up there. He didn't have any nostalgic attachment to his childhood home like he imagined some people had. It wasn't because his childhood had been unhappy; it was just that he'd always felt as though he didn't belong; as though he was destined for something greater than his parents' little life in that little house in Edinburgh.

He hadn't really thought the trip through before getting the flight to Scotland. Besides not particularly wanting to stay with his parents, he'd probably be tempted by the night life, the bars, and so much going on in the city. How did he think he'd recharge his batteries if he was out every night in a bar, probably drinking?

On the other hand, despite his reticence to visit his best friends, rural Suffolk might just be the perfect place to unwind, and as his agent had said, get his shit together – if he had the money to make the trip. Jack and Beth's farm was in the middle of rolling countryside, just a few miles from the sea. He had the impulse to turn around, walk back into the airport, and catch the next flight to London rather than visit his parents.

His phone buzzed with a message that stopped him in his tracks. It was Jack. 'Callum, so sorry to hear about your dad.'

He read the text message, and swore.

'Mate, watch your language?'

Callum was about to turn around and tell the guy who was passing him outside the terminal to mind his own business when he saw that the guy was holding the hand of a young child. 'Shit, sorry,' he said. He shook his head and rang Jack, but it went straight to voicemail.

After all this time away, he really hadn't known what to expect when his mother had told him about the dementia diagnosis the previous year. His father had been having bouts of forgetfulness that increasingly could not be explained away as just old age creeping up on him. But Callum hadn't expected this – for his father to pass so quickly.

He rushed over to the taxi stand and stood in the queue, waiting impatiently for his turn, thinking that this was what he had always been afraid of – that something might happen to one of his parents when he was abroad, and by the time he made it back, he'd be too late to see them before they died. He tried to phone his mum, but that went to voicemail too. He didn't bother leaving a message. He didn't know quite what to say. Besides, he'd be home soon.

Although it felt interminable, it was only ten minutes before he got to the front of the queue. Callum gave the driver the address of his parents' little house, located in an estate on the outskirts of the city. The hour's drive across the city tested his patience to the limit. The traffic was horrendous, and he couldn't even pass the time looking out of the window; it had started to rain heavily, and the raindrops lashed against the window-pane, obscuring his view.

The taxi turned into the cul de sac where his parents' 1930s semi stood in a small crescent of just eight properties.

The driver pulled the car up at the kerb outside his parents' house. He paid the driver, exited the taxi, and stood at the kerb, staring up at the house. It seemed smaller than he remembered. In fact, the whole cul de sac did. But what had really caught his attention was the brand new car on the driveway. It was a little two-seater MG. He scratched his head and turned at the sound of the taxi setting off. Callum turned back to the house; there was no going back now.

He walked up to the front door and rang the doorbell. He stood for a moment, shuffling from one foot to the other. He tried the doorbell again before getting out his wallet. He still had a door key to the house. Callum put the key in the lock, opened the front door and stepped into the narrow hallway, surprised that nothing inside was how he remembered.

Callum stopped in surprise. He knew he had the right house because it was exactly the same on the outside, and his key fitted the lock. But the place had been redecorated; the chintzy wallpaper was gone, replaced with bare walls painted off-white. He glanced up the stairs. The dark wood skirting boards were now glossy white, and the dark brown staircase with the old-fashioned spindles that had been in the house since it was built in the thirties had been replaced by a modern staircase with open-tread stairs.

Walking down the narrow hallway, past the opened doorway to the lounge, he could hear voices in the dining room next door. He recognised his mother's voice. He frowned. It sounded as though she had friends round. She obviously hadn't heard the doorbell. Perhaps that wasn't surprising, considering the chatter and laughter he'd heard as he passed by the door. Callum frowned. How could she have friends round, and be enjoying herself – it was his mother he had heard laughing – at a time like this?

At the end of the hall was the kitchen, and next door was a

small box room, which was his father's study. Callum didn't fancy walking in on her and her friends, so he stepped into the study and closed the door, putting his bag down on the leather chair in front of the desk. He turned full circle, taking in the room. Nothing had changed; his mother hadn't cleared out all his father's stuff as he expected. This room hadn't been touched. It was still just as chaotic as he remembered.

It looked like an old bookshop, with bookshelves lining two walls, and little wooden tables with old books stacked in precariously high piles. Callum looked at his father's desk. He could see that he'd been in the middle of binding a book when ... Callum swallowed. He wanted to know how his father had died – and when. And why his mother hadn't contacted him.

11

Callum could still hear laughter coming from the dining room. He glanced over his shoulder to the door and frowned. It sounded as though whatever was going on in there, they were having a good time.

He shifted his bag, sat down in the chair, and set to work. He was surprised how it easily came back to him. Of course it helped that all the materials and tools were still here, and it had gone quiet in the dining room, so he could concentrate. He hoped they were all leaving.

An hour later, Callum turned the bound book over in his hands, admiring his handiwork. He'd forgotten how much he enjoyed it. He made the mistake of leaning back in the chair – an antique, wheeled leather chair. The chair rolled unexpectedly, knocking into one of the little tables stacked with books.

Callum swivelled round and reached for the stack, but it was too late. They toppled and fell to the floor with a loud thump. He winced.

A moment later, the study door opened. His mother, Moira, a small slim woman, was wearing a figure-hugging floral dress, and Callum thought she looked surprisingly well for someone who'd just lost her husband. She stopped in the doorway. She couldn't have looked more surprised if she'd tried.

'Bloomin hell, Callum!'

'Yeah, I bet the last person you expected to see was me.'

'What are you doing here?'

Callum stared at her. *Is she serious?* he thought. 'What do you think I'm doing here?' he replied. When she didn't answer, he held up the book. 'He must have been working on this. I just finished it.'

She looked at the book in his hands. 'You still remember how to bind books?'

'Yeah – weird, huh? It's been like, years.' He looked at his mother. He could still hear her friends talking in the next room. This must be how she was coping.

Callum didn't blame her for not getting in touch. Even if she had tried to call, he probably wouldn't have answered. Now he was there, he wanted to go and pay his respects. 'Where's Dad?'

'Ah, Callum, we need to talk about that.'

He shook his head. 'Y'think?'

They both fell silent. Callum glanced at the desk and at the piles of books, some already bound beautifully and half-wrapped in brown paper. He wondered whom they had been bound for. 'Those business trips Dad used to go on ...'

The shrill sound of the old house phone in the hall interrupted Callum.

'I'd better answer that.' Moira walked out of the room. Callum heard his mum. 'Hello Doreen. I'm all right, Doreen, sort of. No, no, honestly, you don't have to come over. Oh, all right ... but I'm running my book club this morning. You're welcome to join us.'

Book club? So that was what all the people were doing there.

He shrugged, thinking that perhaps it was for the best that she was keeping herself busy.

He heard her put the clunky phone receiver back in its cradle.

'Everything all right, Moira?' Callum heard one of her friends ask. 'What was that noise we all heard?'

'It's my son. He's home.'

Callum stepped out of the study. 'It was just me.'

'Oh, my goodness. You didn't tell us your famous son was visiting!' His mum's friend rushed forward. 'I'm Eileen. You must tell me when the next season of the show is due to air. Are you busy filming at the moment?'

Callum bit back a sarcastic remark. If he had been, he obviously wouldn't be there.

'I can't wait for the next season to find out if Fergus MacGregor leaves America and returns to his Scottish ancestral home.'

Callum was thinking of his own return to Scotland – except that the home he'd returned to couldn't be more different to that of the character he played, who had inherited a Scottish ancestral home in the heart of the highlands – a castle, no less.

'Wow – talk about leaving the last season on a cliff-hanger.'

And that was the reason Callum wasn't surprised she had assumed there would be another season. Everyone thought it was a forgone conclusion that there would be – including the writers; otherwise they wouldn't have left the end of the last season on a cliff-hanger. He looked at his mum's friend and didn't feel inclined to let her know the show was over.

She linked her arm in his. 'You must come and meet the others.'

'The others?' Callum frowned. 'Oh, I really don't think—' He was already being pulled towards the dining room door.

'Didn't your mum tell you she runs a book club? It's such fun.'

She looked at Moira. 'When were you going to tell us your son was home?'

'I ... er ...'

'She didn't know,' said Callum. 'It was a surprise. I only arrived this morning.' He looked at his mum. She wasn't exactly saying how lovely the surprise had been. She opened the door to the dining room, and he followed her into the room to find six people seated around the dining room table. She and her friend joined them, his mum sitting down next to the only other man in the room.

Callum stood awkwardly in front of the table. He looked at his mother, waiting for her to introduce him.

Eileen said, 'This is Callum, Henry and Moira's son.'

'Say, you look just like—'

'That's because he is!'

'By jove, it is! You're Laird MacGregor from the TV show.'

Out of the corner of his eye, Callum caught his mum frowning. She was the only one who wasn't smiling at him.

'Well, it's nice to meet you all. I'll, er, just go and make myself a cup of coffee.'

'Won't you join us?' Eileen said eagerly.

Callum glanced around the table. They all had a copy of a paperback book. He caught the guy around his mother's age place a hand on her shoulder. 'Everything all right, Moira?'

She turned to him and smiled. 'Yes, why wouldn't it be?'

Callum frowned at the man, thinking, *He didn't waste any time.* Callum didn't know these people, but he expected that as soon as Moira's husband was out of the picture, he had made his move. *But then again ...,* he thought. 'It takes two to tango,' he muttered.

'What did you just say?' his mother asked.

Eileen said, 'It takes two to tango.'

Callum couldn't believe he'd said that out loud. 'Er, look, I'm pretty tired after the long-haul flight, so do you mind if I go and make myself a coffee?'

One of her friends said, 'Perhaps we should go?'

Others in the group started to rise from their chairs. 'You'll want to catch up with your son. We can do this another time.'

Callum started to shake his head. 'No, please don't leave on my account.' He glanced at his mum, who wasn't exactly making a move to leave her seat, or agree that perhaps they should cut their book club meeting short this week. 'Well, it was really nice to meet you folks.'

As he closed the door, he heard one of her friends comment, 'Your son sounds more Scottish on the television.'

Callum hovered outside the door and heard another say, 'Yes, I thought so too. Guess the Californian accent is going to rub off if you're living out there long enough. How long has he been living in America, Moira?'

'A few years, I guess. I really couldn't tell you.'

Callum shook his head, and sighed. That was just what he had expected her to say. In other words, she really wasn't that interested in talking about her son, or his work. He expected she couldn't wait for him to leave. And he couldn't wait to go.

12

Callum opened the door to the kitchen and stopped abruptly in the doorway. It wasn't just the décor that had had a makeover. The kitchen looked brand new, like something out of a home catalogue, or his nice rental apartment in Malibu. Fresh modern white gloss kitchen cabinets, inbuilt appliances and a warm wooden worktop had replaced the old eighties oak kitchen that had been there since they had moved there when he was a young child.

He made a cup of coffee and walked down the hall into the lounge, halting in the doorway. The room had also had a makeover, with the décor, soft furnishings and wall-mounted television bringing the room into the 2020s.

Callum sat down on the new sofa and imagined that when he went upstairs, the bathroom and bedrooms would have had a makeover too. He cast his gaze around the room and wondered where his mother was getting all the money to spend on the house – and on herself. Callum hadn't seen her in several years. She was slimmer, and her outfit looked as though it came from a designer shop, not a high street store. Her hair fell in thick auburn waves past her shoulders, and she looked like something out of *Hollywood Wives.*

He did feel more than a twinge of guilt that with all the money he'd earned over the years, he hadn't passed any their way – apart from birthday and Christmas presents. And he had told his father, the last time they'd spoken, that if he ever needed anything, he should just ask. He had also offered to buy them a bigger house somewhere they'd like to spend their retirement, but they had never taken him up on the offer, and then he had squandered all his money on himself and on a house and friends he couldn't afford. He wished they *had* agreed; then perhaps there would be something to show for all those years in LA apart from the farm he'd saved in Suffolk.

Callum sat looking around the lounge he didn't recognise, drinking coffee from an expensive coffee machine, and listening to the banter next door. He couldn't wait for them all to leave.

As if reading his mind, he heard chairs scraping along the wooden floor, and footsteps in the hall. A couple of the guests looked in to say goodbye. Eileen said, 'Now, when is your show coming back?'

Callum frowned. For one thing, although he was one of the stars, it wasn't *his* show. If it had been, he wouldn't have cancelled it. Although now he thought about it, Callum realised that, if it weren't for the money, after nine seasons, he'd actually had enough. Enough of LA, of his co-stars and their histrionics, and especially of the crazy long days.

Perhaps even if he'd been able to afford a return ticket, Callum would still only have bought a one-way ticket back to Scotland. Deep down, he felt that although it was all he'd ever known – modelling, and then acting – the reality had never lived up to the expectations of what he imagined his life would be in Hollywood; he wasn't fulfilled or happy.

'Eileen, next you'll be asking him to let you in on what's going to happen in the next season,' said one of the passing group members.

'But I was only asking—'

'Now, why don't we leave him in peace? He said he was tired after his long-haul flight.'

'Jetlag,' said a third as they glanced at him, smiled, and said their goodbyes.

Callum rose from his seat with the empty mug in his hands and waited for them to leave. He heard the sound of the front door closing as he walked out of the lounge. His mother put the latch on the front door and turned around. She didn't rush forward and give him a hug to welcome him home. She frowned at him and repeated her question. 'What are you doing here?'

Callum sighed. 'I told you.' He wasn't surprised by her frosty demeanour. It was just the reception he had been expecting. 'Why didn't you tell me about Dad?'

She sighed too. 'How did you find out?'

'What do you mean, how did I find out? Weren't you going to tell me?'

'I knew you'd be upset.'

Callum looked at her stunned. 'Well, of course I'd be upset. It's my da. I missed the funeral, didn't I?'

'What funeral?'

Callum looked at her. 'What do you mean, *what funeral?* Dad's, of course.'

'What on earth are you talking about?'

Callum stepped forward. 'What are *you* talking about?'

'Why, putting your father in a home, of course.'

13

'His dementia is getting worse. I had to do it.'

Callum thought of the text message from Jack. He'd assumed the worst after reading it.

'But you didn't tell me you'd put him in a home.'

'What could you do about it, thousands of miles away? In fact, what can you do about it now that you're here?' She looked him up and down. 'What exactly are you doing here? Has the season wrapped?'

Under any other circumstances, hearing his mother speaking in those terms – *has the season wrapped* – would have made him smile. Not today. 'Yes, it has.' He didn't add that it had wrapped for good; he thought he'd save that conversation until later.

'You don't normally come home when you've got a break from filming.'

'Yes, I know.' Ordinarily, he'd be sitting on a beach somewhere, or throwing expensive parties, or on the road doing press junkets to promote the up-and-coming season. Not anymore.

'So, look … about Dad ...' He followed his mother into the dining room and helped her clear the table of cups, saucers and empty plates with biscuit and cake crumbs.

'The doctors said it was inevitable, the decline.' She turned around with two cups and saucers in her hand. 'Go see for yourself.'

Callum looked at her. 'I will.'

He followed her into the kitchen, and watched her load the new dishwasher. 'Where is he, then?'

'Highgrove House. It's a nursing home.'

Callum sighed heavily. 'Dad's only in his seventies.' He was aware that his father had had memory problems for several years before his diagnosis.

'I know. But as I said, it's getting worse.'

Callum looked around the kitchen. 'How are you affording the care home fees?' he blurted, then cringed, really hoping she wasn't going to ask him for money.

It wasn't the only question that was going through his mind regarding her financial situation, though. He commented, 'The house looks nice.'

Callum wondered again where the money had come from to do it up. His mum was a teaching assistant. He knew she'd worked part-time for years. Perhaps she'd done up the house on a retirement lump sum.

His thoughts turned again to his dad. He hoped she hadn't spent the money on the house at the expense of his dad; it made him wonder where she'd farmed him out to.

'You might want to call a taxi. It's on the outskirts of Edinburgh.'

He noticed she hadn't answered his question about the care home fees, and had appeared to avoid getting drawn into a conversation about the house. He wondered how much the care home was costing. He thought perhaps he could get a job and take out a loan to help her out. He was at a loose end, after all. But the transformation of the house suggested she wasn't short of a bob or two, and wouldn't be asking him for money.

Callum had the card from the taxi driver who had dropped him there from the airport. He scribbled down the address on the back of the card and rang for the taxi. Then he walked into the dining room, and stood there watching his mother wipe the table.

'When you said that he's getting worse ...' ventured Callum. 'How much worse?'

'Sometimes he's okay. Other times ...' she trailed off.

Callum pursed his lips. He understood. She didn't want to talk about it. *All this can't be easy*, he thought – although with her designer dress, her immaculate hair and makeup, and her social life, she didn't appear worried or anxious at all that her husband was in a care home and she was all on her own.

But she isn't on her own, thought Callum. He'd seen the way the man at the book group had placed a tender hand on her arm and kissed her goodbye.

Callum got a text on his phone, informing him that the taxi would be there in five minutes. Moira returned to the kitchen and flicked on the kettle.

'That was the taxi,' he said, holding up his phone. 'Do you want to come with me?'

Moira shook her head. 'No, I'd rather not. I've got some shopping to do in town.'

Callum had seen the brand new car on the driveway, and assumed it might be a friend visiting. 'Is that your car on the driveway?'

'Yes, but before you ask, you can't borrow it. I'm going into town.'

'I wasn't going to ask.' Callum hadn't driven on British roads for years. He knew it would come back to him, but after a long-haul flight, and not much sleep, he wouldn't risk getting behind the wheel of a car, and certainly not a brand new sports car.

'Well, I'll go and see Dad on my own, then.'

'Okay, but don't you want your bags, Cal? You left them in his study.'

'What do I want to take those with me for?'

'I assumed you'd booked into a swanky hotel and you were just here for a flying visit.'

'Ah. No, actually. I was rather hoping I could stay here ...'

She stopped wiping the table and turned around. 'Why?'

Callum sighed, and decided to come clean about the real reason he'd shown up out of the blue. 'The show's over. They are not renewing for another season. I wanted to come home and figure out what's next.'

'What's next? Your agent is going to find you another role – surely.'

Callum nodded. 'Sure.' He didn't want to get into why that probably wouldn't turn out to be the case. Word had probably spread already about him turning up drunk to auditions. He doubted something else would turn up – and if it did, he doubted he'd want it anyway. 'My agent said I was burnt out and suggested I go somewhere to unwind.'

His mum looked at him incredulously. 'And you thought of coming here? What's wrong with a beach in, oh, I don't know, Hawaii or somewhere? It's where you Hollywood types go, isn't it? I mean it is closer. And hotter.'

You Hollywood types. Callum frowned at her. He got the impression she rather wished he had chosen somewhere closer to LA.

Then he wouldn't be in her house. 'Yeah, I thought of that, but then I haven't been home for an age, and I wanted to see you – and Dad.'

She looked at him. 'Are you still single?'

Callum thought the question came across as more akin to an accusation. 'I'm here on my own, aren't I?'

'Well, you're not going to find any of those Hollywood types here in Edinburgh.'

He assumed she meant someone like the actress off the show he starred in. 'Maybe I don't want one of those types.'

Moira regarded him a long moment. 'Well, if you're thinking of Beth, that ship has sailed.'

'I know that!' snapped Callum. 'She's living in Suffolk. And besides, she's married.'

'That didn't stop you—'

'Right,' Callum said, cutting her off, 'I'm leaving now. I presume it is okay if I come back here?' He wasn't sure it was okay with him now, but he didn't have the money for a hotel room, so his former childhood home was it. Unless ... Callum thought of his dad's old VW campervan. He assumed it was still in the garage. He could sleep in that, although it was quite cramped. 'You haven't got a lodger – have you?' Perhaps that was where she'd got the money to do up the house. He thought of the brand new car on the driveway. The money from a lodger wouldn't pay for that.

She looked aghast. 'Of course not.'

'Great – so it's okay if I stay here for a bit?' Callum really hoped she still wasn't going to question him over why he wasn't booking into a swanky hotel, as she put it.

'I suppose. You've still got your key, I see. You gave me quite a fright, you know, turning up in the house so unexpectedly.'

'Sorry about that. I did knock at the front door when I arrived, but you didn't answer. Obviously, you were busy with your friends.'

'When I heard a noise in your father's study, the last person I expected it to be was you. I thought—'

'You thought—?'

She put the cloth down. 'Look, don't ask me how, but during one of your father's lucid moments, he went missing from the care home and came back here.'

Callum looked at her, perplexed.

He phoned for a taxi and came back home. I heard someone in the study and thought there was a break-in happening, so I called the police. That's when I discovered your father.'

'What was he doing?'

She heaved a sigh. 'I don't know. I caught him binding a book. For a split second, when I saw you in the shadows I thought it was him again.'

Callum walked over to the front door and opened it. He spotted the taxi driver, and waved. He turned to his mum, who had followed him to the front door. 'Did something happen that precipitated your decision to send him away?'

'I did not send him away. I decided it was safer all round if he was in a place where they could take care of him, and keep an eye on him,' she said. 'Obviously, they weren't doing their job very well,' she added under her breath.

Callum raised an eyebrow, waiting for her to answer his question.

'Oh, right. Well, it all got too much when I found him in the van, turning on the engine, about to leave.'

'He was going to drive somewhere?' Callum had stepped outside and looked at the garage attached to the house.

'Yes. That really was the last straw. Imagine if I hadn't caught him, and he'd got on the road.'

Callum thought, *Why didn't she just take the keys and hide them, or get rid of the van?* He didn't say that, though. He hadn't been living with his dad. He imagined that the event was just one of many things that had been happening.

'I took the keys, but then I caught him walking down the road. I asked him where he was going.'

'What did he say?'

'Home!' She threw her arms up in the air in exasperation. 'So, you see, I couldn't keep an eye on him all the time.'

Callum caught sight of the taxi driver getting out of his car. 'Do you still want a taxi, mate?'

'Oh, yes. I'm coming.' Callum turned to his mum. 'Is there anything I should take with me for Dad? Anything he'd like?'

'The keys to his van.' The expression on her face said she wasn't joking.

Callum gave his mum a kiss goodbye.

'I'm glad you're home, Callum. It's been too long.'

He looked at her, surprised by the comment. 'Oh, right. Thanks.'

He was about to leave when she caught his arm. 'Is everything all right with you? You're not on anything, are you?'

'What do you mean, *on anything*?'

'You know, you hear about all these celebrities taking drugs, and you look so ... thin. You've got a nice tan, but you've lost weight.'

Callum sighed. He hadn't been taking care of himself; he knew he hadn't been sleeping or eating properly since the show had been cancelled. It was the worry over the work drying up, and over the stupid financial situation he was in. He kept checking his phone, hoping the realtor had some good news regarding the sale of his Beverley Hills mansion. If only he'd invested in a nice little property back home ten years earlier.

'Callum?'

He shook his head and smiled. 'No, Mum. Contrary to what you read in the tabloids, not everyone in Hollywood is on drugs.' In fact, in Callum's experience, nobody was – at least not on the show he'd starred in for all those years.

'Then what is it?'

'What do you mean?' he asked again.

'I know my son. There's something going on.'

Callum kept smiling. He was too embarrassed to tell her he'd been such an idiot with money. He knew he'd be lucky if he did get a buyer on the mansion to pay off the massive mortgage and settle his debts. What would she think if she knew that after all those years, and all that money, he had nothing to show for it, apart from a tan. Callum said, as nonchalantly as he could, 'Of course there isn't something going on.' Unfortunately, his smile dropped ever so slightly.

'I knew it!'

Callum sighed. 'I told you already, the show has been cancelled.'

'Maybe they'll change their minds.'

He had heard of other studios picking up cancelled shows.

'I thought it was popular – *you* were popular.'

Callum shrugged.

'Do you know why?'

'The ratings I guess.' After ten years, and nine seasons, viewers' tastes had moved on – and so had the studio. Of course, there was still the dedicated fanbase who wanted the show to go on, but times had changed, and as the star of the show, although he hadn't changed all that much – apart from some crows' feet around the eyes – he wasn't twenty-something anymore.

He glanced at the cab driver. 'I'd better go.'

'Okay. Well, I hope you catch Henry on a good day.'

Callum got in the taxi, hoping he did too.

14

Callum stepped into the room. He had been relieved when he turned up at the care home and discovered it had once been an iconic hotel on the outskirts of Edinburgh before it closed its doors and was taken over by a company running care homes.

He could see why his mother had chosen the place. His father had always liked old things – old books, old houses, old cars. He thought again of the VW campervan parked in the garage. He was surprised his mum hadn't got rid of it. Perhaps that was on her to-do list for after she'd renovated the house. Or maybe she already had. He hadn't thought to ask. He wouldn't be surprised if it turned out she'd got rid of it after she'd caught his father trying to drive it away. And he imagined she'd want to tuck her new little sports car away in the garage instead.

He glanced around his father's en suite room. It was a decent size, with a double bed and old-fashioned oak furniture. It looked as though the company had purchased the hotel lock, stock, and barrel. He wouldn't be surprised if the room was exactly as the hotel had left it when it was sold.

'Hello, Dad.'

His father had his back to him. He had a small watering can

and was watering some potted plants on the windowsill.

He turned around at the sound of Callum's voice. 'Son, what are you doing here?'

Callum smiled, relieved that his father recognised him.

'I thought you were in America, working on your show?'

'I'm taking a break.'

'Has the season wrapped up?'

Callum grinned. That was just what his mum had asked. Sparing his dad the details, Callum just said, 'Yes.'

His eyes dropped to the watering can. His dad had turned around with the can, and was now watering the carpet. Callum rushed forward. 'Here, let me take that.'

He handed over the watering can and stepped forward, his foot squelching on the sodden carpet. 'Oh, dear – the carpet's wet.'

Callum put the watering can down on the chest of drawers near the bed. He looked at his father.

'Dad, aren't you a bit chilly down there?'

'Down where?'

Callum stared at him. His dad was standing there wearing a shirt, a tie, a jumper and his underpants.

Henry looked down. 'Crumbs, what happened to my trousers?'

'I think you forgot to put them on?'

'Of course I didn't! What a stupid thing to say.'

Callum pursed his lips and turned around, fighting back tears. This was just what he'd feared, seeing the effects of dementia on his father first hand. He walked over to the wardrobe. Inside were shirts and trousers hanging on hangers. He took a pair of trousers out of the wardrobe and took a deep breath, trying to keep it together and not break down in front of his father. 'Here.'

He watched his dad sit down on the bed and put them on.

'Honestly, I have no idea how that happened.'

'It's all right, Dad. It's just one of those things.' Which it was if you had Alzheimer's. He watched his dad do up the zip.

'Callum, you need to do something for me before it's too late.'

Callum walked over and sat down on the chair beside his bed. He leaned forward. 'Too late?'

'You know, before I die.'

Callum leaned back in the chair, and sighed. 'Let's not be talking about dying, Dad.'

'Now, where did I put it?'

'Put what?'

He tapped his temple. 'Memory is not quite what it was.'

Callum heaved a sigh, staring at his dad as stood up and wandered around the room, opening drawers and cupboard doors. 'I know I put it somewhere for safekeeping ...'

'Perhaps I can help you look?'

'No, I'll remember in a minute.'

Callum doubted that.

'Ah ha!' He turned around from the windowsill. 'It was under the flowerpot.' He held up a keyring with some keys. He walked over and handed the keys to Callum.

'Um, okay.' He studied the keys. He recognised two of them. 'Hey, this is the key to the garage, and this one is to your van.'

His father grinned. 'I know.'

Callum stared at his father, who looked very pleased with himself. Was this why he had returned to the house – to get the keys and the van? Callum thought his mum ought to know that his dad had a spare set of keys to his campervan. He shuddered to think what might happen if his dad was let loose behind the wheel of a van.

'I think I'll keep hold of these, Dad. If you don't mind.'

'Of course I don't mind, son. That's the point.

'Is it?'

'Yes, you see I remember now. I remember everything.'

Callum offered his father a weak smile. *How sad that he thinks he does*, he thought. Callum recalled that he had been hosting another stupid party at his Beverly Hills mansion when he had got the call from his mum with the diagnosis. He'd told all those people who'd turned up, whom he barely knew, to piss off; that the party was over.

Then he'd gone and sat by the pool on his own and cried. He knew what the diagnosis meant. It was a cruel disease, making you watch a person you had known and loved disappear bit by bit; the biggest anomaly being that they were still there, walking, talking, alive, but that the person they had once been, that everyone had known, had gone.

Callum looked at the keys in his hand. He frowned. 'What are the other two keys for?' He knew they weren't door keys to the house. He imagined that when his mum had found his father in the study, he had got into the house via the back door, which opened onto a small pathway between the detached garage and the house that led into the back garden. His mum never locked the back door when she was indoors.

'Aha! Now that's the important bit. One of those keys is to my desk drawer. I left something in there for you.'

'When you turned up at the house in the taxi?'

'Yes, I told you, I remember now.'

Callum looked at him quizzically, but decided not to argue. 'All right.'

He was about to ask what the other key was for, when his

father said, 'And in my study is my wallet. I need you to fetch it.'

'Your wallet?' He glanced at his father's wallet on the bedside table. 'Your wallet is right here.'

He shook his head from side to side. 'That's not my wallet.'

Callum breathed a heavy sigh. It had started off so well, his father remembering him and what he did for a living, but the fog that was dementia – at least that was how Callum thought of it – was drawing in once again, enveloping his memories, robbing him of his lucidity.

Callum reached for the wallet. He opened it and got out his bank card. 'See, here are your cards with your name on.' Thumbing through, he found a photo of himself as a boy. He was a little overcome with emotion that his father was carrying it. 'Hey, and look, it's me, your son.'

Unexpectedly, his father grabbed the photo, and the wallet, and threw them on the floor. 'No! That is not my wallet!'

Callum stared at his father. He knew better than to argue about it. 'Okay, fine.' He decided it was time to leave before his father forgot who he was. 'I'd better go now.' Callum stood up.

His father grabbed his hand. 'You won't forget – will you?'

It would have been funny, hearing him ask that question, if it hadn't been so sad.

15

'Callum, are you all right?'

Callum swivelled around. He was seated at his father's desk in his study. 'No, not really.'

'I know … it's hard, isn't it?'

Callum looked at his mum. *That's an understatement*, he thought.

She stood in the doorway. 'How was he?'

Callum decided to spare her the details. He had been about to put the key in his father's desk drawer when she'd walked in. He'd quickly slipped the keys into his jacket pocket. For some reason, he'd thought it best not to repeat the odd conversation, or let her know he had a spare set of keys to the campervan in the garage.

Callum looked around the study, his eyes returning to the desk. He doubted there was anything of much consequence in the desk drawer. His father's words had just been the sad ramblings of dementia. 'What are you going to do with all this, Mum?' Callum was wondering if the books and equipment might be worth something. 'Are you going to clear out the study and redecorate?'

'The thought has crossed my mind.'

Callum wasn't surprised. The study still had the old wallpaper and carpet from years ago. Stepping inside felt like stepping into a room in another house now the rest of the place had been redecorated and modernised.

She sighed. 'I think he'd want you to have all this.'

'You left all this for me?'

She nodded. 'Of course. It's something you used to love doing as a child.' She cast a gaze at the book he'd bound. 'I think you still do.'

Callum offered up a weak smile. It was true, although that was not what he'd been thinking while he was sitting there looking around the study. He felt a little guilty that rather than contemplating the idea of running his father's bookbinding business, he'd been sitting there thinking how much the books and bookbinding equipment might be worth if he sold them to pay off some debts or even to cover a month or two of the excessive mortgage.

'He always said that he didn't see a future for you in show business.'

'He said that?'

'I'm afraid so. He said that you'd need something to fall back on when the show was over.' She cast a gaze around the study. 'That's why I left it all just as he told me to, for when you came back.'

Callum stared at his mum. Perhaps that was why neither of them had been thrilled when he'd announced he wanted to be an actor, and why they hadn't supported him in his choice of career. He cast his gaze around the room, thinking of what she'd just said.

'Well, it's all there if you want it. I'll leave you to mull it over.'

After she had closed the door, Callum got out the key and turned his attention to the desk drawer. He doubted there was anything of value inside; he imagined that all this key business was nothing at all – just something in his father's mind. Although his father had been back there, obviously in one of his lucid moments, and maybe it was true that he had found something and locked it in the desk drawer for safekeeping. Whatever it was, it was Callum's now. Oh, how he'd like it to be a big, fat wad of cash, takings from the business that his father had been squirrelling away, hiding from his wife for some reason.

He put the key in the lock and opened the drawer. It was empty. He shook his head. 'Well, what did you expect?' he said to the empty room. He shoved the drawer shut and thought he heard something move inside. He opened it again, and there was a wallet. 'What the—?'

Callum picked up the old, worn brown leather wallet that must have been at the back of the drawer, out of sight. He pulled the drawer right out to reveal something else at the back; a brown envelope. It was addressed to him. Along with the envelope was a small, single sheet of notepaper, folded in two. Callum unfolded the note.

Callum, I have to write this quickly lest I forget what it was I was writing. The memory is frustratingly not what it once was. But I remember now. After all these years, I remember!

I'm leaving you the bookshop.

Callum frowned. 'What bookshop?' He was beginning to get the feeling that his father's return to the house may not have been during one of his lucid moments after all. None of this made sense.

The van is for the girls.

'The girls?'

I made them a promise, so you must give them the campervan. Don't tell your mother, but promise me you'll look after them. They are—

Callum frowned. The writing had descended into a scribble. It looked like a toddler had scrawled over the page.

'Damn!'

The door to the study opened. 'Everything all right?'

Callum hurriedly swivelled in his chair, hoping his mother couldn't see the wallet and envelope on the desk behind his back. 'Yeah – sure.'

'I thought I heard you call out?'

Callum shook his head.

'Would you like a cup of tea?'

'Maybe later.'

'All right.' She stared at him a long moment. 'Did ... did he say anything when you visited?'

'What about?'

'Um, nothing. I just wondered – that's all.'

Callum stared at her. He didn't want to mention what he'd found in the desk until he knew what it was all about. He was about to ask her if she knew anything about a bookshop when it occurred to him that the room was filled with bookshelves full of books. It was obvious his father had been confused. Poor Dad. He was leaving Callum his books and bookbinding equipment – that much was true – but in his mind this was no longer just a room, his study, but an actual bookshop.

'Well, I'll leave you to sort through his things.'

Callum watched his mother close the door before he swivelled back round in his seat and picked up the envelope on the desk. He unsealed the envelope. Inside was a single sheet of paper. Callum pulled it out and looked at it. 'What the—?'

They were title deeds to a property with his own name on. Callum stared at the official document. 'This can't be right.' As far as Callum was concerned, his dad had never owned a bookshop.

He was about to call out for his mum when he caught sight of the old wallet and note his father had left him about giving *the girls* the campervan and that he must not tell his mother.

Callum glanced over at the door. The conversation with his mother could wait until later. He stared at the title deeds. There was paperwork countersigned by a solicitor.

Callum looked at the old laptop on the desk. He opened it, surprised that after all these years it still worked. He searched on the internet for the solicitor's website, and then phoned their number. As luck would have it, the woman who had apparently dealt with the transfer of ownership was in her office, and could take his call. Callum still felt like it wasn't real, and was just a figment of his father's imagination, even though the title deeds were right there in black and white.

'I understand you transferred the title deeds of a property from my father's name into mine.' Callum gave his name and his father's name. The solicitor asked him some security questions to confirm his identity before she confirmed that it was indeed the case.

Callum asked, 'When was this?'

They responded that he'd visited their office just recently. It sounded as though it was around the time that he'd gone missing from the care home.

Callum didn't want to look a gift horse in the mouth. He had a property in his name that he'd had no idea his father even owned; he could sell it and make money. But he had to say something. 'Are you aware my father has dementia? I would have thought that he wouldn't be able to sign legal documents.'

The solicitor informed him that this was a misconception. 'As long as it is only in the early stages, and people can still sort out their own affairs, understand what they are signing, and convey what their financial wishes are, then there is no reason why they can't sign legal documents, make a will, or transfer property deeds. In fact, it is best that they sort out their affairs sooner rather than later, before … well, before they can't, before their ability to make sound judgements and decisions declines.'

Callum thought of his dad, standing there in the care home with no trousers on. Just how long had he had dementia? He'd only been diagnosed recently, but his forgetfulness had been going on for some time. Had he really understood what he was doing when he had visited the solicitors? Despite his scepticism that his dad was really competent to make these sorts of legal decisions, Callum wasn't about to argue with the solicitor; after all, if it was his father's wishes that he had this property, then so be it.

'If I may say so, your father seemed perfectly capable when he visited our office to organise his affairs. I am aware that dementia sufferers' capacity can vary day by day, hour by hour even, but I was satisfied with his capacity on that day, otherwise I would not have acted on his behalf.'

He'd obviously visited on a good day. 'When was this? Did he visit you alone, or was he with my mother … his wife?'

'He came alone. Let me see. Ah, here we are. I've found the date of the appointment.'

Callum made a mental note of the date to see if his mum remembered when it was that his dad had made an impromptu visit home. It seemed likely that it would tie up with the visit to the solicitors.

'Do you do conveyancing? Will you act on my behalf with the sale of the property?'

'You want to sell it?'

'Of course. What would I want with a bookshop?'

There was a silence down the end of the phone. The solicitor said, 'He must have had a reason for leaving you the shop.'

Callum sighed. As if he'd want to run a bookshop. In any case, what did that have to do with bookbinding and rare books? He looked at the address. 'Where on earth is Aldeburgh?'

'I believe it's a seaside town in Suffolk.'

'Suffolk?' Callum smiled. He remembered Jack mentioning how buoyant property prices in the area were.

'Now, on the subject of you selling the property … I'd like to just add a caveat to what we were talking about earlier regarding dementia. It is possible that in these instances someone might challenge a will or inheritance.'

'Who?'

'I'm not saying someone in particular. I'm just giving you a heads-up, if you like, theoretically speaking. But of course that's why your father consulted a solicitor, and we do take steps to ensure we are satisfied with our clients' mental capacity before progressing with the legal paperwork. So if a person were to challenge the changes made to the deeds or his will, for argument's sake, we can provide evidence on your behalf that his mental capacity was not diminished at the time of signing the paperwork.'

As Callum was listening to all this with his mobile phone balanced in the crook of his neck, he was going through the old brown leather wallet that he'd also found in the drawer. There was some loose change, just coppers, a very old, faint, hardly discernible receipt, and a photo. Callum nearly dropped the phone when he lifted the dog-eared photograph out of one of the compartments of the wallet.

'Is there anything else?'

'No, er … that's all, thanks.' He put the phone down, sat back in the chair and studied the photo. There were two girls standing together. They were obviously sisters because they looked alike, although the youngest had dark hair, the older girl was blonde. The youngest looked around eight or nine, the other twelve or thereabouts. But what really caught his eye was where the photo was taken – outside a bookshop.

He turned it over. There was no date or names, no indication to say who the girls were or when the photo was taken.

'Callum, would you like something to eat?' Moira called from the hallway.

He hastily tucked the photo back in the wallet and stuffed it and the envelope in his backpack. 'No, I'm fine.' He got up and opened the door to the study. 'I'm going to nip out for a bit.'

'Catching up with some old friends?'

Callum thought of the bookshop in Suffolk. If he was going to put it on the market, he should perhaps pay a visit, check it out, and find an estate agent willing to handle the sale. While he was at it, he thought he could pay his best friend a visit. 'Yes, perhaps I will.'

16

Callum was about to ring for a taxi when he remembered he was trying to watch the pennies. He couldn't afford to spend more money on taxis if he could help it. Would the old campervan still work? It would save him waiting for a taxi, and save twenty quid paying for a trip across town. If the engine didn't switch on, perhaps he'd just sleep in there tonight; the thought had occurred to him earlier anyway. Callum couldn't imagine sleeping in his old childhood bedroom. Perhaps it had been redecorated – if so, it wouldn't feel so weird – but maybe, like the study, his mum had left that room stuck in a time warp, with all his old stuff in there along with the original carpet and décor. Either way, Callum didn't feel exactly enthusiastic about finding out.

He grabbed his bag and scooted past the kitchen. He could see his mum behind the frosted glass of the door. 'Would you like me to save you some dinner for when you get back?'

'Yeah – sure.'

'You sounded quite American there for a moment.'

'Oh, did I?' Callum frowned. He rather wished he didn't. It was all he had to show for his time in the States – that and a tan.

Callum got the set of keys from his pocket as he walked out

of the front door. Now he knew what they were for – one to his father's desk, the other one he hadn't recognised must be to the bookshop, and this one, to the campervan. Luckily, there was also the small key that unlocked the garage door. He opened the garage door as quietly as possible. He didn't see why his mum would object to him taking the van out for a spin. She had her car, after all. Even so, he didn't fancy explaining to her that his dad had been in possession of a spare set of keys. She might ask him what else he'd discovered. Callum thought of the old wallet and the photo of two girls. *Who were they?*

As he walked up to the yellow VW campervan, which was in surprisingly good condition considering its age, he put the key in the lock and recalled what was written in the note.

The van is for the girls. I made them a promise, so you must give them the campervan. Don't tell your mother, but promise me you'll look after them, they are—

Callum opened the van door and slung his bag on to the front seat. It had been years since he'd set foot in it. As a child, he'd sometimes played in it and had invited his friends round for sleepovers. He remembered that they'd had secret midnight snacks in there. But, more often than not, his father and the campervan had been gone, driving around the country to deliver rare or recently bound books to his clients. At least, that was what he'd thought his dad was doing. He thought of the bookshop he now owned. Perhaps his father had been there all along? If so, what was the big secret, and why had he never known about the bookshop? His mother, presumably, wasn't aware of it either.

The last thing Callum intended to do was to ask her about the bookshop – not until he had got to the bottom of what was going on. He realised that if she knew all about the bookshop, it would make his life easier. Perhaps she knew about the old wallet, and the photo of the girls. But something told him that was not the case. The fact was, his father had hidden the wallet and the deeds at the back of the desk drawer in his study for a reason.

Callum got in the driver's seat, hoping he remembered how to drive on the left-hand side of the road and use a gear shift. It had been years.

He adjusted the seat, the wing mirror, and the rearview mirror, then put the key in the ignition. The engine started immediately, the loud rumble of the old VW engine startling him. 'Bloody hell – that's loud!' He'd forgotten how loud it was. His mother was bound to hear it. The whole street would. After all this time, Callum had expected it to have a flat battery, but clearly his mother had taken it out from time to time, keeping it in working order, most likely because she knew that it was what his dad wanted.

He slowly backed the campervan out of the garage, down the short driveway into the street, and glanced out of the window to see the front door opening and his mother appearing at the front door. She looked shocked to see the van outside her house. 'What are you doing?' she shouted above the roar of the engine.

He could barely hear her. He wound the front window down. 'I'm taking it out for a spin.'

'No, you can't.'

Callum threw her a reassuring smile. 'It's fine. I remember how to drive it.' Callum had learned to drive in the old campervan. His father had said that if he could drive that, he could drive anything.

She ran down the path. 'But I don't want you to take it for a spin. You've got to put it back in the garage.'

'I'll put it back when I return.'

'No, do it now!'

Callum looked at her and suddenly understood. 'I'm sure Dad won't object. In fact, the van probably needs to be taken out from time to time if you want it kept in working order. I promise I won't prang it or anything.'

'I don't care about that. Just put it back!'

Callum frowned. Now she was just being unreasonable.

She reached for the driver's side door.

Callum quickly pressed the knob down by the window to lock the door, feeling a little childish.

'Callum, get out right now. I don't know where you found another key, but I want that back too.'

'No!' He frowned at her. He didn't get why she was being like this. She had never liked the campervan. She had always wanted a car. His gaze shifted to the sporty car on the driveway.

She followed his gaze. 'Look, take my car. I'll go and get the keys.' She turned around.

Callum said, 'I don't want to take your car.' There was a reason he didn't take her up on the offer; his dad had said something about giving the old VW to the girls. He thought of the photo of them outside a bookshop. He supposed taking the campervan to them, whoever they were, was the least he could do, as his dad had left him the shop. Perhaps they were the daughters of a best mate of his, or a client who had visited him at the bookshop. That might explain where the photo had been taken.

He wanted to visit Jack and Beth in Suffolk. Perhaps this was the perfect excuse to head on down and stay with them for a bit. He looked at his childhood home, which he didn't recognise anymore, and the thought of getting away was even more tempting.

'I'm going to get my car keys for you.'

Callum watched her run into the house. Before he set off, he had the urge to show her the photo of the two girls and ask if she knew them, but his father's words came to mind – *don't tell your mother.*

Callum put the van into first gear, wincing as he crunched the gears, and just as his mother appeared at the door, he pressed the accelerator. He wound the window further down, and called out, 'I might be going on a little trip, so don't worry if I'm not back this evening.'

'What? What did you say?'

He shouted out as the van started to move away from the kerb, 'I'm going to visit a mate, so I'm probably not going to be back for a few days.'

'In the van?'

'Yes – why not?'

Her mouth dropped open. 'Oh, my god. You can't!'

Callum sighed. There she was, being unreasonable again. 'Why on earth not?' Then something occurred to him. He slammed his foot on the brake. 'Have you sold it?'

'No, of course not.'

'Then what's the problem?'

When she didn't answer, he said, 'I'm off now.' Callum wound up the window and moved away from the kerb again.

Suddenly she grabbed the door handle and started running along with the van.

He saw what was happening out of the corner of his eye. 'What the hell ...?' He slammed on the brakes. She almost lost her balance. He wound down the window. 'Oh my god, what has got into you? Mum – let go!'

For a moment, there was a stand-off. She reluctantly let go of the handle. Callum eyed his mother, and thought of what his father had made him promise to do. Did she know something?

'Are you going to tell me what's going on?' He stared at her a full minute, and then watched her back away from the van. 'Go, then,' she said sullenly. She turned her back, strode back into the house, and slammed the front door behind her.

Callum stared after her, wondering if he should pop into the house before he left and find out if she was all right and what the scene in the street had been about. As he sat there debating what to do, he caught curtains twitching in neighbouring houses.

Callum decided that if he didn't go straight away, he'd end up handing over the keys. He could see his mum standing at the front room window, watching him. He waved, and sighed when she didn't wave back. Even if he'd told her that he might be returning without the campervan, he didn't see what the big deal was. In fact, he'd be doing her a favour. She could put her new car in the garage.

It occurred to him that if he sold the shop, he'd pay her back the value of the old campervan. It wasn't worth much. What he couldn't do, though, was repay the sentimental value. He imagined that was what her behaviour was really all about; it was the reason she hadn't touched the study when she had the place redecorated. Soon, there would be nothing left of his father – the dementia would make sure of that – and all she had to hold on to were these few things: his old study with the books and bookbinding equipment – and this van.

Thinking of that, Callum came to a stop at the end of the cul de sac. He had half a mind to turn it around and put it back in the garage. He sat there for some time, torn between his mum and the promise he'd made his father. What if his father's request was just the ramblings of a confused old man? But he had the old wallet, and the photo; that was something. And for some reason, his father wanted those girls to have the van. Before he did anything, Callum decided he was going to see his father again and find out why.

17

'I've never seen those before in my life.'

Callum had the deeds to the shop in one hand and his father's old wallet in the other. He sighed heavily, and tried again. 'Dad, remember earlier today, I came to see you? You gave me these keys and told me to go home and find your wallet.'

'I did no such thing. I don't know what you're talking about.'

Callum put the wallet and deeds on his father's lap and sighed. Then he had an idea. He opened the wallet and got out the photo of the two girls. Perhaps it would jog his father's memory. 'You made me promise to give the girls the campervan. Is this them?' He held up the photo. 'And is that the bookshop – *your* bookshop? Who are they? Why do you want me to find them and give them your campervan?'

Unexpectedly, his father burst into tears.

Callum looked at him, shocked. He'd never seen his father cry. 'Oh, no. Dad, I'm sorry. Please don't cry.'

His father covered his face with his hands and sobbed.

Callum sat down next to him, putting an arm around his shoulders. He'd read about this. Dementia could cause changes in personality, changes in mood. 'Dad?'

The door to the room suddenly opened. A young care assistant pushed a trolley inside. 'Oh, dear, Henry. It can't be as bad as all that.'

Henry looked up and smiled at the young woman with the bright smile and bubbly personality.

'There you are. Now, you haven't had your medication today, have you?'

Callum watched her pass him two pills and a little disposable cup of water. 'Down the hatch.'

Callum frowned. 'What are you giving him?' He didn't want to think they were keeping him sedated, so he drifted through his day drugged up, docile.

The young woman looked at Callum and smiled reassuringly. 'Don't worry. We don't drug him or anything like that, if that's what you're thinking. It's just a very mild anti-depressant to keep his mood up and help with anxiety and depression – something quite common in people with your father's condition. It's prescribed by the GP.'

'All right,' said Callum watching his father take the pills.

The young care assistant stared at Callum. 'I recognise you.'

Callum bit his lower lip. He had hoped she wouldn't. Next she'd be asking when the next season of the show was starting. He'd thought that when he returned to the UK he wouldn't have this – being recognised wherever he went. It hadn't started off well. He'd barely landed when he was recognised in the airport queue.

'Oh, my god. It *is* you.'

'I don't know what you mean.'

She glanced at Henry and shook her head. 'Sorry for the outburst – that wasn't very professional of me.'

'That's all right. But you're confusing me with someone else.'

Callum didn't make a very convincing liar. He sighed, and gave in. 'Would you like my autograph?'

'Oh, my god, really? My friends are just going to die when they find out I met you.'

'Who's going to die?' Callum's father asked.

'Nobody, Dad. It's just a figure of speech.' Callum had brought something with him for his father. He opened the bag and rummaged through.

The young care assistant said, 'I have a pen and paper.'

Callum looked up and caught her taking a small notepad and pen out of the pocket of her uniform. 'Here.' She handed them over. 'Do you know how big your show is in Scotland?'

Callum had no clue, but he guessed he was about to find out. He glanced at her as he scribbled her a note, thinking that perhaps this was another good reason to leave Scotland and head down south for a bit.

'What's your name?'

She pointed at her name badge. 'We heard the show was cancelled.'

'Where did you hear that?' Callum asked, shocked. He didn't think the news had been officially released by the studio yet.

'Social media.' She caught his expression, and shrugged. 'I guess it was leaked.' She brightened. 'I signed the online petition.'

'There's an online petition?'

'Oh yes, there's already thousands of signatures. We're hoping another studio picks it up.'

Callum stared at her, surprised. He thought youngsters weren't into these shows now.

'They have to bring it back. They can't leave it on a cliff-hanger.'

Oh, but they can, thought Callum. He kept that thought to himself as he finished signing his little note with a flourish. 'There.' He handed it over.

She looked at the autograph. 'Thanks, but ... my friends are never going to believe I met Fergus MacGregor. Can I take a selfie?'

Callum nodded. 'Sure.'

She walked over. Callum draped a hand around her shoulder and smiled as she took a selfie on her phone. She walked to the door, staring at her phone.

Callum turned to his dad and suddenly had a thought. 'Excuse me.'

She turned around. 'Yes?'

'Can you do something for me?'

'Oh, anything.'

'Look, do you mind not telling your friends or on social media *where* you met me? I just don't think it would be fair on my dad or the other residents if—'

'Of course. I swear I won't breathe a word.'

Callum exhaled in relief. 'Thanks.'

She opened the door and stepped outside, casting a glance over her shoulder. 'You know, you're better looking in real life – if that's possible.' She blushed as she said it before closing the door.

Callum rolled his eyes and turned to his father, who was standing at the window, watering his plants.

'Dad. I've brought something for you.' Callum picked up his bag and put it on the bed.

His dad turned around. Callum noticed he'd remembered to put the watering can down this time.

'Look what I brought with me,' Callum said, opening his bag. He glanced at the desk near the window and decided to get out all the things in the bag and put them on the table. He smiled as he got out the bookbinding equipment and a couple of books he'd found lying around his father's study. 'I thought we could bind a book together. What do you think, Dad?' Callum carefully laid out an old book and all the materials and tools needed for bookbinding, including a very sharp knife. He looked over at his dad expectantly as he walked over to the table. Henry picked up the knife.

For a moment, Callum wondered if his plan was a good idea. 'Careful with that – it's sharp!'

'I should jolly well hope so,' his father replied, examining the knife in his hand before opening the book.

Callum grinned as he watched his father deftly start to remove the old leather-bound cover. He hadn't forgotten how to do it.

Fifteen minutes later, the old cover had been removed, and his father had started the process of binding the book anew.

Callum smiled. 'Isn't this fun?'

'I'll say,' Henry replied.

'Why don't I come round with more books and we can do them together? I saw a stack of books that I think you intended to do, possibly for some clients.'

'Oh, yes. I need to get those done.'

'We could do them together,' said Callum.

His father smiled. 'It will be just like old times.'

Callum grinned. He loved that his dad remembered. 'Yes, just like old times.' The sound of Henry's door opening interrupted them. Callum glanced over his shoulder to see a middle-aged woman, dressed in a smart, business-like trouser suit, walk in without even knocking or introducing herself.

Callum frowned at her. 'Can I help you? I'm visiting my father at the moment.' Whatever it is, thought Callum, surely it could wait.

'I'm the care home manager,' she said. 'Sorry, but I had to see you for myself. I'm a huge fan.'

Callum wiped the glue from his fingers with an old rag he'd remembered to bring with him and stepped forward, trying not to feel annoyed with the young care assistant, who obviously couldn't keep her mouth shut. At least it was only the manager and not a crowd of other people who worked there.

Callum sighed. 'Do you want my autograph?'

'Oh, yes please.'

Callum stepped to one side, revealing the tools and book on the desk behind him. She walked over to the desk to take a closer look. 'What's going on here?'

'I brought some things for dad. We used to bind books together. He's very good at it.'

'So are you,' Henry added.

Callum turned around and smiled at him. Before they were interrupted, Callum had felt as though he had his dad back. They had been chatting, just like old times – before Callum became famous – when they had enjoyed binding books together.

The care home manager picked up the sharp knife and shook her head. 'I'm sorry, but you can't bring this sort of thing along for the residents.'

'I didn't bring it for the residents. I brought it for my dad. He can't bind books without the right tools.'

'Then I'm afraid this must stop.' She kept hold of the sharp knife.

Callum stared at her. 'You're serious, aren't you?'

'I'm afraid so.'

'Can't you make an exception for my dad?' Callum glanced at his dad, who was carefully gluing the new hardcover in place.

Callum took the manager to one side and lowered his voice. 'It's helping his memory tremendously. It's like he's a changed person – as though the dementia has disappeared, and he's got his memory back.' He smiled, flashing the dead straight pearly white porcelain veneers that he'd gone to the expense of having done at the behest of his agent; apparently no one worked in Hollywood with bad teeth. Callum hadn't had bad teeth, but they hadn't been as straight as they could be, nor as white. They still wouldn't guarantee him another job, though.

The care home assistant relinquished the knife. Callum had known that his engaging smile would work.

'Please put it away.'

Callum frowned.

'The glue has to go as well – in fact, all of it. It's a health and safety thing.'

'Fine.' It wasn't fine, but unless he wanted his father to lose his place at the care home, he'd have to do as he was told. Callum had a thought. 'What if I brought this stuff with me on my visits and supervised Dad? That was my idea anyway – that we'd do it together.' Although he had intended to leave the stuff there when he left so that his dad could do some work if he fancied it, obviously that wasn't going to happen now. 'It's a compromise. What do you think?' Callum flashed that smile again.

This time she relented. 'Oh, all right. As long as you don't leave any of it here, and you supervise, I can't see the harm.'

'Great.' Callum's smile faltered. Wasn't he meant to be travelling to Suffolk in the campervan to look in on Jack and find those girls?

'Now, what about that autograph?' she said, interrupting his thoughts.

'Oh, yes – right.' Callum looked at the newly bound book. He guessed his father's business had been wound down months earlier. There were no clients, no money to be had from binding the books, although he'd rather not tell his dad that. He looked at him. 'Here, can I put the finishing touches on that?'

'Of course.' He handed it over.

Callum opened the book, checked the binding, and patted his dad on the shoulder. 'Good job!' He opened the book to the first page, which was blank. He picked up a pen, asked the manager's name, and wrote in the book, signing it with a flourish. He handed it to her. 'Hope you don't mind the book. I helped Dad bind it, so I thought you'd like a little memento.'

'Oh wow – thanks.' She turned it over in her hands. 'I'll treasure this.' She walked out of the door. Callum saw her glance over her shoulder and heard her mutter, 'If only I was twenty years younger,' before shutting the door behind her.

'Why did you give the book away?'

Callum turned around and sighed. 'Dad, you haven't got any clients now.'

'That can't be right. Where did they all go?'

Callum pursed his lips and sat down in the chair beside the bed. He looked around the room, his eyes settling on the wallet and the deeds that were still on the floor. He bent down and picked them up, wondering whether to broach the subject of the bookshop again with his father, and of the old wallet with the photo inside. He didn't want to. He didn't want to risk upsetting him again. Callum picked up his bag. Perhaps it was all for the best. Although he wanted to see his best mate, just then he knew he should be here, spending time with his dad – not travelling south in his old campervan.

Henry walked over and sat on the bed. 'What have you got there?'

'Oh, it's nothing.' Callum opened his bag to put away the envelope containing the deeds and the wallet.'

'Is that my wallet?'

Callum stopped. He held it up. 'You recognise this?'

'Yes, it was in the back of my desk drawer.'

Callum stared at him. 'He held up the envelope. What about this? It's the deeds to the bookshop.'

'Yes, I know that.'

'You left me a note.' Callum read the note to Henry. '*The van is for the girls. I made them a promise, so you must give them the campervan. Don't tell your mother, but promise me you'll look after them. They are—*' Callum showed him the note. 'You didn't finish the sentence, Dad. Who are they, and where can I find them?'

Henry focused on the note in Callum's hand. 'That's right. You must find them. Find the bookshop. That's where they'll be. The Bookshop of Memories.' He added, 'There's a photo inside.'

'Yes, I know. But who are they?' He stared at his father. A ludicrous thought crossed his mind. His dad had been a travelling bookseller. Callum had heard stories of people who led a double life – who had two families. Was it possible he had met someone else and had another family?

Callum stared at him and thought of what he'd written in the note. *Don't tell your mother.* But he knew his dad. The idea was ridiculous; he could never keep a secret like that. Callum thought there must be more to it.

'Dad, who are they?' Callum asked again.

Someone knocked on the door.

Callum threw his hands in the air. 'For goodness' sake, not

now!' He rolled his eyes when the door opened. It was the young care assistant who had asked for his autograph earlier.

Callum eyed her. 'Yes, what is it?' He hadn't meant to sound rude, but he finally felt he was getting somewhere with his dad. He stood up and walked over, trying to stop her entering the room. 'Sorry, I didn't mean to sound short with you, but I was just having a conversation with my dad ...' Callum lowered his voice. 'It's one of his lucid moments and there's something I desperately want him to clear up.'

The young woman standing in the doorway looked over at Henry. Her gaze shifted to Callum, her big blue eyes staring up at him. She whispered. 'Sorry. I just wanted to come and apologise. I know you told me not to say anything, but I was just so excited, and my boss wondered what was up. I couldn't help myself – I had to tell someone.'

Callum sighed. 'It's fine. Don't worry about it.' He attempted to close the door, but the young woman stood her ground. She smiled coyly. 'There's just something I wanted to ask you.'

Callum frowned. 'Can't it wait until later?'

'Not really. You see I finish my shift in an hour.'

'Yes?'

'And … well I thought, I wondered, after you've visited your dad, you might like to well … go out for a drink … with me.'

Callum stared at her. He didn't want to ask her how old she was, but he bet she wasn't even twenty. He knew she'd dismiss the age gap, if he brought it up, but it wasn't just that. He had a rule: no dating fans. He wasn't being condescending, as though people who weren't in the industry weren't worth his time. That wasn't it. The issue was that they most probably wouldn't differentiate between the character he played and the person he really was.

They wouldn't be dating him; they'd be going out with a fictional character, with Fergus MacGregor, the Scottish laird.

'I appreciate the offer, I really do, it's just that it's not a good time. I've got a lot going on in my life, what with my dad, and the show being cancelled.' It was no lie. Callum knew he wouldn't date anyone right now.

'It's only a drink.'

Callum detected a hint of annoyance in her voice. He looked at her. But it wasn't just a drink. She was saving face.

'I know.' Callum decided to play along. 'I just don't know how long I'm going to be here today. As I said, I've got some things to sort out with my dad.' He quickly added, 'And it looks as though I'll be going on a trip.'

'Really? Is it to do with work? Are you going back to Hollywood?'

Callum shook his head. 'Afraid not. No, it's a personal matter. I have to travel to Suffolk.'

'Want some company? I have some annual leave coming up.'

Callum stared at her. She really wasn't getting the message.

'That's very kind of you, but as I said it's a personal, family matter, so best done on my own.'

Her face dropped. 'Oh, okay. Well, I'm not going anywhere, so I'll still be here when you get back.'

Callum smiled tightly. 'Of course. Thanks.' He shut the door behind him and breathed a sigh. When he turned around, his father was no longer sitting on the bed. 'Dad?'

He turned around with the watering can. 'I'm watering the potted plans.'

'Oh, no not again. Dad you're watering the carpet!'

Henry looked down. 'Oh, dear.'

Callum stepped forward and took the watering can out of his hands. He placed it back on the window shelf. 'Now, Dad, about the girls.'

'What girls?'

'You know the girls in the photo outside the bookshop.'

'What bookshop?'

Callum sighed.

'What are you doing here, Callum? Shouldn't you be in Hollywood – or has the series wrapped up?'

Callum sighed again. He was back where he had started with the conversation that morning. This could go on all week. On the other hand, if he left now, he could be back in a few days' time, having carried out his father's wishes – if he could find those girls. He could also put the bookshop on the market, although he might refrain from telling his father about that part of his plan.

'Dad, I'm going away for a few days. Perhaps when I get back we can resume the conversation we were having about your note and the photo?'

Henry turned around and picked up the watering can.

Callum sighed as he packed the stuff he'd brought with him back into the bag. He walked to the door, opened it, paused and turned around. 'Bye, Dad. See you in a few days.' He watched as Henry put the watering can down and turned to face him. He said, 'Who are you?'

'I'm your son.'

Henry shook his head. 'No, you're not.'

Callum breathed a heavy sigh. 'See you soon, Dad.' He stepped out of the room and shut the door.

It occurred to him that whoever those girls were, they probably wouldn't be interested in an old campervan. Perhaps they wouldn't even be interested in hearing from Henry. And at this rate, with the deterioration of his memory, Henry would be none the wiser if Callum never found them or delivered the van.

A little voice in Callum's head said, *Why bother finding them?* It felt like a wild goose chase. He could be using his time a lot more wisely by just locating the bookshop he now owned and selling it.

Outside the care home, Callum got back into the campervan. He glanced up at the former hotel, spotting his dad standing at the window, looking down. Callum waved, feeling guilty for deciding to ignore his wishes and just concentrate on sorting himself out by selling the bookshop.

But even if that was what he was going to do, he had to find the place first.

18

For the first time ever, Thea couldn't face going into work on Monday. When Gracie knocked on her door and Thea told her she wouldn't be going into work, Gracie didn't sound surprised. In fact, she had a suggestion.

'When was the last time you took some annual leave? I know you love your job, but even you need to take some time out, and have a break, once in a while. I'm pretty certain that under the circumstances, and with all that leave accrued, Edward will just sign it off and let you take it immediately if I have a word with him. When was the last time you saw your sister?'

'Are you suggesting I go and stay with my sister in Suffolk?' Thea couldn't think of anything worse; she'd rather stay in her flat than in her sister's busy household with her two teenagers – not to mention her husband's roving eye. It wasn't something she'd tell her sister, but Thea had caught the way her sister's husband looked at her. It made her feel uncomfortable.

That thought made her think of Miles. Gracie was right; what had happened – what she'd discovered – was for the best. It was just that it didn't feel like that just then. She was heartbroken.

'I think you need to get away from London, and everything

that reminds you of Miles … and he knows where you live. I bet he'll be round.'

Thea shook her head. 'I don't think so. He didn't phone or text me. That was my sister.'

Gracie sighed. 'He didn't call you or text you for a reason.'

'What do you mean?'

'He knows you won't answer your phone or reply to a text. But if he turned up here, in person, and rang your doorbell insistently, there's a chance you might answer that door.'

Thea stared at her.

'Now, you see why I think you shouldn't hang around the flat in case he does come round. You need to get away for a bit.'

Thea nodded. 'All right.' However, she wasn't intending to stay with her sister. Gracie didn't understand; they didn't have that sort of relationship. They didn't have that much in common. When they were younger, she had been the annoying little sister, always trying to copy Jenna; always sneaking into her room and using her makeup. She had looked up to her big sister and wanted to be just like her, but had also been envious of her being older, wearing makeup, having a boyfriend, learning to drive, and going away on holiday with her friends to Ibiza when she was seventeen. Although Thea had known that her time would come, nothing had been able to change the fact that Jenna, being three years older, had always got there first.

But it wasn't just their teenage years that had led to their strained relationship; it was the fact that her sister often expected her to drop everything and babysit her children at weekends, as though the world revolved around her just because she was a mother. And when Jenna had a problem or wanted some advice, she'd be straight on the phone to Thea – but it didn't cut both ways.

Thea knew that there was no point getting in touch with Jenna and explaining what had happened, expecting a listening ear, sympathy, or an invite to go and stay with her. Her sister would be far too busy.

Gracie was still standing at her door. 'Have you got in touch with your sister to find out what she wanted?'

'I think it's probably just babysitting for the weekend, although …' Thea trailed off. Jenna had sounded different on the phone.

'What is it?'

'I'm not sure. She didn't sound herself.'

'Why don't you phone her and find out?'

Thea sighed. She had a lot on her plate. She knew that whenever her sister got in touch it was because she wanted something – or specifically she wanted her little sister to do something for her. Thea wished that just for once, Jenna would be a big sister and look after her for a change. *But I've got Gracie*, thought Thea, her smile fading at the thought that just then, what she really wanted was to speak to her mum.

'Come here.'

Thea stepped forward and got enveloped in a big hug. 'Now, you, my girl, are going to be all right. I'm off to work. I'll let Edward know that you won't be in work today. Phone your sister. If you're not here when I get back, I'll know you've gone to Suffolk.'

'Look, I'm sure I'll still be here when you get back. I won't be going to my sister's.'

'Never say never.' She smiled at her. 'Now, my advice to you is to give her a call. It might be something important.'

Important for her, thought Thea glumly. Even so, she said, 'All right,' knowing that otherwise, Gracie would be on her case. That wasn't the only reason; over the last couple of days, Jenna had left her several messages; in the last one, she had said that something had happened and that she needed to speak to Thea urgently. Thea had rolled her eyes. Her big sister had always been like that – so melodramatic over the least little thing. Although now it struck her as odd that the messages, and calls, had suddenly stopped. Her sister was nothing if not persistent – normally.

Thea took Gracie's advice and phoned her sister.

'Hello.'

Thea was surprised to hear her brother-in-law answer her sister's mobile phone. 'Mark, is Jenna there? She left me a message to get in touch.' Thea didn't mention that she'd left several messages over the last couple of days, before everything had suddenly gone quiet.

'She's in hospital.'

'Oh, god. Are the twins okay?'

'Yes. Why do you ask?'

'Well, you said she's in hospital. I thought something might have happened to—'

'Jenna had an accident.'

Thea swallowed. 'Is she okay?'

'She broke her leg.'

'Oh, no!'

'She needs surgery. I think they're going to insert some pins.'

Thea breathed a sigh of relief. When he'd said the word *accident*, all sorts of things had gone through her mind. 'How did it happen?'

'Hold on, she's waking up.'

'You're in the hospital with her right now?'

'Yeah.'

'Are the twins with you?'

'The neighbours are keeping an eye on them. It's not ideal. I imagine that was what she was phoning you about. I know we can't expect you to just drop everything and come and help out. I told her not to phone you. You've got your own life.'

'I've got a lot of leave, and I'm not in work today.' Thea knew she wouldn't tell him what had happened with Miles. They had bigger issues to deal with. 'Look, I'm taking annual leave for a few days, and I'm at a loose end. I can come down straight away and help out.'

'Would you? Oh, Thea, you're a lifesaver. I've got to work and the kids need taking to school – and stuff.'

He still hadn't told her how it had happened. 'Can I speak to her?'

'Afraid not. She's still drowsy from the pain relief, so now's not a good time.'

'All right.' Thea intended to pop in and see her sister in hospital when she was feeling up to more visitors. She had a thought. 'You have still got a spare bedroom, haven't you?' She'd need to stay at their house, but she thought the spare room might have been turned into a home office. Wasn't Mark working from home part of the week?

They'd moved out of London recently, in time for the kids to start secondary school, and bought a detached cottage in an idyllic little village not far from the coastal town of Aldeburgh. The idea was that Mark would continue with his job in the city, commuting two days a week and spending the remaining time working from home. Her sister's life had turned out just perfectly. Now, she could see the problem; he was still commuting for those two days each week, which meant that someone had to look after the twins.

'Oh, yeah, sure. We've still got a spare bedroom. Look, can you come today?'

'As soon as I've packed.' Thea knew it was lucky she had a very understanding boss who'd let her take leave without notice. It probably helped that her boss was also a family friend, but then again he was such a lovely man that she imagined he'd treat all his staff the same.

'Will you pick me up from the station?' she said. Thea didn't have a car. She had no need for one in London.

'Yes, I'll pick you up from the station. Thanks, Thea. Really, I just can't thank you enough.'

Thea got off the phone. She walked straight into her bedroom and found her suitcase, packing what she needed for a few days. 'A week, tops,' said Thea out loud, wondering what she was going to do there in between school pickups. She looked at her phone, and although she knew she really ought to phone Edward, she phoned Gracie instead.

'Everything all right?' Gracie asked.

'Yes, look – I did what you said and contacted Jenna. She's in hospital. Nothing serious.' Thea frowned. Breaking a leg was pretty serious, and she still didn't know how it had happened. 'So, I'm going to Suffolk to help them out for a bit. Will you tell Edward I've decided to take some annual leave?'

'I already have.'

'What?'

'Well, you weren't in the office this morning, and although you think coming into work tomorrow will take your mind off things, in my experience, it won't.'

Thea knew what she was referring to – her messy divorce.

'Getting away – that's just the ticket.'

She wasn't so sure. Looking after two teenagers, ferrying them back and forward to school, wasn't exactly a holiday – although she would have the rest of each day free to do her own thing. The trouble was, what was there to do in Suffolk? She had no clue.

The last time she'd stayed there, other than for a flying visit to her sister for a couple of nights, had been when she was nine years old and they had lived there. Now she was too old for crabbing in rock pools, and flying kites on the beach, and visiting petting zoos, and all the other things her nine-year-old self had once enjoyed about the Suffolk Coast. Her life in London was a world away, and her recollection of her childhood, although filled with fond memories, would always be tinged with sadness. There was a reason she didn't ever hang around long on the Suffolk Coast. She was surprised her sister had moved there.

'Thea? You're not having second thoughts – are you?'

Gracie, just like her mum, could read her mind. 'I can't back out now. I promised I'd go.'

'Good. I'll let Edward know you're taking a couple of weeks.'

'A couple of weeks! No, that's not what I said. I'm only going for a few days.'

'Well, at least you've got the time off if you need to extend it to help out your sister, and perhaps have a little holiday there.'

'That's not where I'd choose to take a holiday.'

'Why not? I've heard it's a lovely part of the world, bit of a well-kept secret.'

'I do know that. I grew up there.' Thea hadn't meant to snap. She added, 'Perhaps the break from work will do me good.'

'That's the spirit. Send your sister my best wishes for a speedy recovery.'

'Thanks, Gracie. I will.'

'See you in a couple of weeks.'

'Okay.'

I'll be back a lot sooner than that, Thea thought, but decided to keep that thought to herself. 'I'm getting the next train.' She was already on her phone, looking up the next train leaving Liverpool Street Station. 'It leaves in an hour, so I won't be here when you get home.' Thea hesitated. 'Will you let me know if someone calls on me while I'm gone?'

'And by someone, you mean—'

'Yes.'

'Why?'

Thea was surprised by the question. 'I just want to know – that's all.'

'All right.'

She guessed what Gracie was thinking. 'I didn't say I'd consider getting back together with him, did I?' Thea took a deep breath. 'Sorry, I didn't mean to be rude.'

'You don't have to apologise, Thea. I understand.'

Thea wasn't sure she did. It wasn't like Gracie's divorce. She'd been with her husband for what seemed to Thea like forever. They'd drifted apart over several years, then he'd found someone else. She expected they hadn't even been in love anymore when they'd finally divorced.

But she and Miles hadn't fallen out of love. Not until she had found out the truth about him. And still, deep down, she believed him when he said he'd leave his wife. But she wasn't about to tell Gracie that. She knew what Gracie would say: that he wasn't like Mark, who had actually left his first wife.

She did think that Gracie was right, though. Perhaps it was for the best that she had an excuse to get away from London for a bit – because if he did call round, she didn't trust herself not to end up forgiving him.

19

Thea stepped off the train on to the platform and started walking towards the old red-brick building that housed a ticket office, toilets, waiting rooms, and a café. She thought about how different it was to the Tube stations in London. Even the overground ones were nothing like this. These old stations had charm; she loved the potted plants and hanging baskets lining the platform. The stations on the Lowestoft line had remained largely unchanged, apart from the new, trendy coffee shops inside.

Thea could still smell freshly brewed coffee as she walked through the station building and stepped outside into the small forecourt where cars were picking up and dropping off passengers. She waved and walked over when she spotted Mark behind the wheel of her sister's car. Mark got out and walked around to the back of the car, opening the boot. She was expecting him to offer to put her suitcase in when he shut the boot and walked around the side of the car to greet her. He was wheeling a small suitcase.

Thea stopped in front of him. 'Hi, Mark.'

He stepped forward, brushing his dark hair out of his eyes. She guessed his hair must be dyed; he was in his late forties and still had no sign of a grey hair.

He enveloped her in a hug. 'Thea. I'm so glad you've arrived.'

'Me too.' She genuinely meant it. Although her trip wasn't under the best of circumstances, she was surprised at how she felt. When she'd left London behind, and the intercity train had pulled into Ipswich Station, she had quickly made her way down the platform and stepped aboard the two-carriage local service from Ipswich for the next leg of her journey. She had caught sight of the familiar scenery of rolling fields and pretty little Suffolk villages nestled in the countryside and had felt a tingle of excitement at coming back to Suffolk. Although it was now October and the summer had given way to a blustery autumn, she still felt pleased to be there. That was until she had caught sight of the suitcase that Mark had lifted out of the boot.

'What's that?'

He followed her gaze. 'It's a suitcase.'

She looked at him quizzically. 'Wait – are you going somewhere?' She glanced at the train station. 'Are you catching a train?'

'Yes.' He looked at her askance. 'I do have to work, you know.'

Thea caught that note of irritation in his voice – and something else; Mark could be condescending, judgemental, belittling, and downright rude. She'd been in his company for less than five minutes and had already realised that he hadn't changed one bit.

Sometimes she wondered why her sister stayed with him. Apart from the obvious – he was good at his job, looked after his family financially, and for a guy approaching fifty, took care of himself physically; he was tall, slim, and enjoyed riding his bike and training for marathons. Jenna was a stay-at-home mum, managing their sprawling cottage and two kids. Thea knew that helping Jenna out with household chores was not on Mark's agenda.

And it turned out he wasn't going to help Jenna's sister out either. *Wait*, thought Thea, *I wasn't expecting him to help me out; it was meant to be the other way around – wasn't it?*

'You probably remember where our house is, but I've put the postcode in the Satnav just in case.'

Thea followed his gaze to the front passenger seat and the Satnav on the dashboard as he opened the driver's side door.

'When will you be back? I thought you'd take some time off?'

'I did. I had a couple of days.'

Thea frowned. 'You mean the weekend? Wouldn't your job give you some compassionate leave, so you wouldn't have to return to work on Monday?' Thea hadn't expected Mark to return to work straight away today; at the very least, she'd thought he would work from home while his wife as in hospital.

Mark sighed heavily. 'She just broke her leg. It's not like she's at death's door.'

'But what about the twins?'

He shrugged. 'What about them? You're here now, so they'll have someone to take them to school.'

'That's not what I meant!' Thea stared at him as he looked at his watch and glanced over at the train station, obviously longing to get away. 'Their mum is in hospital. It's not the best time for you to go away as well, so there's no one there to take care of them.' Thea had assumed she'd just be doing the school runs so Mark could work from home and visit Jenna in hospital.

'They'll have you. Speaking of which, here is Jenna's mobile phone, just in case the school gets in touch for any reason, or they leave a message. When I rushed her to A&E after the accident, I didn't think to pick up her phone, obviously. Perhaps you can give it back to her when you visit. I've let the school know that their aunt is staying with them for a few days.'

Thea didn't have much experience of looking after children, let alone young teenagers. But that wasn't the point. Didn't he get that this would be an emotional time for them? They'd doubtless want to talk about how their mum being in hospital made them feel – and it was their dad they'd want to turn to.

Mark looked at his watch again. 'Look, I must go. My train is due in any moment. I've got a meeting late this afternoon. The kids should be home from school by now. How come it took you so long to get here?'

Thea looked at him and ignored the comment. She'd had to pack, and get to the train station, and catch two trains. She said, 'I thought I had to pick them up from school?'

Mark shook his head. 'School bus. Anyhow, here are the car keys, and the keys to the house, but the kids will be home before you, so one of them will let you in. They're expecting you.'

'You left them on their own?' Thea said in surprise.

'It's not for long, is it? And they are thirteen.' They both turned at the sound of a train approaching the station from a distance. 'Actually, as it turns out your timing is impeccable. It couldn't have been better.' He handed her the keys.

Thea still couldn't believe he was going. 'When will you be back?'

'I'm not sure. I've got back-to-back meetings and the like.'

Thea frowned at him. He was sounding like Miles, making work-related excuses for not staying.

'You work away for two days – right? So you'll be back on Wednesday?'

'Er, no – I'm now working in London all week.'

'All week? Since when?'

Mark didn't answer that question. 'Look, I've got to dash.'

She said, 'I can't stay indefinitely. You will be back at the weekend, won't you?'

He nodded. 'Of course.'

She decided not to tell him she had two weeks' leave.

'Here's my mobile number.' He handed Thea a work card with his phone number on it.

Thea said, 'I'm sure I've still got the phone number of your London flat somewhere.' She was surprised they'd decided to keep the flat, which belonged to Mark. She'd thought that when they'd moved to Suffolk, he'd intended to sell the flat and work from home permanently – but by the sound of it, that hadn't happened.

'I'd prefer it if you contacted me on my mobile number.'

Thea shrugged. 'Okay.'

He smiled. 'But I'm sure you won't have to.' He grabbed the handle of his suitcase. 'Look, I've got to run. I'll see you at the weekend.'

Thea stood there with her suitcase and watched him hurry towards the station. She sighed, put her suitcase and bag on the back seat, and sat in the driver's seat. She couldn't believe he'd just left her like that without even introducing her to the twins, whom she hadn't seen for months.

She didn't even have time to visit Jenna in hospital. It occurred to Thea that she didn't actually know where her sister was. She assumed she was in Ipswich hospital. Thea still had Mark's card in her hand. She rang his number.

Mark answered, sounding surprised. He couldn't mask the tinge of annoyance in his voice when he said, 'Thea? Why are you ringing me already?'

'You didn't tell me which hospital Jenna is in. I'd like to visit tomorrow when the kids are at school.' She knew that it would mean she could talk to her sister alone. There was something she wanted to ask her. She'd replayed her phone messages on the way there and discovered that Jenna had in fact contacted her *before* the accident. So, whatever it was that Jenna had contacted her about, it was nothing to do with her accident and needing help with child-care while she was laid up with a broken leg.

'She's at the hospital in Aldeburgh, the cottage hospital – it's not far from where we're living in Pettistree.'

'Great.' Thea was so pleased to hear that her sister wasn't twenty miles away in Ipswich; it meant she could pop in and see her every day. She started the car and headed for her sister's house.

As Thea drove, she thought about how it had always been her sister's dream to move back to Suffolk, where they spent their childhood. Jenna had wanted lots of children, but had been lucky to have twins. It had taken her a long time to become pregnant, and after the twins were born, Thea knew she had tried to get pregnant again, but it just hadn't happened.

She was looking forward to seeing the large old red-brick cottage which seemed too big for a family of four. There was an old stable block that she knew they had been planning to convert to either a triple garage, or a stable for a pony for the children – her sister and brother-in-law appeared to be at odds a lot of the time regarding what they wanted to do with the property. She wondered how the renovations were coming along.

Jenna always raved about their life in the country, and said to Thea that she didn't know how she put up with the noise and pollution living in London. Perhaps being older, her sister had more memories of their life in Suffolk before their father had disappeared and they had moved to London.

Thea had been nine when they left their Suffolk life behind and moved into the house in London. It was pretty much all she'd known. She'd never returned to Suffolk until her sister and her family had moved out of London nine months earlier. Their mum hadn't even seen where her eldest daughter had moved too. They'd had a housewarming party, which their mum had been aware of, but she had refused to fly back from Nepal to attend. Thea remembered the email; she hadn't minced her words. Suffolk wasn't a place she wanted to revisit. She'd left that life behind.

Thea remembered that her mum and sister had had a huge falling-out over it, and wondered if they'd patched things up. Her sister had been straight on the phone to Thea, telling her how selfish their mum was; Jenna felt that she should be able to put aside her feelings over their dad's disappearance for once and just return to Suffolk for the party.

Have you ever had your heart broken? Thea had asked her. Jenna had nearly fallen out with her too, saying that Thea always took their mum's side. But Jenna had undoubtedly had a point when she'd said that it had been years and years since he'd gone, and their mum had moved on with her life; why couldn't she just be pleased that Jenna was moving on with her life too?

Thea followed the Satnav directions from Wickham Market train station to her sister's village, Pettistree. It was very pretty, with thatched houses, a village church, a little green, and, adjacent to the church, a pub that served lovely food. There was no village centre, or main street – just a winding road with a handful of large, detached period houses in the middle of countryside, but it was not far from a little market town you could drive or walk to down a winding country lane. Thea liked Wickham Market, a small village with a u-shaped village square around which were several little shops – a butcher's shop that doubled as a baker's, a couple of tea shops, a general store, and a charity shop. It was under ten miles from the station, less than a twenty-minute drive through picturesque countryside. Jenna had the best of both worlds. She wasn't far from the Suffolk Coast and the lovely coastal towns of Orford and Aldeburgh.

She knew her sister preferred Aldeburgh, a twenty-five minute drive from where they lived, with its shops, cafés, restaurants, fish and chip shops, and a cinema. There were more things for her children to do there at the weekend, and they would meet up there with their friends from the local secondary school just ten minutes from Aldeburgh.

She felt like doing a detour to Aldeburgh to visit her sister straight away, but she was anxious to arrive at their house and check on the twins. She hoped they hadn't invited friends round after being left on their own. Thea was worried she'd turn up and there would be a house full of teenagers and a house party in full swing. How would she deal with that? Thea shook her head. She had no clue about how to deal with teenagers.

By the time she arrived, pulling up on to the gravel driveway in front of the impressive red-brick home, she was convinced it wasn't going to work and she'd be straight on the phone to Mark, telling him to come back. How could he do this? Leave her in charge of two teenagers and this house while he swanned off to London?

As she switched off the car engine, the enormity of the responsibility hit home. Would she need to shop for groceries? What would they have for dinner that evening? What time did they need to get up in the morning, and out of the door, to make it to school on time?

Just breathe, Thea told herself, remembering what her therapist had taught her; to do calming exercises whenever she got stressed. *I'm going to need to do plenty of those when I walk in that house*, she thought. She remembered previous visits, and imagined nothing had changed. Whereas she liked her little flat to be minimalist and orderly, with everything in its place, her sister was the opposite. When Jenna had lived in London, her house had just seemed chaotic, and she'd brought that mindset here to the cottage. It seemed to have been made worse by the fact that they'd been in the throes of renovating it.

Thea had commented on the mess on her last visit, and Jenna hadn't taken very kindly to it. She had come back with her own caustic remark; she'd said, *Wait until you get married and have children – you'll find out your priorities change. You won't be cleaning all the time.*

Thea had taken exception. *I don't clean all the time*, she'd replied.

Then she'd caught what her sister had said under her breath: *No wonder you're still single.*

Thea had corrected her on that score.

'Well, you haven't moved in together, have you? You know what your problem is? I don't think you can commit.'

Thea sighed, thinking back to that conversation. Yes, it was true, she shied away from commitment, from change. But now she and Miles wouldn't be moving in together even if she had decided that she was ready to share her life and her orderly flat with someone. She wasn't looking forward to telling her sister that she was single again. She imagined that, like Gracie, Jenna would just tell her the right person hadn't come along yet.

And how was that going to happen? I work in the basement of a museum, locked away in a room with two other people all day, apart from when I do school tours. She knew what Jenna would say to that; put yourself out there. Join a gym or a class; you might meet someone. She wasn't interested in joining a gym or a class. What was the point of meeting someone there? It's not as though they'd have anything in common if she was at the gym or a class she hated.

Thea sighed as she got out of the car and looked at the house. She was not looking forward to this. She was already counting down the days to the weekend when Mark returned.

Thea reached inside the car and grabbed her suitcase, sliding it off the back seat. She shut the car door and locked it. She had expected at least one of the twins to open the front door; she knew they must have heard the car turning up, spewing gravel as she clamped her foot down too hard on the brake and skidded. It wasn't exactly the most dignified arrival.

Thea was already missing London, although she couldn't deny how lovely the location was. She stood for a moment, breathing in the sweet countryside air. There was no traffic noise, no sirens going off in the distance – just the sound of birds chirping and the rustling of the wind in the trees. It reminded her of her childhood.

Despite the blustery October weather, the late afternoon sun had peeked out from behind a huge grey cloud, suddenly brightening up the otherwise grey day. It brightened Thea's mood too. She caught herself smiling at her surroundings. It was a world away from her life, and everything that she was familiar with, and yet this part of the world *was* familiar. It was where she'd spent the happiest time of her life, before everything had changed.

20

Thea walked up to the front door. On the ground floor of the house, there were four floor-to-ceiling Georgian windows – two on either side of the front door – looking over the lawn and the gravel driveway. She didn't see either of the twins looking out of the front windows to see who had arrived. But she did hear one of them, Katie, behind the door.

'Winston, for goodness' sake, let me answer the front door, will you?'

Who the hell is Winston? Thea thought. Did they have a friend round, or was someone babysitting that Mark hadn't told her about?

The front door opened. Katie stood there holding on to the collar of a large yellow dog.

Thea's eyes went wide at the sight of the dog, an excitable golden retriever. Mark hadn't mentioned they'd got a dog. She'd have to feed it, walk it. Why couldn't it have been a cat? She sighed. She didn't know the first thing about looking after a pet.

Katie's fingers slipped from the collar and the dog leapt forward, barking, slobbering, and jumping up at Thea.

Thea took a step back and lost her footing as the dog's weight pushed her backwards before she had a chance to right herself.

She took a tumble backwards, landing on her rump. 'Ouch!'

'Winston! You naughty dog. Come here!'

The dog licked Thea's face before running over to Katie. She wagged a finger. 'You are a very bad dog. How many times have you been told not to jump up?'

Not nearly enough, thought Thea, getting to her feet. She looked at the large, exuberant dog and thought perhaps she had an idea about how her sister might have broken her leg.

'I didn't know you had a dog, Katie.' Thea didn't remember them having a puppy the last time she saw them.

'We got him a couple of weeks ago. He's a rescue.'

'How old is he?'

'Ten months, I think.'

Thea looked at the dog, who still hadn't calmed down. Maybe that was why the previous owners had given him up. Too much energy. Untrained. He looked a handful. A handful that Thea was not prepared for.

Winston's head whipped around to look inside the house. He must have heard something; perhaps Toby. He barked and scampered off.

Thea sighed. She asked, 'Does Winston have a crate or something?'

'What do you mean?'

Thea was wondering whether there was somewhere safe Winston could be left in the house alone while she went out when the children were at school.

Katie didn't answer her question. She folded her arms instead and remained standing in the doorway, blocking Thea from entering the house. 'Dad said you were coming. I told him we don't need a babysitter.'

Thea hadn't been expecting a warm welcome. 'Yes, well, I'm not babysitting. Someone has to run you to school.'

'You don't have to run us to school.'

Thea frowned. 'What do you mean? Your school is in Leiston, isn't it? That's a good half an hour drive up the coast road.'

'Yeah, and we get a coach at the end of the street.' Thea heard her add under her breath, 'Idiot.'

She stared at Katie, but decided to ignore her rude comment. Mark had mentioned that they'd come home today on the school bus, but she'd assumed it was a one-off. Thea much preferred not to have to do the school run. Someone still had to be there for them, though. They were thirteen – although looking at Katie, Thea thought she could easily be mistaken for fifteen or even sixteen. She'd changed a lot in the past few months. She had makeup expertly applied, like a model. Her long, blonde hair was straightened, with a centre parting, and Thea couldn't help but notice her nails, which made Thea feel a little embarrassed at the state of her own; she blamed it on her archiving job and the fact that, unlike Katie, she didn't have time for manicures.

Katie flicked her hair over her shoulder. 'We can take care of ourselves.'

Thea was quite shocked when Katie shut the door in her face. She stood there for a moment, staring at the door. Now would be the perfect excuse just to get in the car and visit her sister. But she'd promised Mark she'd look after the twins. What if something happened while she was gone? They'd obviously been okay since Mark had left for the station. Even so, now she was there, she couldn't just leave them on their own.

Thea rolled her eyes and put the key in the lock. Katie obviously wasn't aware that Mark had given her a door key.

She stepped into the house, expecting Winston to bound over and jump up at her again. Fortunately, this time the dog was nowhere in sight. Neither was Katie.

Thea lifted her suitcase and bag inside and closed the front door. She cast her gaze around the entrance hallway to see what had changed since her last visit. The staircase was still uncarpeted, but the hallway had been laid with light oak flooring leading into the lounge on the left. On the right, a door led through to the kitchen, which looked as though it had been refitted with white shaker-style units. She knew that both rooms were double-aspect rooms. The lounge had French doors on to the pretty back garden, and the kitchen had an extension with a skylight in the ceiling and big patio doors also overlooking the garden, letting in lots of light.

Thea walked into the kitchen and found a glass. She poured herself some water and stared out at the garden. They'd built themselves a summerhouse in the corner of the back garden. She imagined it doubled as Mark's home office. What she couldn't understand was why he'd returned to work in London full-time. She'd thought those days were behind him; that leaving London was the whole point of moving to the countryside. She'd thought he'd have more time for the twins.

Thea decided to take her things up to the spare bedroom she'd stayed in before, and then find Toby. Perhaps she'd get a better reception from him, and even a friendly hello on her arrival. Somehow, she doubted it.

Thea left her shoes by the door, hoping Winston didn't chew them, and made her way upstairs. It was an L-shaped landing, painted in white, the floorboards bare. They were obviously waiting for carpet to be laid. Some electrical work looked as though it still needed doing, by the looks of the wires hanging down where a ceiling light should be. The spare bedroom hadn't changed. The single bed was made up, but it looked as though it had been slept in. Thea raised her eyebrows, wondering who else had been staying there.

'So, you're still here.'

Katie's voice came from right behind her, making her jump.

Thea glanced at her. 'I promised your dad that I'd look after you, and a promise is a promise.' She caught Katie pulling a sour face as she mouthed *a promise is a promise.*

'Well, it is,' said Thea.

'What do you mean, Dad's away at work?'

'He told me when I met him earlier at the station,' Thea replied.

'Not for work,' scoffed Katie.

'Then what for?'

'Oh, my god, how old are you?' Katie blurted sarcastically.

Thea stared at her. 'I have no idea what you are talking about.'

'My dad has not gone to London for work. I'm not surprised you don't know. I mean it's not like you bother to stay in touch with us, is it?'

Thea's mouth dropped open. She didn't know what to say because it was true. 'Sorry,' she mumbled.

Katie glanced at the spare bedroom. 'You'll need clean sheets. They're in the airing cupboard in the bathroom.'

'Which bathroom?'

'The one on this floor.'

Thea glanced up the second flight of stairs. She knew there were two further bedrooms in the attic. She turned her attention to the spare bedroom and walked in. When she turned around, Katie was still standing at the door. Thea asked, 'Have you had another guest?'

'Oh, my god.' Katie stared at her. 'Doesn't Mum tell you anything!?'

Thea watched her stomp off. If Katie wasn't just thirteen, and totally wrapped up in herself, perhaps she'd realise that her mum and sister no longer had the sort of close relationship they'd had when they were children.

'Where's Toby?' Thea called after her.

'How do I know? I'm not my brother's keeper.'

Thea sighed. Toby must have realised she was here. Their house was big, but wherever he was, he must have heard her arriving. *This is going to be a fun week*, thought Thea. She'd been insulted by one twin and ignored by the other. At least she'd made friends with the dog.

Along the landing and around the corner was Toby's bedroom. She left her suitcase, bag and coat in the spare bedroom. Stripping the bed could wait until later. She still wondered who'd been sleeping in the spare bedroom. Her thoughts turned to what Katie had just said. If Mark wasn't working in London, then what was more important than staying with the twins while their mother was in hospital?

Thea walked up to Toby's bedroom door and knocked.

'He's not in that room anymore,' Katie shouted out from her bedroom next door. 'He's in the attic.'

Thea headed up the next flight of stairs and knocked on Toby's door. There wasn't a sound. She opened the door to find him sitting on his bed, still wearing his school uniform. A pair of large wireless headphones covered his ears, flattening some of his wild black hair. He was staring at a laptop screen, playing a computer game.

Thea caught his attention, pointed at her head indicating for him to remove the headphones. Surprisingly, he did as she asked. If it had been Katie, Thea knew she wouldn't have complied.

Unlike his twin, Toby hadn't changed all that much since she'd seen him last. They were non-identical twins; Katie took after her mother with her blonde hair and fair skin. Her brother, born a few minutes after Katie, was just like his father, with his dark curly hair and skin that tanned. What the twins had in common, though, was their large brown eyes.

Toby stared at her sullenly.

'Hi Toby. I expect Mark, er … your father, told you I'd be coming to look—' She stopped abruptly, re-thinking what she was about to say. She decided to avoid using the terms *looking after* or *babysitting*. 'I'm here to hold the fort while your father is away in London. I'm sure your mum will be out of hospital soon.' Thea actually had no idea how long Jenna would be in hospital. She was hoping to find that out the next day during her visit.

Toby's response was to shrug. She remembered him as a happy-go-lucky little boy, always smiling. What she saw now was someone completely different. She was thinking that perhaps it was down to hormones, puberty. At least she hoped it was that, rather than the effect of anything going on at home.

Thea said, 'Your mum is going to be just fine.'

Toby stared at her.

'So, I expect you haven't had anything to eat. I'll go to the kitchen and …

'We had pizza already!' Katie shouted up the stairs.

Thea wasn't surprised that she was listening in. 'All right, well, I guess I'll get myself something to eat.' Thea watched Toby put his headphones back on. She looked at the dog, which was lying on his bed. She'd noticed that Winston's head had shot up at the words, *something to eat.* She ignored the dog and said, 'If you need anything or want to talk, I'll be downstairs.'

She got no response from Toby. He turned to his laptop and resumed the game. She did get a response from Winston, though. He jumped off the bed and came running up to her. For a split second, she thought he'd jump up, but this time, he sat at her feet, panting, and nudged her hand. 'Oh, er … good dog.' Thea gingerly patted his head. She got a paw for her efforts. 'Oh, right.' Thea took his paw and gave it a shake. 'Good dog. Now you stay there.'

Unfortunately, Thea did not speak dog. Winston didn't stay there. Instead, he decided he was following her downstairs.

Thea walked back down the stairs to the landing, the dog hot on her heels, and found Katie standing at her door, leaning against the doorframe, chewing gum. 'So, what did he say?'

'Nothing.'

'Yep, just as I thought. He's such a dumbass.'

This time Thea couldn't ignore her language. 'Really, Katie, that's a bit rude.'

'But he is. His grades are just rubbish, unlike mine. I'm in the top group at everything.'

She frowned at her niece. 'That's no way to talk about your brother.' Thea couldn't abide smugness. 'I bet you're not in the top group for modesty.' Thea said sarcastically.

'What's that supposed to mean?'

Thea grinned. 'Look it up. And while you're at it, don't call your brother a dumbass ever again. I bet he has hidden talents.'

'Oh yeah – like what?'

'Well, that's why their hidden. You'll find out one day, and then you'll eat humble pie.'

Katie turned around and slammed her door shut.

Thea sighed. Perhaps she should have kept her mouth shut, but she hadn't been able to. Did Jenna let her get away with speaking about her brother like that? If Katie's grandmother had been there, she'd have given her what for.

Thea turned from the door. She thought she heard the creak of a floorboard upstairs. When she looked up, she thought she caught a glimpse of Toby. Had he been standing on the landing listening to that exchange? She couldn't be sure.

Thea looked at the dog. 'Well, have you eaten yet?'

Winston barked.

She frowned at him. 'Is that one bark for yes, two for no?' She was joking of course, but Winston barked again – just the once. 'Well, all right then, let's go find you some dog food, shall we?'

She could tell Winston was about to give another bark, so she put a finger to her lips, shushing him, and whispered, 'Indoor voices, please,' just like her sister had done with the twins when they were little and were being loud and obnoxious. Thea smiled at Winston. She didn't know if she was a dog-person or a cat-person. They'd had a cat once, years and years ago when they'd lived in Suffolk. But never a dog. She didn't even know if she liked dogs. What Thea did know was that Winston's company was far preferable to that of the twins.

Winston looked at her, but didn't bark again.

'Good. I think we have an understanding.'

She watched the dog race downstairs. She found him in the kitchen, standing over his food bowl. 'Well, you're one smart pup, aren't you? Now, where is your dog food – eh?'

Winston raced over to a cupboard and nudged the cupboard door. Thea opened the cupboard but didn't find dog food. Instead, there were crisps and chocolate bars. 'Oh, no. They are not for you.' She hunted through the cupboards and didn't find any dog food at all. 'Okay, that's weird.' She looked at Winston. She guessed why Mark hadn't mentioned the dog. It would be just one more thing she was responsible for.

'Good grief. Where on earth is your food?' Thea turned full circle in the kitchen and caught sight of a detached, single-storey red-brick building adjacent to the house. 'The garage – of course!' She'd forgotten about the garage. It was accessed from the street but to the side of the house, so that you had to drive past the side of the house and up a short drive.

Thea opened the patio doors and stepped out into the garden to take the short-cut across the lawn, hoping the side door into the garage wasn't locked.

Winston seemed to know where she was going – and why. He bounded after her and reached the door first. This time, he barked.

21

When she opened the door, Winston barged past her, heading straight to a large plastic storage container, where she guessed the dog food was kept. Thea stopped inside the entrance and waited for her eyes to adjust to the gloom.

She walked over to the plastic container, took off the lid and reached inside for a tin of dog food. She noticed a large bag of dried biscuits and a small empty plastic bowl. There was a plastic scoop, which she used to put some dog biscuits in the bowl.

Winston stuck his snout in the biscuit bag. 'Hey.' Thea nudged him out of the way and put the lid back on the container. She had an idea why the food was kept out here, away from prying snouts.

'Come on.' Thea picked up the can of dog food and the bowl and looked around the garage. There was an old car which belonged to Mark, and in the far corner were piles of boxes. Thea put the dog food down for a moment and found the light switch. She pulled the cord, flooding the garage with light from the single light bulb and walked over to the boxes, which were stacked rather haphazardly. There were a couple of Persian rugs, and a large ornamental lamp, the base in the shape of an elephant's head. It was obviously too large to fit in a box. Thea recognised these. All this stuff belonged to her mum; she was storing her personal belongings in Jenna's garage while she was travelling. Her furniture was still in the flat that Gracie was renting.

She remembered that during her last visit, she'd been into the garage to get into Jenna's car. She'd not taken much notice of the boxes, but she did remember that they had been neatly stacked and sealed; she had carried them in there herself after her mum had packed them, and there had been a small plastic sheet covering them because the garage roof leaked sometimes.

Thea stared at them. All the boxes had been opened, and it had not been done carefully – they were torn in some places, as though someone had opened them in a hurry. They were no longer neatly stacked; each box had obviously been searched through before being haphazardly stacked again, and whoever had done this hadn't even bothered to seal them up. The plastic sheet was dumped beside them. Thea thought of the photo albums, books and personal belongings that should not be open to the elements, or to dust and mice. She glanced inside one precariously balanced box. Inside, her mother's possessions, which Thea had watched being carefully packed, looked as though they'd been pulled out and then just dumped back inside the box. She tidied the contents of the box, thinking *Who would do this? And what were they looking for?*

She was about to walk around to the front of the garage and see if the lock was broken or had been tampered with when she realised that the side door into the garage from the garden was left unlocked, and the garden was not secure; there was just a rickety gate to prevent people wandering off the street into the back garden. She knew why that was; apart from the odd walker, or person living in the village, it wasn't as though they got a lot of traffic – foot traffic or otherwise – past their home.

Thea thought perhaps she'd mention it to Mark. They should get a padlock for the door. And while she was at it, she'd mention to him that someone had been in his garage, rifling through her mum's things. She knew there were some nice ornaments that might fetch some money.

She decided that after she'd fed the dog, she would come back, go through the rest of the boxes, and then tape them up. She'd hate to think of her mum returning suddenly and discovering that her personal possessions were not how she'd left them. The boxes would take some time to sort out, but she had all evening. It wasn't like she had anything better to do.

Winston came running over and poked his nose into one of the boxes.

'Hey!'

She noticed that the dog was licking his chops. She looked at him. 'What have you been up to?' Thea discovered that the plastic pot she'd filled with dog biscuits was empty. She put her hands on her hips. She didn't know much about looking after pets, but she imagined the biscuits were probably meant to be mixed in with the wet food. Thea picked up the tin and looked at the dog. 'Come on.'

She stepped out of the garage with the excitable golden retriever sniffing the tin in her hand as she walked across the lawn.

22

Thea found a can opener and opened the tin of dog food. 'Oh, my god. That smells rank.' Holding it at arm's length, she spooned the congealed meat into the dog bowl. For once, Winston wasn't jumping up at her or kneading her arm with his muzzle. He sat quite still, watching.

Thea placed it on a plastic mat next to a bowl of water. While Winston wolfed down his dinner, Thea went upstairs, thinking of the other possible explanation for the open boxes.

She knocked on Katie's door.

'What do you want now?'

Thea couldn't remember ever being that rude when she was a teenager. Although Thea's mum had been fun, she had also been strict; she'd had to be, raising two teenage girls on her own.

Thea opened Katie's bedroom door. 'I want to speak to you about something.'

Katie was sitting cross-legged on her pink duvet, doing something on her mobile phone. 'Not now, I'm busy.'

'Has someone broken into the garage?"

That question got Katie's attention. She lowered her phone. 'No, I don't think so. Why do you ask?'

'Because your grandmother's boxes have been opened and rifled through.'

Katie stared at her.

'Have you been through Grandma's boxes in the garage?'

'What do you mean – *been through Grandma's boxes*?'

'What I said – have you opened them and rifled through them?'

'No! Why would I be interested in an old person's stuff?'

'That is not a nice way to speak about your grandmother.'

'Well, it's true. She's old. How old are *you*? I heard Mum telling Dad that she doesn't think you'll ever settle down and get married – let alone have kids. Don't you want children?'

Thea ignored the remark. She was not getting into a conversation about her love life with her rude thirteen-year-old niece. 'So, you don't know anything about Grandma's boxes?'

'Of course not.' She furrowed her brow, as though something had occurred to her.

'What is it?' asked Thea noticing her expression.

'It's probably nothing, but Toby is into old stuff.'

'Old stuff?'

'Don't ask – he's weird like that.'

Thea had it on the tip of her tongue to tell her not to call her brother weird, but she let it go this time, interested to hear what Katie had to say about her brother in this instance. 'How so?'

Katie put her phone down. 'He's just into old stuff. When Mum takes us into Aldeburgh to meet our friends at the weekend, I meet up with my friend, but he doesn't. We followed him once to Cobblers Yard. I guess that's where he's been hanging out.'

'Cobblers Yard?'

'Yeah – it's a little shopping street, well, not a street – more like a … yard. There's not much there.'

Thea remembered Cobblers Yard. She hadn't been there for years. That's where her father's old bookshop had been – she was sure of it. Katie hadn't mentioned that her grandfather used to run a bookshop there, so Thea imagined her sister probably hadn't mentioned that fact. There would be little point.

There was no way the bookshop would still there after all these years, so it wasn't as though they could visit the shop and reminisce. 'What does Toby do in Cobblers Yard?' Thea asked, interested to know.

'How do I know? It's so small that if we actually followed him, he'd see us. I think he goes to the old antique shop. That would be right up his street.'

'Why do you think that?'

'Doh! Because it sells old stuff.'

It hadn't taken long for the sarcasm to resurface, Thea noticed.

'I told you he's weird. I wish he wasn't my brother.'

What Thea was gleaning was that she was embarrassed. 'But not everyone can be little Miss Popular.'

'Well, I am *not* little Miss Popular since I started high school.'

Shit, Thea silently swore. She hadn't meant to say that out loud.

Katie frowned at her. 'I never wanted to move out of London. I hate it here.'

Thea thought of Mark returning to London; perhaps the fact that Katie's father had returned to London had something to do with Katie's unhappiness, finding it hard to settle down in her new circumstances in Suffolk. Thea had hardly been here, but she was already gleaning that perhaps her sister's life here wasn't all roses around the door as she'd made out.

'But I thought you were on your phone to your school friends?'

'Doh! No. I do have a friend from school, but she's not my

best friend. I just hang out with her because there's no one else.' Katie made it sound as though she was doing this girl a favour.

Katie suddenly smiled the sweetest smile, taking Thea aback. She was a very pretty young lady when she wasn't pouting. 'Auntie Thea …'

Thea looked at her, disconcerted by the sudden smile, not to mention her niece calling her Auntie Thea – something she had not done since she was little.

'Yes …?'

'Can I come and live with you in London?'

'What?'

'Then I can go to school with all my real friends. I won't be a bother, I promise. You'll hardly know I'm there.'

Thea stared at her, thinking, *You can't be serious.* She wouldn't even consider it. She had enough going on in her life without a teenager living with her. Even so, she said, 'What about your mum and dad?'

'What about them?'

'You'd miss them.'

'Would I? They argue *all* the time.'

'Really?'

'Yeah – since we moved here.'

'What about?' Thea had thought they were happy. That was always the impression her sister gave. Perhaps it was Mark, and he wasn't happy moving out of London. Perhaps that was why he'd returned there to work.

Katie sighed heavily. 'Money – what else? I hear them having rows about the cost of heating oil.'

'Heating oil?'

'Yeah. I mean, we don't have gas here. But it's a village in the middle of nowhere – what did they expect?'

The place wasn't in the middle of nowhere. It might feel that way in the house, which was surrounded by countryside and one-track lanes meandering through the Suffolk countryside, but there was actually a lot to do – nearby Woodbridge had an independent cinema and a public pool, and there was even a private pool and gym at a hotel and spa just five minutes away by car. And the Suffolk Coast was just a twenty-minute drive away. What was not to like? Thea frowned.

'There – you see?' said Katie pointing at her. 'You agree with me. This place is, like, really crap. I mean there is nothing, and I mean *nothing* to do, unless you're my brother and like old stuff. But even he has to be ferried around in the car. We can't walk out of our front door and go anywhere. I'd rather live in a city any day.'

Katie had misread her thoughts. She wasn't frowning because she agreed with her sentiments – far from it. She remembered her father saying when she was little that he was saving up to buy them a family home; he wanted to buy the cottage they were renting in the countryside. It had been an idyllic childhood until they'd moved to London with their mum.

Thea had only been back in Suffolk a short time, but unlike her other occasional trips to see her sister, this time she felt differently here; she felt happy. Perhaps it was the fond childhood memories. Thea tried to ignore her feelings. She thought of her job and her flat. Her whole life was in London. There was nothing for her here – apart from her sister, and her niece and nephew whom she rarely saw, apart from for fleeting visits.

She was surprised that Katie wanted to come and live with her, but perhaps she wasn't surprised that she wanted to return to London. It was where she had been born and brought up. An outgoing young girl, Katie was finding it hard settling into her new circumstances.

It didn't sound as though the rows over money were helping. Looking around their home, which still wasn't finished after all these months, it made her wonder whether, given the escalating bills for running a house this size, they'd run out of money.

She looked at Katie. 'So, you think your brother went through the boxes?'

Katie rolled her eyes. 'Duh! Didn't you listen to a word I just said?'

'Don't be rude, Katie.'

'You're not my mum. You can't tell me what to do.'

Thea had been expecting that. She sighed and closed the door. She glanced up the stairs. Just then, she didn't fancy confronting Toby over the boxes, even though she wanted to know what he'd been looking for. She'd had enough teenage cheek for one day. She looked at Winston. He was standing by her side, looking up at her. 'What do you want?' Thea said, annoyed that since she'd fed him, he seemed to be following her everywhere.

Thea returned to the kitchen and hunted through drawers and cupboards until she'd found what she was looking for; a pair of scissors and some sticky tape. On her way out of the kitchen, she tried to shut Winston in before she went out into the garden, but he wasn't having any of it; he poked his head out of the patio door every time she tried to close it. 'Oh, all right. Come on then, if you must. But you are not getting any more biscuits.'

Five minutes later, Thea found she wasn't getting anywhere with sorting through the boxes because Winston insisted on putting his nose into everything. Thea had put a box on a work bench, and was trying to sort through the contents before repacking and taping it up. 'For goodness' sake! Why do people have dogs? You are beyond irritating!'

Winston nudged her hand for a stroke. Thea had no choice but to pat his head and stroke his smooth fur. 'Now, are you satisfied you've got my attention?'

Winston barked in her face.

Thea looked at him. 'You're not going to leave me in peace, are you?' She glanced over at the plastic container. A moment later, Winston was occupied, eating more dog biscuits outside.

Thea shut the door to the garage, leaving the dog eating his biscuits in the garden. She hoped she didn't regret it. She imagined that in a few minutes she'd hear him howling outside, wanting to be let in.

As Thea started sorting through her mum's possessions and taping up the boxes, she heard a whine outside. She rolled her eyes, expecting Winston to start barking. There was a window next to the door. Thea resisted walking over and glancing outside in case Winston spotted her.

The whining continued, but she ignored it as she took another box and started tidying up the contents. She was still wondering what Toby had been looking for. So far, she couldn't tell if anything was missing. Although she'd helped her mum pack up her things, she hadn't helped her with all the boxes, so she had no idea what was in some of them.

She had suggested to her mum that she let some of the stuff go to charity shops; there were lots of little ornaments she'd collected over time, old dog-eared paperback books, travel books, and a lot of other things that Thea recognised from her childhood. She had asked what the point was of keeping it all. She had thought perhaps that with her mum's new life and her travelling, she would let some things go. She had been surprised when her mum had refused to even consider it; had said she didn't want to hear another word on the matter. It had led to a row and to Thea walking out, because she knew what it was about. Despite appearances, her mum still hadn't let go of the past – let go of her husband.

Thea had also suggested getting rid of her and her sister's old schoolbooks and artwork, which her mum had religiously kept over the years, but she knew her mum wouldn't. Thea taped up those boxes and moved on to the last two boxes, which were full of old clothes, coats and handbags. Like the boxes containing the schoolbooks, the boxes had been opened, but she could tell the contents had been left untouched.

She stood back and surveyed the newly stacked boxes thinking that perhaps when her mum returned from Nepal and started her yoga practice, she would be ready to let all this stuff go.

Thea opened the door and was immediately confronted by Winston, who was furiously wagging his tail, barking, and jumping up at her as though she'd been gone for days. 'Hey!' Thea thought that Winston really needed some doggy training classes. If she had been planning to be around a bit longer, she would have offered to take the dog to a class herself.

She went back to the house and looked at the two boxes of pizza that Mark must have ordered in before he left. She opened them. The twins had ordered one each, which was too much to eat, and both had several leftover slices. Thea chose a couple of slices of peperoni pizza and found a plate in one of the cupboards, along with an open bottle of white wine in the fridge. She poured herself a glass and sat on a stool at the kitchen island in the centre of the room, eating the pizza and admiring her surroundings. She remembered the small, cramped kitchen and original dining room. Now, the white, high-gloss kitchen with its wooden worktop complemented the light oak wooden flooring, and she loved the light and airy space they'd created by adding the dining area extension with its skylights.

She turned in her stool to look out at the garden through the patio doors. The large patio must have set them back a good amount of money, as must the landscaped back garden. Although the garden wasn't very large, it was walled, and had lots of privacy from the road. She frowned at the thought that they hadn't bothered to replace the old rickety gate between the wall and the garage, meaning that anyone could just walk into the back of the house. Getting a padlock would be no good. The gate was so low that anyone could just hop over it.

Thea reminded herself that it was probably Toby who had rifled through her mum's stuff rather than a trespasser. She finished the pizza and the glass of wine and looked at the time. It was seven o'clock. Should she ask the twins if they had homework and remind them to get it done? What time did they go to bed now they were in high school?

Thea had babysat for them before, but when they were younger, they'd had a bedtime routine. She'd give them a beaker of milk each, remind them to clean their teeth, and then read them a bedtime story together in Katie's bed before Toby settled down in his own bedroom next door. She'd tucked them in and give them a kiss goodnight, setting their little night lights so they weren't scared of the dark – or in Toby's case the monster under the bed.

Thea stared into space wistfully. She'd enjoyed those times, and had loved it when they'd gone to sleep. Then, she had always carefully put away all their toys. Everything had become orderly and the house had been neat and tidy. In those moments, she had longed for a family of her own – until the next morning, when there was chaos, and noise, and mess, and she had longed for the haven of her flat and her job at the museum.

Thea's wistful meander into the past was rudely interrupted by Katie shouting out, 'Where is it, Toby? I want it back!'

Thea cast her gaze to the heavens and caught Winston, who was lying on his doggy cushion in the dining room, doing the same. She looked at the dog. 'Do you want to go up there and see what's going on, or shall I?'

Winston put his head back on his paws and closed his eyes.

'I said – give it back!'

Thea downed the last of her wine, realised she felt a little light-headed – it was a huge glass – and reluctantly left the table.

As she walked up the stairs, she heard Katie shouting, 'Why do you always take stuff without asking!'

Thea thought of her mum's things again. She wondered if he'd taken anything.

At the top of the stairs, she saw that Katie's bedroom door was wide open but that she was nowhere to be seen. Thea sighed and started up the next flight. Katie was banging on Toby's door and trying the handle.

Thea noted that the door was locked. That wasn't good. What if he refused to go to school the next day? Thea rubbed her forehead. She wished she hadn't agreed to help out. If she hadn't, Mark wouldn't have been able to swan off to London; he'd be the one dealing with all this.

Katie banged on his door again. 'I mean it, Toby. I need my compass. I've got homework due in tomorrow. What is wrong with you?'

Thea smiled when she realised Katie was doing schoolwork. She was going to tell Katie to leave her brother alone – but not anymore. A stair creaked underfoot.

Katie turned around. 'What do *you* want?'

'I heard you shouting, so I came to see what was going on.'

'What's going on is he's always going through my stuff.' She turned to the door. 'I know you've got it, Toby. Don't pretend like you don't know what I'm talking about.'

Thea was just wondering how to deal with this situation, when she heard the sound of a key turning the lock. Toby opened the door.

Katie unfolded her arms and held out her hand.

Thea noted that Toby wasn't playing computer games. There was an open textbook on his desk, and what appeared to be a paper for school he was writing on his laptop. He walked over to his desk and picked up a compass. It looked old-fashioned, with a gold case and slightly chipped glass casing. The words *North*, *South*, *East* and *West* were in old-fashioned lettering.

'It's mine,' said Toby.

'No, it's not. You said you found it, and I paid you for it – remember?'

Toby slapped it in her hand and slammed the door shut.

Thea stared at the door. She guessed it wasn't the right moment to bring up the subject of the boxes in the garage with him.

'That's just rude,' said Katie.

You should know, Thea thought, but kept it to herself. She looked at Katie and thought how sad the situation was, given how close the twins had been as children. She looked at the old compass. 'You paid him for it?'

'Yes, he wanted some money, and he'd used up all his pocket

money. I needed this for a school project, so it was a win-win.'

Thea glanced at the door. She had got a different impression; Toby obviously regretted selling the compass to his sister. 'Where did he get it?'

She shrugged. 'I don't know.' She frowned.

'But you've got a theory?' Thea prompted.

'I think he stole it from the old antique shop in Cobblers Yard.'

'Perhaps he bought it?'

'How? He uses all his money on video games.'

'I really don't think he'd do a thing like that – stealing, I mean.' She knew the twins were given an awful lot, and never went without – they always had the latest trainers, laptops, iPads, everything. There was no reason for them to steal.

Even so, Thea decided that in the morning, when they'd both cooled off, she was going to ask Toby about his grandma's boxes.

23

'Why would I want to go through Grandma's boxes?'

It was the following morning, and they were all sitting on stools at the kitchen island, eating breakfast cereal. Thea hadn't slept well in the single bedroom; she'd been afraid she'd miss the alarm and had imagined all sorts of catastrophes – maybe the twins wouldn't get up, or wouldn't get dressed in their uniforms, or would refuse to go to school. Then the school would ring her up and tell her off for not making sure they attended. And they'd fine her for every day the twins weren't at school; that's what schools did now – wasn't it? Thea's morning went nothing like she imagined. When she had knocked on the twins' doors to wake them up, they had both already been awake and were showering in their ensuite bathrooms. They had both appeared for breakfast dressed in their school uniforms, with their school bags packed and ready to go. Toby had kept diligently checking his watch to make sure they weren't late for the school bus.

Everything had gone swimmingly until Thea had raised the issue of the boxes.

'I didn't even know they were in the garage. What are they doing there anyhow?'

Thea sighed. She'd known he'd deny it. A sarcastic remark was on the tip of her tongue; he knew Grandma had left them there before her travels.

'Whatever is missing, I did not take it.'

Thea eyed him. 'Why do you think something is missing?'

'Well, that's what you're accusing me of, isn't it? Taking something?'

Before Thea had a chance to say anything, he turned to his sister and said, 'What have you been saying about me?'

'Katie dropped her eyes to the table, looking contrite. 'Nothing.'

'Yeah – right.' Toby got up from the table, picked up his uneaten slice of toast and grabbed his bag.

'Where are you going?' Katie asked.

'To catch the bus – what do you think?'

'But it's not going to arrive for another twenty minutes.'

'I don't care. I'm going to walk to the pick-up point and wait with my friends.'

Katie replied, 'You haven't got any friends.'

'Yeah, well maybe I'll make some.'

'Yeah – right,' Katie said under her breath as Toby walked to the kitchen door. He must have heard her remark because he turned around and glared at her.

Thea decided to try and defuse the situation by changing the subject. She had a question to ask them both. 'Toby, before you go. I'm going to visit your mother today. Would you two like to visit her too after school?'

Toby nodded.

Katie said, 'Yes, please. Um … can we go into town afterwards and get an ice cream?'

'You mean, can you go into town and meet the girls you're so desperately trying to be friends with because they are like, sooo popular.' Toby pulled a face.

Thea looked from Katie to Toby and back again.

Katie said, 'You're just jealous because you haven't got any friends and it means you'll just hang out on your own.'

Thea sighed heavily. She couldn't wait until the weekend when Mark would return and she could go home. Thea had had enough of the twins' squabbling, although it did bring to mind the fights she'd had with her sister when they were young. Her lips curled into a wisp of a smile.

She said, 'That's settled then. Shall I pick you up from school, or can the school bus drop you in Aldeburgh?'

Katie shook her head. 'There is a school bus that goes to Aldeburgh, but that's not our one. We'd have to pay extra for that.'

Thea didn't even hesitate. 'I'll give you the money.'

'It doesn't work like that. You pay termly.'

Thea wasn't about to pay for a whole term for one trip.

'And it needs to be organised with the head so they have the correct numbers for the bus.'

'I see.' Thea stopped reaching for her handbag, disappointed that she had to pick them up from school. 'Where do you go to school, exactly?' She knew it was Leiston, but didn't know the name of the school.

Kate pointed at her blazer. 'Alde Academy. It's not far from Aldeburgh.'

'Okay.' Thea was looking forward to seeing them off and having the whole day to herself. 'What time do I pick you up?'

'Three.'

Thea put her spoon down. She couldn't have heard that right.

'I'm sorry – what?'

'Three in the afternoon. That's when the afternoon lessons finish.'

Thea glanced at Toby, who was standing by the door, hooking his bag over his shoulder and nodding.

'Haven't you got any after-school clubs?'

They both shook their heads. 'We can't afford it,' said Katie. 'I wanted to join the drama club.'

Thea looked at her. Since when were school clubs not free? She asked them that question. And since when did her sister and brother-in-law not have any money? He had a good job in the city.

Katie shrugged. 'I guess because they are a drama group separate from the school, they have to pay for using the facilities, and so the teacher charges for the lessons. I don't really know how it works, but I wish I could afford to go.'

'How much are they?'

Katie frowned. 'A lot.'

'How much is a lot?'

'I don't know really.'

Thea wasn't exactly flush with cash either. The archivist job she enjoyed wasn't the best-paid job in the world, although unlike her sister, she didn't have a mortgage – just bills. It meant she could save a good proportion of her income. She expected that most people her age would love to get on the housing ladder and have their own place. She had it even better – all because her mum had converted the family home so that Thea had one flat, and her sister the other when their mum 'popped her clogs', as she often phrased it, although Thea didn't want to think about that.

As Jenna was married, and had a home of her own, their mum hadn't envisaged she'd need the flat, or the money out of it, just yet. But Thea knew there was nothing stopping her sister from selling it if she wanted the cash.

Their mum had included a legal clause when she'd signed over the property. She had a right to stay in the property until she died. The problem was that the legal document didn't specify which flat she had a right to stay in; just that she could live in the house. She'd set up the legal side of things before converting the house. That had been an oversight on her mum's part. Thea hadn't been unduly bothered about it – she hadn't envisaged that her sister would want to sell up her share of the house just yet. But from some things she'd heard, Thea was no longer so sure.

What if Jenna sold up, and her mum came to live in Thea's flat? If the thought of sharing her personal space with a man she was in love with was a problem, then living with her mum again – who, like her sister, was not the tidiest of people – filled her with dread. She made a mental note to email her mum again; someone had to tell her about Jenna's accident. Not that she imagined her mum would hurry home from her yoga retreat in Nepal, but it was certainly possible.

Thea's thoughts turned to Katie and her drama lessons. 'Look, when I pick you up from school, I'll have a quick word with your drama teacher.'

'I told you – Mum hasn't got the money.'

'Well, I have. So let's get you signed up for those, shall we?'

Katie stared at her. 'For real?'

'Yes, for real.'

And for the first time since Thea had arrived, Katie smiled. Little dimples appeared on each cheek as she grinned at Thea, flashing the orthodontic wires that were straightening her teeth. Thea could still see in her the little girl with the straight fringe and pigtails, and the freckles over her little button nose – freckles that were now hidden by makeup. Thea affectionately returned her smile.

'I can't wait to tell my friend.' Katie got out her phone.

'So, I'll pick you both up after school.'

Katie nodded, already on the phone to her friend, thoughts of her mum stuck in a hospital bed with a broken leg now far from her mind.

'I'll see you at three, then.' She guessed that if it was just a few minutes down the road to Aldeburgh, then getting to Leiston would only take about half an hour. Still, she imagined that it wouldn't feel like very long before she was leaving to pick them up. She was looking forward to having the house to herself – to read a book, mooch around, and just kick back; to do nothing, and think of Miles while wallowing in self-pity. She knew she shouldn't have let Gracie railroad her into taking time off work.

'You will have to get there really early, though, because parking is a bitch.'

Thea raised her eyebrows. 'Katie, language!'

'Well, it is. That's what Mum says, although now they can't afford the school bus, so after this term, Mum's going to have to come and pick us up, in between work.'

'I'm sorry – what did you just say?'

'Mum is going to be taking us to school.'

'No, not that. You mentioned she's going to work?'

Katie nodded.

'What is it she's doing for work?' Thea was interested; her sister wasn't exactly careerist – far from it. Ever since she'd left school and started work in an office, she'd been on the lookout for a husband – or someone else's husband, as it happened – with whom she could have children and who would look after her financially. Jenna once told her that her job was being a housewife and a mother; once she had children, she had no intention of returning to work. Ever. So, this job was news to Thea.

'I don't know,' Katie replied in answer to Thea's question, and returned her attention to her phone.

'Is she working locally?'

Katie shrugged. 'I guess.'

Thea was about to ask Toby, but he'd left for the bus. Thea looked at the clock on the wall.

Katie followed her gaze. She got off the stool and picked up her bag.

Thea had a thought. 'Hey, what about lunch?'

'Oh, yeah – right. We have school dinners.'

Thea wondered why, if money was tight, they didn't just take a sandwich. On the other hand, it saved her from having to make them.

'Until the end of term – then we've got to have packed lunches.'

'I see.' So money really was tight. Jenna had made it sound as though her life had really come together since they'd moved out of London. Thea was starting to realise that was far from the case.

'We should have stayed in London,' said Katie. 'Then everything wouldn't have gone wrong.' She headed out of the kitchen.

Thea didn't know what to say to that. She followed her to the front door. 'Well, um, have a good day.'

Just then, Katie got a text on her phone. She started texting as she walked out of the door. Thea asked, 'Are you meant to take mobile phones to school?' She got no response. She stood at the door, arms folded, watching her niece – who was wearing a very short skirt – heading out of the door and down the lane. She spotted her nephew walking ahead, discreetly hanging back. She guessed he was taking his time, keeping an eye out for his sister. There was no need, really. Thea hadn't heard a single car all morning. She imagined she'd be lucky to see a handful of people all day in Pettistree – perhaps a neighbour, or some walkers venturing from Wickham Market and stopping in the village pub.

Thea closed the front door. She turned around and nearly fell over the dog. 'Winston! You'll cause an accident one of these days.'

Thea's sister came to mind. She looked at the dog. *Perhaps you already have*, she thought.

24

Thea closed the front door. She was looking forward to seeing her sister, but wondering what on earth had gone so wrong with their financial situation that she'd had to return to work – although she wouldn't be working for the next few weeks, unless she could work from home, and her job was desk-based.

Apart from spotting an old laptop gathering dust in the lounge, Thea hadn't seen a spare room set up as a study. She had looked through the window of the summerhouse in the garden, but that wasn't a home office either. Thea found the hoover, and decided to vacuum round the house and nosy around. Half an hour later, she'd been in every room and had found no computers, laptops or office equipment that suggested either Jenna or Mark were working from home.

While she was hoovering and cleaning the bathrooms – there were three ensuites, a family bathroom, and a downstairs cloakroom – Thea found a pile of ironing in the utility room on top of the washing machine. Before she found the ironing board, she used her mobile phone to search for information about the hospital. Despite promising Toby and Katie she'd take them to visit their mum after school, she realised she didn't know the visiting hours. She was hoping to pop along that morning as well; she didn't want to wait all day to see Jenna. However, she was disappointed to learn that visiting hours were in the afternoon.

Thea wanted a private conversation with her sister to find out what was going on; she'd discovered there were none of Mark's clothes in the ironing or the laundry. She finished the piles of ironing and took the clothes upstairs, depositing Katie's and Toby's in their bedrooms.

Thea returned to her room, picked up the pile of used bed-sheets she'd left in a pile last night when she'd made up the bed with fresh sheets, and headed downstairs to the utility room. As she was loading the washing machine, she guessed who had been using the spare bedroom – Mark.

As Thea pressed the start button on the washing machine, she heard the sound of a mobile phone. She knew it wasn't hers; she didn't recognise the ringtone. She raced into the kitchen. It was Jenna's phone. Was it the school contacting her because something had happened to one of the twins? Or maybe one of them had mouthed off in class and was suspended?

If Mark and Jenna had split up, wouldn't that be par for the course, that one or both of the twins would go off the rails? But they'd got up, showered, and got dressed in their uniforms, and they had done their homework the previous night. They were acting like it was another ordinary week in their household. But it wasn't – not at all.

Perhaps she was reading way too much into the situation; Mark had just found a more lucrative job in the city to help pay the bills, so it probably wasn't as bad as Thea thought at all.

She knew why she'd jumped to conclusions; after what Miles had done, Thea couldn't imagine trusting anyone else, not even her brother-in-law. Not any man. Thea grabbed her bag, fumbled inside for the phone, and answered it. 'Hello?'

'Hello Jenna.'

Under normal circumstances, if she'd had to answer someone else's phone, she would have immediately corrected the caller as to the identity of the person they were speaking to – but Thea was so surprised by the sound of the caller's voice on the end of the phone that she barely managed a 'Yes?' The voice sounded inhuman, like something she'd heard once on a Hollywood movie where the caller had disguised their voice. It sounded as though she was talking to a computer.

She wasn't surprised the caller wouldn't question who they were speaking to. Thea knew that she and her sister sounded alike.

'I would like to acquire the package.'

'The package?'

'You know – the book.'

'All right.' Thea didn't know what else to say.

'We talked of a figure before. Is that still agreeable?'

The disguised voice sent shivers down her spine. She had the urge to put the phone down, but if the caller had her sister's mobile phone number, perhaps they knew where she lived too.

Her mum's boxes in the garage came to mind. She rolled her eyes. What would someone want with her mum's old things?

'Are you still there?' the artificial voice on the end of the phone asked.

'Yes.'

'So, what are your thoughts? Are you agreeable to the arrangement?'

Agreeable to the arrangement? Thea had no clue what this was about, but she did get the impression she wasn't speaking to someone of her generation; she imagined they could be middle-aged, perhaps older.

'Remind me what figure we were talking about.'

'I see. All right. I'll up the figure. I remember you asked for more money before. Ten is my client's final offer.'

Thea raised her eyebrows. *His client.* So the caller was a go-between, acting on behalf of someone. What was with all this cloak-and-dagger stuff about for what she presumed was a second-hand book? 'I suppose ten pounds sounds fair,' Thea said.

The caller on the end of the phone started to laugh, the synthesised voice sounding even more creepy – if that were possible. Thea held the phone away from her ear until she heard him – she presumed it was a man, but really had no idea because their voice was disguised – speak again.

'Ah, okay, I get it. We are speaking in code. Now, are we going to make the transaction in the same way as before?'

That's a good question, thought Thea, considering that her sister was laid up in hospital with a broken leg. She presumed the caller had no clue about her accident.

She played along, thinking that perhaps this was her sister's new job, selling second-hand books. It wouldn't exactly make her a millionaire, but she guessed every little helped, especially if Jenna had a lot of books to sell.

Thea frowned. She'd just hoovered around her sister's house and hadn't found any books, apart from some dog-eared paper-backs she'd read in the past and some hardback bestsellers she'd been bought as birthday and Christmas presents.

Thea thought again of her mum's things stored in the garage. She'd been through those boxes just to tidy them up and there hadn't been any particularly interesting books there either –

certainly none that would fetch ten pounds from a strange caller masking their identity.

Thea really wanted to end the call, but she decided that she owed it to her sister to collect the money, even if it was only a tenner. The problem was that she had no clue what book they were talking about. Thea didn't want to lose the sale, but she had to stall the buyer. She was going to see her sister that afternoon. Jenna could tell her where it was.

Thea was still interested to know which book the caller was referring to, in case she did come across it. 'Can you remind me which book we're talking about? I've got other books on the go that I'm selling,' Thea wished she'd just told the person on the end of the line the truth from the off – that she wasn't Jenna.

'You've got other interested parties? I didn't think that was the case.'

Thea frowned. That wasn't what she'd said.

'You want more money?'

'No, no. That's not what I meant.'

'So, it's agreed. 10k.'

Thea frowned. She hadn't heard that synthesised voice right, surely. 'Did you just say ten *thousand* pounds?'

'Well, I'm glad we're in agreement. I will organise the drop and text you.'

'The drop?'

'Yes, like before.'

'Like before?' Thea raised her eyebrows.

'I'll leave the money in a bag by the shop door. You collect the money and deposit the book in the bag. I'll be watching, so I'll know if you take the money and don't leave the item.'

'When will that be?' Thea couldn't believe she was acting as though she was going to go along with this. Ten thousand pounds for a book. As an archivist, she knew this person was either a collector, or working on someone else's behalf. And the only books that fetched that sort of money, serious money, were rare, highly collectable books that normally surfaced at auctions, sold by a collector or a museum.

An auction could be quite the event, with a lot of bidders, and the best way to achieve the highest financial return from the sale. The fact that they were doing this under the radar, rather than in an official capacity through an auction house, meant only one thing: the book's provenance was dubious – to say the least. Thea swallowed. If the provenance of the item was shady, meaning the previous owners were not clear, the chances were that it was stolen, or had been at some point in the past. That meant that if it ever resurfaced officially, the parties handling it could be arrested.

Thea swallowed again, realising she could have no part in this. She didn't want to get into trouble with the law; she couldn't, not even for her sister. *But if I don't follow through, the buyer knows my sister's phone number.* It didn't mean they knew where she lived, though. But they knew her name, so there was always that possibility.

Thea shook her head. If Jenna wanted the money, then she'd have to deal with the buyer herself, broken leg or not. Besides, she had no idea where the drop was; the caller had mentioned something about a shop. She couldn't very well ask him to remind her where it was, otherwise he really would get suspicious. Thea couldn't believe her sister was handling stolen books. Did she even realise what she was getting herself into?

Thea started to wonder where her sister had even found a rare collectable book, and how she would even know one when she saw one. She'd gone to university for the nightlife, and to put off going to work for three more years, and had barely scraped a pass in her degree. She had never been into anything like that.

As soon as Thea ended the call, she rushed out of the kitchen, followed by Winston, who was still following her around like a lost puppy. Thea stopped at the door to the garage at the bottom of the garden. She looked at the dog. 'Stay.'

Winston sat down on his rump.

Thea smiled at him. 'Good boy.'

As soon as she opened the door, Winston lost his manners and barged past her, running straight up to the plastic storage box containing his food.

Thea sighed. Perhaps he'd thought she was holding the door open for him. That was when she realised she'd forgotten to give the dog his breakfast.

She walked up to the plastic storage box and scooped out some more dog biscuits, hoping she wasn't giving the dog too much, causing him to be sick all over the kitchen floor or something from being overfed.

She started to go through her mum's boxes one more time. She hadn't paid much attention to what was inside. There were ornaments and some paperwork, but there were also a few books she hadn't bothered to get out and look at the first time around; she'd just been intent on rearranging the contents so they were neat and tidy before re-sealing the boxes.

Thea felt a little guilty for going through her mum's things, even though she had helped her pack them up in the first place. She'd tried to remember what she'd helped her pack back at the flat in London, but she couldn't. It had been months earlier, and in that time she'd met Miles and been in the whirlwind of a relationship she had assumed was going to change her life. Not that she envisaged leaving her archiving job, or her flat, any time soon, but when she was with Miles, before she'd found out the truth, she had thought about him working abroad, and how her future might not be in London, or even in the UK.

For a creature of habit who craved order, routine, and her own personal space – something her therapist had suggested could be to do with her father walking out, and never coming back, when she was a child – Thea had assumed she was turning a corner by even contemplating a different future to the life she had in London. But now that was all gone.

Thea really did not want to think about Miles. She'd been in her early thirties when they'd first met. Next year she was thirty-four. Before she knew it she'd be forty. By the time her sister was her age, she'd married and had two children, and had moved to her dream house in the country – although it now appeared to Thea that the dream had turn sour.

It's not a competition, her mum had always said to her when she bemoaned the fact that Jenna seemed to have the perfect life.

But what constitutes a perfect life? her mother had once asked her. *I'll tell you what does – finding your soulmate.*

Thea stared at the boxes. If that was true, then her mum had had the perfect life – even though they'd never had much money, and the home of their own her husband had promised her had never materialised – because he had been her soulmate.

Thea sighed heavily and opened the boxes that she remembered had some books inside. There weren't many. After a quick look through them, she was satisfied that she hadn't missed anything; there was nothing of consequence – just some paperbacks she knew were her mum's favourites, a few cookery books, and some travel books. Thea picked up one of the travel books that caught her eye. It had a photo of an old VW campervan on the front. She remembered this one because it was just like the campervan her dad used to drive – except the one the front cover was orange. She vaguely recalled that his was yellow. Before their dad disappeared, her mum had planned for them to do some travelling in the old campervan. They had sometimes taken the van on day trips to beaches up and down the Suffolk Coast, but Thea knew her mum had more adventurous plans. Not as adventurous as Nepal, obviously, but she had wanted to travel more extensively in the UK, and perhaps further afield in Europe.

Thea stared at the travel book, wondering if that was what her dad had done – disappeared in that campervan after all. She raised her eyebrows; perhaps Mum's plans had given him an idea, and he'd decided he'd up and leave his family, and travel alone.

Thea frowned at the book in her hand. She felt cross with her mum for keeping it. She knew it was because it reminded her mum of happier times before her dad went missing – it was how Thea preferred to think of his disappearance, rather than accepting what was most likely the truth; that he'd walked out on them.

Thea didn't even bother putting the book neatly in the box. She threw it in and was about to seal up the box when she had a thought. She stared at the box. Then she felt something by her feet. She looked down to find Winston sitting there, licking his chops and looking up at her.

She smiled at the dog and patted his head. 'No more food, okay?'

Winston's head dropped, sad pleading eyes looking up at her, as though he'd understood every word she'd just said.

Thea ignored the sad, puppy dog eyes and looked at her watch.

She felt like phoning Mark and finding out what was going on. Why hadn't he said something at the train station? She didn't know what she expected he might have said. That he'd left Jenna? But had he?

'I'd rather speak to my sister,' she told Winston as she lifted the travel book back out of the box on her way out of the garage. She hadn't brought a book with her to read. It was something she always felt like doing when she went on holiday; buying some paperback books to read while she was away. Not that she went on too many holidays. She still had a load of annual leave she hadn't taken.

Now she understood why she was lucky if she got a weekend away with Miles. Doubtless he'd told his wife he was away on a work thing; what else could he have told his wife when he was spending a romantic long weekend in a fancy hotel with Thea? A weekend that Thea had paid for.

She winced when she remembered the lies he'd told her, that his money was tied up in offshore accounts, or that he hadn't got any pound sterling to settle the bill, or they wouldn't accept his foreign bank card. What a fool she'd been to believe his lies. Of course he couldn't pay for the breaks away, not on his bank card or even in cash, because his wife was bound to ask where the money had gone or possibly catch him out by seeing it on his bank statement.

She realised that this week away would the most time she'd spent on a break since she'd met Miles.

She returned to the house and stepped into the cosy lounge with its wooden flooring, white sofas, and big wall-hung television. She walked up to one of the windows and opened the curtains, planning to settle herself on the white, squishy sofa with a book.

She fancied a big mug of hot chocolate. She left the book on the coffee table and returned to the kitchen. She found some hot chocolate sachets and even some marshmallows, and there was a can of squirty cream in the fridge – all the things she expected would be around with children in the house.

Thea made herself a decadent hot chocolate with all the trimmings. She tried not to feel guilty about helping herself to their food and drinks. What else could she do? *Go and get some shopping*, thought Thea. But she was tired and didn't feel like it, not just then – although she would have to sort out dinner that evening. From what she had seen as she'd searched for the hot chocolate, there wasn't much for dinner. It was little wonder that Mark had ordered in pizza the previous night.

He hadn't left her any money to do some shopping. She wasn't surprised; if they were struggling for money, he was obviously hoping that she'd go shopping and pay for it out of her pocket. In fact, she realised nothing had really been discussed. Nothing at all. Mark hadn't said when he'd be back or when Jenna would be discharged from hospital. She'd find out, she hoped, later that day.

Thinking of the trip to Aldeburgh, Thea had an idea about dinner. She'd pay for a meal out for the three of them in a restaurant, or a pub – whatever they liked.

Satisfied that she didn't have to go shopping that day, Thea took her hot chocolate, which she'd made in a tall glass, with a pyramid of whippy cream hiding the generous handful of mini marshmallows floating at the top of the mug.

She sat on the squishy sofa and picked up the book she'd taken from one of the boxes. She looked at the front cover, studying the young couple on the front, standing next to their old VW campervan at the side of a road. It wasn't a novel. It was one couple's journey – how they'd met and what had inspired them to hit the road and never look back. Unfortunately, the cover just reminded her of her dad. *So, why pick up this book?* Thea guessed it had something to do with returning to Suffolk. It was bound to bring back memories of her childhood.

Thea looked at the young couple on the front cover. The book had been written years earlier, and she wondered where they were now. Were they still together, still as happy as they so obviously had been when this photo was taken, before they'd hit the road? She knew she could probably Google and find out, but she didn't want to go online again in case Miles had emailed her. Thea had switched off her phone too. She assumed that if Mark or the school wanted to contact her, they'd ring Jenna's phone.

Thea opened the book and started to read. She'd put her hot chocolate down on the side table, and with a spoon she started spooning out the cream. 'Hmm … delicious.' She had to be quick, as the pyramid of cream was already melting into the hot drink.

It didn't take long for Thea to reach the marshmallows. As she sipped the milky drink, she could feel her eyes growing heavy. She finished the drink and put the tall glass back on the side table. The sofa was so comfortable that she decided to put her feet up, resting her head on a cushion. She pulled the throw over her legs and closed her eyes, just for a moment. When she opened them again, the throw had fallen off her legs, and strangely so had the book. Then it dawned on her; she'd fallen asleep. Her eyes went wide when she checked the time.

'Oh, my god. I haven't collected the kids!'

25

Thea couldn't wait to put her foot down on the country road. It had seemed to take an age to figure out the Satnav. *Isn't it always the way*, thought Thea, *that when you want to get somewhere in a hurry, everything but everything will go wrong?* First, it had been the Satnav in her sister's car. Thea knew there was nothing wrong with it; she just had no clue how to set it. After randomly pressing some buttons, she finally figured it out. Next, she'd pulled out of the driveway, and a short distance down the road she'd found herself stuck behind a tractor. She'd hardly driven a hundred yards. And of course, it wouldn't pull over and let her pass. Thank goodness she wouldn't be too late, only fifteen minutes or so. She just hoped they were still hanging around outside the school for her.

Thea had felt like beeping her horn, but the last thing she wanted to do was irritate whoever was driving it. She followed it all the way to the main road, about half a mile. With twist and turns along the narrow country road, she didn't want to risk overtaking and be met by someone travelling in the other direction.

At least when she hit the main road to Wickham Market, it was nice and straight – and wide. She could see right ahead, and overtook.

Her next spot of bother came in the form of two horse riders, who were ambling along the road. 'Seriously!' Thea shouted. Not that they could hear her at that distance. But she saw them ahead, riding two abreast, and knew she'd have to slow down to a crawl. The horse riders were very considerate and waved her on when they knew the road ahead was clear. Thea waved back as she overtook.

As soon as she thought she'd cleared them by a safe distance, Thea put her foot down, hoping she didn't come across a police car hiding up a side road. She was surprised at how well she was taking to driving Jenna's car, considering she hadn't driven for quite some time. 'Like riding a bike,' she said to herself. 'What do you think, Winston?' She glanced in her rearview mirror at the golden retriever, who was looking out of the window. He barked.

Thea winced. 'Oh, my god! Indoor voices, please!'

When she'd left the house, the dog had howled, which wasn't what she had been expecting at all. She'd tried to ignore it as she walked to the car, but she was worried about what Winston might get up to while she was gone. She'd spotted a large wire mesh crate in the utility room that she guessed had been used when he was a pup. He was still a pup, really, but he'd obviously outgrown the crate. In hindsight, she thought she could have shut him in the utility room, where he couldn't cause any trouble.

At the time, though, his cries of loneliness had resulted in her rushing back to the house and giving him a big fuss before taking him with her. She hoped it wasn't going to turn out to be a big mistake. She was wondering what would happen when she left him in the car during the hospital visit.

They'd just have to take turns going inside the hospital to visit. This idea suited Thea anyway; she needed to speak to Jenna alone.

As she drove along the main road, passing cottages and villages on her way to Leiston, Thea was thinking about that strange phone call. In hindsight, she probably should have hung up immediately on hearing that strange, synthesised voice. Whatever her sister had got herself involved in sounded dodgy to say the least.

'Ten thousand pounds for a book,' said Thea out loud, shaking her head and suddenly feeling anxious; what had her sister got herself into? More to the point, who was on the end of that call, and what would they be capable of if she didn't deliver?

Thea passed the turn-off for Aldeburgh and took the next one to Leiston. She remembered Aldeburgh, the little seaside town with the lovely promenade, and recalled its streets full of cottages rising up behind the town and the lovely views over the rooftops to the sea. She imagined there were lots of holiday cottages and second homes. It definitely had a holiday feel about it.

Leiston was different. A short drive inland, it had a more local feel, with a bigger selection of shops and supermarkets. It was a larger town – somewhere Thea could easily drive around and lose her bearings. Fortunately, she'd managed to put the school postcode into the Satnav and soon arrived at a large school on the outskirts of the town.

The school looked deserted, apart from two teenagers sitting on a wall outside – one glued to her mobile phone, the other staring into space, looking bored.

As soon as Toby spotted her, he got down from the wall, heaved his bag over his shoulder, and walked towards the car.

Thea pulled up at the kerb and watched Toby get in the back of the car. She turned in her seat. 'Sorry I'm late.'

Toby just shrugged.

Thea turned her attention to Katie. She was still on her phone.

Thea had spotted her looking up, so Katie was aware she'd arrived. Thea stared at her, realising what was going on; Katie was going to make her wait. Thea waited. So did Toby.

Katie finally got off her phone and graced them with her presence. As she sat in the front seat, she said, 'Where were you? Do you know how long we've been sat out here?'

Thea apologised again. 'Sorry.'

'What the hell?' Katie turned around in her seat when she heard a woof from the back of the car. 'You brought the dog with you?'

Thea glanced at Winston, who was lying on the back seat, his head on Toby's lap. 'I didn't know what to do with him.'

'Why didn't you leave him at home?'

'I was worried what he might get up to.'

'Get up to? Oh, my god. Don't you know anything?' Katie said, her voice full of disdain. 'He's a golden retriever! He just sleeps all day.'

Thea bit her lip. She didn't like being spoken to as though she was an idiot, but she was late, and Katie was back to her usual argumentative self. 'He whined when I went out.'

'Yeah, well that's what they do. Try and pull on your heartstrings. Dad says we should ignore him, otherwise he'll get what he wants all the time.'

Sounds like someone I know, thought Thea, glancing at Katie. She remembered she had promised she'd speak to her drama teacher about enrolling in the after-school drama club. That might cheer Katie up and put Thea back in her good books. 'Now, I'll just nip into the school and talk to your drama teacher about—'

'Don't bother!'

Thea raised her eyebrows. 'Oh, don't be like that. Just because I was late, it doesn't mean the whole afternoon has to be ruined.'

'Yes, it does. The teacher has gone home.'

Thea mouthed a great big, 'Oh.'

'Yeah – *oh*.'

'Well, I'll speak to the teacher tomorrow. I will phone the school. I'm sure I can organise paying for your classes over the phone. When can you start?'

Katie put her phone down. 'There's a class every Thursday.'

'Perfect, then you could join this week if I get it sorted out with the school tomorrow. How does that sound?'

Katie pursed her lips. 'All right, I guess.'

Thea smiled. Now, she was getting somewhere. 'Good.'

'Toby wants to join too.'

Thea turned in her seat. 'Really? Well, I'm sure I can arrange for you both to—'

'No, I don't!'

'Yes, you do.'

'I do not! I've got no interest whatsoever in that stupid drama class.'

'That's not what I heard,' said Katie in a teasing voice.

'What do you mean?' Toby shot back.

Katie turned in her seat and grinned at her brother. 'I heard you fancy Caitlin and she's in the drama class.'

'Well, you were misinformed,' said Toby, frowning at her.

Katie mimicked him, 'Well, you were misinformed.' She narrowed her eyes. 'I think not. I've seen the way you look at her. My friend overheard you telling your best friend – oh, excuse me, your *only* friend – that you like her.'

Thea got the impression that Toby was so used to being insulted by his sister – younger than him by two minutes – that it was now water off a duck's back.

Toby heaved a sigh and said, 'When you start the class, will you introduce me?'

'You must be joking.' Katie pulled a face. 'Do you know who she is? She is, like, sooo popular. There's no way she'd be interested in you.'

Thea looked at her, surprised she was being so mean. 'That's not very nice, Katie.' She glanced at Toby, with his brown eyes, mop of wavy dark hair, and quiet, self-assured disposition. What Katie obviously didn't see was that her brother was growing up into a good-looking young man. Although perhaps she *did* see it, and she didn't want her brother getting in with her potential new friends first.

Thea knew what this was about. Although they had started at the high school in September, they hadn't come up to the school with the friends from primary school they had known for years. They'd only been there a term before the summer holidays. Thea imagined that Katie was still trying to find her feet, navigating new friendships within already well-established little cliques.

Thea and her sister knew all about that. Thea had been lucky. When they'd left the Suffolk Coast and moved to London, she had only been nine. She'd had more time at primary school to make friends that she would go on to high school with, but her sister had had to start in secondary school. Jenna, being the more outgoing one, soon found her feet. Katie was more outgoing than Toby and so already had friends, but it seemed to Thea that she wanted to get in with the popular girl at school, called Caitlin.

Thea started the car. She said, 'I guess you're going to have to join the drama club, Toby.'

'No!' Katie shouted out.

Thea frowned. 'But I thought you said—'

'It was a joke, all right? If he goes, then I'm not joining. And that's that!' Katie put a pair of EarPods in her ears.

Thea heard Toby sigh heavily from the back seat. 'Don't worry, sis, I'm not joining the drama club.'

Winston woofed.

Thea breathed a sigh too. This was all so exhausting. She'd only been gone a day, and she was already missing the simplicity of her life in the flat. She was also missing work. Not having anything to do didn't suit her. Perhaps there was more to avoiding taking annual leave from her job than just the issue of Miles not getting away for longer breaks.

She imagined that was why she'd fallen asleep during the day – it was boredom.

26

Thea stole a glance at the two children sitting glumly in the car before she set off. She turned out of the school parking area. 'Right – next stop Aldeburgh to see your mum.' She hoped that would cheer them up.

She heard Toby sigh again.

'What's the matter – don't you want to see your mum?'

Surprisingly, Toby said, 'Not really.'

'Why ever not? She's had an accident. She broke her leg. I would have thought you'd want to see how she is?' Thea brought the car to a stop at the end of the street and turned in her seat to look at him. She watched him get out a pair of headphones and plug them into his phone. She turned to Katie. 'So, are you coming to see your mum?'

'I don't like hospitals.'

Thea cast a glance at Winston, and said, 'What about you?'

'Dogs aren't allowed in a hospital.'

Thea rolled her eyes. 'Yes, I know that Katie. It was a joke.'

'Well, it wasn't very funny.'

Thea set off, driving back the way she'd come, out of Leiston. She assumed she'd remember the way, but had to ask them to direct her. 'So, am I going to see her on my own, then?'

Katie said, 'I guess so.'

'Will one of you look after the dog while I'm visiting?'

'Toby will.'

Thea drove out of Leiston, but instead of joining the main road again, Katie directed her down a country lane that brought her out to Aldeburgh and the coast road that ran beside the beach from Aldeburgh to Thorpeness. Thea recognised it immediately.

On the couple of occasions that she'd visited her sister since they moved to Pettistree, they had tended to stay local, walking into Wickham Market, or driving to Woodbridge about four miles away. Her sister seemed to avoid Aldeburgh. Last time, Thea had suggested a trip down memory lane, to see their dad's old bookshop, but she'd refused, saying she didn't want to bring up *all that.*

'But we had good times. I remember.'

'Yeah, well, you were younger. I just remember mum being heartbroken when he left.'

'But he didn't leave. He went missing.'

And that had been the end of the conversation. It was something they'd always disagreed on. Her sister reckoned their dad had met someone else, and left them. Thea chose to believe that something had happened to him. *If that's what you need to believe, you keep telling yourself that.* That's what her sister had said.

The trouble with Thea's theory was that it hadn't made her feel any better over the years; it just meant if something had happened, and he couldn't come back, then he was probably dead.

Thea hadn't asked to go to Aldeburgh with her again. She wondered how her sister felt about being forced to stay in Aldeburgh.

'Mum asked to be transferred to Ipswich hospital,' said Katie, as if reading her mind. 'I don't know why. Perhaps she thought she'd get better care there or something. But it's not going to happen, thank god.'

Thea threw Katie a sideways glance, wondering what she knew about her grandfather. With her mum in hospital and her dad away, Thea decided it was not a good time to bring that up.

'It annoyed me,' continued Katie. 'Why wouldn't she want to stay locally so we could visit her?'

Ah, thought Thea. Now she had an idea of why Katie didn't want to see her mum. She asked, 'Can you direct me to the hospital?' She assumed they had both visited Jenna since she'd been inside. She frowned, wishing she hadn't thought of it that way – *inside*. It made it sound like Jenna was in prison. She swept her next thought aside – the synthesised voice over the phone.

She decided to ask the twins a question, but waited while they directed her along the high street to the other end of town, and up a side street to a single-storey red-brick building with a small car park at the front.

The car park was full, so she pulled the car to a stop on the street outside and gathered her handbag. She glanced at Katie, and then turned in her seat to look at Toby. 'Have either of you seen a package lying around the house?'

Toby shrugged.

Katie narrowed her eyes. 'What sort of package?'

'Like a book type of package.'

'Were you expecting something to be delivered to our house?'

'Er, no.' Thea didn't want to give too much away because she really didn't know what her sister had got herself into. 'Are you sure your mum didn't mention what her new job was?'

'No, we don't know what her new job is,' Katie said.

A crook, thought Thea, rather uncharitably. It did occur to her that Jenna may have been to an auction house in Suffolk, or found some old hardback book in a charity shop, Googled it, and discovered it was worth a lot of money. The problem was that didn't explain all the cloak-and-dagger stuff with the synthesised voice over the phone. But then there were a lot of strange people out there, Thea imagined.

She looked at Katie. 'All right. I just thought she might be selling stuff online.' Thea hated lying, but she couldn't exactly tell them about the phone call.

Thea got out of the car. She leaned back in to tell them she wouldn't be long when she saw Katie get out of the car too. 'Oh, have you changed your mind?'

Katie said, 'I guess, but I wanted to go into town and buy my mum something first, like some flowers.'

'That's very thoughtful, Katie. What a good idea.' Thea didn't want to visit her sister empty-handed either. 'Do you know of a nice flower shop where we could buy her some flowers?'

Katie nodded.

Thea turned to Toby. 'Are you okay staying with Winston?'

'I might take him for a walk.'

Thea had had the presence of mind to bring along the dog lead she'd found hanging on a coat hook by the front door. She'd stuffed it in her bag on the way out. 'Here, take this.' Thea handed it over as Toby got out of the car.

Winston woofed and jumped from the back seat.

'Let's all meet back at the car in, say, half an hour – then you can decide if you want to come in with us to see your mum,' said Thea, looking at Toby.

He nodded.

They all walked together down the road to the high street. Toby headed off on his own across the road to the promenade behind the shops to take the dog for a walk on the beach.

She glanced at Katie. 'Did you say that you know where a flower shop is?'

Katie nodded. 'Yeah.'

'All right, let's head there.' She glanced at Katie. She had a feeling of déjà vu. She knew why; Katie was the image of her mother, and the last time Thea had walked down this high street with Katie's mum, Jenna had been Katie's age.

'Here we are.'

'Where?' said Thea, looking at the shops around her. She didn't see a flower shop.

'Oh, it's not in the high street. It's down there.'

Thea turned around. Katie pointed, indicating a narrow lane between two shops that Thea recognised. 'This leads to Cobblers Yard, doesn't it?'

'Yes.' Katie started down the path. 'It's not easy to find. My friend who lives here took me to the antique shop in Cobblers Yard. I don't like the shop much; it just sells old stuff, apart from the homemade amber jewellery. We bought matching necklaces and bracelets.'

Thea nodded as she followed her down the lane. She could see Cobblers Yard ahead. As they entered the small, cobbled square, she saw the old-fashioned shop fronts with bowed leaded windows that she remembered. They looked like something out of a Dickens novel. She expected that most people who ventured into Cobblers Yard had the same reaction. She couldn't believe how little it had changed over the years.

'Oh, look – The Potting Shed is open. My friend took me there too to buy some flowers for her mum. The lady who runs it – Lili, I think her name is – is very friendly. I like her, and her assistant, Zoe.'

Thea's eyes roved around the yard, taking in the flower shop, a music shop next door, and a charity shop. She could see the old antique shop, which looked as though it had changed hands – she noticed the shop sign, which read: *Hannah & Maisie's Art and Antique Emporium.*

The shop next door was new – it was a solicitor's office that offered *Friendly, pro bono legal work*. The sign also said: *No problem too big or too small. Call in for a friendly chat. We are here to help*.

But it wasn't those shops, that really caught her attention; it was the old bookshop, the one her father used to run, that she had expected would be long gone. Thea's gaze settled on that shop, her eyes wide in surprise that it was still there. She started towards the bookshop.

'The flower shop is this way.' Katie let out an exasperated sigh. 'Thea?' Katie followed her up to the bookshop window. She followed her gaze. 'I never liked this place. It gives me the creeps.'

Thea stood staring at the window display. 'I don't understand …'

'What's the matter?'

'This isn't right.'

'I know. I told you it's creepy. Look at those cobwebs. It looks like Hallowe'en, which would be okay if that window display had been done for Hallowe'en at the end of the month, but I know for a fact it hasn't.'

Thea saw paperback books, dog-eared and yellowed with age. They must have been standing in the window for twenty-plus years.

Even so, she asked her niece, 'How can you be so sure this hasn't been set up for Hallowe'en?'

'My friend says it's been like this for years. Nobody knows what happened to the owner, apparently.'

Thea looked at Katie. For some reason, her sister hadn't told Katie who had once owned this bookshop – her grandfather. Thea had no idea why whoever had bought it had not cleared out all the old books. She guessed those books had been sitting in that window display since she used to help her mum mind the shop when he went on his business trips to book fairs across the country. It was all rather strange.

Thea stared at the bookshop. She'd just been a young child when he disappeared off the face of the earth. It was a mystery that had haunted her, her whole life.

Staring at the window display, Thea stepped to one side and grabbed the door handle.

'What are you doing?' hissed Katie. 'You do not want to go in there. Besides, it must be locked.'

Thea tried the door. Of course it was locked. That was just what she had expected. What she had not expected to find was her father's bookshop left exactly as it had been when he'd walked out and never come back twenty-five years earlier. If the window display was anything to go by, then inside was a time capsule; a shop that hadn't changed since she'd last set foot inside when she was nine years old. A bookshop full of memories of a happy childhood.

It didn't change the fact that she was desperate to get inside and have a look. Something occurred to her; if nothing had changed, then perhaps there might be a clue inside as to her father's sudden disappearance.

Thea tried the door again.

'Oh, my god!' Katie threw her hands in the air. 'Will you please stop that!' She sounded exasperated, as though she was talking to a small child who wasn't doing as they were told. 'I said – *leave it.*'

Thea actually apologised as she stepped away from the door.

'Someone might see you and wonder what you're doing!' Katie hissed, grabbing her hand and dragging her away from the shop. 'Come on. I thought we were here to buy some flowers for Mum.'

Thea had forgotten about her sister. Perhaps she'd been to Cobblers Yard and spotted the bookshop that appeared not to have changed in decades.

Thea walked across Cobblers Yard, passing the charity shop. She spotted an old lady peering out of the charity shop window, and hoped she hadn't spotted her trying to get into the bookshop.

27

'Marjorie, come over here – will you?'

'Why? I'm busy.'

'Quick. You've got to see this.'

'Oh, for goodness' sake, Mabel. Do you know how old I am? There is no such thing as quick at our age.'

'Speak for yourself,' grumbled Mabel, thinking that perhaps if her older sister watched her diet like she did, and wasn't carrying around an extra stone or three, she might well move more quickly.

By the time she did join Mabel at the window, the young lady had disappeared into The Potting Shed next door.

'Well, what is it? What have I had to get off my comfy perch and walk all the way over here for?'

'All the way over here? You make it sound as though our little charity shop is cavernous.'

Marjorie ignored her sister. She folded her ample arms and said, 'Well? What is it you want me to look at? Personally, I don't see anything wrong with the window display.'

'It's not about the window display, Marjorie.'

Marjorie shook her head. 'Then what have you dragged me over here for?'

'I didn't drag you anywhere.'

Mabel heard their mother's voice in her head, shouting out, 'Will you two stop bickering for once in your lives and just do as I ask?' followed by the usual grumble, 'I should have had a boy.'

Mabel had grown up often hearing her parents say they wished they'd had a son – her father especially. Mabel stared at the bookshop, memories flooding back of her childhood there.

'Well?' Marjorie said, interrupting Mabel's thoughts.

Mabel sighed. 'It's too late now.'

'Too late for what?'

'You missed them.'

Marjorie followed her sister's gaze out of the window. 'Missed who?'

'The girl.'

'Girl?'

'Young woman. She was trying to get into the bookshop.'

'Really? I think you must be seeing things again, Mabel.'

Mabel turned from the window and threw her sister a stern look. 'I was not imagining it.'

'Really Mabel, we both know that no one has set foot in that bookshop for years. How long has it been – over two decades?'

'I saw a light on.'

'Not that again! That was weeks ago!'

'No, it was just the other day too. And I saw a young man's face in the window.'

'And now a young woman trying to get into the shop.' Marjorie stared out of the window and shook her head. 'There's absolutely nobody about.' Marjorie's voice softened. She knew what this was. Ghosts from the past – from Mabel's past. That was what she was seeing, or thought she was. They weren't really there, just apparitions, memories, waking dreams, whispers; a young man and woman who had met at that bookshop once, many, many years earlier, but were never destined to be together.

'Come on, Mabel. I'll make you a nice, sweet cup of tea, and we can forget all this.'

'But I don't want to forget.'

Well, I do, thought Marjorie, wishing they'd never set foot in this shop. Both widows, with their children and grandchildren off, living their own lives – neither of them saw their family from one week to the next. So, the two sisters had had the most brilliant idea – at least Marjorie had thought it was at the time.

Both outgoing and sociable – they had a reputation in the local community for being quite the town gossips – they'd decided seven years earlier, at eighty years young, that there was still life to be lived. They'd decided to do something neither of them had ever done before – run a shop. Neither of them needed an income. They both had state pensions and widows' pensions. Both Mabel and Marjorie had previously worked, Mabel doing shop work, and Marjorie in a solicitor's office, and Marjorie had a small work pension too. They wanted to give something back to the community they'd lived in all their lives. Running a charity shop fitted the bill perfectly – apart from one thing. The location.

Marjorie frowned at the old bookshop across the yard. Mabel hadn't seemed too bothered by the location when they'd first viewed the shop, but it had bothered Marjorie – and still did. Although she would never voice her opinion; not even to her sister, afraid she might let slip the horrible secret she'd harboured for decades.

'Marjorie, I thought you were making a cuppa?'

Marjorie frowned at that blasted shop, and turned around.

'I'm coming.' She walked to the back of the shop, where Mabel had now stolen her seat, and into the room beyond. It was almost as large as the shop floor. There was a small kitchenette on one side with an old Formica worktop that had seen better days, a sink unit, and just enough space for a microwave and kettle. In the single wall-mounted cupboard they stored the tea, coffee, sugar and the most important thing of all – the biscuits.

You can't have elevenses without a biscuit, thought Marjorie, even though it was late afternoon rather than mid-morning. Marjorie filled the kettle with water and flicked it on, glancing around the room. There were several boxes and black bin liners full of more charity donations to the shop that they still had to sort through. There were too many items for their little shop; people were very generous with their donations – too generous.

A lot of it would be collected by another volunteer and distributed to other charity shops. But they always sorted through the bags to see what treasures might be waiting for them to find.

'I definitely saw a light on in that shop.'

'I can't hear you,' Marjorie lied. She could hear her all too well, even over the sound of the kettle boiling. She did not want to talk about the bookshop. If Mabel ever found out that she had betrayed her years earlier, that would be the end of their close bond as sisters, and friends. Marjorie had to make herself breathe slowly. Just the thought of the truth coming to light, even after all these years, had her heart beating furiously in her chest as though she was going to have a heart attack. It didn't matter how much time had passed; she couldn't imagine her sister would forgive her for what she had done – or more to the point, what she hadn't done. She just knew that no amount of apologies would heal the rift.

'Marge – where's my tea?'

'Coming right up!' Marjorie called out. She walked out of the back room, carrying a tea tray. Even though they were at work, and the facilities were basic, they never skimped on their afternoon cup of tea. *It has to be done properly, otherwise there's no point doing it at all*, thought Marjorie as she set the tea tray down on the desk in front of them. She picked up the tea strainer in one hand and the teapot in the other, and poured a cup of freshly brewed tea.

'The way …'

'… tea used to be,' Mabel chimed in, speaking along with her sister.

'You can never get a decent cuppa in one of these new-fangled cafés. They just don't know how to make a proper cup of tea.'

'I know,' said Mabel, pouring some milk into her delicate china teacup.

'Biscuit?' offered Marjorie, holding up the plate of rich tea biscuits, along with some digestives.

'I say, this is a bit of a departure,' said Mabel picking up a chocolate digestive. 'What's the occasion?'

Marjorie avoided eye contact. She always had a packet stashed in a secret drawer out back that Mabel didn't know about. She'd scoff several while she was making the tea – one rich tea was never enough as far as Marjorie was concerned – but if she did it in front of Mabel, her sister would be on her case about her weight.

Today, for the first time, Marjorie shared her chocolate biscuits, and owned up. 'There's a packet in one of the kitchen drawers.' Since Marjorie was the only one who made tea, she didn't think Mabel would find them.

'You had chocolate biscuits all this time, and you didn't think to offer me one?'

'Sorry.'

'Really, Marjorie. You haven't changed, have you? Still hiding things from me.'

Marjorie's eyebrows shot up. 'What do you mean?' she asked defensively, suddenly afraid that her sister knew. She looked towards the front window, eyeing the bookshop, knowing that it was an irrational thought; neither of them had ventured into that bookshop for years. There was no way her sister would have found it.

Mabel said, 'I'm talking about when we were children and I'd be reading a book, and you'd steal it, and hide it from me.'

'Oh, right. That.'

'Why did you do that?'

'Because I wanted you to play with me and you always had your head in a book.'

'Well, was it any wonder, Marjorie? I mean, we did live in a bookshop.'

They both fell silent, glancing across the cobbled square at the old bookshop where they had grown up. It had changed little over the years, although its name had. When their father ran it, it had been called The Fantastic Book Emporium.

Mabel picked up a chocolate digestive and stared into space, lost in a memory of yesteryear.

❖

'Mabel, you come straight back after you've been to the shop. Do you hear, young lady?'

'Why does she get to go? I'm the eldest. I should go.'

'I need you to stay and mind the shop, Marjorie.'

Mabel threw her big sister a devilish grin. Marjorie usually got to do everything. Go to the shops, go out to play, leaving Mabel in the boring bookshop – at least, that was what she had thought before she discovered that the bookshop wasn't boring at all. There were adventures to be had, amazing facts to learn, and wonderful places to escape to, all within the pages of those books. It had just taken her until she was eight years old to discover that fact – which was just as well, because there were few adventures to be had outside, unless you were old enough to go to war.

Sometimes, Mabel wished she had been. She had been only three years old when the war broke out, and that was all she'd ever known; blackout curtains, and air raid shelters, and the little box containing her gas mask. She hated that thing. It made her feel claustrophobic, trapped. But she never left the shop, which was also their house, without it. Not until that day, when she was going out on her own to collect something special from the butcher's shop for a very special guest. They were going to be welcoming their very first evacuee.

Mabel was so excited that she could barely contain herself. She'd hardly slept the previous night, tossing and turning, much to her older sister's annoyance. They shared a bedroom in the eaves upstairs, both sleeping in the double bed their parents had slept in when their mother was still alive. Their father slept on the couch in the makeshift sitting room at the back of the shop.

Mabel couldn't quite believe that from that night, there'd be a woman living under their roof with them. She wondered what she'd be like. She hoped she was young, like her mum had been. She hardly remembered her mother – just that she had often told them off.

Father had explained that it was because she was sick, and so, so tired – too tired for energetic, loud children under her feet. But then she had always read them bedtime stories, and tucked them in at night. And sometimes, when she hadn't been feeling so bad, she had sung to them.

As she skipped out of the bookshop door, Mabel decided that she didn't want to think about her mum. She'd overheard a conversation on the telephone between her father and someone from the church, who organised the evacuees, and had learned that the woman would be bringing her child with her. She didn't know if it was a girl or a boy. She hoped they were younger; then she wouldn't be the youngest anymore.

Mabel was aware that evacuees had been coming since the start of the war, but so far no one had come to stay with them. Five years into the war, and they were getting their very first evacuees. Father said that no one knew how long the war would go on for, but that they were the lucky ones; although publishers were having problems finding paper to print books, people were buying them by the shedload.

There wasn't much else to do behind the blackout curtains during the war apart from listen to the radio, play parlour games, and read. And everyone, so Father said, wanted to escape into a good book. He said business had never been so brisk. Not that he wanted a war. If it wasn't for Father's weak chest, as a result of a bout of pneumonia as a child, Mabel knew he'd be at war right now, and they'd have no one to look after them. 'Then we'd have been evacuees too,' Mabel had told her sister – although Marjorie had corrected her, saying that one of their neighbours, the other shop owners in Cobblers Yard, would have taken them in.

Mabel was so glad that Father hadn't gone to war. She didn't want to go and live with the old lady who ran the knitting and sewing shop just across the yard.

With all the making do and mending that was going on, Father had said that she was doing well for herself too. The flower shop next door to the old lady's shop had closed during the war; it was shut up because no one wanted to buy flowers, which Mabel thought was a big mistake. Flowers were colourful and smelled nice. Father said you couldn't eat flowers. But they made her feel happy because they reminded her of her mother who, no matter how little money there was, had always had fresh flowers in the bookshop.

The flowers had always made Marjorie sneeze, though. Mabel hadn't heard her big sister sneeze for a long time. She vowed to buy some sweet-smelling, fresh flowers as soon as the war ended.

She supposed that they could have gone to live with old Mr Cribbins, who ran the music shop. She thought that he must like violins an awful lot, because the shop window was full of them. He was too old to be called up. The old antique shop next door had closed during the war. She had overheard Father talking to Mr Cribbins. They'd heard that the young man who had run it had been killed in Gallipoli. She wondered who might buy it. The shop next to that was closed too. She had always liked going into the art shop to buy paper and crayons.

There was nothing she enjoyed more than reading – apart from getting one over on her big sister, as she had today. She had been chosen to go out and fetch the ingredients for the very special evening meal Father was going to cook for their guests. The trouble was, though, that it meant she had to put down the book she was reading.

Mabel stepped out of the shop and ran across the cobbled yard and down the little lane into Aldeburgh's high street. She stopped when she realised she'd forgotten something very important. 'Oh, no!' Mabel didn't have her box with the gas mask inside. She looked up at dark sky. It was October, and she knew it wouldn't be getting dark for at least another hour. There was time enough to run to the shop at the end of the high street and fetch their dinner. 'Well, at least I didn't forget the ration book,' said Mabel out loud, getting a funny look from a man in overalls who was cycling past her.

Mabel looked up, still worried about forgetting her gas mask. She didn't want to go back for it in case Father told her off and sent Marjorie instead. Mabel couldn't stand the thought of seeing Marjorie's smug expression, and hearing her say, 'See, I told you she couldn't be trusted.'

Mabel stood there, indecisive. She didn't want to go back for her mask, but the cloudy skies meant she couldn't see if there were any Luftwaffe circling overhead.

Her sister's scornful voice echoed in her head, 'You'll hear them first, you dummy.'

Mabel stood very still and listened. The only sounds were of seagulls, and of people rushing by, and of a motorbike somewhere in the distance. No Luftwaffe. Not that she'd know what they'd sounded like. They didn't bother with Aldeburgh. They only bombed London – didn't they?

Mabel walked along the high street to the butcher's shop and joined the queue. After worrying that there wouldn't be any meat left when it was her turn to step up to the counter, she eventually bought a piece of lamb shoulder.

Father had told her precisely what to get. Mabel had stood in the shop, watching the butcher slice off the lamb and wrap it in newspaper. She couldn't remember the last time they'd eaten meat.

Her next stop was the greengrocer's shop for some vegetables.

She stood in another queue, thinking what Father had said about the reason Marjorie had to stay at home. Marjorie had an important job to do. Whenever he said that, they both knew what he meant – making pudding.

It was usually spotted dick. Sometimes, Mabel helped her sister make it. She used flour, lard and water, and it was a really special treat if they had some currants or sultanas to add. They always had lots and lots of custard too.

Mabel's mouth watered. It was her favourite pudding – which was just as well, because they had it a lot.

Mabel left the greengrocers and walked along the street, passing a queue at the bakery. She saw a lady walk out of the baker's shop with a large loaf of bread. She knew the name of it too – the national loaf – it was the only bread that you could buy now. She stopped to buy a loaf, just in case they needed extra for their guests.

Mabel knew bread wasn't rationed because they always had a big loaf they could help themselves to whenever they wanted. She preferred to spread margarine or butter on it, and jam was just heavenly, but adding anything to their bread beside dripping was a very special treat. Her sister had once told her that before the war, there had been white bread. 'There's no such thing!' Mabel had replied. She had thought her older sister had just teasing her. Mabel had asked her father, and he had said it was true; they'd had white bread before, but Mabel had been too young to remember. He had told her that as soon as the war was over, he imagined the shops would be allowed to sell white bread again.

Mabel was walking towards Cobblers Yard, trying to imagine what white bread, and butter and jam would taste like. She suddenly heard something. Other people had stopped dead in the street too. The noise was loud, like nothing she'd ever heard before. And it was getting closer.

She followed the gaze of the people around her, tilting her head to look up at the sky. And then it happened – from behind a cloud emerged a plane.

Mabel screamed, dropped her bag and started running. She was looking up at the sky, wondering when the plane would drop a bomb, so she wasn't looking where she was going. She ran straight into a man.

He caught her by the shoulders. 'Hey, little girl – where are you going in such a hurry?'

'Let me go! There's a plane! It's going to drop a bomb, and I haven't got my gas mask, and I'm going to die!' Mabel cried.

The young man got down on bended knee. 'Hey, hey – it's going to be all right. That plane isn't going to drop a bomb – not on us.'

Mabel dropped her gaze and looked at the young man with the blonde cropped hair and big brown eyes. He grinned, showing off perfectly straight white teeth. 'That's not true!' cried Mabel. 'It's the Luftwaffe.'

'Nope, it isn't. They're friendlies.'

The plane flew low, doing a sweep of the high street. People whistled and cheered, and waved. 'There, you see that circle on the plane? They're friendly.'

The plane flew so low that Mabel could even see the pilot waving at them.

'I imagine they've come from an RAF base in Lincoln or Scotland.'

The young man offered her a handkerchief. 'Here. Let's wipe away those tears.'

Mabel took the lovely white handkerchief and wiped her eyes. She then blew her nose, and held it out to give it back to him.

'You keep it – what is your name?'

'Mabel. Are you Scottish?'

'I am.'

'I like the sound of your voice.'

'You like my accent?'

Mabel nodded. That wasn't all she liked; she stared, mesmerised by his lovely eyes and kind, attractive face, and felt something stir in her tummy – a tingly sensation she'd never felt before. She didn't know why, but she dropped her gaze, embarrassed.

Later that evening, when she and her sister were tucked under their covers after the most stupendous meal of their lives, she made the mistake of confiding in her sister that she was in love. Marjorie had burst out laughing.

'What's so funny?'

'You're eight.'

'Yes, I know that! Father says I'm pretty, and I'm going to grow up into a beautiful young woman.'

'He did?'

'Yes, because I asked him if I would.'

'Mabel, you are so silly sometimes – all fathers say that about their daughters.' She added, 'You can't fall in love at your age.'

'Why not?'

'Oh, Mabel. You don't know what you're talking about. You're a child.'

'I won't be a child forever. When I grow up, I'm going to marry him.'

28

Mabel sipped her tea and discovered it had gone cold.

'You look lost in thought. Where were you?' Marjorie asked.

'Back in 1944.'

'Pardon me?'

Mabel dropped her gaze from the bookshop and looked at her sister. She thought of the evacuees who had arrived on the day when she'd assumed the Luftwaffe had finally found Aldeburgh. The evacuees had nearly arrived to find no dinner waiting for them. She remembered that day vividly – not only because of her excitement over their impending arrival, but because she had met Douglas for the first time, and he had saved the day.

Mabel recalled what had happened next, after she'd calmed down. Before she'd run into him, trying to flee home, she'd dropped the bag of shopping. When she'd run back to find it, the bag with the meat, bread and vegetables, and what had been left of their weekly rations, was gone. She'd cried again until the young man had caught up with her and asked her what the matter was. When she'd told him some horrible person had picked up her bag and taken it, he'd stepped in to help. He'd gone to the butcher's, and the greengrocer's, and finally the baker's, and had brought back the biggest cut of meat she'd ever seen, along with vegetables, and an apple pie the like of which she'd never eaten before – it had the most crumbly pastry she'd ever tasted, and so much sugar. She'd thought she wouldn't sleep for a week from the excitement of what had happened that day.

Of course, Father had invited him to join them for dinner – how could he not, after Douglas had brought them so much food?

'Would you like me to make another brew?' asked Marjorie.

Mabel said, 'What do you think happened to him?'

Marjorie followed her gaze. She knew what Mabel was staring at – that blasted bookshop.

Marjorie hoped that Mabel wasn't getting any ideas, after thinking she'd seen a light in the shop, that Douglas had come back. He'd be in his late nineties. It was more likely that he was dead now.

She remembered the tall, dashing young man who couldn't have been more than twenty. He was in the RAF, stationed in Norfolk, and often visited the Suffolk Coast when he had some leave. But he'd never discovered Cobblers Yard, and their little bookshop, until he had accompanied Mabel home after she'd had a fright, thinking the Luftwaffe were going to drop a bomb on Aldeburgh. She also remembered what Mabel had said that night; that when she grew up, she was going to marry him.

Mabel had been eight. It was ridiculous, or so Marjorie remembered thinking at the time. But the years went by and the war ended, and Mabel grew into a beautiful young woman. Douglas often visited their father's bookshop to buy books, but Marjorie guessed it was on the pretext of seeing Mabel. The friendship blossomed, until one day, Mabel confided in her sister that they planned to elope. With the age gap, and the fact that Mabel was so young – just seventeen – they knew that their father would never agree to the match. It meant they would have to marry in secret. Mabel told her sister when they planned to leave together.

It was 1953 when Mabel packed her suitcase in readiness to meet Douglas at the train station so they could run away together. The plan was to go to London and catch the sleeper train to Edinburgh. Marjorie knew he wouldn't be there. The plan had changed; he'd brought the date forward, and the details were in the letter he'd entrusted to Marjorie to give to her sister.

In the letter, although he'd expressed his undying love for Mabel, he'd also expressed his concerns over them running away together, and what that meant; she'd be leaving her family, perhaps never to see them again. He'd said that if she changed her mind and didn't turn up, then he'd know she'd broken it off. They were to meet at midnight under the old gas lamp in the middle of Cobblers Yard. He'd have a car waiting to take them to the train station. Marjorie never gave her the letter. Instead, she whisked her sister to London, on the day she was meant to elope, for a rare treat – a show in London's West End. They hadn't returned until the following day.

Marjorie thought her sister would get over her broken heart in time. She was only seventeen. What did she know about love? Eloping would be the biggest mistake of Mabel's life, and as her big sister, Marjorie felt she had to stop her. And it would have broken their father's heart if his seventeen-year-old daughter had eloped. It wasn't just the age gap; Douglas had claimed to be a Scottish laird, descended from a long line of lairds, who owned a huge manor house in the Scottish Highlands. Their father hadn't believed him. He had thought Douglas was just saying it to impress a gullible teenage girl. Marjorie hadn't cared about that. For her own selfish reasons, she hadn't wanted Mabel to leave. Mabel had been all she had – until she met her own future husband, anyway.

Mabel had eventually married too. Marjorie had thought all the business with Douglas was in the past, and that Mabel's heart had healed over time. But the look on her face made Marjorie wonder if she was thinking of him right now, and that perhaps time had not healed a thing.

Mabel turned to her sister. 'Do you think he'll ever come back?'

'Who – Douglas?'

'Why would I want *him* to come back?'

Marjorie was surprised by her attitude, as she'd assumed Mabel was thinking wistfully about Douglas, but of course as far as Mabel knew, he had never turned up, and had reneged on their plan to elope together.

'Besides, he's probably dead now. And good riddance.'

Marjorie gave her a sideways glance. Her sister didn't really mean that; she could hear it in her voice. 'Sorry, I didn't mean to bring him up. I think we're talking at cross purposes. Who were *you* talking about?'

'Henry – of course.'

Marjorie cast her gaze over to the bookshop. 'Is that why you wanted to come back here, Mabel, and work in a shop in Cobblers Yard; so you could keep an eye on the bookshop?'

'Do you ever wonder what happened to him? He loved that bookshop almost as much as Father did.'

'I know,' said Marjorie. 'That's why Father left the bookshop to him rather than us.'

'I wish we'd made our peace with him over that.'

'You were the one who wouldn't.' Marjorie reminded her.

'I didn't understand. I still don't. Why he left the shop to the evacuee.'

'But he wasn't just an evacuee, was he, Mabel? The young woman left the baby with us, and when she didn't come back, and Father went to London and couldn't find her, then he brought him up. He was like a son to him.'

'But I wanted to run the bookshop.'

'I know. I remember Henry asked you once if you'd like to help him run the shop. You wouldn't.'

'Yes, well … that was just as well, wasn't it? Everyone assumed he would remain a bachelor, but then he met someone and had children.'

'Perhaps if we'd, you know, acted like grown-ups and not held a grudge about the shop, we'd have got to know his family.'

Mabel frowned. 'Yes, perhaps.'

'Didn't she move to London with the kiddies after he disappeared?'

Mabel nodded. 'I believe so.'

'What I want to know,' said Marjorie, breaking her golden rule of never talking about the past, or the bookshop, 'is why it has stood empty all these years.'

'Ray looked into it. You know Ray, the retired police officer who used to run the art and craft shop across the yard, before his heir-hunting business took off.'

'Yes, of course I know Ray,' said Marjorie indignantly.

'He didn't find anything, did he?'

'That's right, nobody inherited the property, which means …'

'Which means – what, exactly, Marjorie? I really wish you'd get to the point sometimes, and not talk in riddles.'

'I am not talking in riddles, Mabel. I thought it was obvious?'

'What?'

'There is some statute of limitations – if you've been missing for so many years, then you can legally be declared dead.'

'I don't want to talk about this. What point are you making, Marjorie?'

'Ray couldn't find out who has inherited the property for one simple reason.'

Mabel looked at her sister, exasperated. 'Which is …?'

'That his wife never filed a claim for declaration of presumed death.'

'But isn't it automatic?' Mabel asked, aware that her sister would have some knowledge of such things, as she had worked as a solicitor's secretary way back when.

'No, it is not.'

Mabel stood up, rounded the counter and walked over to the display window, looking outside and across the yard at the bookshop.

Marjorie joined her.

'His wife doesn't think he's dead.'

'It's obviously what she wants to believe,' said Marjorie.

'I want to believe it too. I miss him.'

Marjorie nodded. 'So do I.' Like her sister, Marjorie wished they hadn't been estranged, and that they'd had a chance to repair their relationship before it was too late. 'I liked her, you know, Henry's mother.'

Mabel smiled, remembering the young lady with the infectious laugh. She stared at the bookshop. 'I think Father liked her too.'

'Oh, I have no doubt,' said Marjorie. 'Remember after the war, she went home, but we were so happy – and so was Father – when they started evacuating women and children from London again, and she returned?'

'I don't really remember. Why did they do that?'

'From what I recall, they still thought there might be bombs dropped on London, even though they had declared victory in Europe.'

'We didn't think we'd ever see her again.'

'That's when we had a party,' commented Marjorie.

'That's right. It was a bit strange really. We were celebrating VE day and the return of the evacuees.'

'Yes. I remember feeling so sad when the evacuees had to leave again.'

'Why do you think she left Henry behind when she returned to London?' asked Mabel.

'She said she had to check it was safe to return to London with a baby. Then she never came back.'

'That was sad for Henry.'

'And for us. I liked having her around.'

Mabel nodded. 'Me too.'

'Things hadn't been the same after mother died. That lady kind of lit up the place, you know?'

'We gained a brother, though, didn't we?' said Mabel.

'We did indeed.'

Mabel turned to her sister. 'I'd like to find him – Henry. If he's still alive.'

Marjorie stared at her sister. 'So would I.'

'I wish—'

'You wish we'd tried years ago?'

She nodded.

Marjorie frowned. 'But where do we start?'

Mabel pointed. 'By keeping an eye on that bookshop.'

'You really believe you saw a light on in there, don't you?'

Mabel nodded. 'I really do, Marjorie.'

29

'I love the flowers.' Thea stepped out of the flower shop holding a large bouquet of flowers. 'What a good idea of yours to get some flowers to take in to see your mum.'

'Shall we get her some chocolates too?' Katie asked.

Thea smiled at Katie as they crossed the cobbled yard. Thea threw a backward glance over her shoulder at The Bookshop of Memories.

Katie glanced over her shoulder too. 'Creepy,' she said under her breath.

Thea looked at Katie. 'Come on, let's go and buy those chocolates.' As they walked down the path and stepped into the high street, Thea said, 'I was thinking that after we visited your mum we could have some dinner at a restaurant in Aldeburgh.'

'A restaurant?'

'Yes. Or a pizza place, if that's what you prefer.' Thea remembered when she was a teenager. Whenever they had eaten out, her mum hadn't had the money for a fancy restaurant, but neither Thea nor Jenna had wanted to eat in one anyway.

'Or a McDonald's?' suggested Thea.

'There isn't one in Aldeburgh. The nearest one is in Ipswich.'

Thea didn't fancy driving all the way there just for a McDonald's.

'What about fish and chips?' said Thea, spotting two chippies. 'Mind you, it isn't exactly the weather for fish and chips.' She looked up at the dark sky. The wind was whipping around her coat and her hair, making walking hard work. She'd also lost some of the petals on a few of the flowers.

'We don't have to eat fish and chips outside,' said Katie.

'But it will be cold by the time we arrive home.'

'They have little cafés where we could eat inside if we want to.'

'Perfect.' Thea hadn't had fish and chips in a long time. She remembered that it was something they had always eaten on a Friday when she was very young. But that was one of many little family rituals that had changed when they moved to London.

Thea didn't want to spoil what was turning out a surprisingly nice afternoon with her niece and nephew by thinking about the past. 'So, Katie, the question is: will Toby want fish and chips too?'

'Oh, yeah. He'll eat anything.'

Thea thought that perhaps she should ask him. Fish and chips wasn't an inexpensive meal anymore, and she didn't want to waste money on a meal he wouldn't eat.

They walked out of the Co-op on the corner with two large boxes of classic Thorntons chocolates. As well as the one for Jenna, Thea had decided to buy a box for the three of them in the hope that her rather nice afternoon would extend to the evening, and they could all sit together and watch a movie.

As they walked, Thea broached the movie idea. 'So, I was thinking that this evening we might want to sit and watch a movie.'

Katie looked at her. 'Who's *we*?'

'You, me and Toby, of course.'

Katie's response was what Thea guessed she should have expected, given the tensions she had witnessed between the twins.

'I am not spending my precious evening with Toby.'

'Why not?'

'I just don't want to. Besides, his choice of movie is going to be very different to mine. And anyway, don't expect me to sit with you. I've got a mountain of homework to do.'

'What about the extra box of chocolates?'

Katie shrugged. 'Just leave them on the kitchen table, and we'll help ourselves.'

'All right.' Thea didn't see how she had a choice.

They reached the car and noticed that Toby and Winston were not back from the walk.

'How long does a walk take!' Katie said.

Thea understood that she was being sarcastic, although she herself had no idea. She expected she'd find out tomorrow when she had to walk Winston. She was thinking that after the kids had left for school, and she'd tidied around the house, instead of sitting there bored, she'd go out and give him some exercise. He'd been good in the car, so she didn't mind.

'I'm sure he'll be back soon.'

'He'd better be. I want fish and chips.'

Thea glanced at Katie's pouting face. She reminded Thea of Jenna when she was cross.

She walked through the hospital door and up to the reception desk. 'Here goes,' she said under her breath. 'Hi, my name is Thea, I've come to see my sister, Jenna.'

'We've been expecting you.'

'Have you?'

'Her husband phoned to say you'd be popping along today.'

'Oh, good.' Thea glanced at Katie. The idea was that they went in one at a time – not only because Thea wanted to have a private word with her sister about that phone call, but because someone really needed to keep an eye on the dog. Although she did ask, 'I don't suppose dogs are allowed in the hospital?'

The receptionist shook her head vehemently. 'I'm afraid that unless they are guide dogs, or therapy dogs, then the answer is no.'

It was what Thea expected. She'd have to send Katie out to see if Toby was back and ask him if he wanted to come in after all.

'Where can I find my sister?' Thea asked the receptionist.

'One moment.'

Thea watched her tap on the computer keyboard. 'Ah, I see she's just come out of surgery.'

'Really? I hope everything is okay.'

'Yes, she's just had a plate and screws fitted in her ankle. It went well.'

'Nobody let us know.'

'We did let her husband know that another patient cancelled their operation, so she was scheduled instead.'

Thea got her phone out of the back pocket of her jeans. When she'd switched it back on, earlier in the day, there had been no text or missed call. Mark hadn't had the decency to let her know.

Thea glanced at Katie, who had her phone to hand too. She frowned. 'Dad didn't let us know.'

'Perhaps he didn't read the message from the hospital.'

'Yeah, maybe.' The look on Katie's face said she wasn't convinced. She looked at Thea. 'What now?'

The receptionist said, 'It will take her a bit of time to come round from the anaesthetic, but you're welcome to take those beautiful flowers to her room. You'll find a vase in her room for those. They will be lovely for her to wake up to.'

'Oh, thank you,' Thea said.

'If you take the first floor to the wards, one of the nurses at the nurse's station will let you know which room she's in.'

'All right.'

They walked up a flight of stairs, and were directed to a side room where Thea found her sister lying in bed. Her leg was in a plaster cast below the knee and was elevated off the bed. The anaesthetic hadn't worn off, so she hadn't woken up yet.

Thea saw a plastic vase on the bedside cabinet, along with a container she guessed was for when Jenna came round from the anaesthetic. Some people were physically sick afterwards. She hoped her sister wasn't one of them.

Thea said, 'I'm just going to find a sink and fill this with water.' Thea filled the vase in a sink just outside the room and returned. Katie was sitting there holding her mum's hand. It made her think that it would be nice if, when Jenna came round, Toby was there too. She wanted to return to the car and see if he'd come back. 'Look, do you mind popping the flowers in the vase?'

A nurse walked in at that moment. 'Well, isn't that the most beautiful bouquet? Here, let me arrange those for you.' She walked over and took the bouquet, and vase. 'I'll get a pair of scissors and cut those stems.'

Thea smiled at the nurse. She didn't think the nurses would have time for that sort of thing. 'Thank you.' Thea turned to Katie. 'Do you mind if I just step outside and see if I can find Toby?'

'I'll call him.' Katie dialled, listened for a minute, then frowned. 'He's not answering his phone.'

'Well, I guess it's back to plan A,' said Thea. 'I'll just nip to the car and see if he's back. Are you okay if I go?'

'Yes, of course.' Katie turned to her mum.

Thea had remembered to bring along her sister's mobile phone. She popped it on the side table next to her bed, along with one of the boxes of chocolates. As she walked out of the room, she looked at the lovely nurse, and decided that the staff deserved a treat too for taking care of her sister. She could always buy another box. Thea walked over. 'Here, this is for you.'

The nurse looked taken aback. 'Oh, thank you. Can I share them with my colleagues?'

'Oh, yes. Please do.'

A little gathering of nurses formed as she opened the box.

Thea left them to their treat and returned the way she had come, down the stairs and past reception. She walked out of the door. As she neared the car, she could see there was still no sign of Toby. She was starting to get worried. Winston was rather big and boisterous for a pup, and she didn't know what he would be like on the beach if Toby let him off the lead. Had he run off? What if Winston got into trouble in the water, and Toby followed him into the rough sea to try and save him?

All sorts of scary scenarios were going through her mind as she looked up and down the high street. She was about to cross the road, aiming in the direction of the promenade and the beach, when she spotted him at the top of the high street near the Co-op.

Was he going in the shop? She waved, but he didn't see her. She blinked, and then he was gone. Perhaps he'd nipped into the shop to buy something?

Thea walked at a pace and arrived at the Co-op, expecting to see Winston sitting outside the shop with his lead tied to the doggy post. *He wouldn't take him inside the shop, surely?* she thought.

Thea turned full circle, her eyes alighting on the narrow lane that led to Cobblers Yard. *Of course*, thought Thea. Katie had said that she wanted to buy flowers. She imagined that he'd gone in there to see if they were still in The Potting Shed.

Thea stepped forward and almost collided with two old ladies emerging from the lane. 'Oh, I'm so sorry,' said Thea.

'No harm done,' one of them replied.

'I don't suppose you passed a teenager with a dog in Cobblers Yard?'

'Yes, we did. We've seen him before, haven't we, Mabel?'

'Oh yes, he often goes into the antique shop.'

Thea nodded. She recalled that Katie had said something about Toby being strange – he liked old things, and often hung around the antique shop.

'We work in the little charity shop down there. We've just closed, but we're open tomorrow.'

'Oh, okay.' Thea had never visited a charity shop before. Maybe she would pop in and say hello to the two helpful old ladies, and buy something, even if she didn't need it. At least she'd be donating some money for a good cause.

Thea caught one of the old ladies, the rather plump one, staring at her. Thea said, 'Well, er … thank you. I must go and find my nephew.'

As she turned down the lane, she overheard an exchange between the two ladies.

'Why were you staring at her, Marjorie?'

'She just reminded me of someone, but I can't think who.'

Thea hurried down the lane and into Cobblers Yard. She walked up to The Potting Shed and looked in the window. It was a small shop, and she couldn't see Toby inside. She turned around and cast a glance about her. There was no sign of Winston waiting outside one of the shops. She thought of what the two old ladies had told her. He had definitely been there.

She made a beeline for the antique shop on the other side of Cobblers Yard. In the window, she could see necklaces and bracelets, recalling what Katie had said about the amber jewellery she and her friend had bought in this shop. The door was open. Thea stepped inside.

'Can I help you?'

Thea looked around the shop. There was no sign of Toby or the dog. Had he left already, passing her by – maybe while she'd had her back to him when she was looking through The Potting Shed window? It was possible. But he would have spotted her. Why hadn't he come over?

Her gaze settled on a young woman sitting on a stool by the counter. She guessed this was Hannah, the lady whose name was stencilled on the outside of the shop – *Hannah & Maisie's Art and Antique Emporium*. 'I'm looking for my nephew. Can you tell me when a teenage boy with a golden retriever left your shop?'

The young woman frowned. 'I'm afraid I haven't had a teenage boy or a golden retriever in my shop today.'

Thea blinked. That can't be right. She peered at the young woman. 'Are you sure?'

'Positive.'

'Oh, well … I'd better get going.'

'Can I interest you in anything?'

Something crossed Thea's mind – the shop sign did say *Art and Antique Emporium*. Was this where her sister might have found a rare book that, unbeknown to the proprietor, was worth a lot of money? Thea asked, 'Do you sell old books?'

The young lady immediately shook her head. 'No, I'm afraid

not. But if you're looking for a gift for somebody ...'

Thea thought that wasn't a bad idea. 'My sister.'

'We make and sell some lovely amber jewellery …'

Thea walked out of the shop with a pretty necklace, matching earrings and a bracelet, all encrusted with delicate orange and yellow amber gemstones. Hannah had even wrapped them in pretty gift paper.

She hadn't found what she was looking for in the shop – namely, Toby and Winston – but she had found a lovely present for Jenna.

Thea crossed the yard and stopped beside the old cast iron lamp post in the centre. She remembered being told when she was a child that it had once been a gas lamp. She walked around it. 'There it is,' said Thea to herself, bending down and scrutinising some initials that two naughty children had carved into the lamp post. Over time, they had started to fade, but she could still just make out her and her sister's initials.

She was just staring at them, trying to remember what they had used to carve their initials, when she thought she heard the faint woofing sound. 'That woof sounds familiar,' said Thea, standing up straight and casting a gaze about her. There was still no sign of Winston. She guessed it was coming from outside Cobblers Yard in the main shopping street.

She was just crossing the yard, aiming for the narrow passageway, when she happened to glance over her shoulder. She thought she saw a faint light coming from inside The Bookshop of Memories.

'But the shop wasn't open,' said Thea out loud, thinking of her visit there a little over an hour earlier. 'I tried that door, and it was firmly locked.'

As Thea crossed the yard, she recalled what Katie had said about the bookshop – *It's creepy. My friend says it's been like this for years. Nobody knows what happened to the owner, apparently.*

Thea's heart was racing as she thought about her discovery of the bookshop in Cobblers Yard, stuck in a time warp. What if her father had come back?

Thea hurried over to the bookshop. She looked in the shop window, but she couldn't see anything. And there was no light on. Had it been her imagination? Was her mind playing tricks on her? She immediately felt foolish. And she felt even more foolish for trying to open the door again. There was no way it would be—

'Open!' Thea exclaimed in surprise when the door opened. She pushed the door wide and called out, 'Hello?'

She cast a furtive glance around Cobblers Yard, checking that nobody was watching. She wasn't exactly sure why. The shop was clearly open.

'Well, that's not strictly true,' said Thea to herself when she realised the old sign in the window still said, *Closed.*

She couldn't resist stepping inside.

30

'You can't park that thing here!'

Callum stood beside the campervan, staring at his best friend. 'But you said I could just drop in.'

'Well – yeah. I didn't expect you to bring your dad's old campervan. How on earth did you make it all the way here from Scotland without it conking out?'

Callum patted the door affectionately. He shrugged. 'Your guess is as good as mine.' He'd honestly thought he'd get as far as Gretna Green if he was lucky, on the Scottish side of the border with England, and that he'd have had to call a breakdown service to have it towed home and tucked back in his mum's garage.

He hadn't done the journey all in one day. He'd discovered that it wouldn't have been possible anyway in the old campervan, which only comfortably reached sixty miles per hour on the motorway. Anything over sixty and the van started to rattle, and he feared it might break down. Splitting up the journey – and staying overnight in a Travelodge just off the motorway – gave him, and the campervan, time to recharge.

Modern cars with power-steering, cruise-control and decent suspension made for an effortless drive. The van would take some getting used to. It was hard work, and not very comfortable at all on a long journey. After his overnight stay, it had still taken the best part of the following day to get to Jack and Beth's farm.

'You father must have taken good care of it.'

Callum nodded. 'Yes, he did.' He didn't add that he suspected the reason for that was the photograph he'd found of the two girls, and his father's instructions to deliver it to them. It was weird. And even weirder that once he'd seen the photo of those girls, he'd felt compelled to come.

'I could park it down the road.' There were no other cars about; the farm, located in deepest Suffolk, looked as though it was in the middle of nowhere – although Callum knew from the occasional trip to see them that it wasn't really the case at all. East Anglia wasn't like Scotland, where you could drive for miles before meeting another soul on the road. Suffolk was all pretty little hamlets, towns and villages just a stone's throw from one another.

Jack and Beth's farm wasn't far from the Suffolk Coast, just a few miles inland from Aldeburgh. Jack had once been a bit of a party animal, and the last thing Callum had expected him to do was to settle down on a farm. And yet here he was, with a young child and a wife he adored.

Callum looked Jack up and down. He'd put on weight, which was a surprise considering all the physical labour he undertook running a farm. But it was a nice weight, a contented weight.

From his last visit, Callum remembered that Beth enjoyed baking. He recalled those hearty meals of savoury pies, baked to perfection, followed by homemade pudding and custard. They were the poster-children for life on the farm; happy with their lot, even though they didn't have much – just each other and a lot of hard work. Oh, and a big investment in their business from their best friend. Callum had never thought in his wildest dreams that he'd envy their life. Not that he had any desire whatsoever to be a farmer – but they had each other, and a home, and a life they were building together. He had realised a bit late that there was more to life than pursuing big dreams.

'Yes, I see your point, Cal, with parking the van, but it will be an obstruction on the road outside the farm. We need to get farm vehicles up and down that road.'

For a moment, Callum had forgotten what they were talking about. 'Oh, yes – I see how it could be in the way.' Jack clearly didn't want the campervan on his own driveway, where Callum was currently parked. 'Or I could move it to one of the parking spots in front of your rental cottages.'

'The thing is, Cal, we've got paying guests arriving at the cottages, so you can't park there.'

'No room at the inn, then,' Callum said, half-joking.

'I'm afraid not. If only you'd let me know you were coming.'

'It's okay.' Callum grinned. 'You know me, always footloose and fancy-free.' *If only*, thought Callum, weighed down as he was by that huge mortgage, and the rent arrears he still owed on the rental. Even though he'd given up the apartment he was renting in Malibu, and handed in the keys to the agency, they were still chasing him for the outstanding payments, and for the rest of the rent money for the six-month contract he'd stupidly signed.

'It's so nice of you to travel all this way to see us.'

It wasn't the only reason I came, Callum thought. He had also travelled all that way to get his hands on a bookshop, sell it, and solve some of his money issues. He remembered the solicitor's words about somebody potentially contesting his father's will. But who would do that? The photo of those two girls came to mind.

Would it be so bad if he didn't give them the campervan? Whoever they were, they might want the bookshop instead – who wouldn't? It was going to be worth way more than the bright yellow VW, even though his dad had done an amazing job with keeping the vehicle so pristine.

Not pristine enough, however, to be parked on his mate's land. He understood; they had paying guests. It would rather let the side down if they turned up to find an old yellow VW campervan with old-fashioned net curtains hanging at the windows parked outside.

'Shame you haven't got a pitch – you know, like a camping field. Then I could set up there.'

'We had thought of that. Glamping is big at the moment. We were thinking of setting aside a field, and buying some pods – Beth's idea.'

'Pods?'

'Yeah, you know little wooden cabins.'

Callum had never understood the appeal. No matter how comfy and cosy they were set up inside, you were still, essentially, sleeping in a shed with no facilities – not even a bathroom. He'd rather have the campervan any day.

'Now, if you've got money to burn, and you feel like making another investment in the farm ...' Jack trailed off, his expression hopeful.

Callum looked at him in surprise. Jack had hated taking Callum's money when their farm had been in trouble a few years earlier.

Jack looked at him sheepishly. 'It wasn't my idea. Beth told me to ask you the next time I spoke with you. And look – here you are.'

Yes, here I am, thought Callum, *without so much as two brass farthings to rub together*. That wasn't strictly true. He did have a little money on him, but he had practically travelled down there on fumes. Callum's fondness for the little VW campervan had waned pretty quickly when he discovered how quickly the thing guzzled gas.

Jack was still looking at him expectantly.

Callum stared at him. Was he expecting an answer regarding investing in their farm business on the spot? Considering what he'd done for them in the past, Callum didn't know why he thought it was unreasonable of his friend to expect him to say yes. After all, he'd always been so generous with his money.

Not anymore. Not because he had suddenly become stingy and tight, but simply because he didn't have any – not until he sold the bookshop. Callum couldn't wait.

He avoided Jack's gaze, and was saved by Beth hurrying out of the farmhouse behind him and waving frantically. 'Oh, my god, Cal! What are you doing here?'

Callum grinned. 'Just in the neighbourhood.'

She ran up to him, and they hugged awkwardly, that night they'd spent together never far from their minds.

They shouldn't have done it. It was completely and utterly wrong. They hadn't been able to help themselves, although they'd both regretted it instantly.

'It's been too long.'

'I know.' Callum threw a furtive glance Jack's way. The mistake would never have happened if he hadn't turned up on that particular weekend five years ago when his best mate was away, taking some cattle to market in the next town. Jack had got caught in a torrential thunderstorm, which had closed a road on his way home, so he'd stayed overnight at a local bed and breakfast.

Callum knew why it had been so long since his last visit. Although the years had distanced them from what had happened that night, perhaps he still wouldn't have come if it wasn't for the bookshop. In fact, he was pretty sure he wouldn't have.

'You must stay for dinner,' said Jack, putting an arm around his shoulder and steering him towards the farmhouse. 'Beth is so right: it's been too long.'

'What about the van?'

They all turned to look at the campervan parked on their gravel drive.

'As long as you're gone before the other guests arrive ...'

'Yeah, don't worry – I will be.' He glanced at Beth, and caught the relieved look on her face. Despite the apparent warm welcome, she probably didn't want him here.

'Shame you haven't got a spare barn I could hide the van in,' commented Callum as they came up to the farmhouse door.

'Oh, I'm not embarrassed about the van.'

Callum looked at him.

'We can't have some has-been Hollywood actor hanging around the place when the holidaymakers arrive.'

Jack was joking, of course, or thought he was, on the understanding that he was in the presence of a successful actor. Callum sighed. If only Jack knew that he wasn't far off the truth with his comment about a has-been Hollywood actor. Callum knew he really should put them in the picture.

He was about to say something, when the farmhouse door flew open and a young boy dressed in a Star Wars outfit – a storm trooper – holding a light sabre, pointed at Callum, and said, 'Who are you?'

Callum took a step back in surprise.

Beth said, 'How many times have we told you to be careful with that thing?'

She turned to Jack. 'I knew we shouldn't have got him that outfit.' She tutted. 'You and your Star Wars obsession. I'd rather you hadn't passed it on to him.'

Jack looked at her sheepishly.

'I'm a Jedi,' said Callum, to the young child, 'I guess as I'm an enemy of Darth Vader, you might have to kill me with your light sabre.'

Beth quickly intervened. 'Don't encourage him!'

Callum exchanged a smile with Jack.

Beth looked from one to the other and shook her head. 'Really, sometimes I think boys never grow up!'

Callum turned to their son. 'I'm Callum. Now, behind that mask, I'm guessing you must be …' He'd seen some of the photos and videos of their only child they'd posted on social media; he'd just never met him in person. He knew they'd had issues conceiving, and obviously he was a little blessing because they hadn't had any children since.

'Take off your helmet, please,' said Beth.

He reluctantly took off his helmet to reveal curly blond hair and brown eyes.

Callum guessed he might remain an only child. He didn't think that was all bad; the upside was that he would get his parents all to himself, with no sibling rivalry. For some reason, Callum's father and the two young girls in the photo came to mind. He thought he had an explanation for who they were; he just couldn't believe it, the possibility that his father had led a double life and had had another family. It meant that it was quite conceivable that he himself wasn't an only child after all.

Callum focused on the small child in front of him, trying to push that thought to the back of his mind.

Fergus suddenly came over shy without his helmet on.

'Say hello to Uncle Callum.'

Fergus lowered his light sabre and looked up at his mum. 'I didn't know I had an uncle called Callum.'

'He's not really your uncle. He is your dad's best friend.'

Callum looked at her. He thought it was telling that she hadn't said he was *their* best friend – just his dad's.

Callum was about to bend down and speak to him when Beth grabbed her son's hand. 'Come on!'

'Let go!' Fergus pulled away. 'What is that?' He ran out of the door, pushing past the adults trying to get outside.

They all turned around as Fergus ran up to the camper van. He turned around. 'I want to go inside.'

He was already pulling at the door handle. The van was open. Callum never bothered to lock it. He couldn't imagine anyone stealing an old campervan.

Fergus pulled the door open.

'Fergus!' Jack called out.

'I'll go and get him,' said Beth.

Callum smiled. 'It's all right, I'll give him a tour.'

'No, I think he should come inside.'

Jack turned to his wife. 'Beth, why not let him have a look inside? What's the harm? He'll only badger us to death to have a look if we don't let him. You know what he's like.'

Callum's gaze drifted to Beth. *Yes, what was the harm? Didn't she trust him with her child?* 'He'll be fine, honestly. There's not much to see.' He glanced in the direction of the van, catching Fergus already climbing inside.

Callum turned to Beth and Jack with a question. 'Say, I've been meaning to ask – why did you call him Fergus?' It wasn't that he didn't like the name – after all, he'd lived with it for nine years while starring in *The Scottish Laird*. He was just intrigued about why they'd chosen such an old-fashioned name for their son.

Jack rolled his eyes. 'That was Beth. She's, like, obsessed with your show. Watches every single episode. And the reruns.'

'Jack! Really, that's not true. I may tune into the occasional episode.'

'The occasional episode?' Jack scoffed. 'Oh, my goodness – if you don't get your fix of *The Scottish Laird*, if you have to miss an episode for an evening out, or something, boy, do you get the hump.'

Callum stared at her.

Beth avoided his gaze. 'I do not.' She folded her arms. 'In any case, it's not like there's much else on television, is there?'

Jack opened his mouth to say something.

'Not anything worthwhile watching, that is,' Beth quickly added. She glared at her husband.

Jack shut his mouth. He got the hint that it was time to change the subject. He turned to Callum. 'You'd better give Fergus that tour before he drives off in it.' Jack motioned in the direction of the van.

A loud horn honked, making Callum jump. Fergus was sitting in the driver's seat.

'The handbrake is on – isn't it?' Beth said in alarm.

Callum gave her a reassuring smile. 'Don't worry, that van isn't going anywhere.' He frowned when he turned in the direction of the van, thinking he'd much prefer it really wasn't going anywhere after dinner. He still had no clue where he was going to park it up tonight. He hadn't really envisaged sleeping in it.

'Don't be long,' Beth called out. 'Dinner will be on the table soon.'

Callum halted and turned around. 'Beth, I don't want to impose. I should have told you I was coming.'

'Yes, you should have,' Beth replied.

Jack said, 'Not to worry, mate – you're always welcome,' before he walked into the farmhouse.

I might be welcome here, thought Callum, *just not the old campervan.*

He saw Beth lingering by the door for a moment. He noticed she did not echo Jack's sentiments. He wasn't surprised. His dropping in had been a mistake in light of the secret he wished he and Beth did not share.

Even so, Callum couldn't help but smile as he turned around and watched Fergus having a great time, honking the horn and pretending to steer the van, even though he could barely see over the steering wheel.

'What's that?' Fergus asked Callum through the open window as he approached.

Callum walked around the van and got into the passenger seat, so he could see what Fergus was pointing to. 'Ah, that long stick is the gear shift. It's antiquated, I know.'

For a moment, Callum forgot he was talking to a four-year-old. He wasn't used to being around children. 'It's old,' he explained. Callum had seen the brand new electric vehicle on the driveway. He guessed their investment, or rather his, in converting the outbuilding and farmhouse was paying off very well indeed.

'No, not the stick.' Fergus pointed. 'That!'

Callum spotted something furry hunkered down in the footwell by his feet.

'Oh. My. God. What the fu—' Callum caught himself in time from uttering an expletive that, he had no doubt, would be repeated ad nauseum by Fergus as soon as he walked in the farmhouse.

Callum scrambled over the front seat into the back of the van, his first thought to get as far away from whatever that was, forgetting that he could just as easily have opened the passenger door and scrambled out of the van instead.

He grabbed Fergus and pulled him out of his seat. He stood stooped in the back of the van, holding Fergus under an arm.

'Let go!'

Callum looked at him hanging there lopsided. 'Oh, yes, of course. Sorry.' Callum put him down.

'I'm going to investigate,' said Fergus, holding up his light sabre.

'Investigate?' He thought it was a big word for a small child. 'No, come here!' Callum wanted them to leave by the sliding side doors.

'Hey, I know what that is.'

Callum couldn't believe he was almost hiding behind a child dressed as a character from Star Wars. If only his fans could see him now, the great Laird MacGregor crouching behind a child, hiding from some little creature in his van.

'What is it?' he asked, peeking from behind Fergus.

'It's a cat.'

'A cat?' Callum heard it hiss. 'So it is.' He stood up to take a closer look. 'What is a cat doing in the—?' Callum stopped short. 'Oh, no.'

Fergus turned around, brushed his blond hair out of his eyes, and cast his big brown eyes up at Callum. 'Is it your cat?'

Fergus asked. 'Can I stroke it?'

'No, it's not my cat.' But Callum knew whose it was.

'Whose cat is it?'

Callum sighed. He hadn't recognised the cat at first – but he should have. He'd grown up with that cat. It was his dad's. He was quite shocked to discover that it was still alive. It must be the oldest cat on the planet. Dickens had obviously lived an awful lot longer than the average cat's life expectancy.

Callum's dad had always taken the cat with him in the camper-van on his business trips. Dickens had been his dad's little travelling companion. His mum had never complained because for some reason, she had hated the cat. But she'd obviously been left with it when her husband moved into the care home.

Callum answered Fergus's question. 'It's my dad's cat.' He stared at the scared little black cat with white paws and a white patch of fur around one eye. Wherever he'd been hiding for the whole trip down from Scotland – curled up fast asleep, no doubt, on the comfy sofa in the back of the van – he'd been well and truly jolted awake by the sound of Fergus furiously honking the horn.

'What's his name?'

'Dickens.'

'What's he doing in the van?'

That was a good question. Callum glanced at the split windows in the passenger and driver door. The little window beside the main one that rolled down, opened out. One of them had been left open a crack, and the wily black and white cat staring at them from the footwell had obviously squeezed in and made himself at home for the day – or as it happened, on a journey all the way from Scotland to Suffolk. And there was a reason he hadn't come out of his hiding place and made his presence known. The silly cat probably thought he was going on a trip with Callum's dad.

Callum stared at the cat. If only he could speak, what stories might he tell about their trips together?

'Can I stroke him?'

Callum didn't even get a chance to say no before Fergus squeezed between the front seats and reached for the cat.

'No, wait!' The last thing he needed was for Fergus to run crying from the van after been scratched or bitten by the cat – or both – when he'd promised his mum that her son would be fine.

'It's okay, Callum, he's friendly – look.' Fergus had already crouched down in the footwell and picked up the little cat. He sat him on his lap and stroked him.

To Callum's surprise, the cat actually purred.

'Oh, okay.'

Callum reached over to give him a pet too, and got swiped by an angry paw, which scratched his hand.

'Je-sus!' Callum snatched his hand back.

'Mummy says you shouldn't say that.'

Callum looked at Fergus. 'Pardon?'

'That's what she tells Daddy if he uses that word. I think it's swearing.'

'Ahem, well, she's right. That was, er … very naughty of me. Um, you won't tell your mum that I said that – will you? It's our secret, eh?'

Fergus narrowed those big brown eyes, and seemed to consider it for a moment. 'Okay. But you mustn't say it again. Unless you're saying a prayer. That's what Mummy told Daddy.'

'Of course. I promise,' said Callum in relief. He looked at the cat, all mush in Fergus' little arms, and frowned. Callum's hand stung where the cat had scratched him. He looked at the cat and thought, *Don't blame me. It's your fault you got into the van, fell asleep, and woke up hundreds of miles from home.*

'Can I keep him?' Fergus asked.

'What?'

Fergus was already opening the van door. 'I'm going to ask my mum.'

'No – wait!'

Surprisingly, the cat stayed in his arms as he walked at a pace to the farmhouse.

Callum quickly followed.

31

'Mummy, Daddy! Look what I found in Callum's van.'

Callum stepped into the farmhouse. 'I think I should put him back in the van.'

When Beth and Jack saw the cat, they readily agreed. 'Son, we can't have a cat on the farm. We've got chickens to think of.'

'But I want one.'

'How about a dog?' Jack said.

'Jack!'

He looked at his wife.

Fergus turned around and thrust the cat at Callum. 'I'm getting a puppy! Yippee!' While Fergus did a happy dance around the kitchen table, Jack got the evil eye from his wife.

Callum looked at Dickens. He expected that any minute now, the cat in his arms was going to lash out again. 'I think I'll go and put the cat back in the van.' Callum made a hasty retreat, not only because he didn't want to be attacked again by the cat, but also because he realised Jack was in trouble for suggesting a pet dog.

Oh dear, thought Callum. *I definitely should not have dropped in unannounced*. He glanced at the food on the table on his way out and wondered if he was still welcome for dinner. He hoped so. He was starving. On his way out, Jack passed him a bottle of water and a small plastic bowl. When Callum had raised his eyebrows, Jack sighed and said, 'For the cat. He must be parched.'

Callum stared at Dickens as he hot-footed it back to the van. He briefly put him down to see if he needed a toilet break, which he imagined was long overdue. Not surprisingly, he did. Dickens took more time clearing up his mess, attempting to bury it under a mound of earth. Callum scooped him up, quickly opened the van door, and gingerly placed the cat inside, along with a bowl of water. He thought he really should buy some cat food; Dickens must be starving too.

Callum shut the cat in the van and checked that all the windows were securely shut. Dickens sat in the driver's seat and looked at him through the window. He hissed.

Callum took a step back, forgetting for a moment that there was a window between him and the grumpy cat. 'Yeah, well, sorry but you're going to have to stay there until I get back. I'll bring you some leftovers.'

Callum retreated from the van, wondering whether Dickens was going to be a problem. How would he drive the van know there was a grumpy cat prowling around in there? Callum heaved a sigh. Unless Dickens was going to curl up and go to sleep, like he had been on the whole journey from Scotland, Callum knew he'd probably need to buy a cat carrier to be on the safe side.

His stomach rumbled loudly. 'Let's deal with one problem at a time.' Firstly, he needed something to eat, and secondly, he needed to figure out where he was going to park the damn van, which he was obviously going to be spending the night in. With Dickens.

Callum rolled his eyes. He really hoped that all this – dropping in unexpectedly on his friends and discovering he couldn't stay with them, along with the discovery of the cat – wasn't going to turn out to be a bad omen. This trip was meant to be straightforward; he was there to find the bookshop and sell it. For some reason, he had a feeling in the pit of his stomach that it was going to be anything but straightforward.

He willed himself not to think about the next potential problem – the bookshop. All he wanted to find out right now was that his invitation to dinner had not been rescinded.

Callum walked up to the farmhouse door, took a deep breath, and gingerly knocked.

The door flew open. 'What are you knocking for?' Jack asked, grabbing his arm. 'Come inside.' He gestured at the kitchen. 'Go, grab a seat at the table.'

Callum walked into the kitchen. Fergus was already sitting at the table. Callum noticed he was drawing something with crayons.

'What are you drawing – can I see?'

Fergus put his crayon down and held it up just as Beth walked into the room carrying a hotpot. Jack brought up the rear with two dishes, one with roasted vegetables, the other with potatoes.

'I'm drawing my puppy, the one I want.'

Callum caught Beth frowning at the picture as she leaned over to put the hotpot on the table. 'Um, that's a nice drawing,' said Callum, smiling weakly.

'Take your crayons and drawing pad off the table please, Fergus.'

'But Mummy, I haven't finished my drawing.'

'Do as your mum asked please, lad,' said Jack, looking sheepishly at his wife.

Callum watched Fergus pick up his stuff and dump it on the

kitchen worktop behind him. The kitchen was new, with expensive granite worktops. Callum hadn't been there since they'd renovated the farmhouse, which had only been possible because of the money he'd sent them to pay off their mortgage and debts.

He sighed, thinking, *Perhaps I should have prioritised my own mortgage first.* But theirs had been a drop in the ocean compared to his own, and at that time, he'd just thought that the good times – meaning the money – wouldn't end.

Had he been happy, though? That was another story. If someone had told him that the show would be over after the last season wrapped, he'd probably have been over the moon, if he'd been in a better financial position.

Callum didn't want to think about that. Instead, he glanced around their cosy farmhouse kitchen. It was small by the standard Callum had been used to while living in his sprawling Beverley Hills mansion. But it was exactly how he imagined a little farmhouse kitchen should be, with an Aga, oak kitchen units, and a big wooden family-sized table seating eight people at least, taking up far too much space in the centre of the kitchen.

Surprisingly, before Beth sat down at the table, she picked up Fergus's drawing of a black dog and stuck it with a magnet to the fridge door. When she sat at the kitchen table, she said to Fergus, 'So, what are you going to call your puppy?'

Callum caught Beth eyeing Jack and throwing him a wisp of a smile. She'd obviously decided there was no going back now – Fergus would be getting a dog.

Fergus put a finger to his lips. 'Um, I don't know. I like Chewie.'

Beth sighed. 'Do we have to name the dog after a Wookie?'

Callum sniggered into his hand as Jack ladled some of the hotpot onto Callum's plate. He could tell Beth lived with a Star

Wars fan; despite not being a fan herself, she clearly knew all the names of the characters.

'What about Teebo?' Jack suggested.

'We are not naming the dog after an Ewok.' She raised her eyebrows at Jack. 'We will have plenty of time to think up a name for the puppy – a *sensible* name.'

As Beth passed around the roast vegetables and potatoes, Jack turned to Callum. 'So, you finally got a break from filming?'

'Yes, of sorts. Quite a long break, actually. They cancelled the series.'

'No way! After all these years?'

'Yes, that's Hollywood for you.'

Beth exclaimed, 'No! They can't do that!'

Callum shook his head. 'I'm afraid they can. I'm not sorry, on one level.' Callum wouldn't tell them what a fool he'd been with his money – helping out his best friends, notwithstanding. 'I'm getting too old for that lark.'

'Too old?' scoffed Jack. 'You're thirty-seven, for goodness' sake, and you haven't let yourself go like me. You don't look a day over… well, thirty-seven.'

'Ha ha,' said Callum sarcastically, smiling at his joke.

'But seriously, what will you do? Actually, that's a dumb question. You could retire – lucky bastard.'

'Jack, language!'

'Oops, sorry.'

Callum didn't know what to say in response to Jack's assumption that he could retire, and the inference that he could sit on his backside for the rest of his life. *If only*. So he changed the subject. 'Look, the reason I've travelled all this way, apart from to drop in on my best friends, is that I'm here to visit a bookshop.'

Jack, who had been about to eat another forkful of stew, lowered his fork. 'Did you just say you've travelled all the way from Scotland to visit a bookshop?'

Callum nodded.

'You do realise that you could have found one a bit closer – oh, I don't know, say in Edinburgh.'

Callum shook his head. 'Very funny, Jack. I'm looking for a particular bookshop.'

Beth said, 'Why? What's so special about it?'

'Well, here's the thing. It turns out that I own it.'

Beth and Jack exchanged a confused glance. 'Pardon?'

'Yeah. I went to visit my dad—'

Jack interrupted. 'How is Henry?'

'Oh, you know …' Callum trailed off. He didn't want to think of his father in that care home. It didn't help that he'd arrived home to his mum running a book club with her friends. He was sure she had a special friend too. Callum thought of the only guy in the club.

It didn't seem right, somehow. He understood she was entitled to move on with her life, but should she have done it that fast? He knew he shouldn't knock her. Perhaps it was her way of coping with such a big change, effectively the loss of her husband. Unfortunately, with the illness his dad had, the grieving process had already begun as they lost him bit by bit.

Callum caught Jack and Beth exchanging a glance. 'So, about this bookshop,' said Beth, changing the subject.

'Yes, the bookshop—'

'May I get down from the table?' interrupted Fergus.

'Don't interrupt while someone is talking.'

Fergus frowned. 'Sorry.'

Callum smiled at him. 'It's okay.' He glanced at Beth.

Beth said, 'All right, Fergus. Why don't you go and play for a bit. It will be bedtime soon.'

Callum watched Fergus get down from the table and run out of the room. When he turned around he caught Beth staring at him. Beth quickly looked away.

'So, about this bookshop,' said Jack, scooping up the last of the hotpot onto his plate. He hesitated, holding up the ladle with the last of the stew. 'Does anyone want some more?'

Callum sat back in his chair, and wiped his mouth with a serviette. 'Nope, not for me. That was delicious, but I'm stuffed.'

Jack put the last of the stew on his plate.

Callum got the photo out of his wallet. 'Ever seen this place before?' The solicitor he'd spoken with about the deeds had given him the address, but there was no Satnav in the van, and the bookshop didn't have a website, which didn't surprise him. 'I know it's in Aldeburgh, in Suffolk. It's called The Bookshop of Memories.'

'The Bookshop of Memories – no way!' Beth looked at him in surprise. 'I know that place. It's opposite The Potting Shed.'

'The Potting Shed?' Callum had no clue where that was.

Jack said, 'We started another side-hustle – well, Beth did. She's very enterprising. We've renovated the old greenhouse in the kitchen garden. Turns out that among my wife's many qualities, she has green fingers. She grows the most beautiful flowers, and sells them to a lovely young lady called Lili, who runs a flower shop in Aldeburgh.' He turned to his wife. 'Why don't you give Callum a tour of our new greenhouse?'

Callum noticed that Beth didn't appear keen to give him a tour. He said, 'Wait, isn't Aldeburgh just down the road from here?'

Beth nodded. 'Yes, that's where The Potting Shed is and your bookshop, in a place called Cobblers Yard.'

'Cobblers Yard,' mused Callum. He imagined a little clique of shops with Dickensian type shop fronts. He hoped it lived up to his expectations because, if it did, the store would be saleable and would hopefully fetch a good price.

Callum decided to show them the photo just to be sure.

'Where did you get this photo?' asked Beth.

'My dad.'

'Who are those girls?'

'I don't know. Anyway, is this the bookshop?'

Beth took the photo and scrutinised it. 'Yes, that's definitely the place.'

Callum grinned.

'But ...'

Callum's smile faded. There just had to be a *but*, a catch. 'What is it?'

'This photo must have been taken some time ago.'

Callum had already presumed that was the case. Something about the way the girls were dressed, and their hairstyles, and the fact that the photo was dog-eared, as though it had been sitting in that old wallet for quite some time.

He looked at Beth, who was waiting to find out what the problem was. He caught Jack, who was leaning towards her, looking at the photo and shaking his head.

Beth handed him the photo back. 'I'm afraid that bookshop has been closed for years. It might take a bit of time and elbow grease to sort the place out.'

'I've got all the time in the world.' And the motivation to get it done. Callum was thinking of the money. He had no intention of reopening the shop; just making it presentable to sell it.

Jack said, 'How did you come to own this place anyway? You know it must be worth a bit of money – right? I mean, the Suffolk Coast, especially places like Aldeburgh and Southwold, are really expensive when it comes to property.'

That was music to Callum's ears. However, he was still looking at Beth's expression, wondering just how much elbow grease would be involved.

She added, 'I'm afraid you'll find the place needs *quite* a bit of tlc.'

Jack nodded. 'I'll say.'

Callum frowned, thinking, *Why am I not surprised?* It couldn't be as easy as just turning up, doing a bit of dusting one afternoon, and putting it on the market as a going concern to bring in lots of cash.

A peculiar thought popped into his head out of nowhere. *I could run it myself, making a decent living.*

'I think it's got a flat above the shop,' said Beth.

'Has it?' Callum said.

'Don't quote me on that. I mean, the other shops in Cobblers Yard have, so I just assume that one has too.'

Callum caught Jack nodding in agreement.

Callum stared at them. A home and a business all in one. Is that why his dad had wanted him to have the place – because he'd known that one day his Hollywood life would implode and he'd need somewhere to live, and something to do?

Callum couldn't believe the thought of running the bookshop himself had even entered his head. That wasn't the plan. The plan was to sell and pay off his debts, or at least carry the mortgage on the house in Beverley Hills until it sold. He wouldn't walk away with much, but at least he'd walk away debt-free – he hoped. It reminded him that he had to check in with the realtor back in LA at some point to let them know where he was – although they still had his mobile phone number; he was sure they'd get in touch if a buyer appeared.

Jack said, 'I've got the most brilliant idea. You could move into the flat above the shop while you do it up. Then you'd be just down the road, and you can visit whenever you like.'

Beth voiced her thoughts too. 'Really, Jack, that's a dumb idea.'

Callum turned to Beth. 'Now, anyone would think you don't want me to hang around in Suffolk.' It was meant as a joke, but the look on her face suggested that it was true.

Beth said, 'All I'm saying is that the shop hasn't been open for twenty-five years, so I'm guessing, going by the state of the shop, that the flat won't be much different.'

'Twenty-five years?'

'Rumour has it,' Jack added, lowering his voice to a whisper, as though he was about to tell a secret, 'that the owner just upped and vanished.'

Callum frowned. 'Pardon?'

'Yes, and hasn't been heard of since.'

Beth eyed Callum intently. 'You didn't say how you came by this place. Have you inherited it from some long-lost aunt – or something?'

Callum pursed his lips. 'Something like that,' he mumbled. The last thing he intended to do was lie to his closest friends, but they obviously had no idea that his dad had owned the bookshop, because he hadn't actually told them yet.

He stared at them, and for some reason felt he wanted to get to the bottom of what connection his dad had to the girls in the photo, and why he'd owned a bookshop for years that Callum had known nothing about.

Another thought popped into his head. Did his mum know about the bookshop? Until he found out what the hell was going on, he didn't feel inclined to ask her that question.

'Something like that?' said Jack repeating what Callum had just said. 'It's quite a mystery among the locals, what happened to the bookshop owner all those years ago – not to mention the fact that it appears no one even remembers who they were. Aren't you going to put us out of our misery and tell us who it is?'

His friends were looking at him expectantly. He was saved from the awkward question by Fergus running into the kitchen. 'I've thought of a name for my dog! I want to call him Luke.'

'Good choice,' said Jack, scooping the little boy into his arms and sitting him on his knee.

Beth rolled her eyes at them. 'May I just ask one question? What if it's a girl dog? Then what will you call her?'

'That's easy,' said Fergus. 'I'll call her Leia.'

Beth rolled her eyes. 'Of course.'

Everyone laughed, even Beth. 'All right, you. Bedtime.'

'I'll do bedtime,' said Jack.

'I'll do the dishes,' offered Callum.

Jack shook his head. 'No, way. You're our dinner guest.' He cast a glance at his wife. 'I'll wash up after I've put Fergus to bed. Right – time for bed, little man.' Jack put him down.

To Callum's surprise, Fergus ran up to him. Climbing on his lap, he flung his arms around Callum's neck and kissed his cheek. 'Goodnight, Uncle Callum, I love you.'

'Oh, er … yes. Goodnight. I love you too.'

Beth reached for Fergus. 'Right, come on, it's bedtime.'

'Can I say goodnight to Dickens?'

'Who?'

Callum sighed. 'That's the cat in the van.' He'd completely forgotten about his grumpy, hissy travelling companion.

Fergus said, 'Callum, will you take me out in your van?'

Callum looked helplessly at Jack and Beth. Of course he couldn't do that. He presumed he'd need a child seat. And besides, although he wouldn't mind at all – in the short time he'd been there, he'd already grown quite fond of the little boy – he got the impression that Fergus' overprotective helicopter parent would say—

'No, absolutely not. Callum is a busy man – too busy to take little boys out for a spin in his van.'

Fergus frowned at his parents and stomped off upstairs.

32

Jack stood up. 'Right, well I'm going upstairs to get him to bed. I think he's overtired. Beth, you can show Callum your pride and joy.'

Callum turned to Beth, raising an eyebrow.

Beth rolled her eyes. 'He's talking about my greenhouse. Cal, you really don't have to see it. It's nothing special.'

'Nothing special?' Jack guffawed.

Callum said, 'No, I'd love to see it, really.'

'Go on, Beth – he said he'd like to see it.'

'All right.'

Callum followed Beth and Jack out of the kitchen. He glanced at Jack, who was carrying a glass of milk up the stairs. 'Fergus, are you changing into your pyjamas? I've got your glass of milk. I'm coming up to read you a bedtime story.'

Callum smiled but felt a little sad when he realised that he'd spent his life chasing a dream, and real life was passing him by. His best mate was married and had a child – that was real life. Sure, he'd had a starring role in a long-running series, but that meant nothing now; pretty soon he'd be forgotten, along with that series – apart perhaps by some super-fans like Beth, who'd watch the reruns broadcast on some obscure network channel relegated to a late-night slot that hardly anyone would tune in to watch.

He had already acknowledged he was a has-been. He had a feeling the door to Hollywood had shut firmly in his face, and that side of his life was over. He'd already thought that perhaps it was for the best. Seeing Jack with his wife and child only confirmed how he'd been feeling for some time; the path he'd chosen in life was not for him anymore – if it ever really had been. He was looking for something else in life; something real that fame or a Beverley Hills mansion would not give him.

As he followed Beth out of the door and across their gravel driveway, passing the campervan and the grumpy cat, which was still sitting in the driver's seat, staring right at him as he passed by, the bookshop came to mind. That was real. But the trouble was that no matter how much the idea of keeping it might appeal to him, he still needed to sell it for the money in order to keep afloat while he off-loaded the stupid commitments he'd saddled himself with across the pond.

'So, this is it,' Beth said, interrupting his thoughts. They'd walked around the side of the farmhouse and through a gate into the walled kitchen garden. At the back of the kitchen garden, where Beth and Jack were growing their own vegetables, was a large, wooden structure.

'It was here when we moved in, but totally beyond repair. I liked the old-fashioned wooden conservatory abutting the kitchen garden wall, so I used some of the money you invested in the farm to have the old structure rebuilt and enlarged.'

Callum nodded. He remembered the last time Beth had given him a tour when he'd visited five years earlier. Had it really been that long? He recalled the state of the outbuildings, including the kitchen garden and the old rundown greenhouse. That was when he'd said he wanted to invest in their farm.

'It's really something, Beth.' He could see several long trestle tables inside where she was growing the flowers she sold to the local flower shop. 'Looks like things are really working out with your side hustles,' he said, genuinely pleased that his investment was paying off for them. He thought that at least there was something to show for the money he'd earned over the years in that show. They had put the money to good use, and it hadn't been wasted, frittered away on things they didn't need.

He liked the thought that they would have something to pass on to their son; something worthwhile that they were building for his future, and that he'd contributed in a small way. Callum had given them a lot of money, but it was up to them to make something out of their new business ventures; from what he'd seen, they were doing really well.

Beth whirled around and folded her arms. 'That's what I want to talk to you about.'

'Pardon?' Callum wasn't sure what she meant.

'You paid for this too, you know.'

Callum looked at the greenhouse. He wasn't sure why she'd brought that up.

'Have you come to collect? I know you said you didn't need money, but why else would you be here? And you would not have travelled all the way from Scotland in that thing if there wasn't something up. I mean what would you care if you inherited some old, rundown bookshop?'

Callum stared at her. Beth was the smart one of the couple; far too perceptive. Unlike Jack, nothing passed her by. She was the reason they'd made a success of the farm.

'There's something going on, Callum, I just know there is.'

Callum knew there was no good denying it. But he was not about to tell Beth about his situation. He wanted to save face. There was no way he would admit to Beth that he was in trouble financially. If she knew that, she'd never believe him when he genuinely said, 'I am not here to collect anything.'

He took a breath, and reiterated, 'I told you from the off that although I invested in your farm, I do not want a penny in return, and never will. That was always the deal.'

'Apart from a percentage of the proceeds of the rental income from the cottages,' Beth reminded him.

Callum raised his eyebrows. He hadn't forgotten. How could he? Right now, he needed that money. He hoped to goodness Beth wasn't going to ask for that money back. 'I don't suppose I need to remind you that it was Jack who insisted that if I was going to invest, I had to take a small cut of the profits. He made me promise. I can't go back on my word.' Callum felt terrible for not revealing why he needed to stick to that agreement.

However, as far as Callum was concerned, things had not changed. He still wouldn't take a penny from their farm, other than that small percentage of the rental income. He'd rather sleep on the streets than do that – or sleep in a campervan, which was where he'd be tonight, and probably for the next few days while he sorted out getting the bookshop on the market. And as soon as he'd sorted his finances, and got a job, that money would go straight back into a fund for Fergus.

'It's guilt money – isn't it? For what we did.'

Callum looked at her, surprised she'd brought *that* up. The thought had never entered his head when he had given them the money. In his mind, all he had wanted to do was help out his best friends. Although, looking back, he wondered if it was true.

At the time, Beth and Jack had been going through some financial troubles, and he had been afraid it might spell the end of their marriage. The farm was a mess. They'd bitten off more than they could chew; although Beth had inherited the farm, she didn't know much about farming. She'd been to university and got a degree, but it wasn't relevant. Jack was just as useless. And to top it all, they were getting nowhere trying for a child.

But all that had changed on Callum's last visit, five years earlier, when he'd seen the state of their farm, and their marriage, and had offered them the money. They hadn't been in a position to refuse – they had been desperate.

And then their fortunes had turned around completely. He guessed that being relieved of the stress of the farm haemorrhaging money and of all the loans and the mortgage payments had helped Beth to finally become pregnant.

Callum's smile suddenly dissipated. He felt that five years earlier, in the midst of Beth's and Jack's marriage going through a rocky patch, he'd taken advantage of Beth. 'I am so sorry. When you were at your lowest ebb, I shouldn't have—'

Beth held up her hand to silence him. 'It wasn't your fault, Callum. Jack and I were … distant. We hadn't … been together for a time. We were going through a tough time, as you know. I needed to feel close to somebody. And you showing up the way you did, out of the blue …' She trailed off. 'I'm sorry.'

Callum stared at her. All this time, he'd felt terrible at the thought he'd taken advantage, but he now realised that Beth thought it was the other way around.

'Can you forgive me?' asked Beth.

'Of course.' Callum was relieved they were putting that one-night stand behind them. Callum stared at her when something occurred to him. 'It was never about me, was it? It was about that character I play.' Beth hadn't slept with him; she'd slept with a fictional character she was in love with. 'You're in love with him, aren't you? My character, Fergus MacGregor.'

'I'm afraid so. He's not real, though. I know that. That's why I married Jack.'

'Because I'm not him, really.'

Beth lowered her eyes. 'I'm so sorry, Cal.' She put a reassuring hand on his arm. 'But you're a good guy, and a good-looking guy.'

Not good enough for you, though, thought Callum. All this time, since way back when he and Jack had first met Beth hiking in Scotland on holiday with her girlfriends, he'd assumed that Beth was really in love with him, but that the reason she'd chosen Jack was because she didn't want to be a Hollywood wife. She had said that herself to his face once, all those years ago, that she didn't want to lead that life. But now he knew she'd only said it because she didn't want to hurt his feelings, as it was obvious he was besotted with her back then.

He thought of the saying that love is blind. He realised that he'd been blind to the fact that if she had been in love with him, then she'd have followed him anywhere – the way Jack had followed her to a life on the farm. That life didn't really suit Jack at all, but he'd made it work, for her – for the person he loved. *That's what love is, isn't it?* thought Callum. *Being prepared to follow someone to the ends of the earth.*

'You're going to find somebody, Callum, I just know you are. And when you do, don't blame me if I feel a little jealous – or maybe a lot jealous.'

Callum managed a smile. She was still trying not to hurt his feelings. He imagined that she might be a little envious of the person who eventually stole his heart, but only because of Fergus MacGregor.

Unfortunately, as much as he wanted to, he still couldn't be honest with Beth about his dire financial situation. It wasn't that he thought they'd turn their backs on him if they found out he needed money. On the contrary, he was afraid they would do quite the reverse, and do something stupid, like re-mortgage the farm to give him back some of the money. And cancel all the holiday bookings in one of the cottages so he had somewhere to live.

On no account was he going to let that happen. For them. Or for Fergus.

33

'Hey, you guys!' Jack appeared by the kitchen garden gate. 'You've been an age. I didn't think it took that long to see the greenhouse.' Jack started walking towards them. 'What were you doing out here?'

Beth quickly dropped her hand from Callum's arm.

Callum turned around and caught a look on his mate's face he'd never seen before – jealousy. He wanted to tell Jack that he had absolutely nothing to worry about. The trouble was, as Beth had said, he was a good-looking guy. And as Jack had said, Callum hadn't let himself go like Jack had.

Callum stepped forward. 'We were talking about the *real* reason I'm here,' he called out. 'I have a confession to make.' He glanced at Beth, who raised her eyebrows, the look on her face afraid what he might be here to confess. She started to shake her head, mouthing *Please don't tell him.*

Callum looked at her in surprise. How could she think that? He would never do anything to jeopardise his best friends' relationship – although he realised it was a bit late for that now; that horse had bolted. But even so, Jack would never, ever find out.

Beth wouldn't tell him, and neither would he, so there was

nothing to worry about. Callum whispered, out of earshot of Jack, who was making his way down the kitchen garden towards them, 'Don't worry. There's no way I'd tell him. And I know you wouldn't.'

He caught something in Beth's expression. She should have been relieved, but she wasn't – not at all. Before he had a chance to ask her what the matter was, he heard footsteps on the gravel path behind him.

Callum whirled around. 'It's about the campervan, Jack, and the photo of those two girls outside the bookshop. You see, I promised my dad I'd find them and give them the van. That's why I've driven all the way from Scotland in it.'

'Seriously? He wants you to give them some old van?' Jack asked as they fell in step and headed back towards the farmhouse. Callum glanced over his shoulder at Beth. Worry lines were creasing her brow. She wasn't listening to their conversation, he could tell. She was thinking about something else – but what?

'Who are they?' Jack asked.

Callum turned to Jack. 'I have no idea.'

'Is Fergus asleep?' Beth asked, catching up with them, and cutting in.

'I think so.'

'You think so? You can't leave him alone in the farmhouse! He could get up to anything.'

'I only walked down here!' Jack pointed out. 'You were out here a long time.'

Beth glared at him. 'I'm going to check on him right now.'

'What's got into her?' Jack commented staring after her.

Callum shrugged.

Jack apologised, 'Sorry, not sure what her problem is. I

thought he was asleep, and I only stepped out of the house for a minute.'

Callum didn't know what her problem was either, although he had an idea as he glanced at the farmhouse. *The problem is me, being here, stirring up a mistake she made five years ago.* He sighed, realising the time had come to leave.

'Do you know how you'll find them, the girls in the photo, and what they have to do with your dad?'

'I don't know.' Callum didn't really want to get into it. He wished he hadn't mentioned it.

Jack said, 'Do you mind if I make an observation?'

Callum raised an eyebrow, wondering what was on his mind. 'Er, no … not at all.'

'Look, mate, your dad is … unwell. Whoever he thinks these girls are, and why he thinks he needs them to have the campervan …' He trailed off. 'What I'm trying to say, and not making a good job of it, I might add, is I reckon it's the dementia messing with his mind, with his memories.'

Callum stared at him a long moment. 'You're saying that however this photo came into my dad's possession, this business about giving them the campervan is nonsense?'

Jack nodded. 'I can't imagine what you're going through. If he can't distinguish what is real and what isn't, how can *you* in terms of what he's saying to you?'

Callum nearly blurted, *I know the bookshop is real because I spoke to a solicitor.* He pushed that thought to one side, and focused on the photo. Was it possible that it was just a coincidence that two girls, perhaps local or on holiday, had their photo taken outside the bookshop? But how had the photo ended up in a wallet in the back of his dad's desk drawer? Perhaps he'd found the wallet, meaning to return it to the real owner. Callum looked at Jack, mulling over what he'd just said. Callum was wondering if he'd got things all wrong. When his dad had told him about the wallet in the desk drawer, and asked him to take the campervan to give it to the girls in the photo, he had assumed his dad was in his right mind. When he'd returned with the wallet to see his dad, and he'd said it wasn't his, Callum had thought that his dad was confused and that it was the dementia talking.

Callum was thinking about a plausible explanation for all this. What if, when his dad had bought the campervan years ago, he'd found the wallet in the van? Then he'd put the wallet in his desk drawer for safekeeping, intending to return it, and had forgotten all about it. That might explain why he thought the campervan should be returned to the previous owner's kids. The fact that the two girls had happened to have their photo taken outside the bookshop might simply be a coincidence.

Callum stared at his best friend. If Jack's theory was true, then all these thoughts going around his head about the possibility his dad might have led a double life with a second family would turn out quite false.

Jack stared at Callum, and burst out laughing. 'Sorry, mate, but what on earth has got into you? I know Henry. There is no way on this earth that your dad led a double life – if that's what you're thinking.'

'But how can you be so sure?'

'Because he is Henry. I mean, I don't think he'd have it in him to do that – do you?'

Callum stared at Jack. 'It does sound ridiculous – doesn't it?'

'Completely. You know what I think? Your show has just been cancelled, you're all over the place, and your dad is messing with your head – through no fault of his own, obviously. I am really sorry to say this, but I think he's led you on a merry goose chase. It's all a load of claptrap, the wallet, the girls, and the campervan. If I were you, I'd forget about it.'

But I can't. What about the bookshop? Callum wanted to ask. That was the huge spanner in the works of Jack's thinking.

'You look tired, mate. I'm really sorry you can't stay. Actually, why don't you stay? Sod the guests, they can think what they like when they turn up to a campervan on the drive. In actual fact, I think I'm going to cancel one of the bookings. The rooms are all taken in the farmhouse too. We're running a bed and breakfast. But I can cancel somebody and you could stay—'

'No – absolutely not. You're not cancelling a guest.' They were not going to get a bad review for cancelling a guest at the last minute, and ruin their business, all because of him.

'Then just stay here, parked up for as long as you like.'

Callum looked at the farmhouse and caught Beth starting out of the window at them. He didn't think that was a good idea either. 'What? And have little Fergus pestering you to let me take him out on a road trip,' Callum joked. 'Seriously, I'm fine. I'm going to drive into Aldeburgh and find a place to park up for the night. I want to check out the bookshop first thing in the morning.'

'Are you sure?'

Callum flashed him a reassuring smile. 'Absolutely.' He turned to the van.

'Wait. Let me go and tell Beth you're leaving.'

Callum caught his arm. 'No, it's fine. Look, I'm sure I'll see her. She takes her flowers to The Potting Shed in Cobblers Yard, right? She can pop into the bookshop and say hi.' Callum doubted she would, but he didn't tell Jack that.

'Oh, yeah – good idea.'

'Well, I'm off now.' Callum was just turning to his van when Jack grabbed him by the shoulders and gave him a hug, patting him on the back. When he drew back, he said, 'You're going to be okay, aren't you? I know what that show meant to you. On top of your dad, it must be like another loss.'

'Actually, it's not. I think I was kind of ready to move on. I just didn't realise it at the time.'

'You know, you could stay here on the Suffolk Coast. It's a great place to live, and you've got a bookshop, although you haven't exactly spelled out how you came to be in the possession of said bookshop …' He trailed off, the look on his face hopeful that Callum would enlighten him.

Callum looked at his watch. 'Another time.'

When Callum wasn't forthcoming, Jack said, 'I remember you used to do bookbinding with your dad. Whoever left you the place, I think it's kind of serendipity that you inherited it, isn't it?'

Not really, thought Callum.

Beth came running out of the farmhouse, surprising Callum. 'You didn't think you were leaving without saying goodbye!'

Jack said, 'He might not be leaving for good. I'm trying to persuade him to keep his bookshop. Wouldn't that be great if he was just down the road?'

Beth shook her head. 'No.'

Jack looked at her in surprise. 'But you always say how lucky we are to live in this part of the world.'

Callum gave her a sideways glance.

'What I meant,' said Beth, 'was that it's going to be quite a change from Hollywood. It might not suit him.'

'But it would suit us. It would be good for little Fergus. You saw how he took to Callum. He's not normally like that. It's great. My brother and sister are all the way up in Scotland, and you haven't got siblings, so it would be wonderful to have more family around.'

'But he's not family.'

Jack stared at her. 'That's a funny thing to say – he's our best friend. He's as good as family.'

Callum butted in, remembering he was on a mission to sell the bookshop. All this talk of him staying in Suffolk permanently to run a bookshop was not his agenda. 'Beth is right: it's quite a change from LA.' He ignored her comment about not being family – it was true, he wasn't.

Jack turned to him. 'But you said yourself you're ready to move on. I think the bookshop would be the perfect opportunity to do just that.'

Callum didn't comment. He could tell Jack wanted him to stay. Beth didn't feel the same way – that much was obvious.

'Well, I'd better head off before your guests arrive.'

As if on cue, Callum heard a car coming up the drive. He checked the coast was clear, glancing in the driver's side window for the cat. Callum didn't fancy being attacked again by Dickens. The cat was nowhere to be seen. Callum didn't feel particularly reassured by the fact that he couldn't see the cat. What if Dickens jumped out at him while he was driving?

I really need a cat carrier, thought Callum as he opened the door and climbed into the van. He was just switching on the engine and waving goodbye when Beth shouted out, 'Stop!'

Callum wound his window down. 'What is it?'

'You won't know how to find Cobblers Yard without directions.'

Callum smiled at her concern. 'I'm sure I will. It's in the town – right?'

'Yes, Cobblers Yard is just off the high street, but—'

'Well, there you go,' said Callum. He could see a car heading up their drive. 'I'd better get going.' He crunched the gears into reverse. 'Send my love to Fergus. He's a great lad. I hope to see him soon.'

Jack said, 'Don't worry, Callum. We'll come and visit you at the bookshop.'

Beth turned to Jack. 'You're far too busy with work on the farm. And Fergus has school.'

Callum started to wind his window up in case Dickens got out. He overheard Jack say, 'But you could visit when you pop in to see Lili with your autumn flowers.'

Callum slowly backed the van out of their driveway, giving the car passing him a wide berth. He happened to glance in his friends' direction, intending to give them a final wave goodbye, when he saw Beth still shaking her head at Jack's suggestion.

Callum continued to back out of their drive. If Jack knew about him and Beth, he wouldn't be suggesting that they all drop by and see him in the bookshop. In fact, this would probably be the last he ever saw of them.

Callum shuddered at the thought. Jack was his best friend, and he didn't want to lose that friendship because his wife had been infatuated by a fictional character in a television show and had acted out her fantasy on one mad night.

Callum berated himself for putting the onus completely at her door after what she'd said during their conversation. *I went along with it, didn't I? Only because I thought I was in love with her, and she was in love with me. How stupid can one person be?* He should have realised that if she had been in love with him, she wouldn't have married Jack.

34

Callum headed down the lane in the direction of Aldeburgh. He thought he heard a grumpy cat complaining from somewhere in the van. 'I'm stopping off to get you some food,' Callum said, feeling foolish for speaking to the cat. Although to his surprise, he did get a response from somewhere; there was a stunted meow. At least that confirmed Dickens was still in the van.

'Whiskas okay?'

Again, Dickens gave that funny stilted meow, as though he was actually answering Callum's question.

'I'll take that as a yes.'

Callum found two grocery stores on the way into Aldeburgh. He quickly popped into one of them, emerging a short time later with some cat food, cat biscuits, bottled water and two cat bowls, along with some cat litter and a tray. They didn't have Whiskas. He also had a four-pack of beer for himself. On his return, he was surprised to find Dickens in the driver's seat again, front paws on the window, looking for him.

Callum opened the driver's side door. He expected Dickens to jump out of the van, but the cat scooted over on to the passenger seat and nosed in the bag when Callum placed it on the seat next to him. 'Yes, it's all for you – apart from the beer, of course. Unless you want to join me for a drink when I finally get this thing parked up somewhere for the night.' Callum couldn't believe he was holding a conversation with a cat. He wondered if this was what his dad had done when he had been on the road with Dickens. Had he held conversations with his cat? *Probably*, thought Callum. He probably stopped in grocery stores to stock up on cat food and treats too.

He recalled what Beth had said about the bookshop – there was probably a flat above it. Perhaps it was furnished. That would be perfect. He'd rather stay there than drive around a place he did not know, trying to find where he could park up overnight. Although it had occurred to him that as Aldeburgh was a seaside town, he could park on the beach and wake up to a beautiful sunrise. *This isn't LA*, he reminded himself. *You can't just drive your van on to the beach, park it up and sleep there*. Although he didn't even know if you could do that in LA; he'd never done it, although he had seen it in the movies.

He looked at Dickens with his nose in the carrier bag. 'Come on – let's find the bookshop.' Apart from anything else, Callum didn't really want to spend the night cooped up in the van with the world's oldest cat. Did he even have control of his bladder anymore? Callum was relieved that he'd had the foresight to pick up some cat litter and a tray when he'd stopped off at the store. He sniffed the air. He couldn't smell anything untoward, for now.

With that thought, Callum put the van into gear and drove out of the small car park, following the street signs for Aldeburgh town centre. 'Not long now,' he commented.

Dickens let out another stilted meow.

He glanced at the cat and saw him standing on his hindlegs,

front paws on the dashboard, looking around.

'First impressions?'

Dickens let out a long meow.

'Yeah, I agree – it is kinda nice. Really nice, actually.' He drove past a large church on the left and then down a small incline, where he reached another road. Neat little red-brick terraced cottages lined the street, but he also spotted some shops and an old Tudor pub on the corner. This was the town's high street, where he knew he'd find Cobblers Yard. He drove slowly, keeping an eye out for Cobblers Yard that Beth had said was up a side street.

He thought of something else Beth had said: *You're going to find somebody, Callum, I just know you are. And when you do, don't blame me if I feel a little jealous.*

Callum frowned. He hadn't spotted Cobblers Yard yet. Looking for the bookshop reminded him of the promise he'd made his father to find the girls in the photo – girls who would now be young women. *No, I don't have to find them*, said a voice in his head. *Remember what Jack said – dad is unwell. Whoever he thinks these girls are, and whatever the reason is that he thinks he needs them to have the campervan … it's the dementia messing with his mind, with his memories.*

Callum thought he'd ask the cat. One stilted meow for *yes* was all he needed. 'Dickens, can I ask you a question?'

A stilted meow followed.

Callum smiled, 'Good.' He brought the campervan to a halt for a moment to let a motorist out of a parking space. He glanced at the cat. 'Now, what say we forget finding these girls and giving them this here campervan, and just get on with the business of preparing the bookshop to sell? What do you say?'

Dickens took his front paws off the dashboard, sat down in the seat, and actually hissed at him.

'Hey, calm down! What's your problem?' Callum actually shuffled over as much as he could in his seat to put some distance between him and the cat. Fortunately, he'd only driven a short distance when the cat jumped over the front seat into the back, surprising Callum with how agile he was for such an old cat. He could see Dickens in the rearview mirror. He was up on his hindlegs again, paws on the back window. He let out a kitty cry.

'What is your problem?' One minute the cat had been meowing quite happily, the next he was hissing; now he was crying. Callum shook his head. He thought of his dad and the mood swings his mother had told him about. Did cats get dementia too? Perhaps the cat would have been better off with dad after all.

Callum sighed as he continued his slow drive down the high street, still no closer to locating Cobblers Yard.

35

Thea glanced out of the restaurant window, her eyes following a yellow VW campervan that was slowly driving down the road. She stared at it, her eyes wide. *He came back*, she thought. Then she saw a young man – a really good-looking young man with a suntan – driving the van down the high street.

'What are you staring at?' asked Katie, sitting next to her brother.

'Oh, nothing,' said Thea, absent-mindedly. *What a stupid thought*, she berated herself. *It was just some guy, probably on holiday.*

Katie turned in her seat to look out of the window too. 'Oh, my god,' said Katie. 'Did you just see that?'

Thea stared at her. Surely, she didn't know that her grandpa had owned a yellow VW campervan. Perhaps Jenna had told her, or she'd seen old photos. Either way, it didn't matter. That wasn't Dad. How could it be? He'd been gone decades. He was never coming back.

Katie turned to her brother. 'Did you see that, Toby?'

'Yeah, it was a yellow van – so what?'

'No, I'm not talking about *the van*, dummy!'

Thea was about to have words about Katie calling her brother names, but Toby said, 'Then what are you talking about? And please stop calling me dummy.'

'I'm talking about the guy in the van – did you see him?'

Thea rolled her eyes. Of course her thirteen-year-old niece, teenage hormones racing, had discovered boys, and good-looking guys passing by in campervans who were way too old for her.

'That's the guy who stars in that American TV drama.'

Thea leaned forward in her seat, 'Who?'

'That guy on American TV who plays Laird Fergus MacGregor in *The Scottish Laird*.'

Thea shook her head. 'I'm sorry, but I don't know what you're talking about.'

'Oh, my god. Who hasn't heard of that show?'

'I haven't,' said Toby.

'Well, that doesn't surprise me, because you're weird.' Katie turned to her aunt. 'But seriously, Auntie Thea, you've never watched that show? He's famous.'

Thea shook her head. 'I'm afraid not.' She looked at Katie, sitting there avidly watching the campervan until it was out of sight. She didn't want to burst her bubble, but if the guy was that famous, what would he be doing in Aldeburgh, driving an ancient VW camper van – even if it did look in good nick? She reckoned that her niece was mistaken.

'I've got the DVDs of all the seasons. You can watch it if you like.'

Toby said, 'You only started watching that show because your friend, Caitlin, loves it.'

'That's not true. Well, perhaps it was to begin with, but now I really like it too.'

'And him,' said Toby. 'Someone's got a crush.'

'Oh, do shut up, Toby!' She turned to Thea. 'Do you want to watch it? You'll find the DVDs in the cupboard by the sofa.'

Thea shook her head. 'I think I'll pass, but thanks for offering.' Thea had no intention of spending her holiday watching some rubbish American TV drama. Besides, she had enough on her mind and doubted she'd be able to concentrate on it. She'd found out her sister wasn't leaving hospital any time soon, which meant that Mark had better step up and start working from home because she couldn't stay there looking after her niece and nephew indefinitely.

It had occurred to her that perhaps Mark was having an affair. But now she didn't know what to think because she'd found out something since visiting the hospital that had thrown her. The operation to insert a pin had gone well, and there had been no complications with the broken leg. That wasn't the problem. But the baby might be.

Thea had not expected to walk out of the visit with her sister finding out that Jenna was in the early stages of a pregnancy. That's why they were keeping her in for observation after emergency surgery; her leg had been broken when she'd tripped over the dog and fallen, so they needed to check there were no other complications.

Apparently, surgery was generally safe for pregnant women, although Thea imagined that her sister would have delayed surgery until she was further along, or even until after she'd given birth, if that had been possible. Thank goodness that so far, things were okay, medically speaking. She hadn't lost the baby. But after speaking with her sister, Thea had got the impression that Jenna was not okay. She'd been in floods of tears when she'd told Thea she was pregnant.

Thea didn't understand. She'd have thought her sister would

be over the moon. It had taken a long time to conceive with the twins, to the point that they'd had to go down the IVF route. She'd always said she'd been lucky on her first IVF round to get pregnant, and to have twins – a boy and a girl. But Jenna had always wanted a house full of children, and now she was getting her wish. That's what Thea had told her sister, thinking it would cheer her up. Instead it had just brought on more floods of tears.

At least the twins had not been in the hospital room at the time. They'd both been sitting in the car after their brief visit, during which Jenna had reassured them that everything was okay, and had not revealed that she was pregnant.

Before Thea had left to take the twins to this restaurant for an early evening meal, Jenna had made her promise not to tell them. Thea sat eating her pudding, a lovely velvety chocolate fudge cake, wondering why Jenna was so upset. And why she couldn't tell the twins. Of course it would be a shock – they were thirteen, and their mum was having another baby – but in light of how difficult it had been for her to get pregnant in the first place, the whole family should be supportive of the new addition to their family – Mark included.

But Mark wasn't there. He should be. Jenna needed him. Thea had asked her what had happened when she'd told Mark she was pregnant. That was when the floods of tears had started again, and Thea hadn't been able to get anything more coherent out of her. At that moment, the nurse had come in; visiting hours were over. The nurse had given her a look as if to say, *your presence is clearly upsetting my patient.*

Thea had slunk out of the hospital room and walked back to the car where she'd left Katie, Toby and the dog. She'd been lucky to fit in a solo visit during visiting hours that afternoon, considering she'd had to leave Katie at the hospital, and go and find Toby, who had seemed to have been out walking the dog for a considerable time. Except that he hadn't been walking the dog; he had been in Cobblers Yard. She'd been so surprised when she'd discovered the bookshop door was unlocked, and had stepped inside to discover none other than her nephew in the shop.

She stared at Toby across the table. Toby stared back. She guessed that he, too, was thinking about the bookshop as they finished their pudding in silence.

Thea glanced at Winston. She'd kept checking he was okay. The dog was sitting outside the restaurant with a chew bone from the local pet store she'd discovered along the high street. He was being very well-behaved; Thea had discovered the way to Winston's heart, and a well- behaved dog, was a good supply of treats.

Her eyes roved back to Toby. He looked uncomfortable under her gaze. As well he might. Her mind replayed her return to Cobblers Yard, when she had thought she might find Toby in the old antique store, but had gone through the open door of the bookshop after spotting a light on.

The young lady who was serving them interrupted her thoughts. 'How is everything? Can I get you anything else – tea, coffee?' She looked at the two teenagers seated with Thea. 'Soft drinks?'

'I'd like another coke,' said Katie.

The young lady wrote it down in her little notepad.

Thea thought she might as well have a cup of tea. She was in no hurry to return to Jenna and Mark's house, have the kids disappear to their rooms, and spend the evening in the company of four walls, a clingy dog, and an endless day of nothing ahead of her. She already longed for something to do.

She thought, I might have to resort to those DVDs of Katie's after all. She was used to her own company in her flat, but that was different. She could do things at home, like tidying up, cleaning, a bit of decorating – if she fancied it. It was different living in someone else's place.

She decided that the next day she could visit some of the beautiful Suffolk Coast and have a long-drawn out lunch, read a book, be on holiday.

Unfortunately, she didn't know how to be on holiday, and the thought of a book brought to mind the bookshop again, and the conversation she was still intending to have with her nephew about what, exactly, he was doing there.

36

As soon as Katie and Toby walked through the door after arriving home from Aldeburgh, they headed towards the stairs, intent on disappearing to their rooms. Thea wasn't surprised. Why would they want to hang around with their aunt? Even so, Thea said, 'Toby, I want a word.'

Her inquisitive niece, already partway up the stairs, halted and turned around when she overheard Thea. 'What about?' she asked.

Toby quickly said, 'It's nothing, just about the dog.'

Katie regarded him a moment. 'Yeah – whatever.' She didn't believe him, but flounced up the stairs, checking her mobile phone.

'Have you got homework to do, Katie?' Thea called up the stairs. Thea heard a door close upstairs without any response.

Toby, who had also been on the stairs, turned around and looked at Thea.

Thea saw the look on his face. He didn't want to talk about it. But she'd kept up her end of the bargain – not to bring up the issue of where she'd found him in front of Katie while they were having dinner in the restaurant. Now, he had to keep up his. She wanted an explanation – the one he'd refused to give when she'd found him in the bookshop.

Toby headed down the stairs. Thea walked into the kitchen and put the kettle on. She waited with her arms folded for him to come in. She shut the kitchen door behind him and beckoned him to sit on one of the stools in front of the kitchen island.

He sat down, elbows on the wooden worktop, chin in his hands. Thea sat opposite him. 'So, let's start with what you were doing in the bookshop, and where you found the key.'

She thought back to that afternoon. When she'd walked into the bookshop, she hadn't expected to find her nephew inside, sitting at the counter at the back of the shop. He looked quite at home there. She guessed he liked the old bookshop, and was sitting there imagining the bookshop open, serving customers.

The bookshop hadn't changed since she'd last stepped foot in it as a child. She'd had an inkling that it might be the case from the window display, but until she had actually stepped inside the shop, she hadn't been sure that it would be just as her mum had left it when she'd locked the door and the three of them had left for their new life in London.

So, Toby must have gone through his grandmother's boxes after all, and found a key to the bookshop. 'I don't understand …' said Thea, wondering why her mum still had a key to the bookshop. Had she kept it for sentimental reasons? Quite possibly. Then again, if she had sold the place, would she really keep hold of a key? Thea raised her eyebrows when something occurred to her. She didn't know why the bookshop had lain forlorn and forgotten for so long. She had assumed that at some point her dad had been declared dead, and that the bookshop had been sold. That would be the sane, rational, sensible thing to do – wouldn't it? Not keep it for years, because you couldn't let go of the love of your life, and believed in your heart that one day he would walk back through that door. Did this mean they still owned The Bookshop of Memories? For some strange reason, Thea's heart leapt at the thought. She suddenly imagined running a bookshop right there on the Suffolk Coast in the heart of Aldeburgh.

She had no experience of running a shop, but she loved books, and she knew how to look after old books, if there were any volumes like that in the shop. She'd seen the bookbinding equipment. Perhaps that was something she could learn too.

But she couldn't leave her job and flat. *I love my job, and I have a life in London*, she thought. *Or do I?* Her thoughts drifted to Miles. A short time earlier, before she'd found out her relationship was a lie, she'd thought she was happy in London – although she had surprised herself by considering giving it all up to travel and live abroad with Miles.

Apart from her job, what was keeping her in London? Thea looked at the key to the bookshop and then thought of her flat and the tidy sum she would get if she sold it. She'd be able to buy a smaller version of Jenna's lovely cottage on the Suffolk Coast. Thea was suddenly contemplating something she would not have considered in her wildest dreams; moving to Suffolk, returning to the place she had spent her early childhood, and running a bookshop.

'But is it still ours?'

'What?' Toby asked.

Thea stopped staring into space and dreaming of a different future, and looked at her nephew.

Thea got the key out of her pocket that she'd insisted Toby hand over and placed it on the table in front of him. Thea folded her arms, waiting for the promised explanation.

Toby looked at the key. 'Can I have it back?'

'The key?'

He nodded.

'No, Toby, of course you can't have it back. It's not yours.'

'Well, no … but it's Mum's.'

Thea stared at him. 'Jenna, I mean your mum, has a key to the bookshop?'

'Yes.'

'And she gave it to you?'

'No, not really.'

'What does that mean?'

'I found it.'

'Wait – you've been through Grandma's boxes?'

'No, of course I haven't. I said Mum had the key.' *Jenna must have been through Mum's boxes and found it*, thought Thea.

'So, you found the key lying around after your mum went into hospital.'

He didn't deny it. But that didn't explain one thing – how did he know it was the key to The Bookshop of Memories?

'She told you about the bookshop?'

Toby studied his fingernails, avoiding eye contact.

Thea stared at him. Jenna knew that their mum had kept the bookshop. *So, why didn't she tell me*, thought Thea. Perhaps she was intending to reopen the bookshop; that was her new job, or she was hoping it would be. Perhaps that was what the phone messages she'd left for Thea had been about.

Toby sighed. 'No, she didn't say anything about the bookshop. I found the key in her handbag.'

You mean, you took it, thought Thea.

He cast a glance towards the kitchen door, and lowered his voice. 'She's been acting really weird lately.'

'Who – your mum?'

'Yes. Anyway, one day she collected us from school and dropped us in town.'

'Town?'

'Aldeburgh. She said she had some errands to run, and gave us money to go buy an ice cream or some chips. She never gives us a fiver each, or any money apart from pocket money. They've been very strict like that lately.'

Toby continued, 'I bought an ice cream, then I saw Mum standing around the high street. I thought she was doing some shopping. I was bored, so I thought I'd catch up with her. Then she disappeared.'

'Disappeared?'

'Into Cobblers Yard. So, I followed her and looked into all the shop windows, but I couldn't see her.'

'Like I did with you when I followed you into Cobblers Yard. So, you found her in the bookshop?'

'Not exactly. I'd walked into each shop, and I was standing in the antique shop when I saw her come out of the bookshop, glance around the yard, and quickly lock up the shop, putting the key in her handbag.'

'Why didn't you walk up to her and ask her about the shop?'

'I don't know. I followed her out of the yard, and she went into the Co-op. When she came out with a bag of groceries, and she saw me, I asked her where she'd been. She said just shopping, and didn't mention the bookshop.'

Thea asked, 'How much do you know about your grandad?'

Toby shrugged. 'Mum doesn't talk about him. I just know that he left years ago, when she was around our age, and didn't come back.'

'Do you know that he owned that bookshop?'

Toby stared at her and sat up from his slouching position on the stool. 'For real?'

'Yes. I assumed your grandma sold it years ago, but it looks like she kept it.'

'Do you think she kept it in case Grandpa comes back?'

Thea looked at him. She couldn't remember a lot about her dad, but Toby reminded her of him. He was quiet and introspective, and she wasn't at all surprised that he was drawn to the old bookshop.

When she'd discovered Toby inside, she hadn't hung around; she had just ushered him quickly out of the shop, thinking they were trespassing. Now, she didn't think that at all. She thought she knew what was going on. 'Katie told me that your mum is starting a new job soon. Well, I think it's the bookshop. She's intending to reopen it.'

'You think that's it?' Theo frowned.

Thea saw him frowning. 'There's something you're not telling me, isn't there?'

'That wasn't the first time I saw her in the bookshop.' He looked at Thea. 'Can I have some juice, please?'

Thea stood up and poured Toby a glass of orange juice from the fridge. She made herself a cup of tea and placed it on the kitchen island before resuming her seat. She looked across the table at Toby. When he'd finished drinking his juice he put the glass down and looked at Thea. 'I told you Mum was acting weird.'

'There's nothing weird about her checking out the bookshop and deciding perhaps to reopen it.' Thea frowned, wondering why her sister hadn't mentioned it to her on her visit that afternoon. Jenna wouldn't have gone through those boxes unless she'd known the key was there. Which meant their mum must have told her. That made sense – didn't it: their mum suggesting that Jenna should run the bookshop and make some money that way?

Of course, there was another solution – sell the shop. But if her mum had kept it all these years, she'd never agree to it – would she? And besides, Thea didn't want it to be sold. She'd come over surprisingly nostalgic after stepping into the shop; it held so many happy memories from her childhood – from when they had been a happy family of four before her father had left.

'But it's still weird,' said Toby.

'What is?'

'They way mum's been behaving. Look, Dad's been working away, and one night I was woken up by a sound of a car. I thought it was Dad, back from London. But when I looked out of the window, I saw Mum backing the car out of the garage.'

'She left you two alone?'

Toby sighed. 'We are thirteen.'

Thea didn't know at what age you should leave children home alone. She guessed that was down to the parent to decide. 'Perhaps she just needed to pop to the shop for something.'

'At midnight? It's not London, you know. There's bugger all out here.'

'Language, please, Toby.'

'Sorry.'

Thea regarded him for a long moment. Perhaps Jenna had just been unable to sleep and had needed to go out for a drive to clear her head. She told Toby her thoughts.

'Yeah, okay, but it wasn't just a one-off.'

Thea knew that Jenna had a lot on her mind, what with the baby, the financial issues, and Mark returning to work during the week in London. It was little wonder she couldn't sleep, and was going for late-night drives. But Toby wasn't aware that his mum was pregnant, and Thea couldn't tell him.

'It had crossed my mind that she was just going out for a drive. I mean, Mum and Dad are, like, rowing a lot when he's home. I'm actually glad he's working away now. At least I don't have to listen to them shouting all the time.'

Thea pursed her lips. Although she loved her job, and was happy in her flat, there were times when she did feel envious about her sister's life – especially when she had moved out of London with Mark and the kids and had bought the farmhouse. But she didn't envy them right now.

'Anyway, one day I decided to find out where she was going.'

Thea sighed. 'Like I said, she was probably just going for a drive. And anyway, how on earth did you follow her?'

'Easy, I hitched a ride in the car.'

'How – without her noticing?'

'She doesn't lock the car when it's in the garage. So, when she thought I was in bed asleep, I stole down to the garage and hunkered down in the boot behind the back seat.'

Thea could see how that could work. Toby wasn't very tall, and they drove a hatchback. 'Where did she go?'

'She went to the bookshop.'

Thea sighed. Of course. She had the key, after all. It was the perfect place for Jenna to clear her head. It occurred to Thea that her sister could have gone there during the day. But whatever she was going through just then, if she was having trouble sleeping, and she needed to get out of the house, it made sense she'd go to the bookshop for somewhere for a change of scene; somewhere calm.

She looked at Toby. 'You know, there's nothing to worry about.'

'Isn't there? Because when I followed her down the lane into Cobblers Yard, I saw that she was meeting someone there.'

'What? Are you sure?'

'I saw a guy waiting for her outside the bookshop.'

37

Callum was about to turn the van around in a small car park by the beach. He was intending to cruise slowly back down the high street and see if could spot the turn-off for Cobblers Yard. So far, apart from the side streets leading to the promenade, he'd seen no indication of a side street that led to a pedestrianised yard with more shops. Callum realised he was assuming he could drive the van into Cobblers Yard.

'I think I would be better off walking down the high street,' said Callum to Dickens, who had re-joined him in the front, having got over whatever huffy mood he was in.

Dickens let out a stilted meow.

Callum smiled. 'Yes, I think it's a good idea too.' He pulled into the car park and discovered it was free to park after six in the evening. 'Perfect.' Of course, he expected that he couldn't park there overnight, but he decided he'd deal with one problem at a time. First, he wanted to find the bookshop.

He forgot about the cat as he opened the van door. The cat jumped over his lap and out of the door. 'No, Dickens!'

The cat stopped and turned around. 'There's a good cat,' said Callum, slowly getting out of the van. 'Now, just stay there while

I—' Callum bent down to pick him up, but Dickens avoided his clutches and walked off. 'Come back here!'

Callum sighed, turned around and shut the van door. When he turned back, Dickens was gone. Callum heaved a heavy sigh. Surprisingly, he realised he'd miss the little black and white cat if Dickens got lost.

Callum walked across the car park and entered the almost deserted high street. The shops were now closed. He waited for one solitary car to pass him by before he crossed the road. And there, sitting on the opposite side of the road, was Dickens.

'Hey!' Callum grinned. The cat hadn't got far – but then, he was an old cat. This was probably the most exercise he'd had for quite some time.

As Callum crossed the road, he said, 'Now, just wait there, will you?' He felt a little foolish talking to the cat, even though there was nobody around. 'Good boy, Dickens. Stay!' *He's not a dog*, Callum thought. *He is not going to do as he's told.*

The moment Callum reached the pavement on the other side of the road, Dickens was off again, strolling down the street. He even glanced behind him as if to say, *Go on, catch me if you can.*

Callum frowned. He didn't feel inclined to chase after the cat. He had a feeling that if he walked more quickly or broke out into a run, Dickens would just quicken his pace and disappear.

Callum ambled along, taking his time, looking for Cobblers Yard with one eye on the cat. Every now and then, Dickens paused and looked around. He did it a few times, giving Callum the impressions that the cat wanted him to follow.

Callum kept his sights on the cat. There was as street rising behind the town, with a café on one corner – The Two Magpies Bakery – and a fish and chip shop on the other. He paused to look up the steep street lined with red-brick terraced cottages. There was no sign of a place called Cobblers Yard.

Callum looked at the cat, who was now sitting on pavement by the fish and chip shop. 'I'm coming,' said Callum. As he strode across the road, and continued along the high street, Dickens continued walking.

'Anyone would think you know where you're going,' said Callum, taking his eyes off the cat for a moment to glance in a shop window as he passed by. 'That's handy.' Callum had discovered there was a pet shop in Aldeburgh. When he looked ahead, the cat was gone. 'Oh, you have got to be kidding.' He'd lost sight of Dickens. 'So, you didn't really want me to follow after all,' Callum said under his breath, feeling foolish for even thinking that might be the case.

He walked on, seeing a Co-op up ahead which looked as though it was still open. Someone walked out carrying a plastic bag full of groceries. 'That might come in handy,' he said to himself. Although he'd had a good dinner with Jack and Beth, and he'd bought food for Dickens and beer for himself, he hadn't thought to pick up breakfast cereal and milk for the morning. This wasn't LA. He might not find a place that served breakfast first thing in the morning, unless he made do with a pastry or scone in a café.

Callum was aiming for the Co-op when a loud meow stopped him in his tracks. He looked about him, but he couldn't see any sign of Dickens – until he heard a meow again, and turned around. That was when he saw the sign for Cobblers Yard pointing down a narrow alleyway. He walked forward two paces. Dickens was sitting in the alleyway, just visible in the dark alley, his two yellow eyes staring at Callum.

'Hey, there you are.' Callum followed the cat down the alley, which opened out into a cobbled yard. He looked about him at the old-fashioned store fronts, his eyes settling on The Bookshop of Memories. Dickens was sitting outside the door.

Callum stared at the cat. He meowed at the door as Callum approached. Callum shook his head in wonder. After all these years, it appeared that the cat had known exactly where he was when they'd arrived in Aldeburgh, and where he was heading – right here to Cobblers Yard, and The Bookshop of Memories.

Callum looked about the yard. All the shops were closed. That didn't bother him. In fact, he preferred it. Cobblers Yard was small and intimate, and he could just imagine the other shop owners being very interested to see who had turned up with the key to a bookshop that appeared to have lain forlorn and forgotten for years.

Although Callum was interested to discover what they knew about his father, he was quite happy to turn up incognito and have a look around without nosy neighbours.

Callum got out the key, hoping that the key fitted the lock and that it hadn't rusted over the years.

Dickens meowed loudly.

'Alright, already! A bit of patience, please.' The key worked. The door creaked open. Dickens squeezed through the gap and ran inside as Callum opened the door. He stepped inside too. His shoulders sagged. 'Oh, dear. It's worse than I thought.' The bookshop wasn't like any he'd been in before. It was lined, floor to ceiling, with dusty bookshelves. He ran his finger along one. It was thick with dust. He sneezed loudly. He'd noticed the books displayed in the window. He imagined they had been bestsellers years earlier.

He weaved in between the bookshelves and saw the counter

at the back of the shop. Dickens was sitting there, licking his paw, already looking quite at home. Not for the first time, Callum thought, *If you could talk, what stories you could tell.* He stared at the cat and sighed. 'I wish you could tell me about this bookshop and the two girls in the photo.'

Callum walked through the shop to a room in the back, where he found bookbinding equipment. There was a dusty sofa, a sink, and an old kettle that had seen better days. That was when he spotted another door, behind which was a flight of stairs. He gingerly walked up the stairs, glanced in the small flat and sneezed again. Although it was furnished, the place was full of dust and cobwebs. Unless he cleaned it from top to bottom, he'd have to make do with sleeping in the campervan for the time being.

Callum decided that the priority had to be sorting out the shop downstairs first, if he was going to sell the place any time soon. Unfortunately, the shop was not exactly in the best position for passing customers. Cobblers Yard had charm, but people had to find the place first. That might pose a problem.

Callum sighed. As with most things in life, it was not quite turning out how he had hoped. But he had to get on with it. 'I'll just roll up my sleeves and get stuck in tomorrow – what do you think, Dickens?'

He turned around to find that the cat was no longer sitting on counter. 'Dickens?'

A mew came from the back of the shop. Callum poked his head around the door and found Dickens curled up on the sofa. 'Well, I'm afraid I can't stay here tonight.' Although the sofa Dickens had bagged did look rather comfy. 'Right, well I'll be back in the morning, so don't go anywhere.' He suspected Dickens wouldn't.

He turned around and walked back into the shop. Standing behind the counter with the old-fashioned till, Callum placed his hands on the dusty counter top and looked at the shelves bulging with books. 'Why did you abandon this place?' He got the photo of the two girls out of the wallet. 'Why did you abandon them?' The younger girl had Henry's eyes.

He shook his head, still finding it hard to comprehend, let alone believe, that his father had two families. Jack had said that it was something Henry just would not have been capable of. Callum agreed, and yet here was this photo. He couldn't help but think it must be true. 'I think I've got a sister – or two,' he said to the empty bookshop. The question was, should he try and find them?

38

'How did you get in?'

Thea had walked into the shop early the following morning, having seen the twins off to school on the school bus before setting off herself straight away to Aldeburgh in Jenna's car. She'd nearly jumped out of her skin when she'd entered the shop and heard a loud *meow*. At the back of the shop, sitting on the counter near the till, was a black and white moggy. The cat stood up and stretched.

Staring at the cat, Thea thought it was lucky she'd decided not to bring Winston. He'd whined something awful when he'd realised he was being left at home alone, but Thea had promised him she'd only spend half a day at the bookshop and would be home by lunchtime. She'd felt a little foolish talking to him, knowing he didn't understand a word, but it made her feel better all the same.

She really wanted to spend all day, but she had the next two weeks; she had decided to stay on even if Mark came back at the weekend. She wanted to spend as much time as possible sorting out the bookshop for Jenna.

She didn't want Winston under her feet that day while she got herself organised. But she intended to take him with her the next day, along with his dog bed, and some treats, in the hope that he'd settle down in a quiet spot and spend the day sleeping, mostly, in between walks to the beach.

She rather fancied having lunch out in one of the little cafés on the high street, and thought she might do that before going back to Jenna's and taking the dog our for a walk. Afterwards, she would visit her sister.

Thea didn't have pets, but she was getting the idea that as with children, your day could tend to revolve around them, and their needs – especially as she realised they needed a routine.

Thea frowned when she thought of the itinerary she'd found scribbled on a piece of lined paper stuck to the fridge door. She guessed it was Mark's handwriting, with things hastily scribbled on a note before he collected her from the train station and handed over the keys – and responsibility for his children – for the week.

When she'd visited her sister in hospital the previous day, she had expected Jenna to be firing commands left, right, and centre about how to manage her house and the kids. That was Jenna – rather a control freak. But Jenna had had other things on her mind – the baby, for one. And possibly Mark.

It was unlike Jenna, but she hadn't been talkative at all. So Thea had done all the talking, reassuring her that the twins were fine, and she'd stay as long as her sister needed her. She didn't mention that it couldn't be longer than two weeks, because that was the longest she could be away from her job. Thea was on annual leave, so her time there wasn't open-ended – as much as she'd like it to be.

Although she'd barely set foot in the bookshop, Thea could tell she was going to enjoy rolling up her sleeves and getting stuck in, even if it meant cleaning to start with. She had loved this bookshop as a child; she remembered hiding in corners and losing herself in her favourite books.

Thea walked up to the cat and gingerly held out her hand. 'Hello. Well, aren't you a friendly cat?'

Dickens rubbed his head against her hand, letting Thea stroke him. Perhaps a window was open a crack and the cat had found a quiet spot out of the rain the previous night. There had been a thunderstorm, and quite a downpour, which had woken Thea up. She'd lain there in the early hours, thinking about the bookshop.

She was dying to ask her sister about the bookshop, and who she was meeting there, but hospital visiting hours weren't until the afternoon. However, Toby had told her that he couldn't say anything to his mum, because then she'd want to know how Thea had found out about her late-night rendezvous with some guy.

Thea smiled when the cat started to purr. Staring at the black and white cat, a memory stirred. 'You know, my dad had a cat who used to live in the bookshop with us. When we moved out of the flat upstairs into a cottage nearby, we took our cat to the cottage, but the cat ran away. Do you know where we found him?'

Dickens mewed.

'You want to know?'

Dickens bumped her hand with his head, wanting more strokes.

Thea gently tickled him under the chin. 'He made his way back to the bookshop. So, that's where we left him with food and water bowls, because our little black and white cat's home was here.' Thea stared at the black and white cat. She could tell he was old because his fur was grey around his muzzle, and so were his whiskers.

Thea suddenly had the most bizarre thought. She shook her head. 'Nope, that is utterly ridiculous. You are not him – are you?' She couldn't remember what had happened to that cat. She knew they hadn't taken the cat with them to London. 'You haven't been living in this bookshop, all that time – have you?'

Of course he hasn't, thought Thea. She imagined that when Toby had been letting himself into the shop with his mum's key, the cat had somehow got in and hidden. Even so, now Thea was thinking about their cat from years ago, she felt she would like to know what happened to it. She decided she'd ask Jenna.

She didn't know why she was bothering. 'You can't be him, can you? If you were, you'd be ancient, for a cat.'

Before Thea rolled up her sleeves and started cleaning, the first thing she decided to do, like any good archivist, was take an inventory and see exactly what was on the shelves.

Thea walked up and down between the narrow bookshelves. There were an awful lot of books there. She didn't know where to begin. 'Easy. I'll start with taking stock of how Dad organised the bookshop. There must be some system.'

By lunchtime, Thea had discovered she was wrong – there was no system. Not one she could fathom, anyway. The books appeared to be shelved in no discernible order; not alphabetically, by subject matter or by year – or even by fiction and non-fiction. By lunchtime, all she had discovered was, 'It's a mess. How did he work like this? And how on earth did he sell anything?' If someone walked into the shop looking for a particular book, exactly how would her father have found it?

Thea put her coat on and walked up to the cat. He'd been sitting on the counter all morning, watching her. 'I can't make head nor tail of all this – can you?'

The cat mewed at her.

'I need some help.' She thought of Toby. He could help out at the weekend, but that was just two days. She could feel that her idea of turning the bookshop around into a shop that actually enticed people in and made money was already looking like a pipe dream.

Thea slipped on her coat and grabbed her bag. There was no good in sitting here with the cat, hoping for inspiration. She needed to go away and think about it. She was considering phoning Edward and letting him know what she'd discovered – that her mum hadn't sold the shop after all.

But was it something her mum wanted Edward to know? They were good friends, but if Edward already knew, surely he would have mentioned it to Thea. That meant that for some reason, her mum didn't want her friends to know. Thea imagined why; everyone thought she'd moved on and accepted that her husband wasn't coming back. This was proof she still hoped he was out there somewhere and might return.

Thea walked over to the cat. 'I'm going now, but I don't want to lock you in.' Thea hadn't found any windows open, so she suspected the cat had got inside when Toby had opened the door to the shop the previous day. She gingerly picked him up, expecting him to wriggle, or even scratch her, but he remained perfectly docile. Thea found herself giving him a kiss on the top of the head. 'You are such a good kitty.'

She walked out of the door with him tucked under her arm and gently placed him on the cobbled yard outside.

He looked up at the door and meowed.

'Well, I don't know where you live, but you can't stay here. Your owner will be missing you. Go on, now, go home.' Thea smiled when the cat stood up, turned around and walked out of Cobblers Yard. She stared after him. She rather liked having a bookshop cat. Would that entice people in? Like a cat café?

'Now, that's a silly thought.' She expected that she wouldn't see the cat again.

Thea put the key in the lock and turned it. She heard the satisfying click of the lock. She checked the door was secure. She knew she wouldn't be back until the next morning. She had a dog to feed and walk, and a sister to visit at the hospital, and two children to be home for when they returned on the school bus.

As she turned from the bookshop, she caught a face in the charity shop window staring at her. Thea waved at the little old lady, who she thought must have been rearranging the window display. She wondered how long the charity shop had been in Cobblers Yard, and whether the lady in the window had known her father.

She had an impulse to walk over and ask, but the clock was ticking, and she still rather fancied some lunch before duty called in the shape of another four-legged friend – Winston.

Thea noticed that the old lady standing in the charity shop window was still staring at her as she turned from the door. When she threw a glance over her shoulder as she crossed the yard, she could see there were now two old ladies standing in the window.

39

Callum stirred. He could faintly hear a mewing, but it wasn't that sound that woke him up; it was a sudden weight on his chest. When he opened his eyes, cat whiskers brushed his face as the cat meowed in his face.

Callum sat up with a start, the cat pouncing off his chest and hissing at him. Callum looked at the cat. 'What the hell? What are you doing here? I thought I left you in the bookshop?' Then he remembered he'd left the cat there with no water or the litter tray. He clocked that the water bowl was almost empty. Little wonder the cat had returned, and was annoyed with him. 'Well, I'm not used to having to having a cat around, alright?' he said to Dickens.

Callum reached for his watch, and was shocked to see he'd slept through to lunchtime. 'What the hell?' he said again. He could hear seagulls and the sound of cars pulling into the car park. So far, he hadn't received a dreaded knock on the campervan door from some official telling him he couldn't park there overnight.

He rubbed the sleep out of his eyes. It wasn't really surprising that he'd slept in so late. The drive down from Scotland had been long and arduous. He'd already been quite tired when he'd called in to see Beth and Jack. But it wasn't the long journey that had really caught up with him – it was the bad night on the campervan bed. He had been up a number of times in the night, finding it hard to get comfortable. He'd also opened the window because it was stuffy, and then he'd been woken in the middle of the night by a thunderstorm battering the van. He glanced out of the window as he stood up and noticed the number of cars in the car park. He shut the window as he eyed the cat.

His thoughts turned to his father. How had Henry got on, sleeping in this thing when he'd been on the road buying and selling books?

As Callum stood up and stretched his sore back, he thought perhaps Henry that had stayed in hotels or bed and breakfasts, and had only slept in the van occasionally. Or perhaps he had stayed with his other family.

Callum frowned at that thought, which brought to mind the photo of those two girls, and the reason he had ostensibly travelled down in the van. Was that the last time his father had seen them – when that photo had been taken? Although there was no date on the back of the photo, for some reason Callum imagined that these girls, if they were his half-sisters, were younger than him.

Callum sat down on the narrow bed and got out the photo. Dickens jumped on to his lap.

'All right, already. I get it. You want breakfast.' Callum picked up the cat on his lap and put him down on the sofa beside him. He stood up and reached for one of the pouches of cat food he'd bought in the supermarket the previous night. He squeezed the contents of the pouch into one of the bowls he'd bought, and added some cat biscuits too.

'Oh, my god. That smells rank!' Callum opened a window. 'Remind me never to get a pet of my own!' Before he'd even finished squeezing out all the contents, Dickens was by the bowl, sniffing it.

Callum said, 'Does it meet with your approval?' *It'd better do*, he thought, because he had bought the most expensive gourmet cat food on the shelf.

Dickens started to eat.

'Good, well that's you sorted.' Callum stared at the cat enjoying his breakfast. He thought of that nice little café he'd passed by the previous evening in the van, and wondered if he could get a cup of coffee and a bagel or croissant. After sleeping in, he knew he'd be getting to the bookshop a lot later than he'd intended, but he decided that stopping for a bite to eat was not going to make much difference. Besides, he'd seen the state of the place last night. If he was considering getting it up and running as a going concern, and making it profitable to increase the potential value, then that was not going to happen overnight.

But perhaps whoever bought the shop wouldn't want to run it as a bookshop. So, why even bother? This possibility had occurred to him before. He could just spruce up the outside, get it presentable, and be done. The trouble was that a part of him already felt a little attached to the old bookshop, even though he'd barely spent any time there.

At the back of his mind was what Jack had said about him staying permanently in Suffolk and running the bookshop. *Perhaps if it had potential, I might not sell.* The problem was, could he afford not to?

'You know what, Dickens? I think I'm going to deal with one problem at a time. First – breakfast.'

Callum left Dickens having his breakfast. He locked the van, although he did leave the little side window open in case Dickens decided he was going to return to the bookshop. He would not be surprised.

Five minutes later, Callum stood outside The Two Magpies Bakery. He looked in through the window and could see friends and couples having lunch. It was packed, which surprised him on a weekday lunchtime, but then the café area was small. There was seating near the counter by the window, and further seating a few steps up on a mezzanine level. He spotted a couple getting up from one of the window seats near the counter.

Callum made his move and walked in. He asked the young lady, 'Is that table reserved?'

She shook her head.

'Great.' Taking a seat, he looked around him at the people seated in the café. Apart from one single young lady, with her back to him, he was the only other person sitting alone at a table.

❖

Thea quickly turned around, her back to the counter. The young man who she'd just seen walk in had taken a table downstairs by the window. 'I don't believe it,' she whispered under her breath. She was sure it was the good-looking guy who'd passed by the restaurant in that yellow campervan the previous afternoon.

He hadn't noticed her when he'd walked in; he had been too busy scouting for a free table. She'd happened to turn around, glancing at the young lady who was serving to see if her sandwich was on the way. She'd seen The Two Magpies Bakery when she'd arrived in the town the previous day with the twins, but there hadn't been a table free. She had been lucky to get a table this lunchtime.

She hadn't been waiting long for her lunch to arrive, but

nevertheless she had Winston on her mind. She was afraid she'd left him home alone too long, and was hoping he hadn't got up to anything while she was gone.

She stole a glance over her shoulder, and saw the guy looking at the menu.

Thea heard the waitress comment, 'Hey, aren't you the guy from that American show?'

Thea turned around in her seat again, staring at him. She saw him smile, flashing perfectly aligned white teeth. Thea thought he had a gorgeous smile. She saw him shaking his head at the waitress. 'You know, I get that all the time, but I'm sorry – I'm not him.'

Thea thought of Katie, who had been convinced he was a famous actor.

'Oh, really? Because you're a dead ringer for that guy.'

Thea noticed that other people in the café must have overheard the conversation. Some turned in their seats too and were looking his way.

He was still smiling. 'I'm sure that guy, whoever he is, will be in Hollywood right now, sitting by his pool in his Beverley Hills mansion, not sitting here in The Two Magpies Bakery in Aldeburgh, as nice as it is.'

The waitress pointed her pen at him. 'Yeah, you've got a point.' She smiled. 'I bet you wish you *were* him, though, sitting in a mansion in Beverley Hills right now.'

Thea caught his smile falter.

'Not really. Um … will you take my order now?'

'Oh, sure, sorry.'

'Just a coffee and a croissant, please.'

'Coming right up.'

Thea saw him flash that grin again, and frowned. She'd be

prepared to bet he would get his order before she did. She forgot she was still staring as the other people returned to their drinks and meals. As he handed the waitress the menu, he glanced around the room and caught her gaze. Their eyes locked for a moment before Thea, feeling the colour rising in her cheeks, quickly averted her gaze and turned in her seat.

❖

Callum watched the pretty young woman with the beautiful brown eyes quickly turn in her seat, looking embarrassed that he'd caught her looking his way. If he hadn't been in a rush to eat breakfast in order to head off to the bookshop, he might have asked her to join him, given that they were the only ones in the café eating alone.

Callum shook his head. This wasn't LA. You didn't just strike up a conversation with a stranger. The fact that it had even crossed his mind to just walk up to her table reminded him that he'd been away living on what felt like another planet for far too long.

He glanced at the waitress, who was heading his way with his order. Even though he'd convinced her that he wasn't who she thought he was, she looked more than willing to strike up a conversation with a perfect stranger, meaning him, after he'd flashed his smile.

Callum decided to avoid any awkwardness and just keep that smile under wraps. 'Thanks,' he said in a perfunctory way when she put the cup of coffee and croissant in front of him. 'That was quick!' he remarked.

'Will there be anything else?' She hovered by his table, twiddling some strands of long, dark hair through her fingers.

Callum stared at her. She was so young – younger than he'd first thought. He was surprised she even knew, or thought she knew, who he was. He had to ask, 'You watch that show with your parents?'

'Well, yeah, it started that way, but all my friends love that show.' She lowered her voice and looked around as though she was about to tell him a secret. 'We read online it's been cancelled. I don't think that's true – do you? It just can't be.'

Callum stared at her.

'Oh, right – sorry. You don't know what I'm talking about, do you?'

Callum shook his head.

She shrugged and turned to go. But before she did, Callum got asked the question he was expecting. 'You're new in town – right? I haven't seen you round here before.'

Out of the corner of Callum's eye, he caught the young woman with the big brown eyes almost imperceptibly turn her head. Was she listening to the conversation? He smiled.

Unfortunately, he realised too late that the very young lady standing in front of him had taken that smile as an invitation to ask, 'Are you, like, single? Because I am, and you're really cute.'

Callum stared at her as she cocked her head to one side and continued fiddling with her hair. She said, 'Would you like to go out with me?'

He should have been taken aback at how forward she was being, but he was used to girls coming on to him all the time in LA.

'I just can't believe how much you sound like that guy too.'

'Ahem,' Callum coughed into his hand, and lowered his voice, trying to disguise his Scottish accent, although he knew it was a bit late for that. 'Look, I'm just getting over a break-up, so although, yeah, I'm single, I'm not really available right now, if you get my drift.'

Even though he had been eyeing the other young woman, the one sitting alone, what he was saying was in fact true. He just wished he didn't have to spell it out in the middle of a café. But he wanted to let her down gently.

She shrugged. 'It's because I'm too young, isn't it?'

Callum pursed his lips. It was true, she was young, but even if she'd been ten years older, she still wouldn't have been his type. Callum kept that thought to himself, and just nodded. 'Yeah, I'm afraid so,' trying his best to look disappointed.

She flicked her long hair over her shoulder, as if to say *your loss*, turned on her heel, and strutted back to the counter.

Callum sighed into his coffee. So much for a discreet coffee and croissant before starting on the bookshop. He glanced out of the side window, down the high street, and caught sight of a black and white cat walking by in the direction of Cobblers Yard. 'Seriously!' Although Dickens was just a cat, he was a bit of a rascal. It made Callum wonder what he might get up to alone in the bookshop while he was gone.

Callum gulped down his coffee, wrapped his croissant in a paper serviette, and joined the queue at the counter. He was served by another young woman, who refreshingly didn't give him a second glance when he asked for the bill.

40

Callum stepped out of the café and followed Dickens. The cat started to quicken his pace, albeit sedately, but keeping ahead of him all the same. 'Oh, no you don't,' said Callum, quickening his pace too. Before Callum broke into a run, feeling very foolish for chasing after a cat, he suddenly realised he had the key. He slowed, remembering that Dickens had been waiting at the shop door the previous day to be let in. Callum grinned thinking, *Go on, then – I'll still get in first.*

Callum rubbed his forehead, suddenly recalling that he'd left the cat in the shop the previous night, and locked up.

He'd had too many beers before he went to bed, virtually drinking himself to sleep, and the coffee was only just starting to kick in. 'How did you get out?' he asked Dickens. *Damn*, he thought, *there must have been a window open. Unless* ... Callum quickened his pace again. 'I'm sure I locked up.' He knew he had been tired when he'd left. *What if I didn't lock up, and someone has been in the shop while I've been gone?* He looked at the cat, and exhaled, muttering under his breath, 'Oh, god. Someone broke in.'

Callum caught an older couple giving him a funny look as he strode by at pace, talking to himself. Callum shut his mouth, but that didn't stop the train of thought. *Why would someone even try the door, let alone walk inside if there was a 'closed' sign in the window?*

Callum rushed down the street, thinking of what he might find, and why it hadn't occurred to him when he was woken by the cat. He was half-asleep, that was the problem. He followed Dickens, who despite his advanced years managed to stay several paces ahead. As they both turned down the narrow lane, Callum could see the bookshop in Cobblers Yard. The door was closed. As he approached, nothing seemed amiss. The window display was just the same – cobwebs and all.

He tried the door and let out a huge sigh of relief when he discovered it was just as he'd left it – locked. He glanced at Dickens, who was sitting by the door, and frowned at the cat, thinking, *I don't get it. If you got out by an open window, why not just enter that way too?*

Dickens meowed at him and turned his head towards the door.

Callum grinned. 'Ah, I see.' He'd forgotten that Dickens was an old cat. *Why would he jump through a window if he didn't have to? He's a smart cat.*

Callum put the key in the lock and was about to step inside when he had a feeling he was being watched. He glanced about him and spotted an old lady standing in the window of the charity shop across the yard. At least, he thought it was an old lady. Or was it a mannequin, cleverly disguised in their charity shop finest?

It wasn't a mannequin. The old lady stepped forward, a hand clutching her chest. Callum stared at her. Was she having a heart attack? Her mouth was wide open. She seemed to be having difficulty catching her breath.

Callum left the key in the door and rushed over. As he approached the shop, staring at her, he realised something definitely wasn't right. He threw open the door, which banged against the inside wall, making a lady he spotted behind the counter at the end of the shop jump. 'Good heavens, young man, where's the fire?'

'The *what*?'

'It's an expression. Is everything all right?'

'No. There's a lady in the window, an old lady. I think she's having a heart attack.'

'What?'

Callum was already rushing to her aid. He caught her elbow as her knees buckled beneath her. Fortunately, there was a stool in the window display. 'Here, let me help you sit down.' He had an arm around her waist, and eased her on to the stool while he shouted at the other lady as she approached, 'Quick, call an ambulance!'

Callum turned to the lady sitting on the stool. He knelt in front of her. 'Where's the pain? Is it in your chest, your arm?'

She stared at him, wide-eyed. 'It's here!' She thumped her chest.

Callum looked up at the other lady. She, too, was staring at him. Callum said, 'Why aren't you calling for a paramedic? Haven't you got a phone? Wait … I've got my mobile. Hold on.'

'She doesn't need an ambulance.'

'What? Didn't you just hear her? She's got chest pain. And listen – she can't catch her breath.' Callum turned to the lady on the stool. He said calmly, 'Breathe. In and out. That's right. Deep breaths.' Callum had no clue what he was doing. He wasn't trained in first aid.

'It's you,' she said, in between deep breaths.

Callum watched her looking at the other lady, who was standing over them. She said to her, 'It's him!'

Oh god, thought Callum. Not in his wildest dreams, or rather nightmares, had Callum ever thought that someone recognising him would lead to them having a heart attack.

He started dialling 911, then forgot where he was. 'Shit.' He was about to dial 999 when the other lady closed her hand around his phone.

'She's not having a heart attack.'

'But she's in pain. She said so herself.'

The lady grimaced. 'It's not that sort of pain.'

Callum frowned, turning to the lady on the stool, who was clutching her chest. 'What do you mean?'

'She's clutching her *heart*.'

'But that's what I'm saying—'

'Mabel, darling, it's not him. You know that. It can't be him, obviously.'

Callum sighed. He turned his attention to the old lady sitting on the stool, and took her hands in his. Unlike the young lady in the café, he decided to come clean. 'I am … him.'

Mabel said, 'But you're still young. How can that be?'

'Well, I guess I've kept myself in shape over the years – had to, with my line of work.'

Mabel looked up. 'Marjorie? Am I imagining all this?' She looked back at Callum, reached out and gingerly touched his face.

Callum smiled at her. 'I'm as real as you or the other lady here.'

Marjorie frowned. 'Look, young man, I don't know what your game is—'

Callum looked up at the large old lady called Marjorie, surprised by her tone when he was only trying to help and was for once telling the truth about who he was. He even gave them his stage name; the surname Joe Public knew him by.

'I am sorry, young man,' said Marjorie, 'but your name does not ring a bell in the slightest.'

'It doesn't?' Callum looked at her in surprise. 'I starred on the hit show, *The Scottish Laird*.' He looked at Mabel, sitting there staring at him. 'You recognise me from that American show – right? I thought that's what all this is about – the shock of seeing me here, in the flesh so to speak?'

Mabel looked up at Marjorie. 'I don't understand …?'

Marjorie said, 'I think I do.' She took a deep breath. 'Why don't we all have a nice cup of tea, and I'll explain. What do you say, Mabel?'

'Well, all right. Do you know what's going on?'

'I do indeed. It's a misunderstanding.'

'He's not—?'

'No, Mabel. As I said before, how is that possible? He'd be oh, how old now?'

Mabel mumbled, 'I don't know, but too old to still be alive.'

A few minutes later, Mabel had gone for a lie-down on the couch in the back room, taking her cup of sweet tea with her.

Callum stared after her before turning to Marjorie. They were both seated by the counter at the back of the shop, a cup of tea and a plate of biscuits in front of them. 'I'm sorry … what just happened?'

'What happened, young man—'

'It's Callum.'

'What happened, Callum, is that my sister thought she saw a ghost.'

Callum stared at Marjorie. 'I remind her of someone?'

'Oh, yes, without a doubt. It's a wonder she didn't actually have a heart attack!'

Callum grimaced and looked at her apologetically. 'Sorry.'

'Oh, my dear, it's not your fault that you look the spitting image of Douglas.'

'Douglas?'

'Yes, he was my sister's sweetheart many years ago, but she married someone else.'

'I guess she never forgot her first love.'

'Apparently not.' Marjorie stared at him. 'I still can't get over the resemblance – it's uncanny. He was Scottish too, you know.'

'Was he? What was his surname?'

'It was a long time ago. Let me think. I'm sure it will come to mind.' Marjorie blinked. 'MacFadden – that was it!'

Callum shrugged. 'I'm afraid that name doesn't ring any bells.'

'Do you know he said he owned a Scottish estate – a castle, I think. Or was it a manor house?' Marjorie shrugged. 'I forget. It was a long time ago. But I do remember he was a Scottish laird; at least, that's what he'd said. Although he seemed sincere, I'm not sure I believed him, and neither did our father.'

Callum got the picture. They probably thought he was just saying that to impress Mabel.

Marjorie lowered her voice to a hushed whisper. 'My little sister was so young, you see, only seventeen. There was quite an age gap, too.'

Callum stared at her. 'I see.' It sounded as though any chance of Mabel having a future with Douglas had been out of her hands. 'Well if he was a Scottish laird with a castle, or a manor house, we are definitely not related. I grew up on a council estate in Edinburgh.'

Marjorie smiled. 'It probably wasn't true, in any case.'

'But it might have been,' said Callum. 'You'll never know.'

'Yes, we'll never know,' Mabel added.

They both turned to look at Mabel.

Marjorie frowned at her sister, who was standing in the doorway to the back room. 'I thought you were having a lie-down?'

'I was. I did. But I heard you talking.'

Callum shook his head. 'I am sorry for … well giving you a funny turn when you saw me.'

She walked up to him and put a gentle hand on his shoulder. 'You don't have to apologise, Callum. They say everyone in the world has a doppelganger, don't they?'

Callum smiled. 'Yeah, I've heard that too. I guess I found mine, although I imagine that whoever invented that theory probably meant, you know, someone my own age – not someone from another generation, who's dead.' Callum stared at her, wide-eyed. 'Sorry, that was a thoughtless thing to say.'

'No, not at all.' Mabel took a seat at the counter with them. 'He was thirteen years – or was it fourteen years? – older than me. We first met when I was eight years old, during the Second World War. He was in the RAF, stationed in Norfolk. I literally ran into him when I went to the shops. It was when our father owned the bookshop, and we lived there.' Mabel pointed across the yard.

'You lived in the bookshop? Really?'

'Yes, when we were children. Well, we grew up there.'

'Wow.' Callum smiled. It was amazing to meet these two old ladies who had once lived in the bookshop. Callum's next thought was that his father would love to meet them – on a good day, when he was compos mentis. But he probably had fewer and fewer such days, and he was all the way up in Scotland. These ladies must be well into their eighties, so there was no chance they would meet. Callum sighed. It had been a nice thought.

'I will tell you something quite strange,' said Callum, thinking of Mabel's first love. 'My character in the American show I starred in for several years was a Scottish laird.'

Mabel and Marjorie exchanged a glance and both smiled. 'Well, isn't that peculiar?' said Marjorie.

'I second that,' said Mabel.

'You should watch it some time. You might enjoy it.'

Marjorie said, 'Oh, I don't have a television.'

'I do!' said Mabel. 'Do they broadcast it on the BBC?' she asked keenly.

Callum smiled at the sweet old lady. 'No, I'm afraid not.' He didn't imagine she had an online streaming service where she might be able to find reruns. 'You might be able to get the seasons on DVD. Do you have a DVD player?'

'I do. That would be so kind of you to get hold of them for me.'

Callum realised he'd just accidentally volunteered for the task. 'Oh, okay.'

'Wonderful!' said Mabel, clapping her hands.

Callum caught Marjorie frowning at her sister for some reason. He thought he'd better add, 'I don't think the last season will be out on DVD, though.'

'The last season?' said Marjorie.

'Yes, I'm afraid after nine years they cancelled the show.'

'Nine years? Goodness, how old were you when you started on the show?'

'Oh, I'm older than you think. I'm thirty-seven now.'

'That's no age,' said Mabel.

Callum imagined to someone approaching their ninetieth decade, thirty-seven must appear so very young. But from his perspective, Callum was feeling as though he hadn't achieved much as he approached his fourth decade. He was thinking of his best friend, married, with a kid and a home.

Callum would rather not be reminded of his good looks and his pursuit of fame and fortune in Hollywood. To borrow a phrase, he had young women falling at his feet, and yet they weren't the right women – they always seemed to confuse him with the character he played on that show.

The problem was, they found out soon enough that the character wasn't him. He was just an ordinary guy, who probably would have been better suited to leading an ordinary life. He thought of the young woman who he'd locked eyes with in the café earlier. Callum cast a glance in the direction of the bookshop, with a question on his mind – should he stay and give it a go?

41

'Is that why you're here?' asked Marjorie, startling Callum, who was lost in his own thoughts.

Callum looked at Marjorie. 'Excuse me?'

'Are you here for a holiday after the end of the show?'

'Oh, right. Er—'

'What were you doing over there? I saw you at the door of the bookshop,' Mabel asked before he'd answered Marjorie's question.

'I … I …' For some reason, Callum thought they'd had enough shocks for one day. Perhaps now was not the time to tell them he was the new owner. He was aware that their charity shop had been closed when he had been there the previous night, so they had no clue he had a key and had been inside the bookshop.

They would find out soon enough. They'd probably spot him going in and out, but just then he decided he'd rather have the chance to get the bookshop in better shape. Then he'd invite them over. Otherwise, they might be sad to find out what state their former home – and their father's former business – was in. He imagined that they had fond childhood memories of the place, and he didn't want those to be ruined.

Callum looked at his empty mug and decided that perhaps

now was a good time to leave. He would have liked to sit and chat to these two interesting ladies, and find out more about their childhood at the bookshop, but he could hear Dickens carrying on outside, his loud meows growing more insistent.

He guessed the old ladies' hearing was not what it was, as neither commented on the annoying cat sitting outside their shop window, looking in.

'Well, I'd better not keep you ladies any longer. You've got a shop to run.' *And so have I*, thought Callum, although he was still wavering over his decision as to what to do with the place. He got out of his seat and thanked them for the tea and chocolate digestive biscuits.

'Are you helping that young woman we saw?'

'I'm sorry – what?'

'The young woman in the bookshop. We saw her leave the shop earlier today.' Mabel looked at her watch. 'You just missed her.'

'That's not true, Mabel. It must have been at least an hour ago – probably more.'

'Well, all right, I suppose it was, but it still doesn't change the fact that if he was here to help out in the bookshop—'

'I'm sorry,' Callum interrupted the two bickering sisters, 'but who are you talking about?'

Mabel and Marjorie turned to look at him. 'The young lady, of course. I thought you knew who she was.'

Callum felt a headache coming on. Dickens wasn't helping. He glanced over his shoulder and glared at the cat. He turned back to the two women. 'I have no idea who she is. Are you saying she has a key to the bookshop?'

Mabel tutted. 'Well, how else would she have got inside?'

Perhaps she broke in, thought Callum, glancing at the cat.

'You know, it's a bit of a mystery, what happened to the previous owner …'

Marjorie shook her head at her sister, Callum noticed, as if to tell her not to talk about it.

Callum was thinking of his dad. He didn't want to talk about it either. But he did want to talk about the woman they mentioned. 'Just run that by me again. You said someone has been in my … er … the bookshop?'

'What were you doing at the bookshop door?' Mabel asked again. 'You didn't say. You're not helping the young woman, then?'

'No, I am not.'

'Ah, you didn't see the 'closed' sign, and you were after buying a book.'

Callum was edging towards the door. 'I really have to go.' He wanted to check nothing was missing – not that he'd know if there was; he didn't have an inventory for the bookshop. But what he did know was that there was expensive bookbinding equipment in the back of the shop.

'Don't you want to stay for lunch?' Marjorie glanced at the clock on the wall. 'We stop about this time, close the shop, and sit in our little office out back to have lunch.'

'You are welcome to join us,' Mabel added.

'No, I had something at The Two Magpies Bakery.' Callum's stomach rumbled, which reminded him he still hadn't eaten the croissant.

'Oh, did you? That is a shame,' said Mabel looking disappointed as she followed Callum to the door. He stepped outside.

She stood in the open doorway. 'Will we see you again?'

Callum glanced over at the bookshop, before returning her

gaze and smiling. 'Oh, yes. You can count on it.'

'Don't forget those DVDs you said you'd sort out for me.'

Callum tried to hide a frown. 'Yeah, sure.' He didn't add that he couldn't afford to spend money on eight seasons' worth of DVDs.

'You'll pop them round? We're here until three. Although we do take our hour lunch break.'

Callum looked at her. 'I'm not sure I'll be able to get hold of them today.'

'Oh, well … all right.'

'Will you lock the door, Mabel, and put the 'closed' sign in the window?'

'Yes, Marjorie,' Mabel called back to Marjorie before turning her sights on Callum. 'I just can't get over how much you look like him. It's as though …' she trailed off.

'As though he came back?'

Mabel nodded.

'You loved him, didn't you?'

'Oh, yes.'

'What happened?' Callum gathered, from what Marjorie had said, that her father didn't approve of the relationship, but he couldn't help asking, his curiosity getting the better of him.

Mabel sighed heavily. 'Father didn't approve. I didn't care a jot. I was young and in love, and I'd have travelled to the ends of the earth with Douglas – or to Scotland, if that was where he wanted to return.'

Callum nodded sadly.

Mabel glanced over her shoulder and lowered her voice. 'I confided in my sister – told her our plan.'

'Your plan?'

'Yes. You see, Douglas and I were going to elope.'

Callum stared at her. *Elope.* It was such an old-fashioned word, but without her father's blessing or approval, he imagined she'd have had no choice in those days, but to escape, flee together before someone stopped them.

'Someone stopped you.'

Mabel shook her head. 'No, nothing like that. We'd agreed when we would meet; it was to be at the train station at midnight. But—'

'He didn't turn up.' Callum guessed what had happened.

'That's right. It was a shock. I couldn't understand it. I thought that if there had been a sudden change of plan, he would have found a way to send word. But that never happened. I thought perhaps there had been an accident. I scoured the newspapers and I visited the hospital and the police station. But he'd … vanished. I was …' she swallowed. 'Bereft for quite some time. I thought I could never trust a man again.'

Callum understood. She had been broken-hearted.

'Then I met my late husband, a very kind, generous, loving man, who loved me so much.'

Callum guessed she had never quite loved him the way she had loved Douglas. He said, 'I'm so sorry.'

Mabel rolled her eyes. 'There's no need to feel sorry. As I said, my late husband … well, a nicer man you couldn't hope to meet. So all's well that ends well.'

But does it, thought Callum, *end well if you lose the person you truly love above all others?*

'It's just …'

Callum looked at her. 'What is it?'

'I'd like to know before I die what happened to him.'

Callum looked at her gravely. 'I wish I could help.'

She smiled. 'I shouldn't have said anything. I've come to terms with the fact that I'll never know.'

Callum didn't think she had.

'It will be just another one of my life's mysteries.'

He looked at her, wondering what other mysteries she might be referring to. Something told him there were things the two sisters were hiding about their life in the bookshop – memories from their childhood that they wouldn't share with a stranger. And who could blame them? They weren't the only ones hiding things.

Callum took her hands in his. Although they'd only known each other a short time, it felt like they'd become firm friends. 'I'll be back, rest assured.'

She looked at him. 'That's exactly what he said to me, the last time I saw him.'

Callum swallowed. He didn't know what to say.

But Mabel did. 'You know what?' She gave his hand a reassuring pat. 'I think someone up there sent you to me, to give me a sense of …. what do the Americans call it? Closure?'

Callum managed a smile. 'Yes, perhaps there's an angel up there watching out for you.' He frowned wondering where on earth that had come from.

Mabel's eyes went wide. 'Perhaps it's Douglas.'

Callum pursed his lips. He didn't believe in that sort of thing – did he? But he'd started it, so he couldn't very well backtrack on what he'd just said. He looked at the sweet old lady and said, 'I bet it is.'

'Mabel? I'm making lunch. Would you lock the door now, please?'

Callum looked over Mabel's shoulder at her sister. He lowered his voice, and said, 'Your sister's a bit of a bossy-boots.'

Mabel rolled her eyes. 'Oh, you don't know the half of it. Sometimes I feel she's been bossing me around, taking charge, my whole life. But she has been a blessing. She introduced me to my late husband.'

'That's nice,' said Callum. He felt something tickle his ankle, and looked down to find Dickens attacking his trouser leg with a paw. 'Well, I'd better get going, and you'd better have lunch, Mabel.'

'Yes, before Marjorie gets ants in her pants.'

They exchanged a smile.

'Shame you don't know that young woman. She looked very pretty. Are you single? You might like her.'

As Callum turned from the door, he doubted very much that he would, considering it sounded as though she may have a key to the bookshop. *Who was she?* Callum knew he wouldn't have long to find out; if she didn't reappear that afternoon, he'd be there waiting for her at the bookshop the next day, interested to see if she did turn up with a key to the shop, as Mabel had intimated – and to find out what she thought she was doing with a key to his bookshop.

42

'Yes, I agree that isn't acceptable behaviour, and bullying can't be tolerated.' Thea rolled her eyes at Toby, who was sitting at the kitchen table looking as though butter wouldn't melt in his mouth. Surprisingly, it seemed he had misbehaved at school.

Thea's plan to return to the bookshop that afternoon after checking in on the dog had not materialised. Nor had her plan to visit her sister. She frowned at her nephew, who was avoiding eye contact.

Thea's afternoon had turned out to be anything but straightforward. First, she'd returned to her sister's house after a lovely lunch at The Two Magpies Bakery and had discovered that Winston had done a big wee on the lovely wooden floor. It stunk. She couldn't blame the dog. He was only young, and it had happened just inside the back door; he had obviously been hoping that someone would return and let him out before he couldn't hold on any longer.

He had cowered, ears drawn back, in the corner of the kitchen when she'd returned. She'd thought his behaviour odd when he didn't rush up to her to greet her like she had expected.

She had given him a fuss, anyway, reassuring the poor dog that it wasn't his fault before she cleared up the mess. Her afternoon had not got any better. What had followed was a phone call from the school to come and pick up Toby.

Thea was still on the phone to the headteacher, wishing she could just put the phone down, but she knew that wouldn't help matters. Out of the twins, it was Katie, with her sharp tongue, about whom Thea might have anticipated receiving a phone call from the headteacher and an excruciating lecture about school policy, followed by a suspension.

Thea frowned at Toby while she spoked on the phone. 'I'm sorry – for how long?'

'Five days is our policy.'

'The rest of this week?'

'Yes, and Monday.'

Thea rolled her eyes. 'Just great,' she commented sarcastically, still eyeing Toby. He started edging off the stool, thinking she wouldn't notice. She pointed at him to stay put.

Toby folded his arms on the table and put his chin on his forearms. He stared at her.

'Yes, I do understand how serious this is. But what you've got to take on board is that Toby's mum is in hospital at the moment, and his dad is working away, so there's been a lot of things going on in his home life right now that—'

'I'm aware of that.' The head interrupted her, making Thea's hackles rise, and making her think that the head could do with some lessons in manners. Thea listened and rolled her eyes. 'Yes, I appreciate that doesn't excuse—'

And she still couldn't finish a sentence without the rude head reiterating her point about school policy. Thea looked at her nephew. They'd had a conversation in the car on the way home, and from what little information Toby had given her, he'd lashed out after being goaded by a boy in the year above who claimed to be Caitlin's boyfriend. The boy wasn't happy that his so-called girlfriend had looked Toby's way. That was how it had all started, apparently.

Of course, it was all down to who the head believed, and unfortunately the evidence – the bloodied hand – was all the head needed to make a decision. Toby hadn't touched the boy, thank goodness, but he had thrown a punch, and the boy had moved to avoid it, tripped over and fallen in the playground, grazing his hand. What had led up to that, the head wasn't interested in hearing. Toby was the party at fault, and he was being suspended.

Thea got off the phone and sighed heavily. 'Your head is an arsehole.'

Toby looked at her in surprise and smiled into the sleeve of his school jumper.

Thea shook her head. 'Now, what am I going to do with you for five days?' The school had organised homework for him to do, but knowing her studious nephew, Thea imagined that he'd probably get that done in one morning.

Toby lifted his head off the kitchen worktop and said, 'We could go to the bookshop.'

She was about to say no, but it actually wasn't a bad idea to have an extra pair of hands to help her start sorting out the shop.

'All right.'

'Really?'

She knew why he was looking surprised that she'd agreed. Being suspended from school was meant to be a punishment, and not an excuse to go somewhere you'd much rather be.

'Can we go there now?'

'No. The school bus will be arriving soon, and I need to prepare some dinner for us.'

'Oh, yeah, I forgot about my sister.' He put his chin on his elbows again.

'And before you ask, we are not returning to Aldeburgh after dinner. You both have homework to do.'

'But I've got loads of time to get it done.'

'Yes, but your sister hasn't. She's got school tomorrow. And besides, I'm pretty sure Katie will not want to spend her evening in a dusty, musty old bookshop.'

'But I would.'

'I know.' *So would I*, thought Thea, but she didn't say that.

Toby exhaled heavily. 'What about first thing tomorrow morning?'

'Yes, that was my thinking.'

Toby sat up and grinned.

Thea didn't. 'Now, don't get any ideas that you're going to be sitting with a book on the couch in the back room taking it easy. You're going to have to roll up your sleeves and do some work.'

Toby was still grinning. 'Fine by me. Although …'

'Although – what?'

'I'd like to know what all the equipment is for in the back room.'

Thea had seen it too when she'd been in the shop that morning. 'It's for bookbinding.'

'Bookbinding? Can you show me how?'

Thea shook her head. 'I'm afraid not. It's a specialised skill. You would need someone trained and experienced in that field to teach you.' Thea thought that perhaps if things had turned out differently, and her dad hadn't disappeared, he might have taught her. But he hadn't, and finding someone with the skills to teach Toby – well, that would be a tall order. 'I'm considering selling that equipment.' Thea knew she'd have to contact her mum first and check it was all right for her to do that. 'I imagine we might get some good money for it to help with sorting out the bookshop.'

Toby looked disappointed. 'All right.'

Thea heard footsteps on the gravel drive outside.

Winston barked.

Thea stood up and walked over to the front window. Katie was home from school.

'Katie is going to be so jealous when she finds out I've got a week off.' Toby sniggered.

Thea turned around and folded her arms. 'I'm going to have to tell your dad about the suspension.'

That wiped the smile off his face. 'Do you have to?'

The head had told her there would be a formal letter sent out. She had no choice. 'I'm afraid so, but I'm not going to tell him until he comes home.'

He brightened.

And Thea wasn't going to tell his mum either – not at the moment. It wasn't the end of the world, as far as Thea was concerned, and Jenna didn't need more worry on top of what was going on with her and Mark. Although Thea didn't think it was her own fault that Toby had been suspended, she did feel kind of responsible, as it had happened on her watch.

'So, what are we going to tell Katie?' Toby looked at Thea anxiously. 'She's going to text Dad when she finds out, I just know she is.'

That hadn't occurred to Thea. She had wanted Mark to come back as soon as possible, but now with the discovery of the key to the bookshop, she'd rather he didn't, so that she had an excuse to stay on. She wanted to do something for her sister, but rather than occupy her time with doing things around the house, Thea had decided that her mission over the next fortnight was to get the bookshop up and running for Jenna, for when she left hospital. She imagined that her sister would be delighted – after all, what other reason would she have for having the key, and repeatedly visiting the shop, if she wasn't intending to reopen it?

She glanced at Toby and thought of what he'd told her about hiding in the car one night and discovering that Jenna had met a man at the bookshop in the middle of the night. Whatever that was, she hoped that for her family's sake there was an innocent explanation.

'Auntie Thea?'

Thea heard the front door open. She looked at Toby. 'Okay, right, well, I'm going to lie through my teeth.'

Toby scratched his head. 'I don't understand …'

'You go to a big school – right?'

'Yeah, well it's an Academy. There's, like, over five hundred students.'

'Good, how many classes are you in with Katie?'

'Well … none, actually. We are in different streams.'

Thea didn't know what that meant, but it wasn't important. What was important was the fact that by the sounds of it, Katie wouldn't think it odd if she didn't see her brother all day. She voiced that thought.

'Actually, she'd prefer not to see me. That would suit her, seeing as she doesn't want her dork of a brother embarrassing her in front of her popular friends.'

Thea ignored that comment, although it did rather play into

her hands regarding what she was about to propose. 'We are going to tell Katie that I'm taking you both to school.'

'What?'

'Listen, your mum was going to start running you both to school at the end of the term to save money. Well, I'm going to start now.'

'But she paid for the whole term.'

'Do you want to hide the fact that you've been suspended or not?' Thea lowered her voice. She could hear footsteps in the hall.

'Yes. I do. I just don't like lying to my sister.'

'I don't see as you've got a choice, Toby.'

He nodded. 'Okay. So what happens when we get to school?'

'I drop you both off.'

'But—'

'Let Katie walk ahead.'

'That won't be a problem. She always does that anyway when we get off the school bus, keeping several steps ahead like she doesn't know me.'

Thea stared at her nephew, feeling quite sad that his sister basically disowned him in public. 'Then when she's out of sight, you get back in the car.'

'But why don't I just get the school bus with her, and then hang around, and you pick me up outside the school entrance when everyone's gone into school?'

Thea could see his point. The problem was that she didn't know whether his name would be temporarily removed from the list of pupils getting the coach in the morning and after school while he was suspended. In any case, even though Toby had few friends, some of his classmates might be on that coach and wonder where he was when he didn't attend lessons.

She explained her thinking.

Toby nodded.

'So, it's agreed,' said Thea. 'The plan for the next few days.'

Toby said, 'Yes.'

Katie walked into the kitchen and asked a question Thea had not prepared for. 'Toby, what are you doing home already? Why weren't you on the school bus?'

Thea sighed. She had never been good at telling lies and hated deceiving people. 'Toby has been suspended from school, so I had to pick him up this afternoon.'

Toby turned around and pulled a face at his aunt. 'But only for today.'

Thea looked at Toby.

'So, you won't tell Dad – right?'

Katie looked at her brother shocked. 'You're suspended? I don't believe it.'

Thea said, 'It's true, I'm afraid.'

Katie said, 'What did you do?'

'I kind of got into a fight over a girl.'

'A girl? What girl?'

'I don't want to talk about it.'

Katie shook her head. 'Well, whoever it is, you know she'll never go out with you, right?'

Toby frowned. 'Why?'

'Because you're a dork!'

Thea stepped in. 'Katie, haven't you got homework to do?'

Katie flounced out of the room.

Thea turned to Toby, who was watching Katie walk out of the kitchen. 'Ignore what your sister said. She doesn't see what I see.'

Toby turned in his seat and looked at her. 'Which is *what*?'

'A boy who is turning into a handsome young man.'

'You're just saying that because you're my auntie trying to make me feel better.'

'No, I'm saying that because it's true. Do not listen to Katie. You're thoughtful, caring, and good-looking, and don't you forget it. Someday a special girl is going to walk into your life.'

'But what if that girl is Caitlin?'

After Thea's disastrous relationships, she really had no business giving her young nephew relationship advice, but she didn't want Katie to knock his self-image.

'Katie is going to drama club with her, but I know she'll never introduce me.'

'Is that why you don't want to tell her it was Caitlin you were fighting over?'

Toby nodded.

'Why don't you try talking to Caitlin? Tell her how you feel.'

Toby shook his head furiously.

Thea understood; he didn't want to risk rejection.

Thea had an idea. 'Perhaps Katie will bring her home for a play date …' Thea quickly rephrased. 'I meant, er … well, you know.' They were too old for play dates. 'Then you'd have a chance to strike up a conversation with her.'

Toby considered this.

'In the meantime,' said Thea, 'Let's not get into any more fights, eh? There are better ways to deal with things, like steering clear of her boyfriend.'

'I don't think he is her boyfriend, but I get that he'd like to be.'

Thea smiled. 'Well, there you go. You've got a chance, then.'

Toby smiled at his aunt. 'So, is the plan still on for tomorrow?'

'Huh?'

'You know, I get ready for school like normal, and you drop us both at the school gate … I did tell Katie I was only suspended for one day.'

Thea grinned. 'That was quick thinking.'

'I know.'

'Now, if you don't make it as a writer, you could turn your creative abilities to becoming a master criminal,' Thea joked. Of all the things he could choose, Toby wanted to be a writer. It was obvious why spending time in the bookshop appealed to him. Thea had once thought that she wanted to be a writer too. Her niece reminded her of her sister, but it was Toby who reminded her of herself at that age.

Her smile faded when something suddenly came to mind; that odd phone call she'd taken, and the huge amount of money that might change hands regarding a book, and how shady it all seemed. Thea still hadn't located the book. It wasn't in their house or the garage. Which meant Jenna had left it somewhere else for safe-keeping. Thea knew where that *somewhere* was – the bookshop.

She decided that when she arrived at the bookshop the next morning, the first thing she was going to do was hunt for that book. She'd know it when she found it. A book with that price tag was what the industry called 'a lost book' – something very precious that hadn't seen the light of day for years.

Thea thought of the old bookshop that had been closed for decades, and imagined what treasures she might find inside. She wondered what treasures Jenna had found; Thea was convinced that was where she'd discovered the book worth thousands of pounds.

The only thing she didn't understand was how her sister would know a rare book when she found one. She was no archivist with a knowledge of rare books and artefacts. Thea thought of the person Jenna had met late at night at the bookshop. Who was that? Did *they* know a rare book when they found one?

'So, we're going to the bookshop tomorrow after you drop Katie at school?' Toby asked, interrupting her thoughts.

Thea looked at her nephew. 'Oh, yes.' She couldn't wait to find out what surprises lay in store, and what discoveries she might happen upon.

43

Callum was woken up again by the cat. He rolled out of bed, his back aching from the hard mattress, the same thought running through his head as the previous morning – that his dad must have stayed overnight in hotels on his travels for his book business, not in the campervan.

Or with his other family.

Callum grimaced at the thought of that old wallet and the photo of the two girls inside. He rubbed the sleep out of his eyes and looked down at Dickens, who was meowing for his breakfast. 'Can you have a bit of patience? I've just woken up!'

Callum hastily got dressed in the confined space. Fortunately, there were public toilets just steps from the campervan and the beach, but there were no showers. After leaving the bookshop the previous evening, he'd driven to the nearest larger town, Leiston, which had a public swimming pool. He'd paid for a dip in the pool, and he'd had a shower too.

Callum stepped forward a pace to the little counter and reached for a pouch of cat food in the small cupboard above. He squeezed the contents into Dickens bowl; the cat was already on the counter trying to get to his food.

Callum yawned. 'I'm still considering checking into a hotel and putting it on my credit card,' he said to Dickens, although he knew he really couldn't afford to add to his debts.

He glanced at his watch. *At least I'm up bright and early this morning*, he thought. It wasn't that early – around nine – but it was way better than the previous day, when he'd been woken by the cat at midday.

The only thing he might not get in a hotel was a gorgeous view to wake up to. Callum poured himself a bowl of cereal from the box he'd remembered to buy from the local Co-op, along with a pint of milk, and slid the side door open to reveal the sea.

Callum had shifted his van the previous night, afraid that someone might spot his van parked overnight in the car park again. He hadn't shifted it far; just a few hundred yards. His thoughts drifted back to the previous afternoon as he stood admiring the view.

Mabel and Marjorie had been having lunch when he'd left the charity shop and crossed the yard, so they hadn't spotted him entering the shop. They had been long gone by the time he'd stepped out again, and he had locked the door before he left.

He hadn't done much; he had been at a loss as to where to start. He'd found himself perusing the bookshelves, chosen a good book to read, and settled on the couch in the back room. He'd spent the afternoon reading, telling himself that he'd be more productive tomorrow, when he'd get an earlier start.

When he'd left the shop, he'd gone for a walk through the town, down a side street and along the little promenade fronted by pastel-coloured Victorian terraced houses and small cottages looking over a pebbly beach.

He had become used to the vast sandy beaches in LA with

their huge modern beach houses and their wide promenades stretching as far as the eye could see. This was another world – cosy, very British, and surprisingly very him.

He bet he wasn't alone in falling instantly in love with the place. 'No, don't do that,' he said to himself thinking about the old bookshop and the flat above it. 'I'm not staying, I'm here to sell the place.' He knew he was trying to convince himself.

He looked at the cat. 'What do you think of the view, Dickens?' He'd left the car park, driving by way of a track that led just a couple of hundred yards along the seafront to free parking he'd discovered near a boat yard, with views on one side of the sea and on the other side of the marshes. When he'd left the car park, he had wondered whether Dickens would find the van if he was let out of the shop.

'Oh, my god!' exclaimed Callum at that thought. Dickens was back, which meant his plan had worked. 'Someone let you out!'

He'd checked last night, and there was no other way the cat could get out unless someone unlocked the front door. Dickens liked his food, so Callum had been pretty confident he'd be back first thing if someone let him out this morning – and he imagined he'd soon spot the campervan just a short distance away from where it had previously been parked.

Callum put his unfinished bowel of cereal down on the counter and pulled the heavy sliding door closed. It made a thumping sound as it shut, disturbing Dickens. Callum spotted the cat turn from his cat food and sniff the bowl of cereal before he started lapping up the milk.

'Hey! Do you mind?' Callum took the dish away. Clearly Dickens didn't mind at all, his nose following the dish as Callum looked around for somewhere to put it. 'Eat your own.'

Callum dumped his bowl in the washing-up bowl. He remembered to put the milk away in the little fridge before grabbing his coat. He left a window open, anticipating that Dickens would be off to the bookshop after he'd finished his own breakfast. Today, Callum was going to get there first.

Oh boy, he thought as he walked at pace down the track and past the car park to make his way along the high street. *I can't wait to confront whoever is in my bookshop right now.* Then he slowed his pace, starting to feel surprisingly anxious. For some reason someone in that bookshop right now thought, mistakenly, that they owned the bookshop. He didn't know why he was feeling anxious. He had the deeds. He'd simply tell them to leave.

But whoever was there had a key. That was what the elderly sisters in the charity shop had told him. But there was something *he* hadn't told *them*. His thoughts turned to that photo. Was it one of those girls? And if it was, what were they doing with a key to his father's bookshop after all these years?

All this time he'd assumed that if they were Henry's kids, he'd had an affair – that was why Callum hadn't mentioned the wallet and the photo he'd found to his mother. But it was quite an assumption. Callum was starting to wonder if he'd got it all wrong. Those girls could be older than him, in which case, was it his mother that Henry had left his original family for?

Callum shook his head. Did it matter? Either way, it was quite possible he'd had two families. He realised that his anxiety was really about whom he was about to meet. Would they resemble his father? Would they take one look at him and guess the truth – that they might be half-siblings? Or were they already aware that their father had another family, another child?

Callum wasn't sure he was ready to be confronted by the truth about his father, but he had no choice. It did cross his mind that he might be reading way too much into the photo. As Jack had said, his father had dementia. The wallet, and the photo, might have nothing to do with Henry whatsoever. But that didn't explain why someone else had a key to the bookshop.

Callum quickened his pace. Up ahead, he could see The Two Magpies Bakery. Outside the stop, sitting patiently beside a bowl of water, with his lead tied to a post, was a sweet golden retriever. Callum stopped to say hello, patting him on the head and giving him a stroke.

He happened to glance in the window, thinking of that pretty young woman he'd locked eyes with at lunchtime the previous day. He'd hoped to see her again, but he hadn't expected to see her this morning. She was standing at the back of a long queue at the counter, which meant she was getting something to go.

Perhaps she works here in town, thought Callum, smiling hopefully.

She happened to glance out of the window, and caught him pausing outside the café, smiling her way. She smiled back.

If he hadn't been on a mission to find out who was in his bookshop, he might have stepped inside that shop and joined the queue behind her. What a perfect way to strike up a conversation.

Damn! He was torn between doing just that and heading to the shop. He said goodbye to the well-behaved dog and stole a glance at the young woman being served fresh croissants at the counter. He wondered where she was headed with those croissants.

You haven't got time for that either, thought Callum, as it crossed his mind that he could wait and find out. Petting the dog would have provided the perfect excuse to hang back outside the shop.

Callum sighed and said goodbye to the dog before heading down the high street. He cast a backwards glance a couple of times to see if he could spot which direction she was headed after she left the café. But by the time he'd reached Cobblers Yard, she still hadn't emerged from the café.

He sighed and turned down the narrow lane, emerging into Cobblers Yard. Callum looked at the charity shop. Neither Marjorie nor Mabel were standing in the window. He couldn't see them. He had thought of popping his head inside their shop and asking if they'd seen someone entering the bookshop that morning, but he really didn't have to do that. All he had to do was walk up to the bookshop and try the door. The only thing was, would whoever was in there have locked it from the inside?

Callum walked up to the bookshop window. He couldn't see anybody inside the shop – not that he could see a lot through the dust and cobwebs that still covered the window. If there was someone in there, what were they doing? They certainly weren't cleaning. He thought of himself lazing on the old couch the previous afternoon, reading a book.

He stepped to the right and looked at the door. The 'closed' sign was still in the window. He tried the door, and was taken aback when he turned the handle and it opened. 'Oh, damn!' he said under his breath. Callum was not a confrontational type. He was not looking forward to having words or getting into a slanging match with whomever was inside, trespassing on his property.

Callum stepped inside. He couldn't see anyone. 'Hello?'

He waited, as though he needed an invitation to enter the shop. *This is stupid. I own the place. What am I doing?* he thought.

He was about to shut the door behind him when Dickens appeared between his legs, meowing at him loudly, making him jump. 'For goodness' sake, Dickens!'

Callum closed the door behind him. He looked down at the

cat. 'So, who let you out this morning?'

Dickens turned his back, put his tail in the air, and sauntered through the shop.

Callum stared after him, and decided to follow.

44

Callum followed the cat, past the bookshelves and the counter with the old-fashioned till, to the door which led to the room out back – the one with the sofa, desk and bookbinding equipment. He stopped in the doorway, surprised to find a young teenage boy lying on the sofa with his head in a book. Dickens had jumped on his chest. 'Hey, you're back! How did you get in?'

The boy hadn't noticed Callum standing in the doorway. He lowered his book and stroked the cat, who settled down, purring.

Callum folded his arms and stared at them, most notably at Dickens, who he felt had defected to the other side. *Traitor* thought Callum. The boy said, 'You know, you're going to have to leave when Winston returns. He doesn't like cats.'

Winston, thought Callum, narrowing his eyes. So it wasn't a woman who had the key to his bookshop. The old ladies' eyesight obviously wasn't great – they'd mistaken a man for a woman.

The boy resumed reading, oblivious to Callum's presence.

'Ahem!' Callum cleared his throat loudly, startling the boy. He sat up quickly, disturbing Dickens, who meowed loudly. He put the book down and stood up. 'Oh, I forgot to lock the door. Didn't you see the 'closed' sign in the window?'

Callum stared at him. What was he doing here? Why wasn't he at school?

'Sorry, but we're not open yet.'

'*Yet*? You mean you're going to reopen the bookshop?'

'Yes, that's the plan. There's a lot of work to do.'

Callum noticed that the boy suddenly looked surprised. 'Hey you're that guy!'

Callum stared at him, hoping he didn't recognise him. 'What guy?'

'The one in the yellow campervan that passed by the café a couple of days ago. We were having dinner when my sister spotted you and swore that you're that Hollywood actor. Are you?'

Callum was about to shake his head, but he thought he'd had enough of lying about who he was, and decided to come clean. 'Yes, I'm him, actually.'

Toby sat up, 'No way!'

Callum couldn't help but smile at the boy's shocked face. 'Yes, way.'

'What are you doing here?'

Callum asked him the same question.

'I told you. We're doing up the shop to reopen it.'

'Shouldn't you be at school?'

He frowned, and said in small voice. 'I got suspended.' He brightened. 'But it means I can spend my time in the bookshop, helping out. I love this place.'

'How long have you been coming here?'

'Since I found the key.'

'*You* found the key? Where?'

The boy clammed up.

Callum wanted to keep him talking until Winston returned,

otherwise he imagined the boy would text and forewarn this Winston that there was some guy hanging around the bookshop.

'What's your name?'

'Toby.'

'What's so special about this place, Toby?'

Toby shrugged. 'I don't know. I guess it's kind of sad that the bookshop has sat empty for years and years, when it could be serving the community, you know. There's nothing like a good book, is there?'

Callum smiled. 'That's very true.'

'I love books. I want to be a writer.'

'Really?'

'Yes. Although I'd like to know about bookbinding too.'

Callum raised an eyebrow. 'Excuse me?'

'Here, look at all this stuff.' Toby pointed at the bookbinding equipment on the desk. 'I think it's a shame.'

Callum looked at him. 'What is?'

'Well, I'd love to know how to repair books, but because there's no one to teach me, we might end up selling the equipment.'

'Oh no you're not.'

Toby turned around and frowned at him. 'What makes you say that?'

Callum couldn't believe he was doing this. He rolled up his sleeves. 'Because I'm going to teach you.'

'Bookbinding?'

'Oh, yes.'

'Right now?'

'Right now.'

'But I don't understand … you're an actor. I thought you needed like special skills, and to have been taught by an experienced bookbinder. There's not many of those around.'

Callum grinned. 'I grew up with a master bookbinder.'

'You did? Who?'

'My father.' Before Toby asked anything more, Callum said, 'Right, let's get to it.' It was what his father had always said to him when he was a child and they were starting a new project. 'Now, first we need to find a book!'

Toby grinned. 'I think I know just the one.' He opened the drawer of the desk. 'I found this at the back of the drawer, wrapped in brown paper.'

'That is one old book,' said Callum, admiring the old, worn cover and the embossed lettering on the inside cover. He knew a rare book when he saw one – that was another skill he'd picked up after growing up with a bookseller.

But he wasn't an expert. He would love to have shown this to his dad and asked him to run his expert eye over it. There were some books, his father had once told him, that should not be rebound, but should be left in their original condition.

He hesitated. Was this one of those books? He looked at Toby, eagerly awaiting his first lesson in bookbinding, and brushed that thought aside. 'Right let's get to it,' said Callum once more, hoping that by the time they were done, Winston would have returned, and he could find out more about how Toby had come by the key, and why they thought they could open someone else's bookshop.

❖

They were partway through Toby's first bookbinding lesson when Callum heard the sound of the shop door opening. He turned to Toby. 'Is that Winston?'

'Yes.' He looked over at the sofa.

Callum followed his gaze to Dickens, who was curled up, asleep.

'I think we need to do something about the cat.'

'Why?'

'I told you. Winston doesn't like cats.'

Callum grimaced. What sort of person doesn't like cats? Callum was not looking forward to meeting this guy. 'Is Winston your dad?'

Toby was just throwing him a bemused expression when Callum turned to the door and saw a golden retriever bounding through the doorway. He spotted the cat.

Dickens was woken from his slumber by an inquisitive black nose approaching the sofa and sniffing his tail.

Dickens meowed loudly and hid behind the sofa.

The dog spotted Callum next and bounded up to him.

'Hey! I know you,' said Callum giving him a good fuss.

'You know Winston?'

Callum raised his eyebrows, and looked at the dog. 'This is Winston?'

'Yeah – where did you meet him?'

'On my way to Cobblers Yard. I saw him sitting outside The Two Magpies Bakery.' Callum didn't mention the reason he'd hung back and given the dog a good fuss; that he'd been watching the young woman in the café.

'Oh, yeah, that makes sense. That's where my—'

'Toby? I hope you're not lounging on the sofa reading a book!' a woman's voice called out.

'No, I'm not,' Toby called out, smirking.

Callum realised that whoever that woman was, she hadn't heard them talking at the back of the shop.

'I'm being productive, Auntie Thea – like you said.'

'That's your aunt?'

'Yes, I'm helping her in the bookshop this week. She promised she'd go and buy some croissants along with her coffee.'

'Toby? Are you talking to Winston?'

Callum turned around. He could smell the freshly baked pastries before a young woman appeared in the doorway, holding a bag of croissants and a takeaway coffee. Callum could smell the freshly ground coffee too.

'I'm binding a book, Auntie – look!'

Callum couldn't have been more flummoxed if he'd tried. The last person he'd expected to see walk through that door was the pretty young woman he'd been unable to take his eyes off in the bakery.

'It's you!' he blurted, feeling surprisingly shy under her gaze. He never usually felt that way. He was a pretty confident, outgoing guy, but not in her presence – clearly. Under her gaze, he felt tongue-tied, embarrassed, and rather intimidated, which was silly – it was just she was even more beautiful up close than he had realised.

She looked just as surprised as he did. 'What are you doing here?'

'He's showing me how to bind books,' said Toby before Callum had a chance to respond.

She cast her gaze down at the desk. 'Um, yes … I can see that. But—'

'It's my fault, Auntie Thea, I forgot to lock the door. He didn't see the 'closed' sign in the window, and just wandered in. But it turns out he knows how to bind books, so he's teaching me book-binding.'

Callum looked at Toby. 'Er, yeah – that's right. I was about to leave,'— even as he was saying it, Callum couldn't believe what was coming out of his mouth— 'but your nephew mentioned that you were thinking of selling the bookbinding equipment. He has an interest in learning how to do it. So as I was here, in the neighbourhood so to speak, I thought that I might as well show him.'

Callum didn't add that he had been waiting for Winston to turn up, thinking he was Toby's dad, in order to have it out with him regarding what he thought he was doing by trespassing. Now he'd found out it was her, he had just clammed up.

'Don't you recognise him, Auntie Thea?'

Callum caught the colour rising in her cheeks as she stared at him. Was she too feeling suddenly shy and embarrassed under his gaze? They had exchanged a smile in the shop. Of course she recognised him.

'He's the guy in the yellow campervan who passed by the café the other day. Remember the one Katie pointed out?'

Callum rolled his eyes. *Oh, no.* He knew what was coming next. This was going to spoil everything. That bloody character he played felt like a curse on his relationships. Not that he was in a relationship right now. He stared at her. But he might like to be.

What about the bookshop? A voice in his head reminded him. Callum ignored it, for now.

Callum looked at Toby, and thought *please don't tell her—*

'He's the guy, the actor. Katie was right!'

Thea looked at Callum apologetically. 'I honestly don't know what they were talking about. I've never watched your show, so I have no idea who you are. Sorry.'

Callum stared at her.

'I've offended you – haven't I?'

'Offended me?' *Oh, my lord,* thought Callum. How refreshing to meet a young lady who had no idea who he was, or what character he'd played, and had no expectations.

'Not at all. I prefer that you haven't watched the show, and have no idea who I am.'

'Why – is it embarrassing?' She offered him a quirky smile.

Callum stared at her. *Is she flirting with me?*

'Embarrassing?' Toby looked at his aunt. 'Of course not. I mean, I'm not into the show, but I've caught some of the episodes when Katie was watching them on DVD and it is good.'

Callum raised his eyebrows. 'Your niece has some of the episodes on DVD?'

'Oh, my god. She has *all* the seasons on DVD,' said Toby. 'The moment the next one is out, she said she's going to buy it.'

The last one, thought Callum.

Thea nodded. 'That's right. She offered to give them to me to watch. Sorry, but I turned her down.' She winced.

'Truly, I'm not offended. So many people just confuse me with the character I play. It's refreshing to meet a woman – er, I mean a person – who doesn't think they know me just because they've watched me on the show.'

'Well, I'd like to get to know the real you.' Thea looked away embarrassed. 'God, I don't know where that came from.'

Callum grinned. 'How about lunch at The Two Magpies Bakery? I'd like to get to know the real you, too.'

They were exchanging a smile when Toby butted in. 'What about me? You were going to take me there for lunch, remember?'

Thea managed to prise her eyes off Callum for a moment. She turned to Toby. 'Oh, yes – of course.'

'I can't wait to tell Katie that I met—'

'Um, Toby … remember the plan?' said Thea.

'Oh, yeah. I forgot.'

Callum looked from Toby to Thea. 'The plan?'

Thea sighed. 'This is going to make me sound a really devious person. I'm not, really I'm not.'

Neither am I, thought Callum, knowing that he had no intention of telling her what he was really doing there in the bookshop – not right now, anyway. He'd made up his mind. Not until he had got to know her better. He grinned at her. 'Do tell.'

'Toby has been suspended for five days, but we didn't tell his sister, Katie, that. Just that he'd been suspended for one day, so she doesn't know he's spending time with me at the bookshop.'

'How come?'

'Well, if it gets back to their father working away in London, he might come back earlier, then I may have to leave.'

'Leave?'

'Oh, yeah, Auntie Thea is looking after us while Dad is working away and Mum is in hospital with a broken leg.'

Thea looked at Toby. 'Yes, I'm looking after them for a few days, which is why I'm here in Suffolk.'

'Oh, you don't live here?'

'No, not normally. London. Although when I walked into this place yesterday, I must admit, I felt like staying here longer. I could do with a change of scenery. Don't get me wrong, I love my job in London, but I needed to get away, and I don't think a few days, a fortnight tops, is going to turn out to be long enough.'

The look on her face said she hadn't meant to come out with all that, but her pained expression suggested that someone had let her down – big time. He guessed, like him, she'd split up with someone recently.

'When I walked into the bookshop yesterday, well, it hadn't occurred to me to run a bookshop …' she trailed of.

Callum's mind was racing. It was ridiculous; he'd only just met her. And yet going through his mind at this moment was the thought that they could run the shop together. And perhaps their work relationship would blossom into something more.

He was about to ask her how Toby had found a key to the shop, when Thea looked at him, and said, 'I will have lunch with you. But there is one proviso.'

'That Toby can come too? Which is totally fine by me.'

'No, it's not that, although Toby is coming to lunch with us.'

'I should hope so,' mumbled Toby, returning to his work, completing the first part of binding a book, which was to carefully cut away the old cover.

'So, what is the proviso?' Callum grinned. 'Anything – name it.'

Thea looked at him. 'You carry on with teaching Toby all about bookbinding. I don't like that he's off school. I want him to do something productive, and learning a new skill would be perfect. Otherwise I know he will just laze around and read all day.'

Callum caught Toby glancing his way with a worried look on his face, clearly hoping Callum didn't mention that he'd caught Toby doing just that.

Callum smiled. 'I'd be delighted.' He was so looking forward to having lunch and getting to know her better.

Toby exclaimed, 'Great!' Although he did frown at his aunt as he added, 'I like reading.'

'Yes, I know, Toby. But there's a time and a place for that—'

He rolled his eyes. 'If you can't do it in a bookshop, where can you do it?'

Callum tried to keep a straight face. Her nephew did have a point. 'You know, I've seen some bookshops with places where people can sit and read, as well as browse the bookshelves. They even provide tea and coffee, which makes it a bit of a community hub.'

He could tell by the look on her face that she liked his thinking. Thea turned around and looked at all the cluttered bookshelves. 'You know, that's not a bad idea. Perhaps when you're done teaching Toby, you could help me out with organising this place?'

She quickly backtracked. 'Sorry, that was a bit forward of me. You're probably here on a well-earned break from filming and have much better things to do than—'

'No, not at all. I'd love to help out.' He tried to brush the guilty thought aside that in fact he wasn't helping her out; she was helping him. He knew he still had to get to the bottom of what was really going on here regarding how they had a key and why they thought they had every right to be there. But just then he was just over the moon to have an invitation, and an excuse, to spend more time in her company.

But what happens when she finds out who you really are – the owner of the bookshop? Callum did not, and would not, think about that right now.

'The thing is, I shall expect lunch every day. You can't expect me to work for nothing,' Callum joked.

She laughed.

He liked that she got his sense of humour.

A loud meow followed by a doggy yelp interrupted his thoughts. Winston had been sitting on the sofa, his muzzle sniffing along the back of the sofa, when a paw had appeared from behind the sofa and connected with his nose. Winston flew off the sofa and ran over to Callum, hiding behind his legs.

Thea looked at her nephew. 'I thought you put that cat out this morning, like I asked. We both know it's not going to take kindly to Winston around.'

'I did. But it got back in.' Toby looked at Callum.

Callum shrugged. 'Must have been me when I opened the shop door,' he said innocently, knowing very well it was him who had let Dickens in.

Thea said to Callum, 'I had no choice but to bring their dog. He's quite young, and I couldn't leave him home alone all day.' Thea's gaze shifted to the sofa. 'I have no idea why the cat keeps turning up here. I don't think he's a stray. He looks well-fed.'

Callum glanced around the room, feigning ignorance.

Thea sighed. 'Well, we'd better put him out again.' She looked at her nephew. 'He seems to be your best friend, so do you mind?'

Callum helped Toby shift the sofa so they could get at the cat hiding. He warned, 'Careful – he scratches, and bites!'

Toby frowned. 'How do you know?'

Callum said, 'Er, well … he's a cat.'

'It's all right. He doesn't scratch me.'

'Really?' Callum raised his eyebrows.

Toby crawled behind the sofa, while Callum winced, and reappeared holding Dickens, who actually purred.

As Toby passed by, heading for the front door, Dickens' paw came out swiping at Callum.

Callum glared at him thinking, *How was I to know they had a dog?*

'Say, about those DVDs,' said Callum, watching Toby put the cat out. 'Your niece wouldn't mind lending them to me – would she?'

'Would she ever?' blurted Toby. 'Oh, my god, when she finds

out who my new friend is, she is going to … well I don't know what she's going to do.'

Callum smiled.

'Toby,' warned Thea, 'remember, she doesn't know we're here, and that goes for Callum too.'

'Oh, okay, yeah … I forgot.'

Thea turned to Callum. 'It's fine, I'll sort it out. You want to watch your show?'

'Oh, god, no. That's the last thing I want to do. Um, the thing is I know two very sweet old ladies who would love to watch it. Mabel and Marjorie in the charity shop across the yard. I met them yesterday.' Callum avoided letting Thea in on exactly how he had come to meet them. 'They asked me if I could get hold of the DVD's. I said of course, but—' *I haven't got the money to go ordering all eight seasons on DVD.* Callum didn't add that part.

'Well, as you're here on holiday, it might be a bit difficult trying to order DVDs online and getting them delivered.'

'Exactly – it's not like I have any DVDs of my show lying around.'

'I'll bring them along with me tomorrow. She told me where she keeps them.'

'Won't she miss them, though?'

Toby said, 'No, they're online now, on a catch-up channel she watches. But I don't expect the old ladies have things like that.'

Callum shook his head. 'That's doubtful.'

Thea said, 'That's fine, I'll put it in the diary in my phone so I remember to bring them with me.'

'Great.' Callum watched her get her mobile phone out. He wanted her number. 'I'll nip across the yard and let them know I'll have the DVDs for them tomorrow.'

Callum was just walking to the door, when Thea said, 'You're an actor, right? How did you learn bookbinding? I know it's quite a specialised skill.'

Callum said, 'My dad.'

'Hey, what a coincidence. My dad used to do that too. He used to run this bookshop.'

Callum swallowed. 'What happened to him?'

'He disappeared when I was nine.'

As Callum stepped out of the shop, he got out his wallet and took out the photo of the two girls. When he turned around, hiding the photo behind his back, he caught her smiling at him through the open doorway. His face dropped when he saw the little girl in the young woman standing before him.

Oh, my god. I think she's my sister.

45

'Hey, it's nice to see you,' said Thea. 'Did it slip your mind about our plan yesterday to have lunch, and then help Toby out bookbinding?'

Callum had just stepped into the shop. Thea was there with a bucket and a sponge. She was wearing a pair of Marigolds. She had already cleared the outdated bestsellers from the display in the shop window and had been scrubbing the window when she'd spotted him enter Cobblers Yard and head straight in her direction. She'd waved and had been relieved when he'd waved back.

The previous day, Thea had been getting on with sorting out some of the books and had been surprised that Callum hadn't returned after visiting the ladies in the charity shop across the yard. She'd wondered if his absence was down to something she'd said. He had seemed surprisingly keen about the plan to help Toby and her in the bookshop – not to mention having lunch together. She'd wondered what had changed his mind.

Toby had been looking out for him too, waiting all day for him to return to show him the next step in the bookbinding process, and Thea had felt guilty that it might have been her fault that Callum hadn't shown up. Perhaps she had been a little too forward yesterday, and had made him feel uncomfortable. Her joy at seeing him again was tempered with the possibility he might just be there to tell her the plan was off, and that he wasn't coming back.

She mopped her brow with the soapy Marigold glove. 'I remembered to bring the DVDs with me,' Thea said hopefully as he walked up to her in the window. Perhaps that was all he'd turned up for.

Callum held up a paper bag. 'I brought croissants, and—' from behind his back he produced a tray with three takeaway cups, 'two coffees for us, and a hot chocolate for my protégé. I am so sorry about yesterday. I …'

'There's no need to explain,' said Thea. She was just over the moon to see him again.

'Well, um … something came up. But I'm here now, ready to roll up my sleeves and get stuck in!'

Toby had been sitting on the couch with Winston, reading a book. They both got up at the sound of Callum's voice and ran into the shop front. Winston ran straight up to Callum for a fuss.

The dog got a hiss for his troubles.

'You're back!' exclaimed Toby. 'And so is the cat!'

'I have a confession to make,' said Callum.

Thea stared at him, noticing that unlike the previous day, when he had been all smiles – and she'd assumed coming on to her – today he seemed … different. She saw him look at the cat by his feet.

'I want to introduce you to Dickens.'

'Dickens?' Toby and Thea said in unison.

'Yes, the cat. That's his name. I should have told you in the first place, but …' he trailed off.

Thea looked at him, relieved. Was that what all this was about?

He felt guilty that he hadn't told them about his cat, and that was why he hadn't come back yesterday afternoon? 'Oh, goodness, don't be silly.'

'I know it's not ideal, with your dog and all, but I'm afraid I just can't keep Dickens away. As you can see.'

'He's travelling with you in your campervan?' Toby asked.

'Yes, I'm afraid so.'

'That is *so* cool. When I'm older, I want to hit the road travelling with my dog.'

Thea said, 'I didn't know that.'

'Like John Steinbeck,' commented Callum.

'You've read that book too – *Travels with Charley*?'

Callum admitted he hadn't. 'No, but I've heard of it.' He smiled at Toby. 'Right, well after we've had a well-earned coffee and croissant, we can crack on. Well, for one of us it's well-earned.'

Thea caught Toby and Callum looking at her Marigolds. 'Yeah, it's just been me working in the shop this morning.'

Toby looked at her sheepishly.

'Well, we can't have that,' said Callum. 'I'll help with some cleaning after setting Toby to work on the bookbinding.' He carried the drinks and croissants over to the counter at the back of the shop, where there were a couple of chairs and a stool, all quite tatty, with seat pads that had seen better days.

Callum offered Thea a coffee, and gave Toby his drink. 'Hope you like hot chocolate.'

'Yes, thank you.'

'Help yourself to a croissant, or a doughnut. I wasn't sure what you'd like.' Callum had thoughtfully brought some paper napkins from the café.

'That's very kind of you, Callum.'

'It's the least I can do after bailing yesterday afternoon.'

Thea glanced at the old black and white cat with the grey whiskers as he jumped up on to the counter top.

Winston thought he'd join the cat, by jumping up, front paws on the counter top. Thea told him off. 'No! Down!'

Winston slunk off to the corner of the room, and sat there panting, staring at the cat.

Satisfied the dog was not going to bother him, Dickens sat licking his paw, looking as though he was minding his own business, which he wasn't. Thea watched in amusement as Dickens started to move closer to Callum's croissant when he thought Callum wasn't looking. The cat moved several inches at a time, then sat there licking a paw as though he hadn't budged.

'I hope you'd be so kind as to accompany me to lunch,' said Callum, picking his croissant up, and shaking a finger at Dickens. 'I booked a table at The Two Magpies Bakery on my way here – my treat.'

Thea looked at her coffee and croissant as she took off her Marigold gloves. She hadn't expected an invite to lunch too. She smiled at him.

He smiled shyly back, but once again she noticed there didn't feel as though there was the same easy banter or flirtatious behaviour. *Perhaps that's my fault.* Thea thought there must have been more to his failure to turn up the previous day than simply the cat.

He was a good-looking actor, and famous, and no doubt used to women coming on to him. Perhaps if he was interested, which she thought he was, he was backing off, wanting to take things slow.

Thea decided that was for the best; she'd just broken up with who she'd thought was the love of her life. She knew Callum had broken up with his girlfriend. She'd broken it off, according to the gossip columns. Thea had Googled him the previous evening; she hadn't been able to help herself. Then she'd asked Katie if she could borrow the DVDs they'd talked about to lend to the ladies in the charity shop.

Katie had shrugged and said okay. Thea and Toby had agreed not to mention Callum. Just then, it had to be their secret, otherwise Katie would find out that Toby was not in school but was spending time with a famous actor in their grandfather's bookshop.

Thea had thought that if Katie bumped into one of Toby's friends, they might mention his five-day suspension, but Toby had assured her that wouldn't happen – he only had one good friend, and Katie avoided him because he wasn't cool.

When Thea had been putting the DVDs in her bag the night before, making sure she'd packed them so she wouldn't forget to take them with her in the morning, once again her curiosity had got the better of her. She'd decided to watch an episode. It had turned into so many that she'd lost count before she fell asleep on the sofa at midnight.

She was enjoying the series about the Scotsman who'd lost his castle and moved to America to make his fortune. There were plenty of opportunities on the ranch in America for the actor to go bare-chested – swinging an axe while cutting wood, saving a calf that had fallen into a reservoir – situations concocted, she imagined, just as an excuse to show the actor shirtless. Not that she was complaining.

It wasn't raunchy, though, which was just as well, given that her thirteen-year-old niece had been watching it. Thea could see how the clean and wholesome television programme could appeal to the whole family.

Perhaps that was why it had been cancelled; times had moved

on. She'd Googled the next series and had come across the announcement by the studio that it had been cancelled. She wondered why Callum hadn't mentioned it. Perhaps he was embarrassed – or, more likely, after so many years starring in that show, it was a sensitive issue; something he didn't want to discuss with a stranger.

Thea looked at Callum. Perhaps that was why he was pleased she hadn't watched the show – then she wouldn't be asking when the next season was due.

The trouble was – and she wouldn't tell Callum this – that she was hooked. She wished she didn't have to hand the DVDs over to the old ladies across the yard. She had asked Katie first thing in the morning which catch-up channel they were on. Katie had laughed, and said, 'You started watching it, didn't you?'

Thea admitted it. Her niece had said, 'See, I told you it was really good.'

Thea smiled when she thought back to that.

'What's so good?' Toby had asked, joining them for breakfast that morning in his school uniform, as planned. When he'd found out what they were talking about, he'd surprised his sister when he'd said he'd been watching it too. Although Thea hadn't been surprised in the least – Toby had made a new friend. His sister would be so shocked if she found out Toby's new friend was in fact none other than the star of that show. She imagined that if Katie knew, she would change her attitude to her brother and be grovelling at his feet for an introduction. Toby would suddenly turn into the coolest brother on the planet.

46

Callum looked at the bag of DVDs in his hand and glanced over his shoulder at the bookshop before he stepped inside the charity shop. He caught Thea standing in the shop window. She waved.

Callum tentatively waved back, a knot twisting in his stomach at the thought that the good-looking girl in the shop window could never be his girlfriend, if she was who he suspected she was – his half-sister.

He sighed heavily. For that reason, he wasn't looking forward to returning to the bookshop after delivering the DVDs as promised, or to going to lunch with her. Then again, if she was his half-sister, it meant he had a sister, and that also meant he was related to Toby – he had a nephew, and a niece.

But when are you going to tell her about your father?

Callum opened the charity shop door. First of all, he had to be sure that she was the girl in the photo – and that Henry was her father. *So, ask her.* But he didn't want to ask her outright – *was your father Henry?* Or show her the photo just yet. There would be time enough, whether at lunch today, or working with her and Toby, to get to the bottom of who he suspected she was, and what she was doing in his bookshop. And once he was sure, then he'd figure out how he was going to tell her the truth – that Henry had two families, and that he was Henry's son. He imagined it would come as quite a shock when she found out.

'Oh, Callum, you came back!'

'Of course I did, Mabel. I had to see you again.' He grinned.

Mabel looked at him coyly. 'Now, you're making me come over all flustered.'

Marjorie rolled her eyes at the pair of them.

'I came bearing gifts.' He walked up to the counter at the back of the shop.

Marjorie looked at the bag. 'You brought some things to donate?'

'Oh, er … no. This is for Mabel.' He smiled as he handed her the bag.

She took it, and looked inside. 'DVDs?'

'Yes, the entire eight seasons of my show. I borrowed them from a friend. She didn't mind me lending them to you.'

Callum caught Marjorie frowning. She said, 'Well, it looks as though I'm going to be here in the shop on my own for the duration.'

'Oh, don't be silly, Marj,' said Mabel. 'I'll get through these in no time. I'll binge-watch them.' She looked at Callum. 'Is that what they call it?'

He nodded. 'That assumes you like the show. You might not.'

'Oh, I'm sure I will.'

Marjorie rolled her eyes in her sister's direction. 'Yes, because Callum is in it.'

Mabel didn't refute that comment. She did ask, 'Are you in anything else?'

Callum shook his head. 'Nothing of note.' He preferred not

to mention the roles he'd had earlier in his career, most of which had been bit-parts in embarrassingly bad movies.

Marjorie turned to Callum. 'Would you like a cup of tea?'

Callum glanced over his shoulder at the bookshop. A part of him still wanted to avoid Thea and Toby, as he had done the previous day after he'd seen Thea's resemblance to the girl in the photo. He was about to turn down the offer, knowing he couldn't do a repeat performance with Thea and just disappear for the rest of the day. But then he thought, *why not?* It was only a cup of tea.

He took a seat. 'Yes, please. But only on the proviso I can have a chocolate digestive biscuit with my tea. Preferably two.' He wasn't joking. Callum had missed so many things when he'd been away living and working in America, like a good old cup of tea and a biscuit. Of course, you could get those in the States, but for some reason they never tasted quite the same.

It turned out that Marjorie had an ulterior motive for inviting him to join them for a cuppa. She made a pot of tea in double-quick time. As she poured the tea into three china mugs, she said, 'So, Callum, we saw you this morning going into the bookshop.'

'Really, Marjorie,' Mabel looked at her sister crossly, 'I told you that in confidence.'

Marjorie eyed her sister. 'Did you now. I bet you're dying to know what he was doing in there – with that girl!'

Callum looked from one sister to the other.

'Didn't we say they'd make a nice couple?' said Marjorie.

Callum tried to hide his frown, but Mabel caught it. 'Has she got a boyfriend already? I wouldn't be surprised. She's a pretty little thing, isn't she Marjorie?'

'Oh, yes.'

They both turned to look at Callum, eyebrows raised, waiting for his response. Before he got on to the subject of Thea, he had a question for them. He got out his wallet and found the photo.

'We're going to visit the bookshop,' announced Mabel.

'Are we?' said Marjorie. 'I thought you said you never wanted to step foot in that bookshop again?'

Callum looked at them in surprise, wondering what they had against the bookshop. He'd assumed they had fond memories of the place and would jump at the chance to get inside for a trip down memory lane. Maybe they didn't have fond memories of growing up there after all – or perhaps Mabel's aversion was just down to the fact that it reminded her of her lost love.

Callum didn't ask. He had his own problems to sort out.

Mabel said to her sister, 'I presume that after all these years the bookshop has changed hands, and she's the new owner. I'd like to meet her.'

He put the photo on the table and slid it towards them. 'Do you recognise these girls?'

Mable and Marjorie exchanged a glance. Marjorie put on her reading glasses and picked up the photo. She asked, 'When was this taken?'

Callum shrugged. 'I don't know exactly. But judging by their clothes and hairstyles, they must be around my age now.'

'Let me see,' said Mabel, reaching for the photo in her sister's hand.

Marjorie handed it over.

Mabel took one look, and said, 'It's them. It's the two girls who lived in the bookshop.'

Marjorie said, 'Are you sure?'

'Oh, yes,' said Mabel.

Callum raised his eyebrows. 'Do you know their names?'

Mabel turned to Marjorie. 'It's Thea and Jenna. I'm sure of it.'

Marjorie studied the photo once more. 'So, it is!'

Mabel said, 'Oh, how I wish we could meet them again. I've always wondered what happened to those girls.'

They both shifted their gaze to the window.

Callum knew he ought to tell them that it was Thea over in the bookshop. They obviously hadn't been over there yet, but they'd find out soon enough, he imagined. He didn't know what they'd think when they found out he knew. 'So they lived in the bookshop with their dad?'

'Yes, Henry. He took over the bookshop after Father passed away.'

Callum swallowed. They'd said – *Henry.* Callum stared at the two ladies, thinking, *Oh, god, so it is true. They are Henry's daughters.*

He caught a look pass between the sisters that he couldn't quite fathom – as though there was something more that they wouldn't say.

Marjorie said, 'They lived there with their mum and dad.'

Callum frowned. They were a lovely little family,' said Mabel suddenly eyeing him warily. 'Where did you get this photo?'

Callum looked at the photo, realising his mistake too late. As soon as Mabel and Marjorie made a visit to the bookshop, and discovered the young woman was Thea, they'd surely mention the photo Callum had of Thea and her sister.

Would the sisters promise not to reveal this conversation, and the photo he had in his possession if he asked them to? They might, but what explanation could he give? They were bound to ask him for one. They were already curious. He'd seen to that by showing them the photo. But he needed more time to get to the bottom of his father's past, and how it came to be that he had two families. It wasn't something he wanted to reveal to anyone just yet.

Callum realised he didn't need to find out from Thea whether Henry was her father. He'd had a lot of questions answered already, apart from one – how had she come by the key? And what was she doing there, cleaning it up, looking as though she was preparing to reopen it?

He reached out and took the photo out of Mabel's hand, aware that he hadn't answered the question. He saw Mabel turn to her big sister.

Marjorie, the more forthright of the two, said to Callum bluntly, 'You've met Henry – haven't you? He gave you that photo, didn't he?'

Callum stared at them.

Mabel reached over to Callum and put a hand on his forearm. 'Please. We want … we need to know what happened to him.'

Callum swallowed. They knew Henry, and Thea and her sister. Thea's mum was most likely still alive somewhere too. He couldn't tell them who he was, or about Henry, not yet. He just felt he needed more time to get to the bottom of why it came to be that Henry had two families before he told anyone where Henry was.

'I … look, I can't. Not yet. Please, you have to give me some time. If I promise to tell you when I'm ready, will you promise me not to tell … *anybody* about this photo.' He put it back in his wallet. 'You have to promise me.' He stared at them. 'Is it a deal?'

Mabel and Marjorie exchanged a glance. Marjorie said, 'Can you just tell us one thing?'

Callum pursed his lips, intending to remain tight-lipped.

'Please just tell us if he is still alive. You don't have to tell us anything else, what happened to him, not yet, just … just give us that.'

Callum stared at them. He took a deep breath, and said, 'Yes, he's still alive, but—'

'Oh, thank the lord!' Mabel shouted out, clasping her hands together. Marjorie and Mabel stood up and hugged each other.

Callum thought it was a bit over the top, their reaction to finding out that the guy who had once run the bookshop was alive. Still, they were old ladies; he thought that this was probably the most exciting thing that had happened to them in years. An age-old mystery of what had happened to the previous owner had partially been solved. He wasn't dead, as everyone had obviously suspected – including, no doubt, Thea and her sister.

But why had he left his bookshop, along with his other family, never to return? If he'd had two families, why stop a deception that had gone on for years?

It was highly likely that Henry would never be able to answer that question now. But Callum knew who might have the answer – his own mother.

He looked at the two old ladies, who were now doing a little dance around the charity shop. He shook his head and managed a smile. A moment later, they had linked their arms in his, encouraged him off his seat, and he joined them, dancing around the charity shop.

'Hey, what's going on?'

They all stopped dancing. Callum's eyes went wide, like a rabbit in headlights, at the sound of Thea's voice behind him.

'Do we have a deal?' he whispered to the old ladies, hoping they had their hearing aids in, if they needed them, and had heard him ask that question again.

The two ladies nodded before turning their attention to the young lady that had just walked into their shop.

'Hi, I'm Thea.'

'Thea?' said Mabel and Marjorie in unison.

'Yes. I thought I'd come and introduce myself.'

Callum, still standing with his back to her, thought *Oh, my god. Why did she have to come over here at this very moment?*

Mabel said, 'You're the young lady I saw going into the bookshop yesterday!'

'Yes – that's me!'

Both sisters shifted their gaze to Callum. Marjorie said, 'Callum here has been telling us all about the lovely young lady he is helping in the bookshop.'

'He has?'

Callum stared at both sisters, mouthing, 'Remember. The. Deal.' He heard Thea say, 'Callum?'

Callum turned around, fixing a smile on his face. The moment he saw her standing there, his heart sank. Why did she have to be so damn beautiful? It was little wonder he was drawn to her – it was a sibling thing. He'd read about this in some article once in a Sunday newspaper supplement, where people got together unknowingly who really had no business being together; who were siblings. Thank god he knew the truth. That did not make him feel any better. He just wished they weren't related.

He sensed that she was drawn to him too; he knew that she felt the connection. She just had no idea of the real reason. *So tell her,* that voice in his head insisted. He willed it to stop, thinking *I can't. Not just like that. She deserves the truth, but I must find out how this all came about first.*

Once again, Callum thought of his mum. Did she know? Something told him she did. Or at least suspected.

Callum brushed that thought aside for now, knowing that he

would be heading back to Scotland soon enough. In the meantime, he wanted to find out more about his sister – if the two old ladies didn't give the game away and mention that photo.

Callum glanced at them, and held his breath, wondering what they were going to say next.

'You must come and have a cup of tea, and a chocolate biscuit,' said Marjorie.

'Oh, I wasn't disturbing anything, was I?'

'Not at all,' said Mabel. 'We've got plenty of tea in the pot.'

They led her to the back of the shop. 'Now, we want to know all about you.'

So did Callum. He thought he'd join them.

Marjorie said, 'Callum – haven't you got something to do?'

Callum frowned. 'What do you mean?' He knew what they meant. They were chucking him out of their shop, so they had Thea all to themselves.

Thea turned in her seat. 'Oh, yes – Callum is showing Toby, that's my nephew, how to bind books.'

'That's good. Off you trot, Callum.' Marjorie flicked her finger at Callum to get a move on.

'You have a nephew?' said Mabel.

'Oh, yes, and a niece, Katie. They're my sister's children.'

'That's lovely,' said Mabel. 'I'd love to meet them.'

'You can meet Toby if you want to pop in and see the bookshop. I'd wait, though. It's a bit of a mess in there right now. We're trying to get it sorted out. Toby's there helping. I'm afraid he got suspended from school, so I've put him to work in the bookshop. He's being productive – well, most of the time.'

'We remember you from when you were little and your dad owned the bookshop.'

'Really? I had no idea. I don't remember a charity shop in Cobblers Yard back then.'

'No, there wasn't a charity shop here back then. We just … knew your father.'

'You did? You knew Henry? I was only small when my dad disappeared,' she said.

Callum was heading for the door when he heard her. He paused and turned around. He caught Marjorie and Mabel glaring at him. He knew why they were giving him a filthy look – for making them promise not to tell a soul about that photo.

He slunk out of the door.

47

'I'm trying to keep it under wraps – the plan to reopen the bookshop. I know that's going to be difficult in Cobblers Yard. I saw one of you ladies at the window, so I imagined you'd seen me in and out. I thought it would be nice to pop over and introduce myself,' said Thea. 'However, it would be really nice if you guys could, like, keep this between us if at all possible – about reopening the bookshop.'

'You're reopening the bookshop?' Mabel and Marjorie exchanged a grin.

'Well, I'm hoping my sister is. I'm doing it for her. She's in hospital at the moment. I wanted it to be a surprise for when she comes out.'

'The bookshop?'

'Yes, her new job.'

'Have you run this by her?'

'Well, no, but she has—' Thea stopped. She was going to say she'd been coming here at midnight, but she wondered what that would sound like.

'I'm sure she will be delighted,' said Marjorie.

'I hope so,' Thea replied. Her smile faltered. Perhaps she

should ask her sister if that was what she wanted. *No, I want to stick to the plan for it to be a surprise*, Thea decided, although in the back of her mind she could see a complication – Jenna was pregnant; how would she run a shop with a baby? *Easy*, thought Thea, *she can bring the baby with her*. She was aware that she hadn't had children herself. Would that work? She had no idea. Perhaps she could take some leave from work and help out when the time came.

Although she had only been in the shop a short time, Thea knew that when the time came to leave she'd miss it, and would take any opportunity to return.

❖

Callum nervously glanced at Thea as she walked back into the bookshop. 'So, how was tea with Mabel and Marjorie?' He winced, hoping they hadn't told her about the photo. They had a deal – didn't they?

'It was great. They are so lovely, aren't they?'

Callum reserved judgement until he knew they'd kept up their end of the bargain.

'They knew my dad.'

'Really?' Callum tried to act surprised.

'They remembered that he'd disappeared, never to be seen or heard from again.'

Callum stared at her.

'Are you talking about Grandpa?' Toby asked, lowering his book. He was sitting on the couch, taking a break and reading a book. Winston was lying on the sofa, his head on Toby's lap. Dickens sat on the sofa back, staring at Winston.

Callum had been busy putting the finishing touches to the book they'd been binding when Thea had walked in.

She glanced at her nephew. 'It's such a shame that Toby never knew him. They are quite alike, you know.'

Callum agreed. 'Yes, they are.'

'Pardon?'

'I meant that I imagine they are because he enjoys bookbinding.' Callum winced realising he'd nearly put his foot in it.

Thea smiled at Toby. 'Yes, that's what I thought too.'

'When are we going for lunch?' Toby asked. 'I'm hungry.'

Thea looked at her watch. 'Not long now. I just want to finish cleaning the window.' She walked over to the sink and poured some fresh water into a bowl with a squirt of detergent.

Callum insisted on carrying the bowl of water. He followed Thea out into the shop, still worried about her visit to the charity shop. He set the bowl of water down on the floor by the window. 'I didn't expect to see you in the charity shop.'

Thea rolled up her shirt sleeves and pulled on her Marigolds. She turned to Callum. 'You were gone so long that I started to think they'd stolen my handsome helper for themselves.' Thea looked away embarrassed. 'I can't believe I said that out loud!'

Callum laughed. 'Well, you were gone so long I began to think they'd stolen my beautiful girl—' He looked at her, aghast. In the moment, with the light-hearted banter, Callum had forgotten himself. 'God, I'm sorry. I shouldn't have said that.'

'Oh, but you should. You can call me that any time.'

'Ahem, well, er … I'll get back to …' he pointed to the back of the shop.

❖

Thea slipped off her gloves. It had taken the rest of the morning, but with a good amount of elbow grease, the window was clean, inside and out, and so was the shelving in the window. The shop had lost its musty odour, which had been replaced with a strong, zingy lemon smell, thanks to the floor and wall cleaner Thea was using, and helped in no small part by having the latch windows wide open, letting in the strong autumn breeze.

The cold air coming through the open window hadn't bothered Thea. She'd slipped on an old jumper of Mark's she'd brought with her – stolen from the clean laundry – deciding she wasn't going to use her nice clothes to clean in. She would put it straight in the wash when she'd finished.

She walked over to the back room to find that Callum had joined Toby on the sofa. Dickens had got his spot back, curled up contently on Toby's lap. Winston was now sitting by Callum's feet, his muzzle resting on Callum's knee.

They were sitting together, examining a book. Which reminded Thea that she still hadn't made time to hunt through the bookshelves in search of that rare book she imagined her sister had left in the bookshop – the one that she had agreed to sell to the stranger on the phone.

'What have you got there?' she asked, shifting her gaze to the book.

Callum covered the book with his hands. 'Ah, we're not quite done. Still some finishing touches to go.'

'Oh.' Thea couldn't hide her disappointment. She rather fancied seeing how the bookbinding was coming along.

Toby said, 'When it's completely finished, then we'll show you.'

'All right.'

Toby added, 'Are we going to lunch now?'

She smiled at her nephew. 'Of course. Let's go.'

Toby got up and took the book over to the desk. Thea made

her way to the front door, taking her coat off the old-fashioned coat stand by the door. She stopped to put it on. Callum joined her by the door, and they both stood waiting for Toby.

'Can you do me a favour after lunch?' Thea asked. She heard Toby shut the desk drawer in the back room.

'Yes, sure.'

'I want to visit my sister in hospital this afternoon. Toby can't come. She doesn't know yet that Toby has been suspended from school. I know it's a lot to ask, but would you mind hanging on here until I get back?'

'Not at all. I'm not going anywhere.' He smiled at her as he took Winston's dog lead from the coat rack and clipped it onto his collar. Toby joined them by the front door, slipping on his jacket. They all stepped outside the shop, and Thea locked up. As Toby and Callum fell in step, Callum holding on to Winston's lead as they crossed Cobblers Yard, Thea paused before she followed, glancing over at the charity shop.

Something the sisters had said when she was talking to them, or rather something they hadn't said, kept playing on her mind.

When she'd walked in on them dancing around the shop together, the sisters had clearly been happy to see Callum – and the DVDs. However when she'd joined them for a cuppa after Callum had left, and had commented, 'Isn't Callum just amazing?', she'd expected them to agree, or at least say something, but she'd caught the sisters exchange a glance before changing the subject. Her mind kept wandering back to that moment. *What were they not telling her?*

48

Callum walked into the library, straight up to the librarian, who was sitting behind a desk. The young lady looked up and smiled. 'Can I help you?'

He glanced at her name badge – *Lexi*. He noticed she had an American accent. 'I want to find out some information about the local shops.'

'Local shops in Aldeburgh?'

'Yes. Do you have any old newspapers on file from, say, twenty-five years ago?'

'That's going back quite a few years. Any shop in particular?'

Callum eyed her. 'Yes, actually. The bookshop in Cobblers Yard – The Bookshop of Memories. I'm also interested in any local news stories from around about that time.'

She pointed her pen at Callum. 'Hey, you're that guy.'

Callum frowned. That damn show followed him wherever he went, even to the little local library in a seaside town in deepest Suffolk. He sighed. 'Yes, I'm the guy from the TV show.'

He noted her bemused expression. 'What TV show?'

'Oh, er … nothing.'

'Aren't you helping someone called Thea do up the bookshop

in Cobblers Yard? I told my grandmother. She's a writer. She's so excited that someone is finally reopening that shop.'

'What?' Callum stared at her. His head was spinning. 'Wait – how did you know about the bookshop?' Callum had heard that news travels fast in small towns, but this was ridiculous.

'Why, The Gossip Girls, of course.'

'The Gossip Girls?'

'Mabel and Marjorie. They run the little charity shop across the yard from the bookshop. Everyone, and I mean *everyone*, in town knows them. You must have met them.'

Callum inwardly groaned. Of all the people, they had to be the town gossips.

'They're lovely. It's such a coincidence, but Mabel was in here just yesterday collecting a library book. Mabel said the young man helping Thea is gorgeous.'

Callum thought for a moment Lexi might start flirting with him, like the young waitress in the café, but he noticed an engagement ring on her finger.

'Do you know Thea too?' Callum asked.

'I'm afraid not. But I'd love to meet her. Will you introduce me? It's all so exciting. In fact, I've got some free time next week. I could pop in and help out. I love bookshops.'

Callum looked at her. It was the weekend, and the week had flown by in a blur as they tried to get to grips with sorting out the bookshop. Working in such close proximity, try as he might, he had failed miserably at keeping his distance from Thea.

He'd been there every day, as he'd promised, but the bookbinding lessons had dwindled as he'd spent more and more time among the crowded bookshelves, helping Thea try to bring some semblance of order to the shop.

It was a losing battle. Although Thea brought some experience of cataloguing through her work as an archivist, neither of them had any experience of this business. He looked at Lexi. Here was a librarian who might actually be able to bring some order to the chaos that was his father's, *their* father's, non-existent system.

They needed a professional. A professional *what*, he hadn't been sure – not until he'd set eyes on Lexi.

'Great!' Callum said in answer to her question. 'I think it would be an excellent idea for you to come and help out in the bookshop.'

'You do?'

'Oh, yes.' He hadn't run the idea by Thea, obviously, but it hadn't occurred to him that he should. It was his bookshop, after all. She just didn't know it yet. Even so, he thought she'd be very pleased to have an extra pair of hands.

Callum also had an ulterior motive, besides Lexi helping to sort out the bookshop. So far, Toby had been there. But from Monday, when Toby returned to school, it would just be him and Thea alone together in the bookshop. And the trouble was that they'd been getting on rather too well.

They were growing close, he couldn't deny that; for him, in a sisterly way, he constantly reminded himself. But things were starting to get awkward. On Friday, she'd asked if he was free at the weekend. She'd said that as they were both there in Aldeburgh on their own, single, and didn't know anybody else besides family, in her case, and Mabel and Marjorie, she'd wondered: why not get together for a day out?

She made it sound all innocent. However, for Callum, it was one thing working in the shop with her, but meeting up at the weekend just felt too much like a date. She'd said that wasn't her intention, but he suspected it was.

Her brother-in-law had been due to return home from work in London. He'd be spending time with his kids, which meant that Thea would have some free time.

Callum really hadn't wanted to hurt her feelings by saying no, but thankfully fate had stepped in. Fortunately for Callum, Thea's brother-in-law had been delayed returning home for some reason. It meant they couldn't get together for a day out, just the two of them. Callum's Saturday was free.

He couldn't exactly meet up with Thea at the bookshop that day either; she would have had to bring along her niece and nephew, which meant telling her niece that she'd been working in the bookshop with Toby and a famous Hollywood star all week; something she was trying to keep a secret from her.

Toby had told him that they were doing up the bookshop for his mum when she came out of hospital. Apparently, money was tight and she needed a job. They wanted it to be a big surprise, but the trouble with Toby's sister was that she couldn't keep her mouth shut. Toby had told him all this when Thea had visited her sister in hospital. Callum had been relieved about the weekend, but more than a little dismayed to find out they were making plans for the bookshop. Thea did ask him for his mobile phone number in case she was free on Sunday, but he was hoping that turned out not to be the case. Callum was going to spend the weekend doing a bit of research into the history of the bookshop and seeing what he could find out about his father's double life here in Aldeburgh.

He frowned. Of course, The Gossip Girls sounded like the perfect resource to approach about all things Aldeburgh, but he wasn't in their good books just then; at least not in Marjorie's, in any case. And he guessed that whatever Mabel's big sister said would stand.

So there he was, in the local library, staring at a young American, wondering how she had come to be in this part of the world, and finding it rather refreshing to meet someone else who had not watched his show.

'I can't wait to meet Thea and see the inside of the bookshop. It's always intrigued me, what might have happened to the last owner,' said Lexi. 'Do you know that it's been shut up, gathering dust, for years? Oh, I expect you know that already. But I wonder how Thea came by the shop?' She stared at Callum, expecting him to tell her.

Callum just smiled at her, hoping that inviting the inquisitive librarian into the shop, and their lives, was a good idea.

'I've just had an amazing idea. You know I mentioned that my grandmother is a writer?'

'Yes.'

She's finished writing her new book. Wouldn't it be amazing if she could do a book signing in the bookshop, and release the book first at The Bookshop of Memories? She'd love that. I'll mention it to her.'

Callum actually thought that wasn't a bad idea. If Lexi was going to roll up her sleeves and volunteer in the shop, that was the least he could do, let her grandmother, a local writer, sign a few copies of her book for her friends in the local bookshop. 'That's a great idea. I'm sure she'd love it.'

'She's quite a well-known author, you know,' said Lexi proudly.

'Is she?' Callum imagined she was quite well-known in her local community.

'Oh, yes. She's Margot Dorey. Have you heard of her?'

'*The* Margot Dorey?' Callum looked at her, shocked. 'My mum used to read me her books as a child. She's bloody famous. Well, she was. I thought she stopped writing. Sorry, but I thought she'd passed on.'

'Nope, not dead. Very much alive. She did stop writing for a while, though. But she's back. And I tell you, if she agrees to launch her book in Thea's little bookshop, she'll have queues right down the street. It would bring people from all over, and would be a great way to really put the old bookshop back on the map. Just imagine it. We could have like a grand opening of the bookshop at the same time. I could invite a few friends. There'll be the press—'

'The press?' Callum swallowed.

'My friend knows a journalist for a local paper. She'd love to—'

'Nope. No. Absolutely not.' Next his face would be all over the papers, along with truth about who really owned the bookshop. *So tell Thea the truth first.* 'Not yet!' he blurted, talking to himself, knowing that meant telling her the truth about Henry.

Lexi said, 'What do you mean – *not yet*?'

'Er, I meant … um … that we're obviously nowhere near ready to reopen the bookshop, so it couldn't be yet, having your grandmother round to do a book signing.'

'Something tells me you're not keen on the publicity.'

Callum felt uncomfortable under her gaze.

Lexi narrowed her eyes. 'Didn't you say you starred in a TV show?'

'Well, yes.'

'Are you, like, famous?'

Callum shrugged, glancing around the small library. It was in a modern, single-storey building, and the open-plan room that housed the library was a bit too small for his liking. He lowered his voice. 'Kind of, I guess.'

'And you're trying to stay under the radar?'

He looked at her, and said, 'Yes.' But not for the reason she might think. He could just imagine some reporter nosing around, getting the scoop on the bookshop that had been dormant for years, and then discovering that it wasn't Thea who owned the place, even if she was clearly under the misapprehension that she did, or her sister did – or was it their mum?

It turned out that Toby had found the key in his mum's possession, who had in turn probably found it in the boxes that Toby's grandmother, who was in Nepal in some yoga retreat, had stored in their garage. That was what Toby had said to him as they spent time bookbinding.

'My good friend, Ray, would love to see the bookshop reopened. He's always been keen to find out more about the place.'

Callum stared at her. 'Who's Ray?'

'Oh, he's such a lovely man. He helped me out no end when I first moved here from America. He lives next door, on a houseboat.'

'You live on a houseboat?'

'Yes, by the quay in a place called Walberswick, a little town just next door to Southwold. Have you been there?'

'Er, no. I'm new to this part of the world.'

'Oh, you'll have to visit. It's amazing. Are you considering moving here, by any chance? You won't regret it. The people are just *so* friendly.'

Too friendly, thought Callum, knowing that it was an unkind thing to think. It wasn't their fault he'd got himself into a bit of a predicament. *Just a 'bit'?* Callum furrowed his brow at the thought that it was turning out to be quite a major one. He cared for Thea, and her nephew, Toby. What would happen, what would they think, when they found out he'd been deceiving them by not telling them about the photo, and what he was really doing there?

Callum shook his head. He knew they were getting off-topic, but he had to ask, 'So, who is this Ray character?'

'Oh, he's a retired police officer.'

Oh god, thought Callum, this just gets better and better. She was good friends with a retired police officer. His mind was racing. He thought of his dad and his double life. Were there laws against bigamy? He didn't know, but he imagined there were. You couldn't be married to two people. Why had it only occurred to him now that his father had broken the law? Good god.

'Ray also runs an heir-hunting business.'

'A what?'

'He finds long-lost relatives of the deceased – heirs. He might see an obituary, and someone might have died without a will. He tries to track down long-lost relatives. He looked into the case of the abandoned bookshop once, but he couldn't find any leads regarding the owner.'

That's because the owner wasn't dead, thought Callum. Once again, he thought that perhaps enlisting Lexi's help was not going to turn out a good idea after all.

'I'm going to make a list of all the people we can invite to the grand opening.'

Callum stared at Lexi's smiling face. This was going to become a circus, if he wasn't careful, and the clown at the centre of it all, him, was going to live to regret it.

'Now if you need any extra helping hands at the bookshop, I know lots of people who would love to help out too.'

Callum thought of Ray, and the reporter who was a friend of a friend, and quickly held his hands up. 'No, I think we'll be fine.'

'Well, if you do change your mind …' she trailed off.

I'm pretty sure I won't, thought Callum. 'Now, about the reason I'm here.'

'Oh, yes. You wanted to see if we've got any archived material, old newspaper articles, about the bookshop?'

Callum nodded enthusiastically. 'Yes, please.'

'We have copies of local newspapers in microfiche format, but I'm afraid you can only search by date, not for a particular article in the newspapers.'

'That will do.' Callum smiled. At least it was something.

'I'll show you where the microfiche reader is.'

Callum followed Lexi to the back of the library, where the machine sat on a desk in a corner behind the library bookshelves. She said, 'Did you say you wanted to search local newspaper archives from twenty-five years ago?'

He nodded. It was around the time Henry had disappeared from Thea's life. Would it have made the local news? Would he find an article about Thea's family, about Henry?

As Callum sat down in the chair, Lexi said, 'Say, wasn't that around the time the bookshop owner disappeared?'

Callum looked up at Lexi. She'd put two and two together. 'Yeah.'

She smiled 'I thought so. I'd be interested if you find out anything. I'm sure Ray did a search way back when. Let me know if you find anything – I'd be interested to know.'

Callum looked at her and decided he was not going to share whatever her found.

Luckily for him, the library was very quiet, despite it being a Saturday. It meant he could take his time and concentrate on what he was looking for.

Callum had a thought. 'You wouldn't happen to know if the archive holds local newspapers dating back to the Second World War – would you?'

'I can certainly find out. Looking for anything in particular?'

Yes, thought Callum. He had a feeling that The Gossip Girls were keeping something from him about the bookshop. What were they not telling him?

He looked at Lexi and decided not to share his thoughts. 'I'm not sure. I'm hoping I'll know it when I see it.'

She grinned. 'How intriguing.'

Callum turned in his seat to look at the large machine in front of him. That was when he heard Lexi exclaim, 'Hey, what do you think you're doing in here?'

Callum whirled around in his seat. He rolled his eyes when he caught sight of Dickens. He'd left the cat in the campervan eating breakfast that morning – or so he'd thought. Callum had driven to the local library in the campervan because it was pouring with rain. He'd parked in the small library car park but had made the mistake of leaving one of the windows open.

Dickens jumped up on the desk in front of Lexi and purred.

Oh, so you can lay on the charm when you want to, thought Callum. All he got was a demanding little fella at breakfast time and a loud meow in his face if he didn't get up pronto and feed him.

Despite leaving the cat behind in the bookshop the previous night, fast asleep on the sofa, with a small window out back slightly ajar, a bowl of water, and cat biscuits ready for the morning, Dickens had still decided to wake Callum up in the campervan bright and early, like a furry alarm clock, jumping on his chest and letting out a shrill meow.

'Hey, aren't you a cutie?'

Callum sighed. He stood up and walked over. 'Sorry, but this cutie is my cat.'

'Really? For a moment there I thought we had another LC.'

Callum looked at her quizzically. 'Pardon?'

'I also work at the library in Southwold, and we have a cat that visits every day and spends time in the library. We call him LC. It's short for—'

'Library Cat, by any chance?'

'How on earth did you guess?' said Lexi straight-faced, showing off some good old British humour.

Callum smiled at her as he reached for the cat. 'Ow!'

'Oh, dear. I think your cat wants you to go away and leave him to make new friends.'

'Y'think?' said Callum sarcastically, nursing another battle scar courtesy of his dad's temperamental old cat.

'Do you need a plaster? We have a first aid kit.'

'No, it's not bleeding.' The scratch stung like hell, but he tried not to let on. 'He's not really my cat, he's my—'

Callum stopped short. The last thing he wanted to do was mention his dad. 'Well, I think I'll leave Dickens to make new friends, then.'

'Dickens?'

'Yes, that's his name.'

'Well, hello Dickens,' said Lexi, stroking the cat.

Callum shook his head at the cat. 'I'll get back to my bit of research.'

'Okay.' Lexi sat down in front of the computer on her desk.

Callum was just heading back to the microfiche machine when Lexi called out, 'Oh, by the way, we have got some local newspapers dating back to the Second World War, if you're still interested.'

Callum turned on his heel and looked at her. 'Oh, I'm still interested.' He wanted to find out more about The Gossip Girls. He was convinced there was more to them, and their story, than they were letting on.

49

'I still can't believe it's my last day,' said Toby, looking miserable.

'You have to go back to school tomorrow, Toby. Besides, it's not your last day at the bookshop. It's Tuesday tomorrow, and you only have to get through to Friday, then you can come back at the weekend.'

'Yeah – right!' he replied sarcastically.

'What does that mean?' said Thea, turning around and eyeing her nephew, who was helping them clear a corner of the bookshop to make a seating area, like Callum had suggested. They were going to bring the old sofa into the front of the shop and make a little cosy corner for people to sit with a book, if they liked, before deciding whether to buy one.

Callum eyed Toby, but refrained from saying anything. He had an idea as to why Toby was being sarcastic about the next weekend.

'What do you think about having a coffee machine?' Mabel asked. 'I think it would be nice if people could sit with a drink too. It's a very nice little coffee machine. Of course you'd have to provide the pods – is that what they call them? It was very thoughtful of my family to buy me one for my birthday, but I'm not a coffee drinker myself. It's such a shame for it to go waste. I was going to donate it to the charity shop, but I think you should have it in the bookshop.'

Mabel was sitting on a chair in an alcove by the window, sipping a cup of tea from the china mug she'd brought with her and enjoying overseeing the proceedings. She'd invited herself in this morning, and hadn't left all day.

'Do you still want that old standard lamp in the charity shop window that we haven't been able to sell?' asked Mabel.

Thea said, 'Yes, please, Mabel. We want this to be a proper cosy corner, reminiscent of someone's living room. And your idea of having a coffee maker sounds rather nice too.'

'Good, I thought so.'

Callum eyed Mabel. During his research in the library over the weekend, he'd spent hours at that microfiche machine until he'd hit upon two articles. There was an article on the bookshop from twenty-five years earlier on the disappearance of one Henry Cavendish. Included in the article was a grainy photo of a family of four, with a young woman in her thirties standing with her husband and two girls. The two girls in that grainy image matched the photo he'd found in a wallet in the back of his father's desk drawer in his study at home.

If Callum had had any doubt that they had the same father, he now knew for certain, because the man in the photo was undeniably a younger version of his father, Henry.

Thea had no clue that they shared the same surname. For years, ever since he left for America, Callum had been known by his stage name, not his given name – Cavendish.

It wasn't very Scottish, but then neither was his father. It was his mother who was Scots. But that was beside the point. The point was that his parents – especially his mother – had insisted that he did not use his real surname if he was going to be an actor. And they didn't want to be photographed, or talked about, by their famous son across the pond. They'd always been a quiet, private couple. He could well understand that the world he moved in was not for them. Although he'd respected their wishes, he'd always thought it was because they were not interested in his career, or his success, or were embarrassed that he'd become an actor. But now he knew the real reason – they had something to hide. Or more to the point, his father did.

But it was his mother who was the one who had insisted he adopted a stage name. Was that just a coincidence, so he didn't embarrass her in front of her friends if his career flopped? Or was it something else – was it because of Henry? The question on Callum's mind was *did she know?* He still suspected she did.

The article about Henry's sudden disappearance wasn't the only discovery he'd made, sitting for hours at the microfiche machine. He'd been rewarded by a small article about another family who'd lived in the bookshop decades earlier.

Callum had found something on The Gossip Girls. They hadn't lied about growing up in the bookshop, but they had omitted to mention one significant fact. They'd had a brother. And his name had been Henry.

Callum had sat back in his chair at that point, realising the reason the sisters had been jumping around for joy at the prospect that Henry was still alive. He was their brother. No wonder they had been overjoyed at the news. They obviously wanted to find him, see him again.

When Mabel had first walked into the bookshop that morning, surprising Callum, he had been worried that she was going to spill the beans about the photo. But thinking about what he'd discovered, he realised that they'd waited so long for news of their little brother that they were hardly going to risk Callum disappearing before he kept up his end of the bargain and eventually told them where Henry was. He guessed that Mabel was there to keep a close eye on him. He was still wondering why neither of them had mentioned that Henry was their brother. Had they been estranged? Callum looked at Mabel, who was watching Thea and Toby. Mabel had no idea that he was related to Henry, but she knew that Thea and Toby were Henry's daughter and grandson. It was little wonder that he'd caught her staring at them affectionately. But they had no idea who she was – Thea's aunt.

Even though Henry had disappeared from their lives when Thea was nine, wouldn't his sisters have kept in touch with his family? The fact that Thea clearly had no clue they were related confirmed his suspicions that Marjorie and Mabel must have been estranged from their brother for many years.

It was no surprise that they desperately wanted to find him. Callum expected that after Henry had disappeared, regardless of what had caused that estrangement, they deeply regretted not having the chance to repair their relationship with their brother.

Callum stared at Mabel. The sisters still had no idea that reconciliation may no longer be possible. Would Henry even remember his sisters, Mabel and Marjorie?

'But what about Katie?'

Everyone turned to look at Toby, Callum included. He felt sorry for him, but his constant whining about the inevitable return to school tomorrow was getting on everyone's nerves.

'How can we come here at the weekend? Look at last weekend. Dad was meant to come home from London, he'd promised, but then he had a work thing.'

Callum caught Thea grimacing. He wondered if she didn't believe it was a work thing at all.

'Which means we had to babysit my sister, and we couldn't come here or see Callum all weekend.'

Thea sighed. 'I know it wasn't the best, sweetheart, but there was nothing I could do about it.'

'Why can't you just bring her along?' Mabel asked. 'I'd love to meet her.'

Callum caught Thea pursing her lips. 'I'm doing all this for my sister, and I wanted it to be a surprise. The problem with Katie is—'

'She can't keep her big trap shut!'

Thea rolled her eyes at her nephew. 'I don't think she'll be very good at keeping secrets, Mabel.'

'I see.'

Callum noticed Mabel staring at Thea at the mention of the word, *secrets*. He caught Thea and Toby exchanging a sigh. This bookshop was their secret – at the moment. Once Katie found out, word would get back to Jenna. As Toby said, his sister just couldn't keep her mouth shut.

Thea said, 'Let's not spend your last day at the bookshop worrying about the weekend, eh?'

'So, it is my last day, all because of Katie.'

'Well, no. Your dad will come back this weekend. He did text and say that, didn't he?'

'But then he'll want to spend the weekend with me and Katie, and we'll have to visit mum. There will be no time to come here. It will just be you and Callum in the bookshop for the rest of the week, and next weekend.'

Thea fell silent.

Callum kept his mouth shut too. Unfortunately, that would probably be the case. He glanced at Thea and caught her smiling his way. The look on her face said she wasn't sorry it would just be the two of them.

'I'll be here,' said Mabel, 'helping out.' She dunked a biscuit in her tea.

Thea's face dropped. 'Oh, I didn't think you would be. I didn't realise you worked at the weekend too.'

'You mean in the charity shop? No, I don't normally. That will remain closed on Sunday, but I'm going to make an exception and work here.' Her eyes roved to Callum.

For the first time all day, Callum was actually pleased Mabel had invited herself over.

Thea turned to her nephew. 'Look on the bright side. Today, Katie is at drama class after school, so at least you get more time here before we go and pick her up. Isn't that nice?'

Toby frowned. 'Yes, I suppose so.'

Mabel said, 'Keep your pecker up, Toby. I'm sure things will work out. You know, in my experience, life can surprise you.'

Callum locked eyes with Mabel.

50

'I need to skip drama class today.' Katie turned around and looked at her friend, Caitlin. They were standing together in the lunch queue at school.

'Why? I thought you wanted to come on Mondays as well. Didn't your auntie agreed to pay for you to attend Mondays as well as Thursdays?'

'She did. It's not about the tuition.'

'Then what is it?'

'I want to find out what's going on. My brother was suspended from school.'

'Yes, I'd heard he'd been suspended.' She gave Katie a side-ways glance. She also knew *why* he'd be suspended. He'd been in a fight with a boy over a girl – over her.

'But did you know it was for *five* school days?'

'Um, I don't know how long suspensions are.'

'He told me it was for *one* day.'

'I did think it was odd that I hadn't seen him around the school all last week.'

Katie looked at her a long moment, surprised that her friend even gave her brother the time of day, let alone noticed him in school. Caitlin's cheeks went bright red.

'So, er, what's your brother been doing while he's been off school all week?'

They both took two steps forward in the slow-moving lunch queue.

'Well, that's the thing. They both told me, my aunt and brother, that he was only suspended for one day, last Monday. But I overheard Toby on the phone to his friend when I passed his bedroom door last night. I heard him say that it was his last day today suspended, and he didn't want to return to school on Tuesday. He was enjoying working in the shop.'

'The shop? What was he talking about?'

Katie shrugged. 'I have no idea. But it gets worse. He has been coming to school in the morning with my aunt, getting out of the car with me, and then scooting back to the car when I wasn't looking.'

'Seriously?'

'Yes, my aunt's been in on it, obviously.' Katie added, 'I did wonder why she'd suddenly insisted on taking us to school in the car and picking us up last week, when Mum and Dad have paid for us to get the school bus this term.'

'But how did you find out this was going on?'

'After I overheard him last night, I got ready for school as normal, pretending like I had no clue what they've been up to. When we arrived at school this morning, I got out of the car, and Toby trailed behind as usual. But this time I ducked behind a group of older kids. He didn't see me watching him as he got back in the car.'

'So, you reckon this must have been going on all week?'

'Yes.'

Caitlin shook her head. 'I don't get it.'

'Neither do I.'

'What's the big secret?' asked Caitlin.

'Good question! Something's going on, I just know it, and whatever it is, they've been keeping it from me.'

'Maybe he was just embarrassed that he'd been suspended for all that time.'

'Okay, I get that. But why carry out that big charade of acting like he wasn't suspended, and getting ready for school, and all that? And why would my aunt agree to do it?'

They both stepped forward in the lunch queue.

'What are they up to, your aunt and brother, do you think?'

'I have no idea, but today I'm going to find out.'

'How?'

'I need to skip drama class. They're going to pick me up from school after drama class.'

'Not if you find them first.'

'Exactly!'

❖

Thea checked the time. The drama class was just starting. Leiston wasn't far down the road, just a lovely, short drive through the countryside. Thea recalled the one time she had been late picking them up from school. That had been before Toby's suspension, so they'd both been together waiting for her. Thea didn't want to risk being late again, aware that her niece would be left waiting outside the school alone.

She checked the time once more. They had a half an hour before they had to leave to pick her up.

She glanced around the bookshop. They'd made good

headway today. She'd never seen Toby work so hard. The shop was now spotless. It helped massively that Callum had come in on Sunday on his own to work in the bookshop, taking more books off the shelves in readiness for today, when they'd finished cleaning and dusting before putting them back.

Thea could have sworn she'd locked up the shop. She had told Callum as much when she'd found out he'd been working in the shop over the weekend when she wasn't there. He'd said he had just turned up on the off-chance she was there, and had found the bookshop open. She liked that he obviously wanted to see her, but it was still bothering her, the thought that she hadn't locked the shop. Although being around Callum, her gorgeous helper, perhaps she wasn't surprised if her mind had been elsewhere, and she wasn't quite with it.

Thea leaned against a bookshelf watching Toby and Callum, who were still hard at work putting the books back on the shelves. 'I think we deserve a break, and a nice cup of tea before Toby and I leave to collect Katie.' It meant they'd all have to call it a day. Thea was going to make sure she locked up this time.

Callum said, 'Great, I'm parched.'

Toby joined in. 'Me too. Can I have a juice, please?'

Thea smiled at her nephew. 'Of course.' Her gaze shifted to the shelves they were restocking with the piles of books on the floor.

There was still no order to the shelving system; it was a mess, and try as she might, Thea just couldn't get a handle on it.

She turned around and glanced at the non-existent window display. Thea had removed all the old bestsellers from yesteryear to clean the window, and saw no point putting them back. She still hadn't figured out what would go in their place. What she needed was to find out where she could buy the latest bestsellers to display in the window.

Thea sighed. There was one thing cleaning the bookshop, but she had no idea what else to stock, and how to get the place up and running. She stared out of the window. She had a feeling that Cobblers Yard was a lovely, friendly place, but it was hidden down an alley off the main high street. In terms of running a business, and passing trade, how would that really work?

It made her wonder how her dad had earned his money, and supported a family, from this shop. She remembered that he used to travel a lot in his campervan. She recalled he visited book fairs. She was sure that was how he'd connected with publishers and probably bought the latest bestsellers to display in the window.

However, looking around the bookshop, that was not the main thrust of the business. He dealt in old and rare books. She was sure he sold them to collectors. Her mum had mentioned that once, when she'd asked why he had been away so much, on the road in his van. Despite going through piles of books, Thea was no closer to finding the book her sister was selling. She still hadn't got around to asking her about it.

When she had visited Jenna on Friday, the last thing on her sister's mind had been work. Her sister was still all over the place about the baby. Mark being away wasn't helping. Thea had asked her whether he knew about the baby. Jenna had looked at her, stunned, saying, 'Of course he knows – why wouldn't he?'

Because you were having late-night, clandestine meetings with a man at the bookshop before you fell over the dog and broke your leg. Of course, Thea didn't say that. How could she? But she did ask when her sister would be discharged from the hospital. She was looking forward to showing her what they'd done with the bookshop.

Unfortunately, there was still no definitive date when she would be going home.

Thea walked into the back room to put the kettle on. While she was waiting, she poured Toby a glass of orange juice.

During the course of the past week, Toby had started to ask questions about his grandpa – things he couldn't ask his mum because she didn't want to talk about it.

Thea didn't particularly want to talk about him either. There wasn't really much to tell – or so she'd thought, until she'd stepped inside the bookshop and the memories of her childhood there had come flooding back. Perhaps it was the same for Jenna; maybe once she'd found the key, she hadn't been able to resist revisiting the place.

She didn't know what had happened to her father. Her older sister told her the most logical explanation – he left us for someone else. That was what she had chosen to believe.

Their mum believed he'd been involved in some sort of accident. She never said the d-word – that he must be dead – she had obviously never believed that it was true, saying she'd have felt it in her heart if he was gone. That was the power of love, she believed; it would be like a stab to the heart. That was why she'd never declared him legally dead, even after all these years, and had obviously kept the bookshop, like a time warp, in readiness for his return.

But what did Thea believe? If he had been in an accident, and wasn't dead, why hadn't he come back? She'd never said that to her mum. She didn't want to destroy the hope her mum had, even though, as the years sped by, and their past life as a family with their dad became but a distant memory, it became clear that they'd never see him again.

Thea turned her thoughts to the shop. She walked over to the doorway and leaned against the doorframe. She was imagining a grand opening, with bunting hanging from the window and a large gathering of excited people outside, eagerly awaiting the reopening – a real buzz.

She looked through the shop, out of the window to the empty yard outside, and sighed. So much for her grand opening. She could see that what she imagined just wasn't going to materialise.

Mabel said, 'Do you want me to make the tea?'

Thea shook her head. I'm just waiting for the kettle to boil.' She smiled at Mabel, who had shifted from a chair to the sofa. Mabel had put the lamp on and brought some cushions from the charity shop, and there was even a coffee table that Callum had carried over from the charity shop, along with a rug. Thea had insisted on paying for the items even though Mabel said she was gifting them to the bookshop.

At least the place was a lot more presentable, and you could actually see through the shop window to the beautiful flowers on display in a large vase.

Thea smiled. She'd met another neighbour in Cobblers Yard today. The young lady in The Potting Shed had popped her head in and had said she'd seen people in and out of the bookshop, and couldn't resist calling in and introducing herself. She apologised for being awfully nosy, finding out what was going on.

Thea noticed that Callum had disappeared into the back room. She guessed why; her famous helper didn't want to be recognised.

The lady's name was Lili, and she'd brought the beautiful flowers with her as a gift for the new owner. Lili had been intrigued to discover people in the bookshop. She'd told Thea that it had always been an added mystery for her and her friend, Abigail, who had invited everyone in Cobblers Yard to her wedding. Abigail had popped an invitation through the letterbox of the bookshop not expecting a reply. To everyone's surprise, she had received a RSVP. It was just signed, 'A.'

Thea had smiled. Her mum's name was Annie, and she must have checked on the bookshop when she brought the boxes to Jenna's before she moved abroad. She'd sent the RSVP back because that's just the sort of thing her mum would do. It explained why the bookshop wasn't full of circulars and old letters when Thea had walked through the door. Her mum must have checked in on the bookshop, over the years, to see if there was any evidence that he'd returned.

Thea heard the kettle boil and went to make Mabel another cup of tea in her china mug. Dickens jumped on the table and meowed at her. 'What? Do you want a drink too? I don't think you deserve one. I haven't seen you hard at work – unless you call testing out the sofa all day work?'

She, Toby and Callum had had a bit of a job shifting the heavy old sofa into the front of the shop. Dickens had stayed put while they shifted it, which had amused everybody – apart from Callum, who'd tried to shift him and had got another battle wound, as he called them.

Thea had found a small first aid kit in one of the kitchen cupboards and had used a cotton wool bud, and a plaster to stem the bleeding from the scratch. She'd insisted. For some reason, Callum had appeared tense the whole time that she was bathing his wound. She knew he felt it too, when they touched, the connection they inexplicably had so soon after meeting. They barely knew each other, but it was there nonetheless, and neither of them could deny it.

Thea smiled when she thought about it as she made the tea. Although Mabel had said she'd be there next week, she imagined that she'd still have to help Marjorie in the charity shop too, but she'd pop in when she could. That had pleased Thea no end, imagining that Mabel wouldn't be around all the time.

Despite spending a lot of time with Callum, she didn't feel he'd talked about himself much or really opened up. She hoped that with Toby back at school, when it was just the two of them, he might tell her more about his life.

Thea was also aware that she was only meant to be in Suffolk for a fortnight. That was the plan. She'd taken two weeks' annual leave. She couldn't imagine returning to London, though.

Gracie had been in touch, asking how she was. She had tentatively asked Gracie if she thought it would be cheeky to ask for more time off if she wanted to extend her stay. Thea had mentioned her sister, and her father's bookshop, explaining that after so many years of it being shut down, she was trying to sort it out to reopen it for her sister to work in.

Gracie had put her mind at ease, telling her she'd have a word with Edward about extending her leave. However, she had said that perhaps it was best not to mention the bookshop. After all, the normal notice period for requesting leave had been waived because of exceptional personal circumstances – the break-up of her relationship, and her sister's accident.

Although her boss was a close family friend, Gracie reminded her that Edward still couldn't be seen to be bending the rules just because of who she was. If she told him that Thea was working, he might have to decline any further requests, and then his most senior archivist would have to return to work.

Although Thea imagined that Edward wouldn't do that,

Gracie was right; he couldn't be seen to be favouring her. Besides, Thea didn't want to put him in an awkward position. She was just rather disappointed that she couldn't tell one of her closest friends, and her father's best friend from years earlier, about the shop. She imagined he'd be over the moon if he found out she was hoping to reopen her father's bookshop.

Thea walked out of the back room carrying a tea tray. There was a cup of English breakfast tea with two sugars and a dash of milk for Mabel, a glass of juice for Toby, and a plate of chocolate digestive biscuits that Marjorie had sent over for elevenses. Thea looked at the biscuits as she set the tray down on the coffee table. It wasn't eleven o'clock in the morning; it was getting on for four o'clock, and she'd have to leave soon to pick up Katie.

Toby's school uniform was in his school bag ready to change back into, just to make it appear that he'd been at school all day and had just come along with her to pick Katie up. Thea was relieved that their little charade had come to an end. What would Katie think if she caught them?

Callum had joined Mabel on the sofa. Toby sat next to Callum. Thea handed Toby his juice.

'Shall I make the coffee?' offered Callum, glancing at the coffee maker that Mabel had collected from home.

'I hope it works,' said Mabel. 'It's never been used.'

Callum turned to Mabel. 'Let's find out.' He stood up.

They'd set up a coffee station on the counter near the till with some glass mugs that Mabel had also brought with her. Callum had popped to a local shop in the town and bought a large box of assorted coffee pods.

He opened the box. 'Café latte for you, Thea?' He'd remembered what Thea had ordered at the café in the town.

'Yes, please.' She smiled at him. It was what she had every morning – a takeaway latte from the café on her way to the bookshop. Now, she wouldn't have to buy a coffee to go. She could have one when she arrived.

Callum made two cups of coffee, and the aroma filled the shop. When they were all seated on the sofa, Callum in between Mabel and Toby, Thea at the other end with the cat curled in her lap, and the dog sitting by Callum's feet, Mabel asked, 'How is it? Does the machine work?'

'I'll say,' Callum replied. 'This coffee is amazing.'

'I'll second that,' said Thea, approvingly.

They all sat there with their drinks, staring around the shop.

Mabel broke the silence. 'What a transformation. And the musty smell is well and truly gone.'

There were murmurs of agreement all round.

'The thing is,' said Thea, voicing her thoughts, 'the bookshelves are still a mess. I'm worried that if we do get customers, they won't buy because they won't be able to find anything. And that's even if there's anything here they want to buy. All the books are so …' she glanced at Mabel, '… old.'

Mabel put her cup of tea on the table and turned to Thea at the other end of the sofa. 'Would you like my penny's worth?'

Thea nodded.

Mabel glanced about her. 'This isn't called The Bookshop of Memories for nothing. Everyone has a favourite book that resonates, that they remember. Perhaps it's not necessary to stock all the new releases and bestsellers. There's nothing wrong with stocking books from yesteryear.'

Thea glanced at the bookshelves.

Mabel smiled. 'In fact, it's the bookshop's strength. Imagine –

people can come in and browse, and discover that annual they remember from their childhood, or that favourite book they thought was out of print.'

Thea stared at her. Toby and Callum turned to look at Mabel too.

Thea looked again at the bookshelves surrounding them. Perhaps Mabel was right, it was a place to browse, and find the unexpected, and lose yourself in the past.

For someone who worked with old books, maps and artefacts for a living, Thea couldn't deny that this was right up her street, and it turned out that it was right up Toby's street too.

'I just love this place,' said Toby, voicing all their thoughts at that moment.

Thea smiled at her nephew. When he was little, his parents had had him tested for autism. Thea could have told them they were wasting their time; not that she was an expert on the spectrum, not at all. But what she suspected was that her nephew, unlike his twin sister, was just an introvert who enjoyed, and preferred, his own company, and got immersed in subjects he loved. It was just his way. Thea could relate because her nephew reminded her of herself. Her mum had said that Katie was just like Jenna.

Thea looked around the bookshop and thought back to the same time last week, when Toby had been suspended from school, and Thea and her nephew had made a plan. They were going to revive the bookshop somehow, reopen it, and surprise Jenna with a business she could run, and earn money from, when she was up and about.

It was such a good idea, in theory, and she absolutely understood, and agreed with Mabel, about the point of The Bookshop of Memories. But even so, she was back to worrying whether all their hard work would be for nothing. She still had to get people through the door. She imagined that was what all those bestsellers had been doing in the window – enticing people inside. After all, it was still a shop, and they had to sell books to survive – or rather her sister did. Not everyone would appreciate a bookshop that didn't stock the new releases if that was what they wanted.

'That's all well and good, Mabel, but I still think I need some modern books in the window. I just have no idea how to get hold of them, who to approach for some stock.'

Thea frowned, wondering why she wasn't thinking about Jenna running the bookshop, but was instead picturing doing it herself – with Callum. She stole a glance in his direction and caught him grinning at her. Was he thinking the same thing?

Mabel had noticed his expression too. 'What are you grinning like a Cheshire cat for?'

Dickens lifted his head at the sound of the word, *cat*.

'I've got a surprise for Thea tomorrow.'

'You have?' said Thea. 'What is it, Callum?'

'*Who* is it?'

'Huh?'

'I've enlisted some help.'

'What do you mean?'

'In the bookshop.'

Thea looked at him. It was *her* bookshop. Shouldn't he have run it by her first?

She was about to say something, but stopped short. He'd worked hard. Without his help, they wouldn't have got this far so quickly. He was a famous Hollywood star. He didn't have to be here in this old bookshop, spending his downtime scrubbing filthy bookshelves. She was sure he had better things to do with his time, like perusing scripts, and talking to his agent about upcoming projects. She smiled to herself. She knew why he was doing this, spending his time here – it was for her. He was attracted to her, just like she was to him.

Even so, she wanted to know who would be turning up. She asked him.

'As I said, it's a surprise, Thea. But all your worries about the bookshop will be over – you'll see. She's going to put this place well and truly on the map.' Callum's smile slipped.

Thea stared at him. If this surprise was so wonderful, why had she caught a worried look crossing his face? She wondered what was going through his mind.

Callum was thinking about Lexi's famous grandmother, the writer, and the huge buzz it would create if she were to debut her new book at the reopening of The Bookshop of Memories. Callum frowned. There was one obvious problem he just couldn't ignore; the more people who knew about this place, the greater the possibility that somebody, somewhere would find out who the new bookshop owner really was.

51

Despite her reservations about having someone she didn't know turning up at the bookshop the next day, Thea knew it wasn't really about that; she was grateful for all the help she could get. However, the time in which she was envisaging having Callum to herself, once Toby returned to school, was dwindling by the second. But putting that aside, she was starting to feel far more confident about this venture – all thanks to Mabel and Callum.

As if it was a sign, she heard the door to the shop opening.

'There you go,' said Mabel, 'sounds like your first customer.'

Thea put her empty cup down on the coffee table. She glanced at her watch. She still had a few minutes before it was time to leave and pick up Katie from drama class. She looked over at Mabel. 'It can't be a customer – we haven't opened yet,' she whispered.

Mabel whispered back, 'Perhaps someone looked through the window, spotted us, and didn't see the 'closed' sign.'

Thea frowned. This wouldn't do at all. She called out, 'Sorry, we're closed at the moment, but we will be opening soon.' She couldn't see the front of the shop from the cosy corner between the bookshelves.

She heard the door to the shop close.

They remained seated on the sofa. It was Winston who sniffed the air, barked, and suddenly ran off.

Thea was just rising from her seat when Winston returned, wagging his tail. 'Hey, where did you go?'

'He came to greet me!' Katie emerged from behind the bookshelf. She looked at her aunt and said, 'What the hell has been going on?' Her gaze shifted along the sofa from Thea to her brother, then to Mabel, and then – 'Oh, my god!' Two teenage girls squealed at the top of their voices when they spotted Callum.

Toby stared at his sister, heaved a sigh and rolled his eyes. 'Callum, meet your biggest fan.'

'Oh. My. God. It *is* you!'

Callum smiled at the two young teenage girls standing before him. 'Hi, you must be Katie.'

Thea noticed Katie suddenly came over all shy in the presence of her biggest crush. For the first time ever, she appeared lost for words. She looked at Toby. 'You know my brother?'

'Of course.' Callum put an affectionate hand on Toby's shoulder.

Toby puffed out his chest. 'Yeah, we're good friends.'

'I've missed you at school,' Caitlin said, smiling shyly at Toby.

Thea looked at her nephew and smiled. She knew that Katie's friend, Caitlin, was a big fan of Callum's too, but it was very telling that she only had eyes for Toby.

'Have you?' said Toby, looking surprised. 'Would you like a juice?'

'Yes, please.'

'I'll get you one.' He stood up. 'If you come with me, I could show you what I've been doing. Callum's been teaching me bookbinding. Would you like to see?'

'Oh, yes please.'

Toby disappeared into the back room.

Thea caught Katie staring after her brother. Thinking of Toby learning new things reminded her – wasn't Katie meant to be in drama class with her friend? How had they got to the shop, and more to the point, how had Katie found out what they were up to?

Callum stood up. 'You know, I've still got some bits and pieces to finish off, so I think I'll take my coffee and finish off.' Before he disappeared down another aisle, sensing that Thea had some explaining to do, he stopped and looked at Katie. 'It's very nice to meet you, Katie. I hope we can be friends too.'

Katie's mouth dropped open. 'Oh, er … yes. I'd like that.'

Mabel stood up too. 'Well, hello Katie, I'm your … I'm Mabel – I work across the yard in the charity shop. I've been helping your aunt too. It's lovely to meet you. Well, I'd better get going. I've got a shop to run.'

Thea had never seen Mabel move so fast. She frowned as she was left to explain her little deception to Katie.

Katie's eyes followed the others. She slowly turned around and folded her arms – the little diva was back. She cocked her head to one side, and tapped her foot, waiting.

Thea looked sheepishly up at her niece. 'How did you get here from Leiston?'

'I'll ask the questions, if you don't mind,' said Katie, sarcastically. She stared at her aunt, and said, 'Caitlin's big brother is in the sixth form. Lucky for me he's just passed his test and got a car.'

Not so lucky for me, thought Thea. 'But you're meant to be in drama class.'

'We told him it's been cancelled. I said you'd be here, at the bookshop, and he just dropped us both off. Caitlin lives in

Aldeburgh, a couple of streets away, so she's going to walk home.' Katie added, 'Do you want to know how I found out?'

It didn't take long for Katie to explain that she'd overheard Toby on the phone to his best friend.

'So, when you heard mention of a shop, you guessed it was here?'

'Well, I know at the weekends, when we come to Aldeburgh, sometimes he disappears, and I caught him walking into Cobblers Yard. I didn't bother following him into Cobblers Yard. I just assumed he was visiting the old antique store. But then it dawned on me that perhaps it wasn't that shop, but the one next door.' She wriggled her little button nose. 'Why didn't you just tell me?'

Thea was honest, and told her the plan for her mum to run the bookshop, but that they were getting it all set up as a surprise. 'I just didn't want—'

'Me and my big mouth to ruin the surprise?'

Thea looked at her. 'Sorry.'

'Apology accepted.' Katie unfolded her arms, and sat down on the sofa next to her. 'I know I've got a big mouth.'

Thea smiled at her. 'I didn't say that.'

'You didn't have to.' Katie smiled back. 'How on earth do you know that guy – Callum?'

'He walked into the shop, thinking it was open, because Toby left the door open when I went to get some croissants one morning. We just got talking. He said he's here visiting friends in the area.'

'He's on holiday here, then?'

'Yes, I guess so.'

'Why does he want to spend time here, in Grandpa's old bookshop?'

Thea smiled. She knew why, but she wasn't about to confide in her thirteen-year-old niece – not yet anyway – that Callum was here because he wanted to spend time getting to know Thea. She didn't answer Katie's question, although Thea did raise her eyebrows, surprised that Katie already knew this was her grandfather's bookshop.

Katie cast her gaze around the shop. 'I like it. I've never been inside. Mum mentioned Grandpa ran a bookshop years ago. I knew it was here. The shop that's been abandoned for years.'

'She told you that?'

'Yes. I ask her things about him, but she doesn't say much. He disappeared, didn't he?'

'Yes.'

Katie nodded. 'Can I come here too?'

'You want to help out too?' As Thea was talking, she heard Callum arranging some books at the other end of the shop.

Thea whispered, 'You want to see Callum again, don't you?'

'I guess. But I really want to help, for you and Mum. And Grandpa.'

Thea looked at her in surprise. 'Why Grandpa?'

'In case he comes back.'

'Katie, I really don't think after all these years—'

'Who's this?' Katie asked, suddenly noticing the cat on her lap.

'Ah, this is Dickens, Callum's cat.'

'Dickens? What a funny name for a cat. He's cute.'

Dickens stood up, stretched, and walked over to Katie, rubbing his head against her hand. 'Hey, little guy. Do you want a stroke?'

Thea smiled. 'I think he does.'

'Aww, I've always wanted a cat. You are so sweet.'

Dickens purred loudly.

Thea looked up in time to see Callum's head pop round the bookshelf. He glanced at his hand and frowned at the cat.

Thea said, 'I think he's quite an old cat, so you just have to be a bit careful. He can be a bit temperamental.'

A bit? Callum mouthed at Thea.

'Oh, you wouldn't hurt me, would you?' Katie picked Dickens up and gave him a cuddle. 'Is he staying with Callum in that yellow campervan?'

'Well, sometimes. He seems to like the bookshop, though. Spends most of his time here.'

Katie held him up, turning him this way and that. 'Why does he look familiar?'

'Um, careful.'

Dickens just hung there in mid-air, paws and claws hanging limply by his side before she put him on her lap. 'I was going through some old family photos.'

'You were?'

'Yeah. We're doing a project at school, genealogy and family history.'

'Sounds interesting.' Thea noticed Callum's head pop out again from behind the bookshelves. He was listening to their conversation. She said light-heartedly, 'Callum, would you like to join us?'

'No, no. Still busy, busy.'

Katie continued. 'So, we're using a website where you can do some research on your family history to construct a family tree. It's kind of fun, because the teacher asked us if we can add photos of our relatives too, from when they were children, if we can find any.'

'Would you like a photo of me when I was a child?'

'No thanks. I've got a photo of you and mum when you were children. I found it in an old photo album in Grandma's stuff.'

Thea raised her eyebrows. 'So, it was you who—'

'No, I did not open those boxes – I swear. But Mum and Dad aren't around to ask where they might keep old photo albums. I suspect they're stored up in the loft. So when you mentioned those boxes in the garage were open …' she trailed off. 'Are you cross with me?'

'No, no not at all, Katie. In fact, it would be kind of nice to have a look at some of those old photo albums from my childhood. We could go through them together.'

'Do you know that when you were a child, you had a cat that looked just like Dickens?'

A loud bang, followed by a doggy whimper, suddenly interrupted them.

'What the hell was that?' explained Katie, looking at the bookshelves.

'Callum, is everything okay?'

Winston came scampering out from the behind the bookshelf. He ran straight up to Thea and offered her his paw. 'Aww, what happened? Did you hurt your paw?'

'Yeah, er, sorry … I dropped a load of books,' said Callum.

'On Winston's paw,' commented Thea. 'Do you need a hand?'

'No, no … er, I've got this. I'll just put them back.'

Thea rubbed Winston's paw. She turned to Katie. 'You were saying?'

Katie looked at the cat on her lap. His tail was swaying from side to side as he eyed Winston. 'Yes, I found a photo of you with a black and white cat.'

Thea looked at Dickens. 'You know, he looked familiar to me too. I did have a cat when I was little. You must show me the photo.'

'I will.'

'If you'd like some help with your school project, you only have to ask.'

'Well, that's the thing. I don't really know anything about Grandpa's side of the family. It's hard because it's, like, blank.'

'Oh, I see.'

'Yeah.'

Thea didn't know what to say. Unfortunately, it was a blank for her too. 'I'll email your grandmother.'

'All right. But she's, like, incommunicado most of the time, isn't she, in Nepal? That's what Mum calls it.'

'I'm afraid so. They discourage the use of modern tech at the retreat, apparently. She tends to get online mostly when she makes a trip into the nearest town, where there's an internet café.' Thea had emailed her about Jenna's accident, but so far had heard nothing.

'Yes, that's what Mum said too.'

They both fell silent, Thea stroking Winston, who was sitting by her feet, and Katie tickling Dickens under the chin, which he seemed to enjoy; he was holding his head up and closing his eyes.

'So, can I come at the weekend and help out?'

Thea looked at her apologetically. 'Your dad is coming home from London at the weekend, I'm afraid.'

'So what?'

'He's going to want to see you guys.'

'That's okay. He can come and help in the bookshop too.'

'Oh, er … I suppose you can ask him.'

'You're not going home yet are you, Auntie Thea? You don't

have to, you know. Daddy is working away. Even if he comes back at the weekend, he'll most likely have to return to London on Monday. And even if Mummy is out of hospital next week, she's going to need help for a bit, until the cast comes off. Will you stay? Please say yes.'

Toby walked out of the back room, hand in hand with Caitlin. He'd overheard his sister pleading for Thea to stay. 'You can't go now. We've still got things to do before the bookshop opens.'

Thea looked from her niece to her nephew. Even Winston seemed to be pleading for her to stay. The dog put his head on her lap, puppy dog eyes staring up at her. Thank goodness she'd already spoken to Gracie to extend her stay.

'I'd already decided to stay on a bit longer.' She stared wistfully around the bookshop, wishing that she could stay there forever.

'What about Callum?' Toby asked.

Callum reappeared. 'Um, what about me?'

'Are you staying until the bookshop reopens?'

Thea hadn't thought to ask him how long he was staying in Suffolk. She suspected it was because she was afraid to ask when he was planning to return to America.

'Yes, of course I'll stay.'

'Good.' Toby ran up and gave him a hug.

Callum patted him on the back.

Katie stared at her brother and shook her head in wonderment.

Thea saw the look on Katie's face; her brother wasn't such a dork after all. In fact, Thea imagined what Katie was thinking – that she had the coolest brother in the world.

52

'So, this is Lexi. Lexi meet Thea.'

It was Tuesday morning, and Callum had been alone in the bookshop with Thea for the best part of the morning – just what he was afraid of. Thea had started to ask him questions about his life, his childhood.

He'd been saved by the sound of the door to the shop opening. Just as she'd promised, Lexi had arrived after her morning shift at the library. She had the afternoon free, and she was going to spend it with them.

Callum noticed Thea's expression change the moment she set eyes on the young American.

'You're very pretty,' said Thea.

'Why thank you – but it takes one to know one.' Lexi grinned, pointing at her.

Callum saw something glinting in the autumn sunshine coming through the gleamingly clean bookshop window.

So did Thea. 'Wow, that's a lovely ring.'

Lexi looked at her ring. 'Yes, it is – isn't it? It's my engagement ring.'

'You're engaged?'

Callum caught the relief in her voice.

'Yes. The moment I set eyes on him, I knew he was the one.'

Callum caught Thea glance his way.

'Ahem.' Callum coughed into his hand. 'Well now the introductions are out of the way, why don't we crack on? Lexi said she'd help out getting the books into some sort of order.'

'Yep, I can do that. I can also source suppliers for any books you'd like to display in your window. I noticed it was empty. The flowers are lovely, but I think books would be better for a bookshop – don't you?'

'Oh, well yes. They're only there because Lili popped in to introduce herself, and gave me some flowers.'

'I know. I was kidding. Lili told me she'd introduced herself with flowers.'

'You know Lili?'

'Oh, yes. We're good friends. She's one of the people who helped me out when I moved here from America.' Lexi turned to Callum. 'It's a great place to relocate to. I can vouch for that.' She looked at Thea and Callum. 'You make such a cute couple. Have you guys just moved here?'

Callum looked at her wide-eyed, 'Oh, we're not—'

'Well, you should be.'

Callum caught Thea grinning. She linked her arm in Lexi's and took her for a tour of the shop. 'So, Callum tells me you've got a plan for opening the shop.'

'Oh, boy, have I ever. I told my grandmother about the bookshop, and she is totally on board.'

'Your grandmother?'

'Now, have you heard of the writer, Margot Dorey?'

Thea said, 'Of course. I loved her books when I was a child.

Such a shame she stopped writing. I always wondered what happened to her.'

Callum shut the bookshop door and smiled. Thea was about to find out.

'No way!' he heard Thea exclaim.

He continued smiling as he walked into the kitchen to put the kettle on. He left Lexi sitting with Thea on the sofa, telling her all about the plan for Margot Dorey to release her new book in the bookshop.

'She thought it would be quite exciting for her book to go on sale at The Bookshop of Memories first, at one minute past midnight. She'll be there to do a book signing too. It's going to be pandemonium, I imagine, with the press, and loads of people queuing down the street to get their copy – hope you don't mind.'

'Mind? Oh, my god, it's going to be … well, I haven't got the words.'

'It will turn out quite the opening day for your little bookshop. Really put it on the map. Everyone will know about it.'

Callum winced when he overheard that.

'And then the following day,' continued Lexi, 'my grandmother thought of doing a reading. She used to do that at the library, which I imagine she will ask me to organise at some point. But she thought it would be a wonderful idea if she could do a reading from her book for local children right here in the bookshop.'

'Oh, that sounds—'

'Thea, are you all right?'

Callum furrowed his brow, wondering why Lexi was asking her that.

'Sorry. I am so sorry, Lexi. I just came over all emotional for some reason. I wish my dad could be here to see all this.'

'Oh, right. Um … I'm sorry for your loss.'

'Thanks.'

Callum was in the middle of pouring the tea. He stopped and looked miserably at the wall. *For god's sake, tell her!*

His eyes dropped to the teabag floating in the teacup. *Let her have this, the grand opening of the bookshop she's worked so hard for before you go and spoil it by telling her that you've been deceiving her all this time over who you really are. And what you're really doing here.* In any case, Callum knew they'd be no point in Henry being there at the grand reopening; he wouldn't understand what the hell was going on – the noise and the strange people would just confuse him.

'Callum, everything okay?'

He whirled around at the sound of her voice behind him. 'Oh, yeah, sure. I was just finishing making the tea.' Along with debating what exactly he was going to do about the bookshop. 'I won't be a minute.' He watched her walk back into the shop and heard them talking about the finer details of the grand reopening of The Bookshop of Memories.

He frowned. *I'm a terrible person. When she finds out, she's going to hate me. She's going to think that I've just been using her to do up my shop. Although … haven't I?* That little voice in his head wasn't helping. It was all well and good if he turned around and said, *Here, have the keys – the bookshop is yours*. But how could he? He needed the money.

It sounded as though her sister needed this shop. Maybe Thea did too – he'd seen her looking downcast, as though something had happened recently that had cast a shadow over her life, but here in this bookshop, she was a different person; light-hearted, as though the worries of the world had lifted from her shoulders. Perhaps she needed it more than her sister did – and more than he did. 'Oh, god, I wish I'd never come here,' said Callum under his breath as he finished making the tea. He slapped a smile on his face as he took the tray of tea out to Thea and Lexi. Whichever way he tried to wriggle out of this now, he knew it wouldn't end well.

He heard Thea say, 'So, Lexi, how did you two meet? Callum never said.'

He stopped like a rabbit in headlights. The trouble was that he hadn't mentioned his visit to the library because Thea might wonder why he wanted to research the bookshop.

'Callum wanted to do some research on the bookshop.'

'Really – why?'

'I don't know, Thea – why don't you ask him?'

Callum stopped behind the bookshelf with the tray in his hands and closed his eyes.

'Callum?'

He heard Thea calling. 'I'll be right there?' He was trying to think how he was going to answer the question.

He walked around the corner of the bookshelf, smiling.

Thea said, 'I heard you were in the library at the weekend doing some research on this bookshop.'

He tried to sound as nonchalant as possible. 'Funny thing. I was at a bit of a loose end on Saturday, and for want of something better to do I thought, why not find out a bit more about the place?'

Callum could not believe the whopping lies that were coming out of his mouth. Mind you, he'd been lying to her all along. What was another one, when all was said and done?

'And what did you discover?' Thea asked.

'Interesting fact. This bookshop used to be owned by Mabel and Marjorie's father during the war.'

'Hey, really?' Thea looked taken aback. 'What a small world. I wonder why they never said?'

Callum bit his lower lip and stared at Thea.

Lexi said, 'You were also trying to find articles about the bookshop from around twenty-five years ago – weren't you?'

Callum stared at Lexi. For some reason, he happened to glance out of the shop window and saw another train crash heading his way. 'Oh, no.'

'Callum, what's wrong?' asked Thea.

What was wrong was that his two best friends were heading towards the bookshop. 'Not now, not today,' said Callum under his breath. He quickly plonked the tray down on the coffee table, slopping the tea. 'One sec, I'll be right back. Er … help yourself to biscuits.'

Callum dashed out of the shop.

'Callum!' Jack spotted him. 'There you are. We came to Aldeburgh today.'

'And we spotted your van parked along the beach near the car park,' commented Beth. 'Or rather, Fergus did.'

Jack added, 'We thought we'd find you here, in your bookshop. How's it going? Got a buyer yet, or have you decided to stay on after all and run it yourself?'

Oh, god. Oh, god. Callum glanced at the bookshop. He could see Thea sitting on the couch, craning her neck, looking his way. He turned back to his friends. It had never occurred to him that they would turn up. But it should have. He'd told them where he was; it was only a matter of time before they showed their faces, especially as Beth did business with Lili across the yard in The Potting Shed.

'Aren't you going to show us around?' asked Jack.

Callum vehemently shook his head. 'It's not ready. Come back on opening day. I'll be in touch and tell you when that is.'

Beth frowned. 'But we're here now, and I can see people in your shop.'

'Oh, er … they're just friends, helping out.'

'You've made new friends? We'd like to meet them.'

Callum was still shaking his head. 'No, that's not a good idea.'

'Why ever not?'

Callum caught Jack staring at him. 'Oh.'

Beth looked at her husband. 'What do you mean – oh?'

Jack said, 'It's her – isn't it?'

Callum took a deep breath. 'Look, she doesn't know – all right. She found the keys. She thinks … she doesn't know about me, about the fact that dad …' he trailed off.

'So, you think it's true.'

Callum nodded at Jack. 'I do.'

Beth looked from Jack to Callum. 'What's going on? Did I miss something?'

'Please, please, don't say anything,' said Callum cupping his hands together. 'She knows I'm famous, and I grew up in Scotland. That's it. Don't, for god's sake, mention Henry!'

Jack nodded. 'All right. But when are you going to tell her?'

'After the reopening of the bookshop.'

'Is that before or after you put it up for sale?' Jack glared at him. 'You've got to tell her, mate.'

'Guys!' Beth got their attention. 'What is going on?'

Jack turned to Beth. 'I'll tell you when we get home. But if we're going to go in the shop, just keep your mouth shut.'

'What?'

'Callum?' Thea called out. 'Are these your friends?'

Callum turned around to find Thea standing at the shop door. He took a deep breath. 'Er, sorry, yes. I was trying to persuade them to wait until the grand opening to see the place.'

'Oh, don't be silly. Come in. Callum has just made a pot of tea. Or we have coffee, if you prefer? Come and join us.' Her eyes roved to little Fergus. 'I have chocolate biscuits.'

'Mummy, can I have one?'

Beth smiled. 'All right.'

Callum stood there in the middle of the yard and watched them all troop inside. He glanced around the yard, thinking, 'Can my day get any worse?' Across the courtyard, he caught Mabel standing at the shop window staring his way.

He took a deep breath before he walked back to the shop. He wasn't looking forward to the grand reopening. He'd heard Thea and Lexi setting a tentative date, in a week's time. As far as he was concerned, it couldn't come soon enough. It was going to be a fiasco. If he got through the day without anyone finding out the truth, he'd be the luckiest man alive.

He took one last look at Mabel across the yard. If his secret was going to be revealed, then he was taking them with him. He had the copy of the newspaper article revealing that their brother was Henry. He was going to confront them with it. Just not straight away. He had enough on his plate for one day.

Callum stepped inside the shop, hoping his friends did as he asked and didn't let on that he owned it.

53

'When are you going to tell them, Mabel?' Callum had a rare moment alone with Mabel in the bookshop when Lexi had to return to work in the library, and Thea was paying another visit to her sister. The week had flown by, and the opening night was upon them.

'Tell them what?'

'That you're their aunt?'

'Why, whatever do you mean?'

'Henry is your brother, isn't he? I saw an old article about the bookshop that had been written after the Second World War. There was a photo of you and your sister, with your father and brother.'

Callum waited for her to deny it. She didn't. Not at first. Mabel said, 'But you don't understand, we're not related. My father just brought him up as his own.'

'What are you talking about?'

'Henry was adopted by my father. Towards the end of the war, we took in an evacuee – well, two – a young woman and her child. Then, after the war, there was another round of evacuations. You probably aren't aware. You see, although the war had officially ended, the government believed there might still be further bombs dropped on London. So the evacuees returned. She was pregnant, and she stayed and had Henry.'

'Okay.'

'But then she left the baby with us, and returned to her husband.'

Callum didn't want to be the bearer of bad – or maybe good – news, depending on how they looked at it, but there was no denying the resemblance between the picture of Mabel as a young child and the childhood photo of Henry's daughters – especially Thea.

Although the image was black and white, and a bit grainy, Callum had printed off the article. He showed it to Mabel, and got out the photo of Thea, pairing them up so she could see the photos side by side.

Mabel stared at the photos. 'No, no. I don't … I can't believe it.'

'You said that your mum had died before the war.'

'Yes.'

'I don't want to state the obvious,' Callum said, 'but it looks like your dad had an affair with the woman who was evacuated here. She got pregnant, and left the baby with him to bring up, and most likely returned to her husband. He's your brother, Mabel – your and Marjorie's brother.'

Mabel looked at him, wide-eyed. She clutched her chest.

Oh, god! She really is having a heart attack this time. It's the shock of finding out her father had an affair. Oh, god, I shouldn't have just come out with it like that.

'Mabel, speak to me? Have you got a pain in your chest or arm? Having trouble breathing?'

Mabel shook her head.

'Do you need a glass of water?'

'A stiff drink, more like!'

Callum breathed a huge sigh of relief. 'I think I need one too.'

Mabel said, 'It explains everything.'

Callum furrowed his brow.

'It explains why our father left him the bookshop. I always thought he'd leave it to us, to me. But he didn't. He left it to the evacuee. He wasn't even his own flesh and blood – or so I thought.'

'You were wrong, Mabel.'

'Oh, my lord. All these years we've been estranged. We never knew.'

Callum looked at her. 'I think your father owed it to you, Marjorie and Henry, to tell you all the truth.'

He thought of Mabel and Marjorie, and their estrangement from their brother because he had been left the bookshop. Callum knew he'd been sent to give Thea and Jenna an old yellow campervan, whereas Henry had signed over the bookshop to him. How could he possibly tell them that?

Mabel said, 'But how can I be sure?'

'How can you be sure of what?' a stranger's voice said. A gentleman appeared from behind a bookshelf.

Callum said, 'I didn't hear you come in the bookshop.'

'Ray!' Mabel got out of her chair.

Ray walked over. 'Now, I could have guessed you'd have something to do with the rumour around town that the bookshop is reopening.'

'Oh, it's no longer a rumour. There are flyers all round town, on lampposts and in shop windows, announcing the big event tonight.'

Callum looked at her. 'Are there?'

'I heard Margot is going to be the star guest,' said Ray.

'She certainly is. It was Lexi's idea, but Margot is really excited about it. Lexi tells me she's so happy to be releasing her first book in years right here in her home county.'

'I bet she is.'

Callum stared at Ray.

Ray looked at him. 'Oh, excuse me – I'm Ray. I've come to lend a hand if the new owner needs one.' He looked around the shop.

'Oh, Thea isn't here at the moment,' said Mabel. 'She's gone to see her sister in hospital.'

'Oh, dear. Nothing serious, I hope.'

'I don't think so. She broke her leg, although …' Mabel lowered her voice. 'I heard she's pregnant.'

Callum looked at Mabel in surprise. 'Really? How do you know that?'

Mabel tapped her nose. 'I have my sources.'

Ray sighed. 'I'm afraid nothing is a secret in this town.'

Callum thought, *You wanna bet?*

'Hey, your face looks familiar,' said Ray, eyeing Callum. 'You star in that show! My wife is such a big fan. You're a long way from Hollywood. What are you doing in these parts?'

'Callum's been helping out at the bookshop. I think he's got a thing for Thea.'

Callum rolled his eyes. 'I have not got a thing for Thea.'

'I see the way you look at her,' said Mabel.

'Well, you're wrong. I can't look at her that way.'

'Why – are you gay?'

'No. She's my sister!' blurted Callum. He stopped, and stared at Mabel in the heavy silence.

Mabel said slowly, 'I'm sorry – what did you just say?'

'She's my sister.'

Mabel shook her head. 'But how can that be?'

'Because before Henry met their mother, he was with mine.' In conversation with Thea he'd found out her age. It all made sense now. 'Henry is my father too. He sent me here with the yellow campervan to give to the girls. That's how I have the photo of the two of them.'

Mabel was still shaking her head. 'No, he was a bachelor in his late thirties before he met their mother.'

Callum slowly shook his head from side to side, and said, 'Just how well did you really know your brother? You said yourself you were estranged from Henry for years.'

'But I never saw him with another woman besides the mother of those girls.'

'He went travelling, didn't he? In his campervan for weeks on end.'

'Yes, they were business trips.'

'Were they, now?' said Callum.

Mabel was still shaking his head, looking at Callum sceptically. 'Well, if that's all true, why on earth did Henry leave it this long to tell you about his other family?'

'I'm sorry to intrude on this conversation,' said Ray, 'but I know there's one way to clear all this up.'

'How?' said Mabel and Callum in unison.

'Take a DNA test.'

Callum rolled his eyes. 'I do not need to take one of those. I know who I am.' He looked at Mabel. 'I think *you* should take one. I know you don't believe me that Henry is really your brother.'

'No, I don't.'

'Take a test then, to be sure.'

Ray said, 'Is Henry around to take the test with?'

Mabel swivelled her head in Callum's direction. 'Where is he? You promised you'd tell us.'

Callum sighed. 'He's in Scotland.'

'What's he doing all the way up there?'

'I told you, he's with my mother. Well, he was.'

'They're no longer together?'

Callum nodded. 'I guess you could say that. He lives in a care home.'

'A care home?' Mabel looked at him in disbelief. 'At his age?'

Ray said, 'Sorry to intrude again, but what about Thea? She could take a test too, because if you're both related to Henry, then that will be a sure-fire way of clearing things up.'

They all fell silent. Mabel finally said, 'But how will I get her to take a test?'

Callum said, 'Tell her the truth.'

Mabel raised her eyebrows at Callum. 'Well, you're a fine one to talk, aren't you? Giving me advice about telling the truth …'

Callum looked away, embarrassed.

Mabel said, 'Show me that photo and the newspaper article again.'

Callum handed them over and watched her study the two photos – the one of her as a child, and the other of Thea and her sister. She passed them to Ray. 'Do you see the resemblance?'

Ray smiled. 'I do. But I still recommend the test, to be sure.'

'All right, Ray. But on one condition,' said Mabel, turning to Callum. 'You take the test too.'

'I told you, I don't need to.'

Mabel regarded Callum for a long moment. 'Thea doesn't know, does she? About you and Henry.'

Callum sighed heavily and took a seat on the sofa. 'That's the reason I made you promise not to tell her that I had the photo of her and her sister. I wasn't ready to tell her about Henry.' He stared forlornly at his hands. Winston appeared, jumping on the sofa and putting his head on Callum's lap. He whined. 'It's all right, boy,' said Callum, patting his head.

Callum looked up at Mabel. 'There's something else she doesn't know, too.' Callum swallowed. He couldn't believe he was telling her this. 'I own this bookshop.'

Mabel furrowed her brow. 'What do you mean?'

'Dad, Henry, signed the bookshop over to me.'

This time Mabel was the one who needed to sit down. 'Why?'

'Maybe he thought my showbusiness career would falter and I'd need a back-up plan. Maybe because I'm his firstborn, and his only son. Who knows.'

'Well, didn't he tell you?'

Callum really didn't want to get into the reasons why Henry couldn't tell him, unless he caught his father in a rare lucid moment. Mabel had had enough shocks for one afternoon, without being told about Henry's condition.

Mabel stared at him. 'I want you to take the DNA test.'

He stared at her. 'Oh, you have got to be kidding!' he exclaimed when he realised what it was about. 'You think I'm related to Douglas.'

'It's possible.'

'Now you're saying my mother had an affair?' Callum shook his head from side to side.

'You see, anything's possible,' said Mabel. 'Now, how about it?

Shall we do one together?'

Callum sighed. 'Okay, let's do it. But you can't let on with Thea the reason why I'm doing one.'

'Why?'

'Because I need to tell her in my own time who I am, and about Henry. She's going to hate me when she finds out how I've deceived her. I just want her to have the opening day, all right?'

'I understand.'

Ray looked from Mabel to Callum. 'I'm not sure I do.'

Mabel smiled at her friend. 'I'll explain everything. But first we want to do those tests, and find out the results.'

Callum wasn't bothered by the results. He knew what they'd be. But perhaps it was better to be armed with the results when he told Thea the truth, because it occurred to him that she might not believe him when he did.

'So, it's decided then,' said Mabel.

'What's decided?' said Thea, walking in on them.

'Oh, I thought you were seeing your sister?'

Thea looked at her watch. 'I went along to the hospital, but I've got to go back in about an hour because they hadn't done the discharge paperwork.' She looked at Ray. 'Oh, hi there. I'm Thea.'

'I'm Ray. We were just talking about my job heir-hunting. Mabel and Callum want to do a DNA test.'

Callum heaved a huge sigh, and turned wide-eyed to look at Ray. Why had he said that?

Thea looked at them. 'Why do you want to take a DNA test?'

'I'm just in it for the fun of it,' Callum lied, wincing.

Mabel frowned at him. She turned to Thea. 'For my part, I think you and I are related.'

'I'm sorry, what did you say?'

'Your father, Henry, might be my biological brother.' Mabel proceeded to tell her about her childhood at the bookshop, and the evacuee. 'Show her the newspaper clipping, Callum.'

Thea turned to him. 'I remember Lexi mentioned you'd been researching the bookshop.' Thea smiled at him, breaking his heart. Very soon, he'd never see her smile at him again.

54

'Are you nervous?' Jack whispered in his ear.

He turned to look at his best friend and grimaced. 'What do *you* think?'

'The shop looks amazing though, doesn't it?' He looked at his watch. 'Not long to go. I hear the famous writer is on her way. What was her name?'

'Margot Dorey.'

'I saw the queues building up already when I walked in this afternoon.'

'How did I get myself into this mess?'

'You're doing the right thing.'

'Am I?'

'Yes, it's strange the way it came about, but perhaps it's for the best that the truth is revealed by a DNA test.'

'I'm not going to show her the result until after the grand opening.'

'Suit yourself, but you're only prolonging the inevitable.'

'I know.' Callum didn't actually have the result yet, but that didn't matter. He knew what it would be anyway; he'd just been railroaded into taking the test.

'Is that when you're going to tell her about her father? About Henry?'

'Yes.'

'Have you decided what's happening about the bookshop?'

'Even if I give the girls the bookshop, do you know how it's going to make them feel when they find out their father had another child, and left it to me rather than them?'

'Not good, I imagine.'

Callum looked at Jack, thinking that this was an understatement. All their childhood memories in that bookshop would be forever tainted when they found out that Henry was not the man, the father, they'd thought he was.

Over the past week, Jack and Beth had helped out with the preparation of the grand reopening of the bookshop too. They had kept his secret, as he'd asked. They weren't the only ones helping out. Katie and Toby were there too, along with Toby's new girlfriend, Caitlin, and his best friend.

Lexi had spent all her spare time on it too, and had sourced the bestsellers. The boxes of books had arrived just in time to display them in the bookshop window, along with reams of bunting that Marjorie had found in a bag in the back of the charity shop. And somehow, in that short space of time, Lexi had managed to bring some order to the cluttered bookshelves.

Lili had brought over more flowers, along with hanging baskets and potted plants, making the outside of the shop look the best in the yard. Someone had donated a couple of small outside tables and chairs so that people could sit outside with a book and a coffee in the nice weather.

When word had started to spread through the small seaside town, so many people had got involved in the bookshop, one way or another, by providing either a bit of spare time or bits and bobs they needed, that Callum had lost track.

The only person who had refused to have anything to do with it, surprisingly, was Thea's brother-in-law, Mark. He had been down from London at the weekend, and his reaction had surprised everyone – especially Thea, who had expected Mark to be over the moon at her efforts to get the shop up and running for her sister when she left hospital.

Callum had overheard some snippets of the conversation between Mark and Thea as they talked privately – or so they'd thought – in the room at the back of the shop, and he did wonder whether this might not turn out to be the lovely surprise Thea had anticipated for her sister.

When Thea, Katie and Toby had told Mark what they were doing there, he'd overheard Mark asking Thea if she'd talked this over with her sister. She told him she had not. Mark had said something about *other plans.* Callum wondered whether Thea would decide to talk to her sister who was being discharged from hospital before they turned up for the reopening. Callum had a horrible feeling in the pit of his stomach that the conversation was not going to go well.

Callum thoughts turned to Mabel and Marjorie. If he was going to tell Thea about himself, then he wanted Mabel and Marjorie to tell her about their link to Henry too – tell her that they were all one big happy, or not-so-happy, dysfunctional family.

And now he was waiting for a DNA test result to prove it.

55

'I'm sorry, Thea, but I don't want to come to the reopening of the bookshop.'

Those were the first words out of Jenna's mouth when Thea walked into her hospital room.

'Mark told you about the bookshop. It was meant to be a surprise!'

'Yes, well I think he wanted to forewarn me.'

'Forewarn you?'

Thea watched Jenna packing her toiletries and nightie into her overnight bag. She stopped to look at her sister. 'It sounds as though you've done an incredible amount of work. And I really appreciate the thought.'

'The thought?' Thea couldn't believe it. She had been *so* looking forward to seeing the look on her sister's face when she told her about the bookshop. It was what she had worked so hard for. She couldn't get over the fact that her sister had pretty much just dismissed it with a flick of the hand.

Thea remembered something Mark had said about having *other plans* when she'd told him about the bookshop. The last time she'd visited Jenna in the hospital, Jenna had confessed that she thought Mark was having an affair. 'Don't get involved with a married man. They might leave their wives for you, but then eventually they'll leave *you* for someone else,' she'd sobbed.

That conversation had made Thea even more determined to get the bookshop up and running in case her sister was left with the twins and a baby to raise on her own.

'I don't think he wants this baby,' Jenna had said on that last visit Thea had made.

'Is it his baby?' Thea had blurted.

'What are you talking about?' Jenna had replied.

That was when Thea had told her, 'Toby saw you with a man at midnight, outside the bookshop.'

Jenna had looked at her, shocked. 'How? When?'

Thea had had no choice but to spill the beans regarding Toby discovering her late-night escapades, when she'd thought she was stealing out of the house unnoticed. 'That's how he'd discovered you had a key to the bookshop,' she'd told her.

'It's not what you think,' Jenna had said. 'Someone had gone through Mum's boxes.' Jenna had no idea who. The children had denied it, and of course Mark wouldn't be interested in their mum's things stored in the garage. Then she'd got a weird phone call, which only raised her suspicions that someone had been looking for the key she already had in her possession; the key their mother had given to her for safekeeping.

'The synthesised voice?' Thea had asked, telling her she'd answered her sister's mobile and heard that voice too.

Thea recalled that conversation with the weird voice on the phone. Jenna had money worries, and this person had offered her a lot of money for a rare book. And by the gist of the conversation, Jenna had done this before – met this stranger and handed over a rare book. When Jenna hadn't commented on what Thea had told her, Thea had said, 'But you did meet someone at the bookshop?'

Jenna hadn't denied it.

'But who was it? And why all the cloak-and-dagger stuff?'

At that point, her sister had clammed up and had said she didn't want to talk about it.

Thea stared at her sister, thinking back to that conversation on her last visit. She saw no point in raising the subject again. Her sister clearly had other things on her mind – namely getting out of the hospital. Her discharge was long overdue.

Jenna said, 'Right, I think I'm ready to leave.' She zipped up her bag and looked at Thea. 'Did you find a book wrapped in brown paper in the bookshop? I'm sure I left it in the back of the desk drawer in the shop.'

Thea shook her head.

'It doesn't matter now.'

'I thought you needed the money? I heard how much you were getting for selling the rare book.'

When she didn't respond, Thea said, 'I thought after our conversation last time that Mark might leave you, and clearly you had money worries. I couldn't believe it when I discovered we still had the bookshop, and I worked so hard to try and get it up and running again as a going concern, as a job and an income for you.'

Jenna patted the side of her bed for Thea to sit down next to her. She took her hand. 'You are the best sister, you know that – right? I don't think I've ever told you what a wonderful, supportive little sister you are.'

No, she hadn't.

'I just wish that I'd been a better big sister to you. If I have a problem, I'm straight on the phone to you. Thinking back on it, I feel so guilty that they are really the only times I'm in contact with you.'

Thea looked at her sister – it was true.

'You've always been the strong one out of the two of us. Mum said so too. I'm sure you've had your problems, but you've never come to me about them, and you should have. I just haven't been there for you like you have for me.'

Thea thought of what had gone on with Miles. She still hadn't told Jenna. As usual, she had put her sister first, thinking she had enough on her plate without being troubled by Thea's own problems.

'Look, I want all that to change.' Jenna put an arm around Thea, surprising her. Jenna hugged her close. 'I love you. I am so sorry about the bookshop. I can't come to the reopening.'

'But it's going to be an opening night to remember,' said Thea, still gutted that her sister really had made her mind she wasn't coming.

'I bet it will be. But it's your opening night, Thea. I want you to have the bookshop.'

'You want me to have the bookshop?' Thea shook her head in astonishment. 'You can't be serious. But … but what about the money? It must be worth a lot, a property in Aldeburgh. Don't you want to sell it, and share the—?'

'No. I do not. I discussed it with Mark. In fact, I didn't discuss it, I told him that the shop is yours. I emailed Mum too, and told her.'

'But the money …' Thea said again.

'It's fine. Mark and I can manage.'

'You're having a baby. And if money is tight now …' she trailed off.

'We don't need the bookshop, Thea. Or the money. We have other plans.'

Other plans. 'What are your plans?'

Jenna told her that Mark had been shocked to find out that he was going to be a father again at his age. He had already been an older father when they'd had the twins. Jenna had said she'd get a part-time job. Money would be tight. But they'd survive.

The trouble was that Mark didn't just want to survive; he wanted to live, have experiences. It wasn't that he didn't want the baby – he just wanted things to be different this time. He wanted an adventure.

It all sounded like a mid-life crisis to Thea.

'That's why we're packing up and moving to New York.'

Thea said, 'What?'

'Mark has been working hard in London, networking, going to a lot of job interviews. He's secured a very well-paid position, working for an international bank in the city, and he's heading up the opening of their new international offices in the States. First stop New York, then the new Chicago office. And we're all going with him.'

'You're leaving?' Thea couldn't have been more shocked. 'But your dream was to live in Suffolk and bring up your kids here.'

'Dreams change, Thea. Look at you. You once wanted to be a writer, then you wanted to be an archivist, like Dad's best friend. I know why that was – he was the father you never had growing up; it's little wonder you followed in his footsteps. But now it's time to find your own way, follow your own dreams. I see the way your face lights up when you talk about the bookshop. Your dream life is here, Thea. This is your future. Mine is with Mark and my family in America.'

'But what about all this? The house you've always wanted. You love that house.'

'It will still be here when we get back, sometime in the future. Perhaps we'll retire here, or if we return in a few years, my baby will go to school here when the twins have gone to university. Who knows what the future holds, Thea. You can't plan for every eventuality. However, right now we're going on an adventure together, as a family.'

Thea knew it would take some time to sink in. 'Did you have any clue what he was up to in London?'

'Not at all. It was the biggest surprise! I was so happy and relieved when he told me. And he told me something else.' Jenna grinned. 'He got the idea from you.'

'Me? I swear I never suggested you move abroad.' Thea started to feel a bit tearful at the prospect that they were moving thousands of miles away. She'd just started to get to know them, her niece and nephew, and now her sister would be having a new baby. She wanted to be part of their lives.

'And you will be, Thea,' Jenna replied when Thea voiced her thoughts. 'You can come and visit us. And there's always Skype, and of course in the holidays we'll be back.'

'But how come you said it was me who gave Mark the idea?'

'It wasn't actually you. It was Miles.'

'Pardon? Mark hasn't even met Miles.'

'No, I mean what Miles does, jetting abroad, living and working in—'

'It's not true.'

Jenna stopped short. 'What are you talking about?'

'I've taken some extended leave from my job. I found out it was all lies. He lives with his wife and two young kids in London.'

'Oh, my god, Thea. Why didn't you tell me?'

'Jenna, I've been such a fool. Why did I end up meeting a man who told me lies, and turned out not who I thought he was.'

Jenna hugged her close. 'I know this won't help right now, but you are my beautiful little sister, and I'm telling you that someone else will come along – just you wait and see.'

Thea brightened. 'I think they already have!'

'Where? When?'

'Right here. Right now.'

'Here – in Suffolk?'

'Yes, I met him in Aldeburgh. He's been helping me in the bookshop. I mean, there's no other reason why anyone would want to spend their time scrubbing bookshelves and working for free. He's been doing it all for me.'

'Oh, how wonderful,' said Jenna. 'It sounds like a love story to me.' She grinned. 'Are you in love with him?'

'I've only known him for a short time.' Tears of happiness rolled down her face. 'But I am, Jenna. I've never felt like this about anyone before. Oh, I am.'

56

It's quite the turnout, isn't it?'

Thea smiled at the reporter. It was almost midnight. She had been counting down the minutes until The Bookshop of Memories reopened.

Margot Dorey was already there, sitting on the sofa in the bookshop, with copies of her new book piled up in several big stacks on the coffee table. A crowd of people were waiting in the yard, the queue snaking right out of Cobblers Yard and round the corner into the high street.

The coffee machine was working overtime, and Lexi was delivering coffee in takeaway cups to customers outside. They were grateful for the hot drinks as they waited in the chill autumn air. There were children there too, wrapped in gloves, scarves and hats, enjoying the chocolate digestive biscuits that Marjorie was handing out.

People had come from miles around to be the first few to get their hands on Margot Dorey's new book when it was released at a minute past midnight in this little bookshop in Aldeburgh.

'And what does the new owner think of all this?'

'Well I—'

'Where is he, by the way?'

'Who?'

'Callum.'

Thea had been asking herself that question. She wanted him to be there by her side when she cut the ribbon that Lexi had placed across the door to the bookshop, marking the bookshop's official reopening. Thea had been asking everyone where he was, but bizarrely no one had seen him.

'It's a bit strange the new owner disappearing like that – don't you think?' the reporter asked.

'I don't know what you mean.' *I'm right here*, thought Thea, looking at her, bemused.

'I'm talking about the guy you've been working for this whole time to get the bookshop ready.'

'I'm sorry, but I think you're confused. My father used to own the bookshop.'

'Well, that's all very interesting, but I'm talking about the *new* owner.'

'That's me,' said Thea, getting a bit frustrated and annoyed with the confused reporter.

The reporter stared at her. 'Well, this is all rather strange. I've done my research on the bookshop and, according to the official paperwork, it's not you but the guy, Callum, who owns the shop.'

'You're mistaken.'

'I think not. I got hold a copy of the title deeds of the shop from HM Land Registry through the government website. Callum's name is on it in black and white – his *real* name, not his stage name.'

Thea hadn't realised he had a stage name. But that was beside the point. She suddenly felt sick. 'I don't understand …'

The reporter opened her handbag, had a rummage, and said, 'Ah, here we are.' She handed Thea a copy of the paperwork.

'Oh, look, there he is now!'

Thea turned around and looked at the crowd of people gathered outside the bookshop. She spotted Callum heading her way, grinning.

He waved. As he joined them outside the shop, he said, 'This turnout is amazing – isn't it?'

Thea still had the form in her hand, although she hadn't had a chance to look at it. 'Where were you?' She noticed he had something behind his back.

'I was just in The Potting Shed.' Callum revealed a bouquet of flowers, holding them out to Thea.

The reporter said, 'Oh, how wonderful, giving your employee flowers to thank her for all her hard work.'

Callum looked at the flowers, and turned to the young woman standing beside Thea. 'I'm sorry, who are you?'

'I'm Clarissa, a journalist for a local newspaper. I'm writing an article about The Bookshop of Memories.'

Thea glanced at the copy of the title deeds in her hand, and said, 'Tell me it isn't true.'

Callum's head turned to Thea. 'I'm sorry – what?'

'The bookshop.' Thea held up the paperwork. 'Do you own it?' The words caught in her throat. She couldn't bear to look at it, to see his name in black and white on the deeds.

Callum took the copy of the title deeds, his eyes wide. 'Where did you get this?'

Thea caught his expression. 'Oh, my god. It is true!'

Clarissa looked at them bemused. 'I'm sorry – did I miss something?'

Thea and Callum both turned to Clarissa at the same time, and said, 'Shut up!'

Callum reached for Thea's hand. 'I can explain …'

'This is *your* bookshop.' She stared at him, having a very hard time getting her head around this revelation. She still thought it couldn't be true.

'I was going to tell you after tonight – I swear. Look, after the opening night has finished, I'm going back to Scotland. You have to come with me.'

'You're going back to Scotland? Oh, my god, you were only down here to prepare the bookshop to sell. I've been such fool.'

'No, you haven't.' Callum furiously shook his head. 'Please, you must come back with me. There's someone—'

'Let go of my hand! I don't want to go anywhere with you!'

'Thea!' Callum watched helplessly as she disappeared into the crowd of people in the yard.

57

'Where's Thea? Did you find her? Did you give her the train ticket?' Callum shifted his gaze from Mabel to look around the train station. He desperately wanted her to come with him so he could take her to see her father. He imagined that she hated him right now, knowing that he owned the bookshop. Worse still, his heart was broken over the fact that he'd deceived her, and as siblings they could never be together. It didn't take him long to scan the small railway station in Saxmundham, the nearest train station to Aldeburgh, and realise she was not there.

Mabel shook her head. 'I'm sorry, Callum.' She asked, 'Did you check your DNA results?'

'Oh, Mabel, how could you bring that up now?'

'Because …' She swallowed. 'I'm a match with Thea. It was true, Henry is my brother.'

'Well, good for you.' Callum looked at her and sighed. 'Sorry, I'm acting like a jerk.'

'It's all right. The thing is, Callum, you didn't turn up as a match with me on the database. You did submit a test, didn't you?'

Callum rolled his eyes. 'Of course I did. Ray can vouch for me. I did it.'

'But don't you see? If you're not related to me, then—'

Callum was distracted. He was still looking around the train platform, hoping she'd turn up. 'What are you saying, Mabel?'

'I'm saying that I'm related to Thea, but not to you, which means—'

Now, Mabel had his attention. She said, 'Thea is not your sister.'

Callum stared at her.

Mabel said quietly, 'It also means that Henry isn't your father.'

Callum swallowed. 'No, that can't be right.' He regarded Mabel for a long moment as the truth sunk in. 'Then who is my father?' Despite everything, he managed a smile. 'And don't mention Douglas, for god's sake. I have never been and never will be the descendant of a Scottish laird. I mean, can you imagine if it were true? I played a laird on my show. It's just ridiculous.' He shook his head, dismissing the possibility. 'But seriously, where do I go from here?' It wasn't just his biological father he was thinking about. How did he get Thea, the love of his life, back?

She's not my sister!

He knew he should be jumping for joy at finding out the incredible truth. If it wasn't for Mabel making him take a DNA test, all because she was convinced he was not related to Henry and might be a descendant of Douglas, he might have never known.

'I'd suggest contacting Ray.'

'Hmm, Ray. Good idea.'

'But actually, in your case, you don't need to do that.'

'How come? He finds long-lost relatives, doesn't he?'

'Yes, but you don't need Ray. All you have to do is ask your mum.'

Callum stared at Mabel. 'Right, I'm going home.'

Mabel looked at the ticket in her hand. 'Do you want some company while you wait for the train?'

Callum smiled, and held out the crook of his arm. 'Yes, why not.'

They got some strange looks as they walked along the platform, arm in arm, but neither of them cared. Mabel glanced at Callum and imagined just for one glorious moment that she was seventeen again, and she had got that note from Douglas, and had met him at the train station. How would her life have turned out if her sister had given her the note from Douglas telling her about the change of plan? Perhaps she would have lived in a Scottish castle. Or maybe her sister had been right, and he'd only said that to impress her.

Mabel looked up at Callum as they waited together for the train to pull into the station. It would take him to London, from where he'd catch the sleeper train to Scotland. Oh, how she wished she could accompany him! But Mabel knew she was far too old for such a long journey, and besides, she wouldn't have had time to pack a suitcase for the trip.

Mabel was there to see him off. Her taxi was waiting outside the station to take her back to Aldeburgh.

Callum had entrusted her with a note, along with Thea's train ticket, asking Thea to meet him at the station. Meanwhile, Callum had had to take the cat and the campervan to his friends, Beth and Jack, to look after while he was gone.

Mabel thought of her sister, Marjorie, whom she'd implored to try and help her find Thea. When she'd told Marjorie about the note and the train ticket that Callum had entrusted to her, her sister had broken down and had revealed a terrible secret she'd harboured for many years – something truly awful she'd done. She hadn't given Mabel the note from Douglas about the rendezvous.

Marjorie had even visited the bookshop back when Thea had first arrived, saying she too wanted to introduce herself to Thea, and perhaps find a book. Mabel recalled minding the fort while Marjorie had nipped across the yard. But she hadn't been there to find a book; she had been looking for a note – the one from Douglas, which she'd hidden in an obscure book. Miraculously, she had found it.

Mabel had the book, and the old note from Douglas, in her handbag. She'd treasure it; of course she would. But as she'd told her sister, she'd married a lovely man, and had wonderful children and grandchildren. She had no regrets. And she didn't want her sister to have any regrets either. All was forgiven. But that didn't mean she hadn't always wondered what had happened to her first love, Douglas.

Mabel clutched Callum's arm as they stood waiting for the train. He was the spitting image of Douglas – even Marjorie had said so. She stared at him.

He turned his head to look at her and smiled.

Callum even had Douglas's smile. She thought of the journey he was about to make, in search of his real father. Was he a descendant of Douglas?

Mabel smiled up at him, thinking, *Anything is possible.*

58

'Mabel?'

Mabel turned and looked at her sister, who had joined her in the charity shop window. Mabel sighed. 'He's back again.'

Marjorie looked over at the bookshop. 'What a silly cat. When will Dickens get the message that the bookshop is closed again, and won't be reopening any time soon?'

'If ever,' said Mabel sadly.

Her sister looked at her and nodded. 'It's so sad.'

They both turned to look at the bookshop. The new blinds that a local shop had donated for the grand reopening were pulled down, the bookshop all closed up. The only visitors were Lili, who walked over there every day and watered the potted plants and hanging baskets outside, and of course the black and white cat now sitting outside the shop, meowing at the door.

'He can meow until the cows come home,' commented Marjorie, turning from the window. 'But it's not going to change a thing.'

Mabel looked at her sister. 'I'm sick and tired of people coming into the charity shop just to inquire when the bookshop will be open again.'

'I know. When will everyone get the message that The Bookshop of Memories is just that; an abandoned old bookshop just full of memories of what was.'

'And what will never be,' Mabel added.

Marjorie looked at her sister. She didn't have to ask her who she was thinking of; a young couple whose paths had briefly crossed in the bookshop – Callum and Thea.

Mabel heaved a sigh. She was about to turn from the window when she spotted two people entering the yard. The window was open. She heard them as they passed by. 'Are you sure this is the place? I left my taxi idling at the kerb outside. I don't want to leave you here if you're not sure. Sorry, but you seem a bit confused.'

The old man turned to look at the taxi driver. That was when Mabel saw his face. 'Marj. Marjorie!'

'What is it? What's the matter?'

'Come quick!'

Mabel returned her gaze to the man passing her window and overheard him say to the taxi driver, 'I'm not confused anymore. I'm exactly where I need to be. I'm back where I belong.'

'Well, if you're sure.'

Marjorie joined her sister in the window again. They both watched the old man walk up to the bookshop. Before he'd even got to the front door, Dickens darted over and started circling his legs.

'Who is that?' Marjorie asked. 'We'll have to go and tell him that the bookshop is closed.'

Just as she was saying that, the old man got something out of his pocket and put it in the door.

Marjorie gave her sister a surprised glance. 'Has he got a key to the bookshop?'

Mabel smiled.

Marjorie studied her face. 'What are you smiling about? Is there something you're not telling me?'

Mabel watched him step into the shop. 'Remember I said to you that we must go to Scotland and visit Henry? I knew it would be a very long, arduous trip at our age, but I desperately wanted to see him again. And I know you want to finally meet him too after all these years.'

'What about Thea? She doesn't know yet, does she?'

'I wrote her a letter. I assumed she'd be in touch by now, wanting to see her father too.'

Marjorie was just nodding her head, staring at her sister, when she happened to glance back out of the window. She caught Dickens walking into the shop behind the old man. 'What the—?'

Mabel saw it too. She smiled. 'So, as it happens none of us have to travel all the way to Scotland to see him. I think I'll write Thea another letter telling her the incredible news.'

Mabel had told Lili in The Potting Shed about the first letter she'd sent Thea, telling her that Henry was alive. She imagined that if Thea did not open her letter then at least she might hear the news from Lili or Callum's best friends, Beth and Jack.

However, Mabel decided that until Thea had been in touch, she would keep the news in the family, and wasn't going to tell another living soul what she had just witnessed. She told her sister the plan.

Marjorie wasn't listening. Her focus was on the shop door closing, and the sign in the window being flipped to *Open*.

59

Thea sat on the sofa, staring at the clock on the wall. For some reason that she couldn't fathom, this morning she had no interest in going into work. She'd been back in London for a month, and had got on with it, trying really hard to put Aldeburgh, the bookshop and Callum behind her. It wasn't proving easy. And then, the previous night, her world had been turned upside down again when her sister had phoned her to tell her that their flight was the next day. They were all leaving England. She'd known it was coming, but she'd said to her sister, 'So soon? I thought it would be months away to get everything organised.'

Thea picked up a tissue and wiped her nose. 'I really don't feel like going into work today.'

Winston whined.

She stroked his head. He lay sprawled along the sofa, his head on her lap. 'Well, at least you're not going anywhere.'

Winston licked her hand.

'Aren't you a good boy?' Thea had worried how he'd get on, moving from her sister's rambling cottage and garden in the Suffolk countryside to a small cramped flat in Pimlico. It wasn't ideal, but Thea just couldn't bear the thought of him being rehomed.

He was part of the family. They couldn't hand him over to strangers. And so she had taken him home with her before she'd thought through the practicalities. What would he do all day in a little flat when she was at work?

She had persuaded Edward to let Winston come to work with her. He'd been no trouble, lying in a dog bed under her desk. She took him for walks in Russell Square Gardens at lunch time. She wasn't surprised he was now well-behaved; the doggy training classes she'd been taking him to had paid off. So far, things were working out – as much as they could, considering …

Her mind kept wandering back to the bookshop. She knew it was all shut up. Nobody was there. The new owner certainly wasn't.

She realised she was feeling sorry for herself. Just as she'd heard no more from Miles, she'd heard nothing from Callum, apart from an official letter from a solicitor in Scotland enclosing the deeds of the shop in her name.

There was no note, no letter from Callum with an explanation. She looked at the other letter that had come in the post that morning. It was from Mabel – again. She'd written two letters now, neither of which Thea had opened. She knew they were from her because she'd written her name and return address on the back of the envelopes.

Thea didn't have the heart to open them. She knew what they were about – the sisters wanted her to come back. She imagined Callum had told Mabel and Marjorie that he'd given the bookshop to her, and she knew that if she opened those letters, they would pull at her heart strings when they mentioned the abandoned bookshop.

But she couldn't go back there. Didn't they understand? She was in love with Callum, but the bookshop was full of memories of their time together, the man she loved, the man who had deceived her, betrayed her. He was just like Miles.

Did he think giving her the bookshop could make up for that? He'd made a fool out her, leading her on, letting her believe her family still owned the bookshop and she was doing it up for her sister. It was no wonder he had been in the library, researching the history of the shop, seeing how it had come about that her still had the keys.

The question remained, though: how had it come about that Callum owned the bookshop? He'd never spoken much about his past.

She looked at Mabel's letters. 'I should write back to Mabel and tell her that I'm never coming back,' she told Winston. 'Then maybe she'll stop writing.'

Thea heard a knock on her door. That was Gracie, expecting her to be ready to get the bus to work as usual. Thea left Winston on the sofa and walked over to the door. When she opened it, Gracie looked her up and down. 'Is everything all right?' she said, her voice full of concern when she saw that Thea wasn't dressed for work.

Thea looked down at her old jogging bottoms and baggy sweatshirt. She hadn't told Gracie everything about her stay in Aldeburgh. She'd told her about her sister moving abroad, but she hadn't mentioned Callum.

'I just got a call from my sister. They're going away today.'

'Oh, Thea.'

'I don't feel like going into work.'

'I understand. Shall I let Edward know you won't be in?'

Thea shook her head. 'It's okay. I'll phone him.'

'All right.' Gracie was about to leave, when she said, 'I don't want to bother you with work stuff, but I've been doing some auditing, and I can't find some of the artefacts – a journal and a few rare books that were in the database.'

For some reason, Thea thought of the occasion, which seemed like a lifetime ago, when she'd taken Miles to show him her place of work late one evening and had discovered Edward in the archives. It had been a bit of a shock to find someone else in the bowels of the museum that late at night. And all rather odd. Edward had said he was doing some overtime, but no one ever stayed after work and did overtime.

Gracie said, 'I'm sure it's nothing. One of us probably misfiled those items somewhere, or entered their whereabouts incorrectly in the database.'

Thea stared at her. 'Yeah, it's probably nothing.'

'Are you sure you don't want me to let Edward know you won't be in today when I arrive at work?'

'No, I'd like to speak to him.'

'Suit yourself.' Gracie smiled warmly at her. 'It's lovely that you're back. I was missing my downstairs neighbour.'

Thea returned her smile. 'I've missed you too.' She was just closing her door, when Gracie said, 'Nothing else happened while you were away – did it?'

Thea looked at her. The trouble with Gracie was that they'd known each other far too long. It was very, very difficult not to lie. 'I met someone.'

'You did? Well that's wonderful—' Gracie must have caught her expression. She halted.

'It's not wonderful.' Thea tried to keep her emotions in check. 'I don't want to talk about it. It didn't work out, just like all my relationships.'

'I'm sorry, Thea.'

'So am I. Look, I'd better go and phone Edward.'

'Will you be okay, here on your own today?'

'I'm not on my own.'

Gracie glanced at Winston as Thea shut the door.

Thea stood there for a moment with Winston by her side, wagging his tail. 'Walkies?' She smiled at Winston's reaction as he ran around in a circle in excitement. She reached for the vase on the side table in the hall, picking it up just in time before his tail knocked it off. Thea had dog-proofed the flat as much as possible. She'd forgotten about the vase.

Winston disappeared into the lounge, returned with his lead and dropped it at her feet.

'Good boy! But first I've got something to do.' Thea took a seat on the sofa and phoned Edward's home number. He wouldn't be at work yet. He answered on the second ring.

Thea sat bolt upright when she heard that synthesised voice on the end of the line. She tentatively said, 'Edward – is that you?'

She heard a funny sound, like Edward was fiddling with his phone, then his normal voice saying, 'Ah – hello, Thea. I think there was some interference on the line a moment ago.'

Thea sat back on the sofa and narrowed her eyes. A few minutes later, she'd persuaded Edward to come round to her flat for a conversation about the synthesised voice. That wasn't all she intended to talk to him about. She didn't mention her mum's open boxes stored in Jenna's garage, and a package, in the shape of a book, that he'd arranged to buy from Jenna, who'd found it in her dad's bookshop. That was all going to wait until she could speak to him in person.

She also didn't mention the missing things from the archive

that Gracie had discovered. She was saving that until he arrived too.

Thea sat on the sofa, waiting for Edward to turn up. She didn't have to wait long. She opened her flat door and Edward slunk in, glancing at her sheepishly.

Uncharacteristically, Winston growled.

Thea looked at Winston in surprise.

Edward nervously side-stepped the dog. 'Do you mind shutting him in the kitchen? He's making me nervous.'

Thea looked at the dog and imagined that the feeling was mutual. She gave Winston breakfast and patted him on the head before she walked out of the kitchen and closed the door. In the lounge, she found Edward pacing up and down. He stopped and turned around when she walked in.

Thea folded her arms. 'Do you want to tell me what is going on?'

'No, not really.'

Thea waited. 'That wasn't really a question, Edward.'

Edward breathed a huge sigh and flopped down on the sofa. 'I've been a very bad boy.'

He spent the best part of the next fifteen minutes telling her everything, most of it spent pacing up and down. Eventually, he stopped by the lounge window overlooking the street outside. He looked at her sitting on the sofa. 'Aren't you going to say something?'

Thea regarded him for a long moment, still taking in what he'd just told him. She hadn't expected that what he'd been up to had been going on for decades. Thea slowly shook her head from side to side. 'Oh, Edward – why did you do it?'

It turned out that he'd been stealing rare books, papers and artefacts from the museum – the very things that had been entrusted into his care as a senior archivist. The worst part was that he'd dragged her father into it, enlisting his help to sell the stolen items.

'Did my dad know he was handling stolen items from museums and libraries?'

'Of course not. But I couldn't sell the items myself, because of my position; it would be too suspicious.'

'And you might be caught,' said Thea.

'Yes, more than likely.'

'But my dad could have been caught out? Didn't you think of that?'

'Yes, but he was renumerated very well.'

'That's not the point, Edward. He obviously didn't know what he was being renumerated very well for. You didn't give him the option to make that choice, to take that risk.'

'When he disappeared, I thought he'd been caught by the police, like a sting or something. I knew he travelled around the country selling them to wealthy collectors. I trawled the newspapers and watched the news on television avidly, but there was nothing about a man and a yellow camper … van.' Edward furrowed his brow. He had his back to Thea, looking out of the window.

'You weren't worried about my father.'

'I was. Of course I was,' said Edward, still looking out of the window.

'I bet you were more worried that if he got caught, they would trace the items back to you.'

'There was always that possibility,' said Edward, moving the net curtain aside.

Thea glared at him. 'Some friend you are.' Thea slowly shook her head from side to side. 'Oh, Edward, why did you do it? You love your job. You are dedicated, conscientious. This isn't you. I know it isn't.'

'My wife was sick. There was potentially a cure for her type of cancer in America. They were holding trials of a new drug, but it would cost a small fortune.'

'She survived,' said Thea. She knew that Frances hadn't died all those years ago. 'It worked.'

'It did. We had twenty-five wonderful years. Then, just a few months ago, we thought it had come back. You still can't get the drug on the NHS.'

Edward moved closer to the window. 'I had to find the money again. I knew when your father disappeared, I'd given him a couple of books to sell. I needed them back.'

'So, you were the one who went through Mum's boxes in the garage of Jenna's home?'

Edward turned around and looked at Thea. 'Yes, that was me. But she didn't have them.'

'So, you thought they were in the bookshop? Why didn't you just go and get them?'

'I didn't have the key, and it would look suspicious if there was a break-in. I did not want to get the police involved.'

'So, you got Jenna involved instead.'

'Yes. I was prepared to give her a commission. She had the key to the shop, and needed the money.'

'Then you could offer them to a private collector for a small fortune.'

Now Thea understood why Jenna hadn't wanted to talk about it, because it would have meant telling her that Edward, the man she looked up to, and respected, and who had been a father-figure to her while she was growing up, was a thief.

'You met her at the bookshop, didn't you?'

'Yes. I guessed they must still be in the bookshop. We had to meet when the other shops in Cobblers Yard were closed so we didn't arouse any suspicions by going into a shop that had been abandoned for years.'

Edward continued, 'There's a wealthy collector in Scotland who usually bought the items, but of course Henry always dealt with them. He'd travel up to Scotland to deliver the items in person, so they could inspect the condition of the books before committing their money. I needed a go-between to handle the sale, otherwise …'

'Like you said, they might get suspicious where you acquired these items if they discovered a museum archivist was trying to sell them.'

'Yes. Well, that was the plan, anyway, but Jenna backed out. Instead I handled the sale of the first book.'

Thea guessed why she'd backed out. She was pregnant. Why would she travel all the way up to Scotland?

'What about the second book?' Thea was thinking of the one wrapped in brown paper that Jenna mentioned she'd left in the shop.

'It took her time to find it in the bookshop. I told her what she needed to look for.'

'But if Jenna knew it was you, why the synthesised voice over the phone?'

'It was one thing meeting in the dead of night, at the bookshop, to hand over a book, but it was in case anyone was listening in. You never know with technology these days, so I thought it was prudent to disguise my voice over the phone.'

'But you rang her from your home phone number. There was no point disguising your voice – the police could simply look up phone records if it all came to light.'

'Oh.'

Thea sighed. 'Goodness, Edward – some criminal you are.'

'So, what are you going to do? Are you going to turn me in?'

'For loving your wife, and doing anything you could to save her?'

A wisp of a smile crossed Edward's face. 'When you put it like that …' He turned back to the window.

Thea frowned at him. She was trying to have a conversation with him. Why did he keep turning his back on her? 'Edward, what on earth is so interesting out that window?'

Edward scratched his head. 'The yellow campervan.'

'I'm sorry – what did you just say?' Thea jumped out of her seat and ran up to the window.

60

‘Oh, my god!’ said Thea when she spotted Jack and Beth peering out of the campervan at the house. They spotted her at the window and waved.

‘That’s Henry’s campervan,’ said Edward.

Thea frowned at him. ‘No, it’s not. And before you say anything, yes I know he had one similar.’

Edward turned to Thea wide-eyed. ‘I’m telling you – that is Henry’s van.’

‘No, it is not. It’s Callum’s van, all right?’

‘Who?’

‘Before you ask, it’s a long story, and I don’t want to talk about it.’ Thea had barely finished her sentence when she heard the doorbell. She rolled her eyes. She knew why they were there; to take her back to Aldeburgh. They were about to find out that they’d had a wasted trip. She was not going back.

Now she wished she’d opened Mabel’s letters and replied. Perhaps then word would have got back to Beth and Jack, and they wouldn’t have turned up in person.

Thea had a lump in her throat. When she’d first caught sight of the van, she’d thought it was Callum. Despite convincing herself that she never wanted to see him again, her heart had leapt.

But it wasn't.

Thea felt like hiding in her flat, pretending she wasn't there, but they'd seen her. *So, you can still hide in your flat and not answer the door.* Thea decided that was the plan.

'I want a closer look,' said Edward.

Before Thea could stop him, he was already out of the flat door and heading to the front door of the house. She caught up with him on the front steps.

'Thea!' Jack and Beth stepped aside as Edward barged passed them.

'Edward!' Thea called out. She shook her head.

Jack and Beth glanced over their shoulder at the stranger examining the van.

Thea said, 'Look, guys, it's really nice of you to come and see me, but—'

Jack and Beth exchanged a glance. Beth said, 'Have you read Mabel's letter?'

Thea looked at Beth. 'How did you know Mabel had written to me?'

Beth looked at her sheepishly. 'Mabel told Lili next door in The Potting Shed, who told me. So, have you read it?'

Thea pursed her lips. 'No, I haven't even opened them.'

'*Them*?' Beth looked at her. 'She sent you another one?'

'Yeah. I got it in the post today.' She looked at the van. 'Is Dickens with you?'

Edward overheard her. 'Dickens! Ah ha!' he exclaimed.

Jack and Beth turned around to look at Edward.

'Goodness me, I can't believe it, that old cat is still alive! He must be ancient, probably one of the oldest cats in, well, the world!'

Thea shook her head at Edward again and turned to Beth and Jack. 'That is Edward, my boss and good friend. He's a senior archivist at the museum. He's having a bit of a moment, because he thinks this is Henry's, my dad's, old campervan. He used to have one just like it. Edward and my dad were best friends.'

Jack and Beth stared at her.

Thea suddenly felt uncomfortable under their gaze. 'What is it?'

'I'm telling you,' said Edward, 'This is Henry's van, and Dickens was … is … his cat.'

Thea furrowed her brow, thinking of something her niece had said when she'd bunked off drama class and discovered them in the bookshop. She'd held up Dickens and thought she recognised the cat from an old childhood photo of Thea and her sister. Thea had dismissed that comment; didn't all black and white cats look alike? Although for the life of her, she could not remember the cat's name.

Edward was still over-excited at seeing the van, and wouldn't let it go. He ran back up to Thea. 'There is no doubt in my mind that this van belongs to Henry.'

'And I told you, it's Callum's.'

'Who?' he said again. 'Oh, never mind that. Look, there's one sure-fire way to know. Just look inside. You'll find you and your sisters initials carved on the wooden seat under the seat cushion. I'll never forget you girls doing that. Henry was quite displeased that you'd defaced his van, even though you'd been very thoughtful and did it where no one would really notice.

'I am not looking for initials carved anywhere,' said Thea.

Jack and Beth exchanged a glance before Beth said, 'You don't have to. I can categorically say, without a doubt, this is Henry's van.'

Thea did a double-take. 'I'm sorry, are you seriously having a joke over all this right now?'

Beth put her hand on Thea's arm. 'This is no joke. You really didn't read Mabel's letters, did you?'

'I told you I didn't.'

'You should have. So, nobody told you and your sister?'

'Told us what?'

'About Henry. Your father.'

'I don't understand …'

Beth offered her a reassuring smile. 'You will. Come with us.'

Thea backed away. 'I'm not going back to Aldeburgh with you.'

'Who said anything about Aldeburgh?' Beth replied. 'We're going to Scotland, and we want you to come with us.'

Thea frowned. 'First, Callum wanted me to come with him to Scotland, now you guys. I don't want to see him.'

'All right. Well, if you don't want to see Callum, what about seeing your father instead?'

'My father?' Thea looked from Beth to Jack. They were nodding their heads.

'Wait. Are you saying … he's still alive?'

'I knew it! I just knew it!' Edward slapped his knee and did a little happy dance right there in the street.

Thea said, 'Is that where he is – in Scotland?'

'Yes.'

Edward said, 'I'm coming too. He's my best friend. I want to see him.'

'But how did you find him?' Thea was having a hard time taking all this in. 'How do you even know about my father?'

'Thea, have you got some chocolate biscuits?' interrupted Fergus, looking out of the window of the camper van.

'Oh, er … sure. Wait right there, I'll go and fetch some.'

Thea dived back into her flat, grabbed her coat and bag, and then remembered the dog. 'Oh, crumbs. Winston!' She flung open the kitchen door. Winston had just scoffed his breakfast. She caught him with his jaws around a kitchen cupboard door handle, trying to get at the biscuits. The clever dog knew where they were stored. Thea had had to put child locks on her kitchen doors.

She walked over and put her fingers around his collar, prizing him away from the cupboard. 'Come on, you – we're going on a trip.' She grabbed his lead and the packet of chocolate biscuits for Fergus. Thea locked her flat door and walked out of the house. She looked at Winston and said, 'Is there room for one more?'

Edward frowned at the dog.

As they all piled in the campervan, Fergus promised his mother he did not need the loo before they set off again. They'd stopped at a service station just down the road, where they'd filled up the van with petrol.

Edward said, 'I can't wait to see Henry again.'

Thea was just taking a seat in the back of the van next to Fergus, with Jack and Beth in the front seats, when she overheard Jack say to Beth in a hushed whisper, 'It's little wonder that Callum didn't want to tell her about his mum.'

Beth turned in her seat and caught Thea staring at her. 'Oh, dear. You overheard that, didn't you?'

Thea eyed her. 'What exactly didn't he want to tell me about his mum?'

Beth sighed. 'I imagined that Mabel wrote about that in her letters.'

Thea had meant to collect them when she'd gone back inside, but had been distracted by Winston.

'I forgot their letters.'

'It doesn't matter,' said Jack. 'We can fill you in on what we know on the way. We've got plenty of time.'

'Will this even get us there?' Beth asked, looking around the old campervan.

'Well, it got Callum down to Aldeburgh from Scotland, and we arrived here, so let's hope so.'

Thea sat back in her seat as Jack pulled the van into the Monday morning traffic. He took a fleeting glance over his shoulder at Thea. 'Mabel told us about Callum and his mother. We've been seeing Mabel most days when she returns Dickens.'

'She returns Dickens – what do you mean?'

'Callum left the campervan with us, along with his cat – well, Henry's cat. Every day, Dickens disappeared from the farm. Turns out he must have been spending his days making his way back to the bookshop in Aldeburgh; it's not too far, but for an elderly cat, it must have been quite a trek across the fields. Each afternoon, when the charity shop closed, Mabel brought Dickens back to the farm. I couldn't understand how such an elderly cat could manage to walk that far every day, until I figured out that most days, the clever moggy hitched a ride, hiding in the van which I borrowed to deliver flowers to Lili in Cobblers Yard. He must have escaped each time when I wasn't looking, and hid until I left.'

It was pulling at Thea's heartstrings – the thought of the little cat sitting outside the bookshop each day, waiting in vain.

'You know, Callum grew up with Henry, thinking he was his father. He didn't go into too much detail, I'm afraid, concerning the visit to see his mother when he returned to Scotland after he'd discovered that Henry was not his biological father.'

Thea remembered Mabel and Callum taking DNA tests.

Beth looked at Jack, and added, 'When you met Callum, Henry had sent him back to Suffolk with the campervan and a photo of the two of you as children. We guess it was the last photo Henry had of you girls before he … disappeared.'

'So, you're saying Callum thought he was my brother?'

'He realised you were Henry's daughter, and assumed that you were his second family, and that he'd been living between two families.'

'Had he?' Thea swallowed. That would make her father a bigamist. She couldn't believe what she was hearing. It can't be true.

'It's a little more complicated than that.'

'How so?' Thea hoped there was some other explanation.

Edward piped up, 'But Henry loved their mum to bits. It's just not possible he had another wife. Honestly, Henry didn't have it in him. He doesn't have a crooked bone in his body.'

Jack exchanged a glance with Beth. 'Mabel told me that when Callum returned to Scotland, he had it out with his mum because he found out from the DNA test that Henry wasn't his father, and you weren't his sister after all. You see, that was the problem. He thought you were his sister, and he didn't know how to tell you about Henry.'

'That's why he wanted me to come to Scotland, to see my dad.'

'That's right. Apparently, when he confronted his mum, she told him who his real father was.'

Thea slowly shook her head. This was the last thing she'd expected Beth and Mark to turn up and tell her. She didn't bother asking who Callum's real father was. She didn't care. Callum's past didn't concern her.

What she was concerned about was her own father. Something didn't make sense. 'I still don't understand why my dad just disappeared from our lives like that. We were a happy family. He loved us. Why would he do that to us?'

'He didn't,' said Beth, turning in the front seat to look at her.

'But that's not true.' Thea frowned. 'You just said—'

'It wasn't intentional – is what I meant,' said Beth. 'It wasn't a choice.'

'How can you say that? He had another woman – a wife, I assume. Callum's mum.'

Jack cut in. 'Henry had an accident in his van years ago, up in Scotland, which explains—'

'Why he disappeared one day,' said Edward, listening from the back seat.

'Are you saying that he had amnesia, he lost his memory?' asked Thea.

'That's right.'

Beth took up the story. 'Over some years, he'd been visiting Callum's father to sell him rare books. Having young children of his own, he'd grown fond of Callum over the course of these visits. That's what Callum's mother said. When she left Callum's father, Henry stayed in touch with her, and visited when he could, helping out the single parent and her young son.'

Edward interrupted, 'That sounds just like something Henry would do.'

Thea glanced at Edward before returning her attention to Beth.

Beth had turned around in the front seat while she spoke to Thea.

Thea said, 'Go on.'

Beth sighed. 'I'm afraid that one day Henry had an accident in his van.'

'While he was on the road, visiting them?'

'That's right.'

'So, he ended up living with Callum and had no memory of us? Is that what you're saying?'

'Yes.'

'But his memory came back.' Thea was aware that she was stating the obvious.

She noticed Jack and Beth exchange a glance again before Beth replied, 'Yeah, I suppose you could say that.'

Thea wanted to know why, if his memory had returned, he hadn't got in touch. And there was something else bothering her. 'If that was the case, and he knew Callum wasn't his son, why would he give him the bookshop, and give just this old campervan to me and my sister?'

'That's the question Callum grappled with. He was in pieces over how to tell you all this. Had been the whole time, especially when he was falling in love with you, but mistakenly thought that you and he could never be together.'

'But we can now.'

'He thinks you'll never forgive him.'

'Well, he's right,' Thea said petulantly, not sure if she was more upset with him for not telling her the truth about her father, or for the fact that he'd got to spend time with Henry growing up that she and her sister had been robbed of.

Jack said, 'I told him to tell you about Henry straight away, but he didn't. I could understand. It meant telling you that your father had been alive this whole time and living with someone else; living with his mother. But now he's paid the ultimate price – he's lost you, the love of his life.'

Beth turned in her seat to look at Thea. 'You can see that all this isn't his fault, right? Do you think you can find it in your heart to forgive him?'

Thea glanced at Edward. Everyone deserved a second chance – didn't they? Especially if their heart had been in the right place, even though they'd done the wrong thing.

'Do you want to see him, your father?' asked Beth.

Thea nodded. 'I do.'

61

'Gone – what do you mean *gone*?'

'I'm afraid Henry absconded from the care home, in a taxi.'

Jack turned to Thea. They were standing in the entrance hall of the care home, at reception. 'Don't worry. I know where he went.'

'But what was my father doing here?'

'That was the other thing that I'm afraid Callum was going to have a hard time telling you …'

❖

An hour later, they turned down a long drive winding through incredible Scottish scenery into a private estate. Thea was still trying to come to terms with the news of her father's early onset dementia. Her sadness at finding out this fact was tempered by a theory of Callum's that Jack had told her about. Callum had wondered whether Henry was remembering his life before the accident because of his condition; maybe those old memories about his past life had resurfaced as the fog of dementia closed in on the present.

Thea noticed a large sign reading *Private Property*. She whispered, 'Did you take a wrong turn?'

Jack glanced at Beth. 'No.'

Beth said, 'It's so much bigger, grander than I ever imagined.'

'But where are we?' asked Thea as Jack drove the van along a deserted, winding single-track road through a pine forest.

'It brings to mind that family curse, though,' said Jack.

Thea frowned. 'What are you talking about?'

'Doesn't it?' said Beth, looking at her husband. 'It's so bleak and cold.'

'And quite austere,' added Edward, shivering.

Thea didn't feel that way about the beautiful Scottish scenery, although she realised they were referring to the huge, rambling grey stone house with its turrets and gables that had come into view at the end of the road. There was no denying that the scenery surrounding the house was stunning, but the huge house at the end of the drive sent shivers down her spine.

'I don't like the creepy house,' said Fergus.

'Neither do I,' commented Thea. 'Would you like a chocolate biscuit?'

He nodded. 'Yes please.'

'Me too,' said Edward.

Once they'd arrived in front of the house, everyone helped themselves to a nice, comforting chocolate digestive. It reminded Thea of the large country estates and houses that she sometimes visited in England belonging to The National Trust. Except this place, apart from the scenery, didn't feel welcoming. She said, 'What is this place?'

Jack switched of the engine and turned around in his seat. 'This is Callum's ancestral home.'

Thea stared at the house.

'Turns out he is a laird – for real! Talk about life imitating art.'

Jack shook his head.

'The family curse,' Beth breathed.

Once again, Thea asked, 'What are you talking about?'

'Mabel went with Callum to the train station to see him off before he left for Scotland. She tried to find you, but you must have jumped on a train and returned to London.'

Thea kept her mouth shut. That wasn't exactly what had happened. Mabel must have kept that to herself, to save Callum more heartbreak. Mabel *had* found her. She'd tried to give her the train ticket, telling Thea that she had to go with Callum to Scotland.

Thea had asked her why, but all she'd said was that Callum had something so, so important to tell her. Now Thea knew what that *something* was. She cringed when she thought back to that short, sharp conversation …

'You have to go with him,' Mabel had insisted.

Thea had yelled at her, 'I'm not going anywhere with him. I don't believe a word that comes out of that man's mouth. I'm returning to London to the job I love and the friends I can trust.'

'But you love the bookshop. You love Callum.'

Thea remembered the tears as she turned away, rushing out of Cobblers Yard to the waiting taxi, her world feeling as though it had fallen apart around her.

Jack said, 'We're worried about him, Thea – the thought that this is his future, living here in this place all alone. We're afraid he'll die here of a broken heart, like Douglas.'

'Douglas?'

'Yes, Douglas was his grandfather. He had a son, Duncan. Turns out that although Douglas married, his heart belonged to another. He was pining over his lost love – Mabel.

'Mabel?' said Thea in surprise. 'Mabel from the charity shop?'

Beth nodded. 'That's what Callum told us. It's a small world, isn't it?'

Thea stared at her. 'It certainly is.'

'It's so sad to hear that Callum's father, Duncan, grew up here, just him and his broken-hearted father, Douglas.' Beth shook her head, remembering what Callum had told them on the phone from Scotland when he'd found out his family history. 'You see, the woman Douglas did marry died in childbirth. It sounded like a very lonely life for Duncan with a distant father, growing up with a succession of nannies, and then eventually being sent away to boarding school.'

'How did Callum's father and mother meet?' Thea asked.

Beth said, 'It sounds as though Moira, that's her name, went to work as a secretary on the estate, and obviously thought that she had done pretty well for herself, marrying Duncan, a laird. However, the marriage didn't last long. The honeymoon period was soon over when she found herself a virtual prisoner, along with her infant son, Callum, and soon dreamt of an escape from a possessive, reclusive husband who was unfortunately an alcoholic – and not a very nice man, by the sounds of it, when he was drunk.' Beth had lowered her voice, whispering to Thea as she leaned forward in her seat, out of earshot of Fergus.

'How did she escape?' Thea asked.

Beth and Jack exchanged a glance before she continued. 'Moira found her escape route in the form of a bookseller who often visited her husband, selling him rare books.'

'Henry.' Thea narrowed her eyes. 'I see.'

Beth caught her expression. 'There wasn't anything going on between Moira and Henry when he came here to sell books, although when Callum talked to Moira about it recently, she did tell Callum that she was always drawn to the kind, thoughtful man, and used to look forward to his visits when he travelled from his bookshop in Suffolk to deliver the rare books. Over the course of those visits, he grew attached to her son, Callum, and agreed to help them flee. They escaped to Edinburgh, where she changed her and her son's surname by deed poll.'

'To Cavendish,' said Thea, thinking of Henry's surname.

Jack said, 'Yes – unbeknown to Henry, who was still living with your family in Suffolk at this point. It was obviously a conceit because they were never married.'

At least that's something, thought Thea.

Beth added, 'Callum's mum was afraid that if she didn't take Callum and disappear when she had the opportunity, then she'd be forced to leave him behind in this big old place, and history would repeat itself – he'd grow up a very lonely little boy with a distant father.'

Thea stared at the house. 'What are we going to do?'

Beth turned in her seat and looked at Thea. 'It's not what *we're* going to do, Thea. It's what *you're* going to do.'

Thea stared at Beth. She didn't have to say it. Although they were all there to rescue Callum from a lonely life in his Scottish castle, it was only Thea who could really do that. She needed to forgive Callum, and tell him the truth – she was in love with him, and wanted him back.

Thea got out of the van. She stepped on to the gravel drive and walked up to the huge wooden door. She turned around and looked at the occupants of the van. Jack, Beth, Edward, and even little Fergus were waving their hands, egging her on to pick up that big brass knocker and knock on that door. Winston barked.

It felt like she waited an age after knocking on the door, but slowly, the heavy door opened. Callum, dishevelled and sporting stubble, his once short blond hair looking as though it needed a cut, appeared. He looked her up and down, clearly shocked to see her. 'Thea?'

Thea stepped forward and flung her arms around his neck.

He tentatively put his arms around her, and started to cry into her shoulder.

Thea was crying too, but she knew that both of them were crying tears of joy. 'I love you, Callum.' When they'd finished hugging each other tightly, afraid to let go, Thea stepped back and grabbed his hand.

A moment later, Thea was pushing him into the van. Winston wasn't making it easy. His tail was thumping furiously as he jumped all over Callum, who took a seat in between Edward and Fergus. Winston licked his face and tried to get on his lap. Thea said, 'Quick, let's get out of here!'

Callum turned to look at her wide-eyed.

'What?'

'I just remembered something from my childhood.'

❖

Callum thought back to recent events as everyone got themselves settled for the journey. What Callum had remembered from his childhood was leaving this place, being bundled into the back of a van just like this one when he was a small child. The memory aligned perfectly with what his mother had told him had happened, and how it had come to be that he, his mother, and Henry had lived together as a family.

When Callum had left Mabel at the train station and returned to Scotland, the first thing he had done was to turn up at his mother's house to confront her. Unsurprisingly, she'd broken down, unprepared for the fact that he'd discovered the truth, but incredibly relieved that the secret she'd kept from him for so many years was finally out in the open.

She'd told him about the day she'd finally summoned the courage to leave her loveless marriage and take her five-year-old child with her. She had known that if she didn't do it covertly, her husband might not be able to stop her from leaving, but he would prevent her from taking their child with her.

It had turned out that her ticket out of there, that place in the middle of nowhere, had been in the shape of a yellow VW campervan and a man called Henry, a collector of rare books, who often visited her husband. She told Callum that she'd always looked forward Henry's visits. He was kind, and caring. And it wasn't long before she was falling in love with a married man.

Of course, she had known they could never be together – he loved his wife so very much – but would he help her, and her son, escape the place? And so, one blustery October day, Callum had been bundled into the back of this very van, two suitcases next to him on the back seat, and they'd sped away down this drive, never to return.

Callum looked out of the window at the house as Thea pulled the van door closed. That was the last time he'd set eyes on the place until his mother had told him who his father was, and that his real surname was MacFadden. Callum had swiftly returned to meet his father here. It turned out that he'd given up the bottle years earlier when his wife and child had disappeared, realising his behaviour had been abhorrent. He had stayed sober from that day forward, knowing it was his only chance of getting them back. He'd spent years looking for them, but to no avail.

Callum's mother told him that Henry, ever the gentleman, had helped her find somewhere to live – the council house in Edinburgh where Callum had grown up – and had visited often in the first few years while on his travels. In those early years in Edinburgh, when Callum had asked after his father, she'd lied to him, and told him it was Henry. And for some reason, in their house, in those early years Callum never called Henry *Dad*. He had always just been Henry. His mother had told her neighbours that her husband was a travelling book salesman.

Then, one day, fate had stepped in – in the form of a boy racer at the end of their street, who'd driven straight into Henry's van as he turned out of their cul de sac after one of his visits. She'd heard the almighty crash at the bottom of their street, and, along with the other neighbours, had gone running out to see what had happened. She accompanied Henry to hospital, and the doctors had told her she could stay with her husband overnight if she wished. Thankfully a neighbour had looked after Callum while she was at the hospital.

And so the lie had begun, and it continued through a quirk of fate – as a result of a head injury, Henry had lost his memory. The doctors said he'd regain it bit by bit, with the help of his nearest and dearest – his wife and children. Except that Henry's wife and children were hundreds of miles away in Suffolk and had no clue about the accident.

The woman sitting at his hospital bedside, and who took him home with her to live as if he were her husband, was going to spend the next twenty-five years worried he would remember his other family. She knew that if or when that happened, he'd never forgive her. She knew she must do everything in her power to convince him that the head injury had muddled his memories. After all, she had photos of the three of them from birthdays over the years, and from the weeks leading up to Christmas each year, when he'd always popped in on his travels. Henry never realised that those old photos, which appeared to depict a happy family of three, did not show the truth.

Callum recalled her words. *I did love him, Callum. And I still do. I didn't want to be alone. Can you ever forgive me?* When she'd asked that of him, Callum's immediate reaction had been *How can I?* She'd stolen someone else's husband, and two children's father. Now he also knew that she hadn't supported his choice of career all because she was trying to keep her secret. And then he realised it wasn't just his career in the limelight that had been a problem; as Callum had grown older, he had begun to look more and more like his father, the man she hated – the Scottish laird. It was little wonder she hadn't wanted to see her own son and had discouraged his visits home. Callum knew it was more than that; his face might stir a memory in Henry of the laird and of the house he'd once visited regularly.

'I knew if I told Henry the truth, about his other family, I'd lose him, Callum. And as much as it broke my heart that I was lying to him, I just couldn't risk it.'

When she'd said that, of course Callum had thought of Thea. Despite everything, he'd empathised with his mother's predicament. He'd found himself in similar circumstances, knowing that if he told Thea he'd been deceiving her, he'd lose her.

And then his mother had said, 'Henry got ill with early onset dementia, which they presume was as a result of the head injury he'd suffered. I'm ashamed to say I was utterly relieved that all my fears of him remembering his past life were over. That's how it was to begin with, but as things progressed, to my utter astonishment, the memories of his past life started flooding back. After so many years, it was the last thing I expected to happen. Trying to convince him those people didn't exist and were all in his imagination just made him agitated, and so hard to live with, and that's when I had to send him to that home.'

Callum did wonder why she'd put his father in the home when he wasn't really a danger to himself or her, and the disease had not advanced to the point where he needed constant care. It had always baffled him, and he had thought she'd just wanted to get rid of him from under her feet so that she had the house to herself, and could spend time with her friends. Now, he knew the truth.

'Right let's go!' Jack said, interrupting Callum's thoughts.

Beth said, 'We passed a hotel not far from here with vacancies, according to the sign.'

Jack glanced at his wife. 'Good idea. It's getting late and we need to find somewhere to have an evening meal and get Fergus to bed. Then we can do the drive home tomorrow. Let's hope they've got enough free rooms for us all.'

Jack already had the engine running. He was just putting the van into gear when Edward exclaimed, 'Wait! What about Henry?'

Callum looked at him. 'Who are you?'

'I'm Edward, Henry's best friend.'

Somehow they managed to shake hands in the cramped confines of the back of the van. Callum said, 'Now, what about Henry?'

Edward said, 'Isn't he here?'

Callum frowned. 'Why do you think he's here?'

Jack said, 'Because we took Thea to see her father in the care home, and they said he'd absconded, in a taxi. We thought he'd come here to see you, Callum.'

Callum shook his head, looking worried. 'He's definitely not here.'

Thea said, 'So, where would he have gone?'

For the first time since she'd seen him, Thea saw him smile. 'He went home.'

'To your mother?'

Callum took Thea's hand. 'No, Thea. He went home.'

'So, after our stop-over tonight, where to?' Jack asked.

Thea stared at Callum. He nodded and continued smiling. She turned to Jack, and said, 'Take us home to The Bookshop of Memories.'

Epilogue

Thea watched her father, who was talking to a customer. He was putting a book they'd just bought into a small paper bag emblazoned with the words *The Bookshop of Memories.*

She left him at the counter and walked over to sit down on the couch, taking a break with a cup of tea. She recalled the surprising discovery little Fergus had made on their journey back there in the campervan from Scotland.

Beth had told her son not to touch anything, but curious little fingers had found a secret compartment in the van, and the mystery of why her father had wanted Thea and her sister to have his old campervan had been solved – along with the reason Callum's mother had been desperate for Callum to return the van to her.

Henry hadn't wanted Thea and Jenna to have the van for sentimental reasons. It had never been about the van, but what was *in* the van; something Moira had discovered too.

Over the years, Henry had been using the campervan as his own personal piggy bank, squirrelling away a lot of cash from the sales of his books. It turned out that Callum needn't have felt guilty over the fact that Henry had given the bookshop to him rather than his girls. What Henry had left them more than compensated for the loss of their inheritance. Thea knew why her father had been saving up for so many years, even when he lost his memory and no longer remembered – it was the promise he'd made their mother to buy her a cottage. Callum wasn't best pleased when he realised where the money had come from to do up his mum's house, but she had also used some of it to fund Henry's place in a lovely care home. There was still enough money left in that hidden compartment for when Thea's mum found the cottage where she wanted to live out her days.

Thea smiled at her dad and got out her mobile phone. She had a phone call to make. A few moments later, when she'd got off the phone with Gracie, Callum came over and joined her on the sofa. 'I heard you on the phone. Everything okay?'

'Oh, yes. All thanks to you.'

Callum grinned. 'Okay, I'll take the credit, even though I have no idea what you're talking about.'

'I'm talking about Edward.'

'Ah. Is that who you were on the phone with?'

Thea shook her head. 'No, I phoned Gracie for a catch-up.'

'Just for a catch-up?' Callum lifted an inquiring eyebrow guessing that wasn't the only reason she'd called.

'Oh, all right, it was an excuse to check that our plan has worked.'

'And has it?'

'Oh, yes. Nobody is any the wiser. Gracie apologised for bothering me with work stuff that day I didn't go into work – the day she said she'd discovered some inconsistencies, stuff missing, during an audit. She told me that she'd found the missing items, and that Edward had admitted he'd logged their whereabouts in the database incorrectly. Gracie said she understood – it must have been years earlier. She knew it was around the time his wife was ill, and his mind was elsewhere, obviously.'

Callum smiled. 'Good.'

'I must admit, I was a bit worried about him getting caught returning the books and other items to the archives in the dead of night – you know, like a security guard thinking something suspicious was going on.'

'Yes, but that didn't happen. So, all's well that ends well.'

'All thanks to you, Callum.'

'Really, you don't have to thank me.'

'I do. And your mum. I'm glad she spotted them still in your father's private collection in Scotland before anyone else did.'

'Yeah, that would have been a bit tricky.'

Thea readily agreed. 'I'll say.' Not long after Callum had left, his father had died. That was when Thea had discovered that the things that Edward had stolen, and that Henry had unwittingly sold to the Scottish laird, were still in his private collection.

They both knew that if someone had looked into their provenance, it was highly likely the police would have got involved when it was discovered they'd been stolen from a museum. And it was just as likely that an investigation would point the finger at Edward – and Henry.

No one could afford that. Thea had had to tell Callum everything about what Edward had done. Callum had gladly handed them back to Edward without a penny in recompense. And now they were back where they belonged with no one any the wiser – and no one serving a prison sentence.

'What about the book Toby and I bound – you know, the one that Toby found wrapped in brown paper at the back of the drawer?'

'How could I forget?' It was the last rare book that Edward had stolen from the archives and passed on to Henry before Henry had disappeared. Edward had wanted it back to sell himself. The plan had been to buy the book from Jenna, but he was going to get a generous commission when he sold it on to a rare book collector.

That had never happened. But Edward had nearly got caught out at the last hurdle – returning that last book to the archives. Unlike with all the others, Edward had become too blasé, and had just brought it along with him one morning to work, thinking he could quickly put it back when Gracie stepped out of the office to get a coffee.

Unfortunately, Gracie had nipped back for her cardigan and had caught him in the act. Poor Edward had said he didn't know how to explain what he was doing – no one was allowed to take anything home with them from the museum archives. But then Gracie had seen how it had been so beautifully bound, and Edward had admitted that it was the first book Toby and Callum had ever bound together.

At first, when Thea had heard that Edward had implicated her nephew and boyfriend, she had been livid, and just a little scared of what the repercussions might be. That was why she was checking in with Gracie. But Gracie had said it was so beautifully bound, and such amazing work, that it was little wonder Edward had seen the state of the book and had wanted to have it professionally bound. It wasn't something they necessarily did with rare books, but this book had been in such a bad state of repair that it was an exception.

All Gracie said was that next time, Toby and Callum would need to visit the archives to do their work.

Thea smiled. 'I think you and Toby might be making some trips to London together to work in the archives of the museum.'

'Really? That sounds amazing. I can't wait to tell Toby. He will be beyond excited.'

Thea knew he would. Toby had loved working in the bookshop, but he had started to question Thea about her job as an archivist, showing an immense interest in her work.

Thinking of Toby, Thea looked at her watch. 'I've got to go soon,' she said.

Callum looked at his watch too. 'Crumbs, where does the day go, eh? School's out soon, then.'

'Yes. I'll bring Toby back here though, as usual. You know how he loves to spend some time in the bookshop after school before we all go home.'

Callum smiled. 'Yes, I know. I'm so glad he came back – and everything worked out for him.'

'Yes, me too.' She thought back to a few weeks earlier, soon after she and Callum had returned to the bookshop to find Henry there. Callum had already guessed that was where he'd be. Mabel recounted the surprise arrival of their brother. He'd walked straight into the bookshop, put the *Open* sign in the window, and it was as though he'd never left. Of course, Thea would have already known all about that if she'd just opened Mabel's letters.

Thea thought back to their return to Aldeburgh. Although they were now officially a couple, back then, on their return, they hadn't sorted out anywhere to live together. It would take time to sell her flat in London to buy a place of their own in Aldeburgh. In the meantime, the flat above the shop would have been ideal, but that was where her father was living. Mabel and Marjorie had enlisted the help of everybody in Cobblers Yard, and they'd fixed up the flat, cleaned it, redecorated, and furnished it for their brother, all in the space of one incredibly long weekend.

Callum had parked up the van again in Aldeburgh, where he'd been before, and had planned to live in it. Thea still had the keys to her sister's place, and she'd asked Jenna if she could stay there for a bit while she sorted out where she and Callum could live permanently. Jenna had insisted that she and Callum must both stay in her house for as long as they wanted.

Although Jenna had invited Callum to live there too, and he did stay over a lot of the time, he'd said he didn't want to take advantage of her sister's generosity and just move into her house. But eventually, Callum spent less and less time at the van and accepted that they just had to be together. The van was left parked permanently on Jenna's driveway.

The news of Henry's miraculous return to the bookshop had quickly spread to Thea's sister and mum. When she'd heard the incredible news, Thea's mum had asked her to take some items that were stored in Jenna's garage to the flat for Henry– a lamp, some spare linen, cutlery and crockery, a rug, and some ornaments from her mum's far-flung travels; things she no longer needed, as she didn't envisage returning to her flat in London any time soon. Those extra bits and bobs had made the place cosy and comfortable; the little flat above the shop was now just perfect for Henry.

Thea knew that while her mum was overjoyed at Henry's return, her mum and dad wouldn't get back together. Thea understood. It wasn't just about his health. In the intervening years since his disappearance, although her mum did love him, and had never given up hope, inevitably she'd moved on. She wasn't the same person she had been twenty-five years earlier. They couldn't go back to the way they had been.

Thea had talked to her when she'd returned briefly from Nepal for the reopening party they'd held in Henry's honour, even though Henry had already opened the shop. Unlike the first reopening, it was a very small, intimate affair, with just family. Mabel and Marjorie were there, along with Jenna and the twins, who had flown back from America. Henry, understandably, confused Katie with her mother.

Even though they had wanted to invite Ray and his wife Sarah, along with Lili from The Potting Shed, and especially Lexi and her grandmother, the writer, it wouldn't have been fair on Henry to confuse him with new faces.

The question at the back of Thea's mind had been whether he would remember his sisters, Mabel and Marjorie. At the small family gathering, Henry had surprised them all by remembering his two older sisters. Aware of his condition, both Mabel and Marjorie hadn't held out much hope that he would. Thea had thought otherwise. She'd seen first-hand how stepping into the bookshop brought back vividly memories of the past, so she wasn't at all surprised that he remembered Mabel and Marjorie – especially given that he was meeting them again in the place where they grew up together, The Bookshop of Memories.

Some weeks later, after the party, Thea had got a big surprise when her mum returned to England – with Toby in tow. They just turned up at the house in a taxi with their suitcases.

When she thought about it, though, it was really no surprise to Thea that Toby had wanted to come home. Toby had been deeply unhappy living abroad. He missed home. He missed his girlfriend, and Thea and Callum, and wanted the chance to get to know his grandfather, Henry. But what Thea suspected was that he missed The Bookshop of Memories more. It hadn't helped at all when he'd briefly returned to see his grandfather, only to have to leave again.

Although Thea's mum had promised Jenna that she'd stay in Suffolk and see Toby through school, it was barely a fortnight later when Thea came downstairs one morning and found her mum sitting at the kitchen table, staring forlornly out of the kitchen window. Thea had followed her gaze to the yellow campervan sitting in the driveway. She'd wondered what was going through her mum's mind.

She'd soon found out.

'I can't do this, Thea,' her mum had said. 'I'm torn. I want to stay here – for Toby. His life is here. I understand that. I can't send him back to America. I don't know what to do.'

'I do,' Thea had said. And so it had transpired that her mum sorted through her boxes in the garage and took a lot of spare clothes, and other items to donate to Mabel and Marjorie's charity shop. Then she'd hit the road, with her yoga mat, looking forward to exploring her own country, with only the possessions she could fit in the van. And at some point in the future, when she was ready, she'd use the money from the campervan, which was now in a much safer place in her bank account, to buy her dream cottage in a place she would call home.

Thea didn't share her thoughts with her mum, but she had a feeling that sometime soon, after she'd travelled the length and breadth of the country, looking for her happy place, she'd be back, settling in a cottage on the beautiful Sunrise Coast.

Thea smiled. Thinking of home, Thea now called Jenna's cottage home. She lived there happily with Toby, Dickens, Winston – and, of course, Callum.

She smiled at Callum, who took her hand as he joined her on

the sofa. He put his phone down on the coffee table.

'Who was that?' Thea asked, hearing him on the phone a moment earlier. 'Was that your agent in Hollywood?'

Callum raised a questioning eyebrow. 'Why would you think that?'

'Remember, you told me he wanted to be a screenwriter, and was writing a film script. He's finished it – hasn't he?'

Callum smiled. 'Oh, yes. He's now approaching studios to sell the rights, on the proviso they offer me the leading role. He still wants me to play the lead.'

Thea's smile faded. 'Really? I didn't know that. Will you be going back to LA then?'

Callum squeezed her hand and grinned. 'I bet it's going to turn out one hell of a movie. If they offer me the role, I've already made my decision. I'm not going anywhere.'

'Are you sure?'

'Thea, I've never been so sure of anything in my life.' He glanced at his phone. 'That was the real estate agent. I sold my Beverley Hills mansion. I won't get a cent after I've paid off the mortgage, the IRS, and the rent I owed on that apartment in Malibu.'

'How do you feel?'

'Relieved.'

'And your Scottish inheritance?'

'I'm property rich and cash poor. I can't afford that house, Thea. But more than that, I don't want the place.' He frowned. 'I've just got shot of one property, and now I've got to do that all over again.' He sighed heavily.

'Have you thought of giving it to the National Trust for Scotland? It's a huge property, with an interesting family history. I mean, you're a real-life Scottish laird.'

Callum rolled his eyes. 'Don't remind me. Talk about life imitating art.'

Thea smiled when she recalled Jack saying the exact same thing. 'Just imagine people, families, enjoying the house and the grounds,' Thea said. 'It would bring the place to life, finally, instead of just one sad lonely man being there.'

'Are you talking about me?'

'No, your father, when he was still alive. Although I kind of was talking about you turning into your father.'

Callum thought of the curse of the MacFaddens, as his mother had called it. He squeezed her hand tightly. 'With you by my side, there is no fear of me becoming a lonely old man.'

'Why the frown, then?'

Callum was thinking that like the Beverley Hills mansion, the large Scottish estate was a weight on his shoulders. 'You're right.' He grinned. 'I'll do it! I'll give the place to The National Trust for Scotland.' He looked at Thea, his smiled fading. 'Can you ever forgive her?'

'Who?'

Callum frowned. 'Moira – my mother.'

Thea bit her lip. She knew he'd ask the question one day.

'Sorry, that was a really dumb question. She took your father away from you.'

'I know. It's true, she did. I missed him so very much, Callum.'

Callum slowly nodded his head sadly.

'But, on the other hand …'

Callum caught her smile. 'On the other hand …?

'I think if you hadn't grown up with Henry as your father, you wouldn't have turned out to be the wonderful man I love.'

'A slightly confused man.'

'Huh?'

'Do you know how many surnames I've had?' He started to reel them off, 'There's my real name, MacFadden, then Henry's surname Cavendish, then the show's character name, Fergus MacGregor.'

'And don't forget your stage name!'

He shook his head. 'Yep, that too. Do I need to change my name back to MacFadden, do you think?'

Thea looked at him. 'I think not. If we were to marry—'

'What do you mean *if*?'

'*When* we marry, I rather do like the name Cavendish.'

Callum grinned. 'So do I.'

They both turned to look at Henry.

Thea said, 'If it wasn't for Henry's business selling books, which brought your mother and Henry together, and The Bookshop of Memories, perhaps I would never have met the love of my life.'

Callum knitted his eyebrows. 'Who's that, then?'

Thea nudged him playfully. She knew he was joking, but she said it anyway, 'Why, it's you, of course.'

They stared at each other, thinking about how fate had brought them together. Thinking of Mabel, Callum smiled. Perhaps it was inevitable.

Callum broke the silence. 'I wonder how Edward is finding retirement,' he said off-hand.

Thea smiled. Soon after he had returned everything he had stolen, Edward had decided to retire from the job he loved. 'I think he's finding it just fine.' Thea understood why Edward had resumed trying to sell stolen books again years and years after

Henry's disappearance; Edward thought his wife's illness had returned, and she'd need expensive treatment again. But it had been a false alarm. She was quite well.

Edward had decided to look at it as a wake-up call. He was the type who had always said he'd never retire. But retire he had, to spend time with his wife. He'd said that nobody knew how much time anyone had, but finding Henry had put things in perspective. He and his wife wanted to make the most their twilight years, making memories together.

Thea smiled. 'He's found a new lease of life – well, they both have.'

'What are they doing? Taking up golf, or something?'

'Or something …' Thea repeated. 'They're going to a yoga retreat.' She grinned.

'A yoga retreat?' Callum couldn't help but smile. 'In Nepal?'

'Oh, no, a bit closer to home. I think they're off to Cornwall.'

Callum laughed. 'Good for them. I imagine your mum had something to do with encouraging them to give it a try.'

'She certainly did.'

Thea heard her father greet another customer and ring up the cost of a book on the old-fashioned till.

The customer said, 'Bye! Thank you, Henry,' and walked out of the shop. She'd worried about her dad living here on his own in the little flat above the shop. She still did. 'Will he be okay?' she asked Callum, not for the first time.

'Who – Henry?'

Henry appeared. He smiled at her. 'Look, I've got some pocket money for you. Would you like to go and buy some sweets?'

Thea smiled affectionately at her father as she took the pennies from his hand. She would be forever nine years old in his eyes now. 'Are you binding another book, Daddy?'

'Oh, yes. That's the plan for this afternoon. Well I'd better get to it.'

She smiled. 'All right, Dad.'

Henry hesitated. He raised his eyebrows. 'Where's your mother?'

Thea replied with the same response she gave every day when he asked that very same question. 'She's out in the campervan, selling your bound books. Remember, it was agreed that she'd get on the road and do that now, so you can stay in your shop?'

Dad was back in business, but there was no way he could go out in the campervan ever again. So the plan was that her mum would come back, now and again, to collect the bound books and deliver them to some of her dad's clients around the country. There wouldn't be that many books. It took her dad a lot longer to bind books than it used to. But he still had a handful of loyal customers who were so pleased to find out The Bookshop of Memories was back in business.

'Righty-ho.' He turned to go, but before he did, Henry had another question that Thea heard every day too. 'Say, where's that lad that helps me with the bookbinding?'

'Toby will be back soon.'

'Ah, right you are. He's a good-un, he is. Do you know, he reminds me of someone …'

Thea squeezed Callum's hand as her father's eyes roved over to him before he walked off into the back room. Since returning to the bookshop, they'd discovered one downside of her father being there; Henry no longer recognised Callum. He had no idea who he was.

Callum just smiled. 'Like I said before, when he's in the

bookshop, his memories from his time here are perfect; he never misses a beat, because this is his past. With dementia, it's where he lives now, in his memories. If he steps out of the door … well, you know.' Callum trailed off.

Thea knew. Her father would get confused, agitated; he couldn't cope with the outside world now. It was a wonder he'd made it back there.

When she'd first asked Callum about her dad's condition, he'd said it was progressive, dementia; there was no sugar-coating it. But he had a theory; in this place full of memories of his past life, he would defy his prognosis and keep it in abeyance.

Callum smiled at her reassuringly. 'Here in The Bookshop of Memories, he can live out his days.'

Thea smiled. That was only possible because they'd already put a plan in place. A carer came in, whom Henry thought was an assistant working nights in the bookshop, minding the store. The lovely carer was, in actual fact, minding Henry so that he didn't have to cook for himself, shop, or take care of himself, and gave Thea and Callum peace of mind that he was never truly on his own.

Callum looked at Thea. 'I have a proposal.'

'What is it?'

'That we make new memories in this bookshop, you and me. What do you think?'

Thea grinned at him. 'I think that is the best idea ever. Where shall we start?'

'With this.' Callum stood up, then slowly lowered himself down on one bended knee.

Thea stared at him. 'What are you doing?'

From his trouser pocket, he produced a little felt box.

They both knew that in the years to come, they would remember this moment and treasure the start of their journey making memories together. Their journey would always be bound up with this bookshop, The Bookshop of Memories.

The Sunrise Coast Series continues in

The Beach House

Paperback and Kindle eBook available soon from Amazon

I hope you enjoyed *The Bookshop of Memories* and would be grateful if you wish to leave a review on Amazon.

For further details about the author and her novels please visit the author's website: www.elisedarcy.com

Printed in Dunstable, United Kingdom

68373805R00302